# The Darkroom
# Of Damocles

*Also by W. F. Hermans*
Beyond Sleep

# Willem Frederik Hermans

# The Darkroom
# Of Damocles

TRANSLATED
FROM THE DUTCH
BY

## Ina Rilke

The Overlook Press
WOODSTOCK & NEW YORK

This edition first published in the United States in 2008 by
The Overlook Press, Peter Mayer Publishers, Inc.
Woodstock & New York

WOODSTOCK:
One Overlook Drive
Woodstock, NY 12498
www.overlookpress.com
[for individual orders, bulk and special sales, contact our Woodstock office]

NEW YORK:
141 Wooster Street
New York, NY 10012

The publishers are grateful for the support of
the Foundation for the Production and Translation of Dutch Literature.

Cataloging-in-Publication Data is available from the Library of Congress

Manufactured in the United States of America
HC ISBN 978-1-59020-062-9
PB ISBN 978-1-59020-081-0
10 9 8 7 6 5 4 3 2 1

# The Darkroom
# Of Damocles

'. . . He drifted around on his raft for days, without a drop to drink. He was dying of thirst, because the water of the ocean is salty. He hated the water that he couldn't drink. But when his raft was struck by lightning and caught fire, he scooped up the hateful water with both hands to try and put out the flames!'

The teacher was the first to laugh, and finally the whole class joined in.

Then the bell rang. The children got up from their desks. Henri Osewoudt was half a head shorter than all the other boys. They trooped down the corridor in single file, breaking into a run as they reached the exit.

Mulling over the teacher's story, Osewoudt became separated from the others by the arrival of a blue tram. He didn't bother to catch up with them once the tram had passed. His eyes lit on the NO OVERTAKING sign which he read every day as he came out of school. The sign stands at the entrance to the narrow high street. The street is so narrow that the tramlines sidle towards each other until they overlap in a single track. Trams coming from opposite directions have to wait for their turn to cross the centre of Voorschoten.

The tobacco shop kept by Osewoudt's father was at the other end of the high street, not far from the point where the tramlines diverge again. Drawing level with the School with the Bible, he saw a crowd gathering by the entrance to his father's shop: neighbours jostling and chattering and craning their necks to peer inside. Two policemen were standing by.

Turlings the chemist caught sight of Osewoudt, left the crowd and came hurrying towards him.

'Quick, take my hand, Henri! You must come with me. You can't go home now! There's been an accident, a dreadful accident!'

Osewoudt said nothing, took the extended hand and allowed himself to be led away. The street was choked with people. Turlings pulled him along so quickly that he couldn't hear what they were saying, but he was sure it was about him.

'Has something happened to Mother?'

'Poor lad! It's too awful for words! You'll hear about it later. A dreadful accident!'

'Is Father dead?'

'How could you say such a thing? It's awful! Awful!'

Turlings' shop was close to the tram stop, diagonally across from the tobacco shop belonging to Osewoudt's father. Osewoudt looked back, but all he could see were the people and the other NO OVERTAKING sign, identical to the one at the far end of the high street.

They went inside, and the chemist took him through to the room at the back of the shop. The chemist's wife wore a white lab coat. She ran to him.

'Oh you poor boy! What a terrible accident!'

She kissed him on the top of his head, fetched him a roll of liquorice sweets from the shop and sat him down on a chair by the stove, which was not burning.

There was a smell of cough drops and chamois leather, even in the living room.

'How dreadful! How could anyone do a thing like that? Poor boy! Poor, poor boy!'

Osewoudt took a sweet from the roll he'd been given.

'Did Mother do it?'

'What on earth . . . ? How does he know?' the wife said to her husband. 'And he's not even crying!'

Turlings bent down and told Osewoudt: 'Your uncle will be coming to fetch you in a while. He'll be taking you to Amsterdam.'

He went back into the shop and made a telephone call.


'Mama! There's blood on the street! I saw it!'

Their son Evert was twelve years old, the same age as Osewoudt, but he attended the School with the Bible.

'Did you see my mother?'

'Hush, the pair of you! Evert, go and wash your hands before you have your supper.'

It was beginning to smell of potatoes and cabbage in the room.

The chemist, his wife and their son took their seats at the table, leaving Osewoudt by the stove. He had stopped asking questions, just put one liquorice after another into his mouth.

The chemist and his wife said grace out loud before beginning; Evert read a passage from the Bible when they got to the pudding. Finally, thanks were given, also aloud.

It was past closing time when Uncle Bart rang the doorbell. The chemist's wife let him in. He was clutching his hat in one hand and a white handkerchief in the other.

'How did it happen, Uncle? Tell me. I'm a big boy now, Uncle!'

'Your father's not well,' Uncle Bart said, 'and they've taken your mother to the institution, like five years ago, remember?'

Outside, darkness had already fallen. They boarded the tram to Leiden. Osewoudt looked out of the window, and when they passed his father's shop he saw that all the lights were out.

He tugged at Uncle Bart's sleeve.

'I don't believe Father's ill, how could he have got ill at the same time as Mother?'

'That's enough, Henri. I'm not prejudiced. I'll tell you everything, all in good time.'

'Mother often said she'd kill Father with the crowbar.'

'The crowbar?'

'The crowbar that's kept under the counter, Uncle. It's a crowbar at one end and a hammer at the other.'

'What a thing to say! Your mother isn't well. Try to think about something else. You'll be staying with us for a while. You can go to school in Amsterdam. You'll like that, won't you?'

They took the tram all the way to Leiden station, where they caught the train to Amsterdam.

'Teacher told us a story this afternoon,' Osewoudt said. 'It was about a shipwreck and a sailor on a raft. He had nothing to drink, and he hated the ocean because the water was salty. But then his raft was struck by lightning and he scooped up the water even though he hated it, to put out the fire.'

'And did he put out the fire?'

'He may have done, but he died anyway, of thirst. We had a right laugh.'

'Does your teacher often tell you stories like that?'

'Hello Aunt Fie!'

'Hello Henri! Poor lamb.'

She kissed him at length, but she didn't smell nice.

'Hello Ria!'

'Hello Henri.'

Ria hugged him just as long as her mother had, but she smelled much nicer.

Uncle Bart said: 'He's looking forward to going to school in Amsterdam. Off to bed with you now, Henri! Ria will show you the way.'

Ria was nineteen years old. She led Osewoudt up two narrow flights of stairs to a small room with a made-up bed. She showed him where to put his clothes and where to wash. He got undressed and had a wash, but when he lay in bed he couldn't sleep. He heard his uncle and aunt go to bed, then the door opened a little and Ria looked in.

'What's this? Light still on? Not asleep yet?'

'I'm scared.'

She pushed the door wide open and pointed behind her to the landing below.

'That's my bedroom, down there. You can come to me if you like, if you have trouble sleeping.'

When he went to her she was in bed.

'Here, get under the covers or you'll get cold.'

As soon as he was in bed with her she switched off the light.

'My mother always lets me get into bed with her, too.'

He began to sob.

She slipped her arm beneath his head.

'I've always wanted a little brother. You can stay with me tonight. Nobody will notice. Anyway, Papa won't mind.'

'He wouldn't tell me how it happened. Won't you tell me?'

'I don't know either, Henri. You shouldn't think about things like that.'

'I'd like to know.'

'Don't you think my hair smells nice?'

'Yes, it smells nice, but I'm scared.'

'Try and get some sleep.'

'I can't.'

'You're just a little boy.'

'No I'm not. I'm a big boy, I'm just small for my age, and that's not my fault.'

'Oh? You're a big boy, are you? Are you quite sure? If you're such a big boy, then why don't you give me a kiss?'

He went outside with Ria and looked back at the house. 'It's such a long time since I was here last,' he said. 'I'd forgotten what it looked like.'

It was a tall, narrow canal house. Beside the door was a black marble plaque with gilt lettering: BELLINCOFF LTD., HABERDASHERS.

'Why doesn't it say Nauta?'

'Bellincoff's just the name of the firm.'

'Why does it say haberdashers? Is that the same as birds' feathers?'

'No, it says haberdashers, but practically the only things Papa sells is birds' feathers.'

'Can it make you rich?'

'Papa does quite well out of it. A hat with feathers costs an awful lot of money, and not many people wear hats with feathers these days. So Papa's the only one in Amsterdam still selling feathers.'

'Why is the street along this canal called Oudezijds Achterburgwal? What does it mean?'

'It means that this was a rampart in the old days.'

'Why are those ladies sitting in the windows wearing pink petticoats?'

'They're ladies who do it for money.'

'What do they do for money?'

'They're nice to men.'

'Like you're nice to me?'

'Shut up, will you? Or I won't let you near me again, do you hear?'

Uncle Bart thought Osewoudt should go on to university when he was old enough, so he sent him to secondary school.

Osewoudt proved to be an amenable but quiet pupil.

Every night he slept in Ria's bed. When he turned fifteen he realised he found her ugly. And then he also realised why the other boys' furtive gossip didn't interest him. Why listen to ill-informed whisperings about things he had been doing for ages, night after night, without any qualms? This wasn't what worried him, what did worry him was that he was apparently the only one doing these things, and also that Ria was the only girl who would let him do them. He thought of ways of getting rid of her, but getting rid of her was not the main thing, the main thing was how to replace her.

Somewhere near Landsmeer, not far from Amsterdam, he found a spot quiet enough for his purpose.

They got off their bikes and lay down in the lee of the dyke. The girl's name was Clelia Bieland.

'You're revolting!'

'Revolting? But my uncle says it's a matter of natural selection!'

She jumped up, grabbed her bike and rode off as fast as she could.

The next day he was summoned by the principal. For a secondary-school principal the man was remarkably young.

'Look here, Osewoudt, Clelia Bieland's father complains you've been telling his daughter smutty stories.'

'But sir, I only told her what my uncle says about natural selection . . .'

'I know your uncle very well, as it happens. Bart Nauta. Good man; used to be a Communist. He feels bad about having turned his back on a revolution which, in its pure form, has long ceased to exist. He realises that, but he's sorry all the same. Puts out the flag on the queen's birthday, votes and pays his taxes like everybody else, but tries to ease his conscience by clinging desperately to ideals that don't stand much of a chance in society at large: abstinence from spirits, no smoking, and discussions about sexual liberation. Hard ideals to live up to, at least for anyone who's addicted to drink and tobacco and lives a monogamous life. What good would they do anyway? Your uncle talks about natural selection, but the books he reads are all out of date.'

'What about anti-militarism, then?'

'Anti-militarism? Germany and the Soviet Union are busy building the mightiest armies the world has ever seen! Hitler wants to conquer the whole world, ditto Russia. Are we to be anti-militarists and let ourselves be killed off as saints? Don't get me wrong, your uncle's a fine man, but don't believe everything he says. Promise?'

The principal held out his hand.

After school he saw Clelia Bieland cycling off with another boy, the same age as him but a head and a half taller.

That same week he joined a judo club. He stopped taking down books from his uncle's shelves. He did his homework with listless diligence, got reasonably good marks, but he was only really interested in judo. Sometimes he thought of paying a visit to one of the whores along Oudezijds Achterburgwal, but although he knew several by their first names – they were neighbours, after all – none of them ever came on to him. And why put himself out? At night, after his uncle and aunt had gone to bed, he would rumple his sheets and creep down to Ria's room.

Exactly how his mother had killed his father he still did not know.

One Ascension Day he went on his own to his childhood home in Voorschoten. First he took the blue tram to Haarlem. There he changed to another blue tram, which took him to Leiden. In Leiden he caught yet another blue tram in the direction of The Hague.

He got off in Voorschoten, at the north end of the high street. He took in the surroundings as if he were a stranger. There stood the house with the municipal coat of arms on the front: three chewed fingernails. In the same building, or in an annexe, were the school he had attended and the police station. Slightly closer to the centre was the Reformed Protestant church, with its steeple like an upright Zeppelin. Further along rose the medieval tower of the St Willibrord church. He headed towards the narrow high street, his eyes fixed on the NO OVERTAKING sign.

The tram he had travelled on came past, darkening the street. Each house smelled of crime and murder. He looked in all the windows, but there weren't any whores. He felt as if something awful would befall him. At the tobacco shop he slowed down, but didn't dare stop. Blinds covered the door and the display window. EUREKA CIGARS AND CIGARETTES, it said in silver letters on the glass; had the E and K been just as tarnished in the old days?

\*    \*    \*

Sluimer's garage, next door to the tobacco shop, was closed. Across the way was a new sweet shop belonging to the C. Jamin chain. The small white building opposite the other tram stop still had a sign saying CENTRAL SHOE REPAIRS. Central, they called it . . . yet it was at the far end of the high street, by the stop where the tramlines diverged again.

Should he step into the chemist's and see how Evert Turlings was doing? But just then a tram from The Hague arrived, and Osewoudt got on, feeling as if he'd shaken off a pursuer. He took a window seat and stared outside. Again he went past the tobacco shop. He now saw, along the top of the display, a yellow sign: NORTH STATE CIGARETTES.

His Aunt Fie did not like him.

She often received women friends, and he began to notice that they stopped talking the moment he entered the living room.

He therefore often gave in to the temptation to linger in the passage and put his ear to the door when his aunt had visitors.

'Don't you ever worry about him?'

'Well, what can I say, with a mother like that? It's a wonder he's alive at all.'

'How do you mean?'

'Didn't I tell you? He was a seven-months baby. Yes, and do you know, he wasn't even born properly. His mother just dropped him into the po one day, along with her stools.'

'Really?'

'Well, he looks it, too.'

'He won't make old bones, I shouldn't think.'

'That pale girlish face of his, and the wispy fair hair.'

'Is he really getting on for seventeen?'

'Yes, and still not shaving.'

'What? My boy was shaving at fourteen!'

'Well, it isn't normal, is it? He got off to a bad start. We'll have to wait and see whether he grows into a proper man.'

'Does he step out with girls at all?'

'Girls? He's just not interested!'

Osewoudt looked in the mirror and touched his cheeks,

which were still soft, fleshy and smooth. At school he would glance about in case anyone was laughing at him, prick up his ears when his classmates huddled together, but they left him alone because they all knew he could wrestle any boy to the ground with ease, including the biggest. He was still a regular at the judo club. Doing judo was altering the shape of his feet, which were growing wide and very muscular in the arches so they resembled suction pads, on which he stood fast, unshiftable. Normal shoes no longer fitted him; he had to have special ones made to measure.

A diminutive freak, a toad reared upright.

His nose was more of a button than a nose. And his eyes, even when not focussing, seemed forever narrowed, as if he could only leer, not look normally. His mouth recalled the kind of orifice through which the lowest forms of life ingest their food, not a mouth that could also laugh and talk. And then there were his round cheeks, and the pale silky hair he kept cropped short in the vain hope that it would stick up.

'What are you doing here? Why are you looking in the mirror?'

'Oh, is that you? Nothing.'

Ria grasped his head, saying: 'Got something in your eye then?'

'No, just looking in the mirror.'

She gave him a kiss and thrust her groin against him. He now knew that she was too ugly to attract any other man, and also that she would otherwise have dumped him long ago. He also knew that she wouldn't get pregnant, because there was no way she could.

There was not a single part of her body that was not hard and bony to the touch. Her hair was the colour of wrapping paper, her chin long and jutting, and her teeth were also too long. Her teeth were always on show, even when she wasn't smiling, and she never smiled. They overlapped slightly, and rested permanently on her lower lip. Her teeth did not enhance her mouth, nor did they make it look fierce, they merely clamped it shut, rather like the clasp on a purse.

'It's definite now, isn't it Papa, that they're discharging Henri's mother from the institution next month?'

'Yes.'

'Then Henri and I have something to tell you. We're getting married!'

'Married?'

'Henri and I have decided to get married, Papa. Henri wants to carry on his father's business. We'll take his mother to live with us over the shop.'

'But Henri! Have you suddenly changed your mind about university?'

Osewoudt said: 'Suddenly? I gave up on the idea a long time ago. I don't think I'm cut out for it. I'm eighteen years old and I want to stand on my own two feet. Who else will look after Mother?'

His voice was still high-pitched, like a child's.

'But Henri . . .'

Aunt Fie began to weep.

'Ria!' she sobbed. 'You're throwing your life away! You're seven years older than him! And he's your first cousin!'

'Oh Mother, you can't talk! You think I don't know, don't you?'

'Don't know what?'

'That I was already two by the time you and Father got

married! Took the pram with you to the registry office and left it with the porter!'

'You don't understand a thing, Ria. Your father was an idealist!'

'Listen, Ria,' said Uncle Bart. 'At heart I've always been against rules and regulations. And I still am!'

'Oh Father, leave off. Who cares what anyone is at heart? Rules or no rules, you got married all the same!'

'And I'm telling you it's not going to happen!'

Aunt Fie stood up and left the room.

Before the month was out she died from a heart attack.

Osewoudt and Ria were married on 25 August, 1939. Six days later the radio announced that Hitler had invaded Poland with aircraft and tanks.

The tobacco shop was refurbished and painted at Uncle Bart's expense. An electric connection was installed in the door frame to make a bell tinkle each time the door was opened or shut. The sales area was so small that the counter, which was by no means large, left scarcely any room to spare. All the woodwork was painted dark brown. The sliding doors to the back room were fitted with leaded panels of frosted glass. As a finishing touch, Osewoudt screwed a small plaque saying HAVE YOU FORGOTTEN ANYTHING? to the inside of the shop door, just above the handle.

They ate and sat in the back room. Upstairs were three small rooms, one for Ria and him, one for his mother, and the third for a student lodger. Moorlag had started out as a cabinetmaker in Nieuw-Buinen, but had felt so drawn to studying theology that he had taken a room in Voorschoten, from where he could commute to the university. He didn't want to live in Leiden itself because he hadn't yet matriculated, which disqualified him from sitting exams. Taking lodgings in the university town at this point seemed to him sacrilegious. He was over thirty, studied day and night, but had failed to matriculate three times.

Sometimes the three of them would go for an evening stroll, and once in a while Moorlag came along too. They went up the narrow high street, greeting the other shopkeepers left and right, stepping out of the way of the blue tram when it passed. When they reached the north end they sometimes went as far as the silver factory, but never further.

'Mother, isn't it rather tiring for you?'

'What gave you that idea, my boy? I'm not an old woman.'

'Of course not, but we're all ready for bed,' Moorlag would say.

Then she would give in.

Moorlag had a soothing influence on her. She sometimes got up in the middle of the night to wander around the house wrapped in a sheet, her face covered by a mask cut from an old newspaper. In a tone as if she were doing the dusting she would say: 'There it is again, I'll just chase it away.'

On such occasions Moorlag was able to get her back to bed again with a few words.

What was she chasing away? Osewoudt didn't ask. He had never discovered how she had killed his father. She was an ordinary fifty-year-old woman with a girlish face covered in wrinkles and a mouth so thin it looked like just another wrinkle. She talked a lot about his father, and always quite matter-of-factly.

'Then your father would say: you only get to kiss the queen if you use stamps costing five cents and over. Because the queen isn't on the cheaper ones, he said. A kiss on the right, he said, because the left cheek's on the front of the stamp. Always one for a laugh, your father.'

Her chortling reminded him of the squeak of chamois leather on a wet windowpane.

On Sundays he sometimes took Ria and his mother to Ypenburg airfield. In the evenings they would listen to the radio. No one had much to say. They didn't speak during meals. Shifting around on his chair, Osewoudt lifted the food to his mouth. His mind was focussed on strange visions: across the room there were railway tracks on which he made long trains thunder by. He imagined aeroplanes with roaring engines waiting outside the shop, or enormous field guns with jolting barrels firing non-stop.

Osewoudt turned nineteen, and had the feeling that everything that needed doing had already been done. All the obstacles that would normally have stood in his way (other people spend a lifetime overcoming them) had already come down: his father, his aunt, both dead. Ria was a woman with whom he had done everything he could think of, including getting married.

He was turned down for military service: he was half a centimetre too short.

Once a week he spent an evening at his judo club in The Hague and another on drill practice with the Home Guard. He learned how to load an old rifle, he learned to drive a car, and on one occasion he got to fire an old revolver.

'Henri! Who can be phoning us in the middle of the night?'

The alarm clock said quarter past four. Outside it was already light. There was plenty of birdsong but also the drone of aircraft — several of them.

Now he heard the phone ringing, too.

'How should I know?'

Osewoudt got out of bed and went downstairs. As he stepped into the shop he saw a big lorry full of soldiers drive past. The phone rang again.

'Osewoudt tobacconists.'

'Osewoudt, this is your Home Guard commander speaking! Get your uniform on and come to the town hall as quick as you can! It's war! The Germans have attacked, they're dropping parachutes all over the place. Come at once!'

From the bottom of the stairs he shouted: 'Ria! The Germans have attacked! They want me at the town hall!'

He went to the back room and took his uniform from the cupboard. The uniform was dark green, like a forestry man's. A German helmet went with it, army surplus from the Great War.

Walking down the street, he hoped the Germans had adopted a new style of helmet in the interim. If they hadn't, who knows what might happen to him?

Three big, black aeroplanes appeared, flying low. Not far off he could hear the pounding of field guns. There were a lot of people about, talking and pointing at the sky.

Until late afternoon he stood guard at the post office, where crowds were gathering to draw out their savings. From time to time the Germans left big white mushrooms behind in the blue, cloudless sky. The people pointed. Dutch soldiers on motorcycles came past on their way to investigate. The blue trams continued to run as usual. All Osewoudt was allowed to do was stand guard with an old rifle, on the sidelines as usual. In the blazing sunshine, to the accompaniment of birdsong, he was obliged to visualise the monstrous guns for himself. No one had any intention of attacking the post office.

Afterwards, when he got home, he gummed strips of brown paper crosswise over the shop window.

An army lorry pulled up outside. The soldiers jumped down and came into the shop. Osewoudt gave them everything they asked for and refused to take any money.

'There's no need for you to do that!' said a lieutenant.

'Why not? Just doing my bit. What would you like for yourself? Have these cigars.'

The lieutenant looked at the price and gave Osewoudt one guilder. Then he said: 'You develop and print photographs, don't you?'

He pointed to the cardboard sign hanging on the shop door. The sign had several snapshots pasted to it, and announced that rolls of film left in the letter box would be developed, printed, and ready for collection in forty-eight hours.

The lieutenant took a roll of film from his pocket.

'Just leave it to me,' said Osewoudt. 'I'll do my best, but I can't promise the pictures will be ready the day after tomorrow. What's the name?'

'Dorbeck. With ck.'

Osewoudt wrote 'Dorbeck' on the film, with ck.

'My name is Osewoudt, with dt,' he said, putting the roll in the drawer under the counter.

'Then our names have something in common.'

The officer shook hands with Osewoudt, looking him straight in the eye. Osewoudt noted that the man's eyes were exactly level with his. They were grey-green eyes, and seemed surprised at what they saw. He had never felt anyone's eyes on him in this way, except when he looked at himself in the mirror.

'You're the same height as me,' Osewoudt said, 'and I was turned down for military service.'

'So was I, almost. But I stretched myself.'

Dorbeck laughed. His white teeth were so even and close-set they looked like two transverse blades of ivory. His hair was black, and a shadow of stubble tinged his jawline with blue. This made his face look even paler, although there were spots of red on his cheekbones. He had a voice like a bronze bell.

'Thanks,' he said. 'They don't need to be ready the day after tomorrow, as I shan't be back by then. But I'll be back, you can be sure of that.' He walked out of the shop and jumped into his lorry.

Osewoudt followed him with his eyes. When he turned round he saw Ria standing between the sliding doors.

'Who was that?'

'Oh, nobody in particular.'

'He looked exactly like you, the way a photo negative looks like the positive.'

'He was passed for military service and I wasn't.'

'No wonder. You look as much like him as a pudding that hasn't set properly looks like a ... let's see ... like a pudding that *has* set properly. What a scream! Did you let them all go off without paying?'

'What business is that of yours? You take money from the till without asking.'

'Yes, I do! It's my father's money! I can do what I like with it! Who do you think you are? What would you and your mother live on if you hadn't married me?'

The Germans arrived in the backs of dusty lorries. The blue tram service had to stop running. The Germans wore the same steel helmets as in the Great War. They confiscated the Dutch Home Guard's helmets, as well as their uniforms, pistols and old rifles.

Soon the blue tram was running to its normal schedule again. Everything returned to normal, only things were somewhat busier for a while.

Two days later a Dutch army officer on a motorcycle stopped in front of Osewoudt's shop. When he dismounted, Osewoudt saw it was Dorbeck.

Dorbeck dropped the motorcycle halfway across the pavement and went into the shop.

'Sorry, your film isn't ready yet,' said Osewoudt. 'I don't do the work myself, it's done by somebody in The Hague, but he hasn't called — because of the war, I expect.'

'Doesn't matter.'

Dorbeck sat with one thigh propped on the counter.

'Is there anyone back there?' he asked, glancing at the sliding doors.

'No, my mother's in bed and my wife is out.'

'Good. I thought of you because you're the same height as me. I need you to lend me a suit. I want to get rid of this uniform. I can't go and give myself up as a prisoner of war. I know Holland has capitulated, but that doesn't mean to say I have. I'll capitulate in my own good time.'

Osewoudt went to the room at the back where the wardrobe stood. Dorbeck followed him, already undoing the buttons of his tunic.

'There was some trouble. What happened was this: I'm on my way to Rotterdam. There's a bunch of sodding German paratroopers blocking the road. Shots are fired, vehicle kaput, my whole division incapacitated. The Germans make me hand over my pistol and take me with them. But then the bombs start falling and I escape. I flag down one of our trucks and get to Rotterdam. I walk down a street, don't hear any more bombs, but what do I see? One house after another bursting into flames, just like that. I ask myself how this can be. Great crowds everywhere, people pushing prams loaded with bedding, people with pushcarts and bicycles. Everyone running and shouting. I spot two men in brown overalls. I know right off what their game is, and I stop them. Krauts, of course! They give me a long spiel. Say they're paratroopers, that they were captured two days ago by our marines and taken to an ordinary prison, for want of a better place, where they were stripped of their uniforms and made to wear those brown overalls instead. When the bombing started the prison governor opened the gates, which is how they came to be walking the streets again.

'Do you know what I told them? I said: what do you take me for? For an idiot who never reads the papers? The pair of you were smuggled into the country on some freighter before the invasion began! You're saboteurs! You can start saying your prayers if you're that way inclined, because you're about to meet your Maker!

'I happen to see three of our soldiers carrying rifles, and I get them to finish off those two jokers pronto. If I'd had my service pistol I'd have done it myself!'

The wardrobe was still open. Dorbeck reached inside for a

pair of shoes. His boots thudded to the floor. He knotted one of Osewoudt's ties around his neck and went back into the shop.

'Hey!' Osewoudt called after him. 'Don't you want an overcoat? It gets cold on a motorbike.'

'No need, and thanks a lot. Hide the uniform. I'll send your suit back as soon as I can.'

Dorbeck righted his motorcycle and started the engine.

'Where did you get that motorbike?'

'Commandeered it!'

He laughed, the engine roared. As he rode off he threw Osewoudt a look over his shoulder.

Osewoudt gathered up the uniform and the boots and took them down to the cellar, where he hid them beneath a pile of old packing material.

Evert Turlings returned from the prison camp with a deep suntan.

'Fine chaps, those Germans, Osewoudt! Another three months and they'll have beaten England too! It's the strongest army in the world! Hitler's a genius! Who'd have thought he'd let all the POWs go?'

The chemist's son helped himself to a packet of cigarettes without asking, and tore it open.

'I'm completely converted,' he said. 'They've taught us a lesson and we'd better take it to heart! We've seen what a rotten democracy is worth. The whole lot packing off to London, leaving the fighting army in the lurch. It was criminal to make us fight the Germans without weapons, without aircraft, without anything. And then running away the moment things go wrong! I've got the message. It's the dawn of a new age, all the little states will have to go. We're heading for a united Europe. A Europe led by Germany, of course. The Germans have shown what they're worth, they're entitled to take the lead. The more we Dutch get together with the Germans, the better it'll be. Hitler's good-hearted. The Germanic brother folk, that's what he calls us. He praised the Dutch rank and file for their bravery, he's released the POWs. There's work to be done, he said, and he's right.'

'I've no head for politics,' said Osewoudt.

'You're not the only one here in Holland. Did you read about that officer?'

'What officer?'

'In the paper last night. While Rotterdam was being bombed, a Dutch army officer ordered two innocent German POWs to be shot in the street, just like that. The very idea! Hitler's too good-hearted, I'm telling you! That officer's got a lot coming to him when they catch him. Shooting harmless POWs! Only a Dutchman would do that. Turns tail on the battlefield at the first shot, but doesn't think twice about shooting defenceless POWs. He'd better give himself up as soon as possible. Otherwise the whole Dutch nation will be made to pay.'

'Perhaps we're not a very manly nation,' Osewoudt said, lowering his eyes.

Turlings slipped the cigarettes into his pocket and reached for the handle of the shop door.

'I'll be back! Bring you a couple of interesting articles from *Volk en Vaderland*, good plain-speaking stuff. It's a month now since the capitulation, and it's time to take a stand. *Stop and think* – that's the watchword these days!'

The door opened, setting off the electric bell. Evert Turlings left and the bell tinkled again.

Just as Osewoudt turned back towards the counter, the bell tinkled for a third time.

There stood Dorbeck. He wore a pale grey summer suit that looked brand new. He did not give the impression of being as short as Osewoudt. He came in, leaving the door open. He deposited a large parcel wrapped in brown paper on the counter.

'Morning, Osewoudt, I've brought your suit back.'

'Dorbeck! Do you know they're looking for you? There's a bit about you in the paper.'

'They can look wherever they like. If I don't want them to find me, they won't.'

'Do you want the uniform back?'

'No, never mind about that.'

'That's easy for you to say, but I don't know what to do

with it either,' muttered Osewoudt, heading for the sliding doors.

But when he returned with the uniform over his arm, Dorbeck had gone. The door was still open.

Osewoudt dumped the uniform on the counter and went out into the street. Just then the blue tram slowly came past, blocking his view. He didn't see Dorbeck in the tram either, but that didn't mean to say he wasn't on.

The sun shone. It was a fine day. There were people walking about, including some unarmed German soldiers. It was almost as if nothing had changed, as if things would stay the same for ever. Maybe Evert Turlings had a point. And maybe even now Dorbeck was on his way to give himself up. Osewoudt took the uniform, put the shop door on the latch, and went out into the back garden. He used the coal shovel to dig a hole in the ground, wrapped the uniform in newspaper and buried it.

Not until evening did he get to open the parcel Dorbeck had left behind. It turned out to contain more than his Sunday suit. There were also two metal canisters, a ten-guilder note, and a typed message: *Osewoudt, develop these films asap. No need for prints. Cut them into strips, put in an envelope and send to: E. Jagtman, Legmeerplein 25, Amsterdam. Post them tomorrow night at the latest.*

Osewoudt examined the canisters and saw they were not ordinary films but so-called Leica films. Not that he was an expert.

That same evening he went to The Hague, to see the man who had given him the cardboard sign about developing and printing for his shop. But when he arrived at the address there was another name on the door, and nobody answered when he rang. Try a different photographer? He didn't know any, and besides they would be closed by now. In Voorschoten there was only Turlings the chemist who knew anything about photography. Ask him to do it? But what about his son?

And so Osewoudt decided to have a go himself. He'd developed the odd film or two back at school. In the cellar he found a red lamp that had belonged to Uncle Bart, and a couple of bowls in a crate. All he needed now was the chemicals. He didn't dare buy them from the chemist. So the following morning he cycled over to Leiden, having asked his mother to look after the shop as Ria was in bed with flu.

When he returned half an hour later, the shop was closed. Even the blinds over the window and the door had been lowered, which he never did in the old days. Since the invasion, though, he had been obliged to lower them after dark because of the blackout. His mind went back to that Ascension Day when, aged fifteen, he had come to scout around Voorschoten for clues to his father's murder, and had seen the shop looking exactly as it did now. He was overcome by a sense of all being lost — what he had lost he couldn't tell — as he put the key in the lock. His mother opened the door, saying she had heard him coming. In a rage, he fell to raising the blinds, but the cord of the blind over the door snapped, so it stayed down.

His mother declared that she had let the blinds down to keep out two men, two men who had a message from somebody called Dorbeck which they wanted to pass on to Osewoudt in person. She had said he didn't live here any more, that the name on the shop meant nothing. After that she had locked the door and lowered the blinds. 'Clever of me, wasn't it, my boy?' She was greatly excited. He almost had to force her to go back to bed, and on the stairs she burst into tears, saying she had felt it coming and that it had to be stopped, stopped.

'You won't help me! Packing me off to bed like this as if I'm ill! You'll come to grief if you don't listen to me!'

She ranted on, but nothing she said gave him any idea of what the two men might have wanted to tell him from Dorbeck. When they did not return in the afternoon, as he had hoped, he decided they had probably only come to ask if the films were ready. Straight after supper he went down to the cellar, dissolved the developer and the fixing salt in tap water and lit the little red oil lamp. Muddled visions of German defensive works, artillery positions, airfields, photostats of secret weapons and other classified material flashed across his mind as he took the first film from its canister. His heart raced, he could scarcely breathe imagining everything that was about to be revealed thanks to a bit of simple chemistry, pictures that would be pored over by the Military Command in London. But when he started unrolling the film he broke out in a sweat. He gauged its length to be two metres. The celluloid was very stiff; it kept slipping from his fingers, coiling around him like a snake.

He struggled on; no images appeared. He tried holding the strips up to the red light. Nothing happened, other than that the films, which were milky white to start with, turned completely black. Finally he hung them up to dry and went to bed. When he looked at them again in the morning all he could see was dark smudges. He cut the strips into sections and put them in an envelope, which he laid in the drawer under the counter. But because he assumed they'd be no good and didn't want to appear totally inept, he did something that could be interpreted as a deed of desperation: he withdrew his working capital (600 guilders) from the bank, went to The Hague, stepped into a camera shop and within five minutes had bought himself a Leica, which he paid for in cash. He took the tram to Scheveningen in the hope of photographing German military installations: anti-aircraft batteries, army encampments and vessels being fitted for the invasion of England. But when he got there he saw very little of potential interest. There were indeed a few ships in the harbour, but he had no idea whether they had anything to do with the impending German offensive against England. He photographed a few lorries on the off-chance, and also took a picture of the German sentry outside the prison. This was seen by the German. Instead of raising the alarm, he stood yet more stiffly to attention. Osewoudt returned home having taken no more than six photos, none of which he thought would be of any use. He was supposed to have sent off Dorbeck's films the day before. As a last resort he took the envelope containing the botched negatives from the counter drawer, wrote E. Jagtman, Legmeerplein 25, Amsterdam on the front, stuck a stamp on it and dropped it in the letter box. For the next few days he left his mother in charge of the shop, only returning home at night to sleep. He wandered around taking photos at random, for what purpose he did not know. No Germans took any notice of him, which strength-ened his feeling that he could not have photographed any location of significance, simply because he was so ignorant about military affairs. But in any case he would be able to show Dorbeck he had tried his level best not to let him down. After three days he felt he had sufficient grounds for a reprieve, should he be called to account. Besides, he had run out of ideas about what to photograph (the first film still wasn't used up). If they came again and said: what's going on? We send you two rolls of film for which people risked their lives and all you do is ruin them — he would be able to prove he had spared neither money nor effort to repair the damage. He went back to running the shop. No one came. One evening a week later there was a storm. In between thunderclaps he heard a ring at the door. He crossed to the front but couldn't see who it was. He decided to take the chance and unlocked the door, turning the light switch at the same time. But the light didn't come on.

It was Dorbeck, in a long raincoat, dripping wet.

'Dorbeck, the photographs—'

Dorbeck placed the flat of his left hand against Osewoudt's chest and pushed him backwards. Tight-lipped, he barely looked at Osewoudt. He shut the door behind him and strode to the darkest part of the shop, at the back by the sliding doors.

'Where's your wife?'

'Upstairs, in bed with flu. The photos—'

'Is there anyone else around?'

'No, but listen—'

'I'm sorry you went to all that trouble for nothing. The films were worthless. They were put into our hands by a German provocateur. There was nothing on them, of course. I sent two people to tell you, but your mother wouldn't let them in. Did you know that?'

'Yes, but—'

'I haven't much time. I need your help. I want you to be in the waiting room of Haarlem station next Tuesday at 2.45 p.m. Look out for me. I'll be sitting at a table with someone else. Here . . .' Dorbeck took Osewoudt's hand and pressed a heavy object into it. 'Here's a pistol. Bring it with you.'

Outside, the storm intensified, the shop grew even darker than before.

'All right? I must go now,' said Dorbeck.

The pouring rain made a hissing sound. A flash of lightning lit up the interior, but not Dorbeck's face, which was in Osewoudt's shadow.

'Hadn't you better wait for the rain to stop?'

'No time. Catch you later.'

Dorbeck went round the counter towards the door and out into the street. Just then the electric light came on of its own accord. A long slab of light fell across the black asphalt paving.

Osewoudt put his head round the door to look for Dorbeck, but couldn't see him anywhere.

'What's the idea? Don't you know there's a blackout?'

A policeman with a bicycle stood in the next doorway, water pouring from his cap.

'So sorry, officer, I was just showing someone out. I tried turning the light on five minutes ago, but the current was down. And now it's suddenly come on again.'

Osewoudt turned the light switch.

'I don't think I've seen you before. Posted here recently, were you?'

'Yes, not long ago,' the policeman said. 'Don't let it happen again, sir.'

The tramlines were still flooded with rainwater, but the sun shone. Osewoudt was halfway up a stepladder behind the door fixing the broken cord of the blind. Evert Turlings came past, and pointed to the cardboard sign with the snapshots on it. He asked: 'Get much call for that, do you?'

'Not much. I don't do the work myself, actually. I ought to take that sign down, because the bloke who did the developing for me has given it up.'

'Good!'

'Why?'

'I'm starting in the developing and printing business myself. So if anyone comes asking, just send them on to me. I'll make you a present of some shaving soap! But you wouldn't have any use for it would you, ha ha!'

Osewoudt came down the stepladder, and asked: 'Is it difficult to learn? I don't know the first thing about it. Doing all that stuff in red light, don't you get exhausted?'

'Red light, did you say? That was how they did it in your grandfather's day. Modern films are sensitive to all kinds of light, including red.'

'So what happens if you develop them in red light?'

'They go black, of course. They're ruined.'

'Is there no chance of getting them to turn out right after that?'

'None at all. Why do you ask?'

'Just wondering. What with everything they can do nowadays. What I mean is—'

Evert Turlings squeezed his arm. He was almost a head and a half taller than Osewoudt.

'We're living in great age, in every respect. You'll see. I was saying so to Ria only yesterday. How is she, anyway? Still in bed?'

'Her temperature was down this morning.'

'I'll just pop in and say hello.'

Evert Turlings squeezed past the stepladder into the shop.

Tuesday, 23 July was a sweltering day.

At 1 p.m. Osewoudt locked up. He changed into a white shirt, white shorts and tennis shoes.

In this outfit he walked along the high street, a rolled-up towel under his arm containing his swimming trunks wrapped round the pistol.

He took the tram to Leiden, and there he took the train to Haarlem.

At 2.45 sharp he entered the waiting room at Haarlem station. Dorbeck was occupying a table beside a tall potted palm; there was another man with him. Otherwise the waiting room was empty. Dorbeck laid his lighted cigarette on the ashtray, half rose from his seat, and signalled to him.

Osewoudt went to the table, passing the towel from his right hand to his left. The other man, who had remained seated, looked up.

He had a large, despondent head oozing perspiration. His black hair was slicked down from a centre parting. On the table in front of him lay a small briefcase.

'This is Zéwüster,' Dorbeck said.

Osewoudt shook hands with him, but did not mention his own name.

Zéwüster was at least thirty-five years old. He wore a thick suit of brown serge.

'The address we're going to,' Zéwüster said, 'is Kleine

Houtstraat 32. Just follow me. Better stay a few paces behind. There's a fish shop near there where I'll wait for you. We go inside together. As soon as we're in the living room, you shoot. Shoot whoever's nearest to you. Mind you don't make a mistake, because if we both shoot the same man the other one'll take us out.'

Dorbeck called the waiter and paid the bill.

They all shook hands deliberately, as if they were saying goodbye for a long time, then left the waiting room. Dorbeck in the lead, Zéwüster following some ten metres behind. Osewoudt brought up the rear.

When he emerged from the station, Osewoudt didn't see Dorbeck anywhere. He could still see Zéwüster, though.

Walking on opposite sides of the street, they went down Kruisweg and then on in a straight line. Osewoudt was in the shade, Zéwüster in the sun. How light Osewoudt felt in his tennis shoes, compared to Zéwüster! It was like being on another planet, where the force of gravity is only a fraction of the earth's.

Zéwüster's wide body lumbered forward under the oppressive sun. The buttons of his jacket must all have been done up, for the thick fabric strained across his back and his pockets gaped. His left hand gripped the handle of the worn black briefcase. He held his arm pinned to his side, as if the briefcase contained dynamite that might explode at any moment, which gave him a strange, jerky gait. He did not look back.

They came to the side street where the terminal for the blue trams to Zandvoort, The Hague and Amsterdam was. Zéwüster stopped outside a fish shop. He still didn't look round, seemingly engrossed in the window display. Osewoudt crossed the street and joined Zéwüster in front of the window. Walking side by side they came to a tree-lined square.

'The public swimming pool's over there,' Zéwüster said.

'You can take a dip as soon as we're done. Was that what you had in mind?'

'No, I just took the towel to make the folks in Voorschoten think I was going to the beach. The son of the chemist across the street is a Nazi.'

Kleine Houtstraat 32 was on a corner. While Zéwüster rang the bell, Osewoudt looked in all directions, but didn't see Dorbeck. The door opened almost at once, and a spongy, bald man with a red face stood before them in the hallway.

'May we come in for a moment?' Zéwüster said.

Introductions and handshakes were apparently not expected. They filed down a cool but stale-smelling corridor. Zéwüster in front, then Osewoudt, and finally the man with the red face.

The door at the end of the corridor was ajar. Zéwüster paused by this door for Osewoudt and the other man to catch up. The man with the red face pushed the door wide open and they went in.

They found themselves facing a conservatory where, indistinct against the light, two figures rose from their chairs. Before they were fully upright Zéwüster said: 'Aunt Amelia sends her regards,' and immediately shots rang out. Osewoudt could no longer see a thing. He had his right hand in the rolled-up towel, which he held with his left hand to his chest like a muff, and through the towel he fired three shots at the red-faced man standing next to him. The man opened his mouth wide as if about to vomit, reached out to grab Osewoudt's shoulders, but missed and fell to the ground.

In the room hung a grey vapour that stank of cough drops.

Osewoudt ran into the corridor with Zéwüster at his heels.

Once outside, they saw Dorbeck across the street, bending over someone who was clinging on to his leg. Osewoudt saw Dorbeck kick the man's head. That was all he saw. He ran back to the square, slowed down, and walked calmly to the swimming pool.

The entrance hall of the swimming pool was crammed with maybe more than a hundred smelly German soldiers. Osewoudt leaned forward to the girl behind the ticket window.

'Do you have a *Wehrmacht* card?' asked the girl.

'No.'

'The pool is reserved for the German *Wehrmacht* today. Always is on Tuesday afternoons.'

He walked evenly out of the building, glanced around and strolled in the direction of the tram stop at the junction. A tram was just moving off, to the accompaniment of long-drawn-out whistles. Osewoudt broke into a run and jumped on. Not until the conductor approached him did he notice that the tram was going to Zandvoort.

He bought a return ticket to Zandvoort and headed for the 'Smoking' section. How could this be? There, sitting by the window, was the chemist's son. Evert Turlings was looking outside, unaware of Osewoudt. Go up to him and start a conversation? No, better get off at the earliest opportunity. But Turlings was on the right-hand side of the car, and people sitting there tend to notice passengers getting off. So he would be bound to see Osewoudt.

Osewoudt turned back and stayed in the 'No Smoking' section for the remainder of the journey. He had picked a seat as far away from the door as possible. At the Zandvoort terminal he waited for everyone to get off. When at last he left the tram there was no sign of the chemist's son.

He would have preferred to return by the same tram, but didn't dare. He might be recognised by the conductor, who would wonder why he had come to Zandvoort with a towel but hadn't gone for a swim. Just the kind of detail that would come back to him when the police started offering a reward for his capture.

So Osewoudt went down to the beach and sauntered along the seashore without bothering to take off his tennis shoes. He saw ships on the horizon; he also saw the black streaks his sweaty hands were making on the towel, and felt how tired they were from carrying the heavy object rolled up in it.

After an hour he turned his back on the sea and returned to the tram terminal. There was Evert Turlings, coming towards him. Evert's hair was sopping wet and plastered down on his head. Like Osewoudt, he carried a towel.

'Henri! I saw you!'

'No need to shout.'

'I saw you having a fight with someone in Houtstraat!'

'I didn't have a fight in Houtstraat. I wasn't there.'

The Nazi son of the God-fearing chemist looked down on him for a moment or two, raising the corners of his mouth. Then he began to whistle.

'You got changed quickly!' he said. 'You don't fool me, you know.'

'When would I have changed my clothes? Don't be daft! I haven't been anywhere near Houtstraat.'

'You got changed. You were wearing a grey suit before, with long trousers.'

'But I've been here for the past half-hour!'

'Liar! Otherwise you'd have been on the same tram as me coming here, and I didn't see you.'

'What does that prove? Trams take a lot of passengers.'

'You only just got here. Your hair's dry. You haven't been for a swim.'

'I was not involved in a fight in Houtstraat. You must have seen someone else. Where could I have changed, anyway?'

Evert slapped him on the shoulder and laughed.

They travelled back to Voorschoten together.

*　*　*

That night Osewoudt could not sleep for the cramp in his left hand. From the moment he ran into the chemist's son he had not dared transfer the towel with the pistol in it to his other hand.

For a whole week he thought almost continually of Dorbeck, hoping to hear from him. But Dorbeck did not turn up, nor were there any messages or notes. Not a word about the incident in the newspapers either. He racked his brains for some way of getting in touch with Dorbeck, but couldn't think of anything safe enough to try.

One Sunday night he finally had an idea. He remembered the roll of film Dorbeck had given him when they first met, that day in May when the Germans invaded. It was still in the drawer under the counter, undeveloped. He went down to the cellar and fetched out the developer and the fixing salt left over from his first attempt. It was a film that could be developed in red light, the label said, so this time it worked. All at once pictures appeared on the wet celluloid. He saw:

a big snowman with a helmet and a rifle

three soldiers wearing gas masks, their arms round each other, in pyjamas

a blurred image of someone who had moved during the exposure

a bare-chested soldier manning an anti-aircraft gun

another botched photo – several superimposed images.

The last one was a snap of Dorbeck standing in a street with his arms around two girls. It was so sharp that he could make out the number of the house behind them: 32. Naturally he thought of the address Kleine Houtstraat 32. He held the film up to the lamp for a closer look.

KLEINE HOUT he read at the edge, with some difficulty as the letters were in reverse. But it was the same house on the corner, there was no doubt about it.

He cut the film into manageable lengths, laid them in the fixing bath, and was still holding the section with the picture of the house when the door opened and the electric light was switched on. It was his mother, in one of her strange get-ups. She gave him such a shock that he did not call out, only went up to her with the negative still in his hand. She stood halfway down the steps, draped in a sheet, with a hat folded from newspaper on her head. She said she could feel it again and had come to scare it away. She pointed to the red oil lamp and asked what he was holding. 'Nothing,' he said, looking down at the negative, and then he saw it had turned quite black. He put it in the fixing bath, switched off the light and took his mother up to bed. He lifted the witch's cap off her head and screwed it up into a ball. When she was under the covers she began to sob, saying she couldn't do anything for him now. Then she had an attack of the hiccups. He tried giving her water, but that didn't help. Ria called 'What are you up to?' but didn't venture upstairs. Moorlag was out. The doctor came, but achieved little. All night his mother was kept awake by the hiccups. He crawled into bed beside her. As he couldn't sleep anyway, he got up every half-hour to look at the negative, in case something of an image had been saved after all. But the next morning, inspecting it for the last time, there was nothing, not even when he held it up to the sun; no house number, no Dorbeck and no girlfriends. The other shots were all right, and he made a set of prints of them.

At the end of August he read in the newspaper that a plane had been shot down in flames over Amsterdam. It had fallen on Legmeerplein, where it had completely destroyed one building and started fires in three others.

Osewoudt went to Amsterdam the same day. He took Dorbeck's photos with him.

The explosion must have been huge. Glass crunched under his feet as he approached the square, curtains flapped in the windows. Furniture, some of it charred, had been stacked in the middle of the road, which was closed to traffic.

He began to take note of the house numbers: 21, 23, 25. All that was left of number 25 was the porch.

'Excuse me madam, do you happen to know if there were many casualties?'

'Twelve dead, sir. The Jagtman family on the third floor, all of them dead. And then there's old Mrs Sevensma, and . . .'

On his return home he put away the photos in a safe place, as a memento of the only man he had ever admired.

The next few weeks he kept hoping, and dreading, that something would happen, or that someone, maybe Zéwüster, would get in touch, but these thoughts, too, evaporated, and in the years that followed it was as if the war simply faded from his existence.

In his left hand he held the sign he had just unwrapped: a smart plaque, made of some sort of ruby-red artificial glass. Painted on it were the words: EMPTY PACKAGING.

In his right hand he held the receipt for the sum of twelve guilders and fifty cents, dated 28 June, 1944. A reasonable price.

He went over to the window and slid aside the half-curtain that served as a backdrop for the display. Leaning forward carefully over the artful arrangement of empty cigar boxes, tobacco pouches and cigarette packets, he reached for the old card with the same inscription, grimy after three years propped in the window.

As he strained to reach it, head down, he had a vague sense of someone passing back and forth outside the window. He looked up, but saw no one. Yet he was sure there had been someone there, and also that they hadn't paused to look in the window before walking on in the *same* direction.

Straightening up again, he looked outside. But all he saw was the milkman on his delivery bike across the street, pedalling backwards to brake.

Osewoudt put the old card on the counter. Turning back to the display window, he noticed a brown envelope lying on the doormat.

He ran to the door and out on to the pavement, setting off the electric bell. There was no one hurrying away. He stopped for a moment and waved to the milkman. Once more he looked up and down the street, but there was no one who could have dropped off the envelope within the last minute.

What do I care, he thought, went back into the shop and opened the envelope.

It contained a white slip of paper bearing a message: *Have you developed my photos yet? Send them to PO Box 234, The Hague. Regards, Dorbeck.*

The entire message was typewritten, including the name at the end.

Osewoudt went to the post in time to catch the early mail collection, carrying an envelope in his hand. At the letter box he took a final look at the three snapshots in the envelope:

a snowman with a helmet and a rifle

three soldiers in pyjamas and gas masks

one bare-chested soldier in pyjama trousers manning an anti-aircraft gun.

Osewoudt checked the adjustable number on the letter box: 3, signifying yesterday's last mail collection. He slid the pictures back into the envelope, stuck it down and pushed it through the slit.

Just before five that afternoon he entered the main post office in The Hague. Looking constantly about him, he sauntered towards the wall of post-office boxes. Almost immediately he spotted the small metal door with the number 234. He waited.

There was the usual post-office fug of damp sacking, drying ink and endless yearning, but it seemed to him that he smelled it for the first time. From outside came the clanging of tram signals and the afternoon sunlight shafting into the airless, twilit space.

There were other people besides him waiting for the last

delivery. Some went straight to their box, key in hand, removed a small batch of letters and vanished.

By quarter past five Osewoudt was the only person left.

Maybe there's been a hitch and now Dorbeck can't come, Osewoudt thought, maybe he wants me to stick around near the post-office boxes for a couple of days until we manage to meet.

He felt his knees beginning to quake. If only he weren't so conspicuously alone! He had every right to stand there, of course, but wouldn't people notice him and wonder what he was doing? The last delivery had been made. What was he waiting for? Osewoudt turned round slowly, suddenly afraid that he was being watched, that it was perhaps a trap.

He stood where he was, his hand on the butt of the pistol in his trouser pocket. There were two exits, left and right, and he glanced continually from one to the other. The post office was now practically deserted.

Then he saw a woman enter. He thought she was coming straight towards him. She was wearing the Salvation Army uniform. He couldn't see her face as the light was behind her, only the shape of her bonnet with the bow, her dumpy figure belted tightly in her navy raincoat, her spindly black-stockinged legs. A shopping bag hung from her left hand. She marched up to the wall of post-office boxes and opened number 234, as if she came here every day. She put something in her shopping bag, shut the metal door with a click and walked off.

When she reached the revolving door Osewoudt went after her. She had a head start of some twenty metres. In the street too he maintained the same distance.

She crossed the street just before a yellow tram came past, clanging loudly. Osewoudt had to wait. When the tram had gone the Salvation Army woman was nowhere to be seen.

\* \* \*

The following day, at the same time, Osewoudt went to the post office again and waited by the boxes. But no one came to unlock number 234. He went back two more days; on the last day he was there at one o'clock and again at five. He waited until half past five, but no one turned up.

He went to the porter and asked which window dealt with post-office box rental. The porter pointed it out.

The window was empty. Osewoudt drummed his fingers on the slate counter and craned his neck to see as far inside as he could. At last a clerk arrived and asked what he wanted.

Osewoudt took a deep breath and said: 'Could you give me the name of the owner of box number 234? I can explain. That box number belongs to an acquaintance of mine, or rather, I believe it does. But I never get replies to my letters. So now I think I may have the wrong number.'

'Number 234, did you say?'

'Yes! 234!'

The clerk consulted a list, narrowed his eyes, shook his head.

'That number is not currently in use,' he said. 'If you have a moment I'll get your letters and return them to you.'

Off he went.

Osewoudt also went off, to the exit, out of the building.

And yet, the next day he was back again, hanging around the post-office box rental window in the hope of seeing the clerk who had told him that box 234 was not in use. That man surely knew more. That man was an accomplice, it was an inside job, because how else could the key of 234 have been in the possession of a Salvation Army woman only two days ago? That man had lied. There had to be some way of getting him to talk.

But someone else was on duty at the window the whole time. Osewoudt had hardly noticed what the man he had spoken to looked like, but he was sure it wasn't the one there now. Wait for the other one to come on duty again? But what would he say?

He got on the blue tram, got off at Voorschoten, waited for it to leave again, crossed the street and paused outside his shop to study the display.

In front of him, up against the glass, stood the plaque: EMPTY PACKAGING.

As if I'm running a shop selling packaging materials, he thought – everything I have on offer is empty, null, void. A tobacconist with an ugly, cheating, penny-pinching wife who's seven years older, a mother who's mental, and a father who was murdered – so much the better, too. Not that I had a hand in it. Shame. What is there left for me to do? I've got a Leica and a pistol stashed under the counter. But I don't know what to photograph and no one will tell me who to shoot. Things just happen. Nothing I do ever makes a difference. No news from Dorbeck for four whole years, and now that he's back he still hasn't shown his face.

He stepped to one side and opened the shop door. As if in response, the telephone began to ring.

He let it ring a second time, closed the shop door, waited for the phone to ring yet again and then lifted the receiver.

He didn't say a word, only listened.

'Hello? Is that Mr Osewoudt? I'd like to meet you. I beg your pardon, but I would really like to meet you.'

Osewoudt kept silent.

'I can't explain everything on the telephone, sir. My name is Elly Sprenkelbach Meijer. You have never heard of me. The thing is, I'd like to meet you, but you don't know me by sight.'

'Come to the shop tomorrow morning then.'

'I'd rather not. Can't we meet somewhere in The Hague? I have an important message for you.'

'About what?'

'Oh, that doesn't matter. What matters is how you will know it's me. I've thought of something. Could you come to the yellow-tram terminal at Voorburg this evening at eight? It's right by the viaduct. Be there at eight. I'll be holding a rolled-up copy of today's *Telegraaf* in my left hand.'

The line went dead.

He looked down at his watch. It was quarter past seven.

His watch showed five past eight when he got off the blue tram at Voorburg.

Through the underpass, over the level crossing, and there, a bit further on, is the yellow-tram terminal. Blue trams, yellow trams, trains, nowhere is there such a concentration of rail transport as in the suburbs of The Hague – and all of it crawling with Germans. How am I to spot a woman holding a rolled-up newspaper, how can I be sure she's alone? There could be two or three armed Germans watching the terminal, ready to pounce the moment I address her. Quite possible. They could be lurking among the other waiting people.

But rather than slowing down, he quickened his pace. He went through the underpass, nipped across the thoroughfare, arrived at the level crossing where the barriers were up, and came to the other side of the track.

Now for the clump of trees marking the terminal of the yellow tram. He could see the shelter clearly, and also the tram wires, starkly defined against the dark grey sky. But he couldn't get a good view of the people. A yellow tram rolled up and halted. I'll wait for it to go, he thought, then she'll be left standing there on her own. It's too crowded now. If she still isn't alone when the tram's gone I'll know how the land lies.

But the tram, having reached the end of its route, was in no hurry to depart. Osewoudt turned round, went back over the level crossing and struck left, thinking to keep an eye on the terminal from there. But he couldn't see it: there was a mass of new bricks stacked up along the railway line. He walked on, only to find his view blocked by the small station. Bells began to ring, a railway signal dropped. When he got back to the level crossing, it was closed. A rumbling in the distance. Hanging over the barrier, Osewoudt focussed his eyes on the tram shelter. The tram whistled and set off.

A car pulled up beside him, followed by a second. When the train finally thundered past dozens of cyclists were standing around him. The cars started up and the cyclists pushed off, one foot on the pedal.

In the middle of that small flow, hampered by a similar flow coming from the opposite direction, Osewoudt crossed the tracks and walked without hesitation to the now deserted tram shelter.

There she was. As soon as he saw her she met his gaze and held out a rolled-up newspaper.

She was hatless, her hair was long and sleek, and she wore a white raincoat.

He saw nobody else at the stop.

In lieu of a handshake he grasped the newspaper, saying: 'Elly? Are you the Elly who rang me up?'

'Yes, that's me. I wanted to speak to you.'

'I've never seen you before. Why did you phone? Why me?'

'I'll tell you later. Not now, not here. I've been here for ages, and I'm a bundle of nerves as it is.'

Her face was round and very pale, her mouth was small with red lips, which she moved slightly as though shaping words under her breath.

Osewoudt looked in all directions, but saw nothing alarming.

'Fine, we'll go somewhere else.'

He took her elbow and steered her along, away from the

tram stop and past the nursery garden at the corner of Prinses Mariannelaan.

'Now, will you tell me how you got my address?'

He was still holding her elbow and could feel her arm trembling. She was short, even shorter than him; he actually found himself looking down into her face. Her big, bulbous blue eyes stared up at him, unblinking, as she said: 'I was given your address in England.'

'When were you in England then?'

'I left the day before yesterday.'

'By train, I bet,' he muttered, letting her go. He thrust his hands in his pockets, his right hand seeking reassurance from the pistol.

'I have proof, you can trust me!'

He didn't reply for the next few minutes; then, at the corner of Laan van Middenburg and Prinses Mariannelaan, he pushed her into a café. He made sure they took a table near the door. She said: 'Why are you so pale? Your hands are shaking, it isn't malnutrition, is it?'

'No, things aren't that bad yet. Is that what they're saying in England? That people aren't getting enough to eat?'

'Yes, they say all sorts of things in England that aren't true.'

She couldn't be older than eighteen.

She now opened a bag that hung from a strap over her shoulder.

'They told me to show you this.'

Osewoudt almost gasped but took the photograph from her anyway. He had immediately seen what it was: a snowman wearing a Dutch army helmet and holding a rifle instead of a broom.

'I don't know what it means. They said it didn't matter, they just told me to show it to you and you'd know I was safe!'

'Who do you mean by "they"?'

'You know, back in England.'

He slipped the photo into his pocket.

'How did you come to be in England?'

'I was there already at the end of '39. I was staying with a family to improve my English. My father and mother are in the East Indies.'

'I didn't catch your name when you phoned. Would you write it down for me?'

Osewoudt took out the photo again and laid it face down before her. She fished about in her bag and brought out an unusual-looking writing tool. It resembled a propelling pencil, but the writing appeared to be in ink.

'What have you got there?' He snatched it from her. At the pointed tip he noticed a tiny ball.

'It's a ballpoint pen. What's so special about that?'

'We don't have them here. Don't ever use it again! The Germans haven't got anything like that. Have you gone mad? What will they think if they see you with that?'

'In England they never said I shouldn't take it with me.'

'Could you tell me a little more about the organisation that sent you?'

'No. They told me not to.'

'How did you get here?'

'In a dinghy.'

'When was that?'

'They put me ashore last night, at Scheveningen.'

'So where did you spend the night?'

She began to laugh.

'You're only asking because you want to check me out, naturally. You knew I'd phone, of course you did. You knew what was going on.'

'I don't know anything. Explain it to me.'

'In England I was given an address, an address in

Scheveningen. But the people weren't living there any more. So I went to an aunt of mine, here in Voorburg.'

'What did your aunt say?'

'Not much. But I've got to find somewhere else. On no account am I to stay with relatives. It's the rule.'

'Where will you go?'

'That's for you to say.'

'Is that why you phoned?'

'No, that wasn't the only reason. I wish you'd stop fussing! It was all arranged long ago!'

'I don't know what you're talking about. The first time I heard your name was this afternoon.'

'You don't expect me to tell you my real name, do you?'

'So it isn't your real name?'

'Are you saying you thought agents would ever use their real names? Are you having me on or is there something wrong with you?'

'I think there's something wrong with you, not me. You're telling me you just arrived from England on a boat. Nobody's allowed on the beach, it's swarming with Germans, and you say you came in a dinghy, just like that? You expect me to believe you? Well, well. Next you show me a picture which is totally meaningless as far as I'm concerned. Where did you get it? In England? When was that?'

She twisted her hands and lowered her eyes.

'Yesterday!' she said. 'Just before I boarded the dinghy, which was at half past eight. I was taken across the Channel in a motor-torpedo boat, then they rowed me to the beach. They gave it to me just before I got into the dinghy.'

'Are you sure?'

'Almost sure!'

'Not absolutely sure?'

'No, not absolutely sure. There was such a lot to remember,

I didn't think I was expected to remember when I got the picture. Stupid perhaps, but not unreasonable for someone who thinks others share their ideals. That's my biggest weakness.'

'Keep your voice down. Do you want the whole café to hear?'

'You make me want to scream, going on like that. You're making excuses because you're scared.'

Osewoudt jumped up, walked to the bar, paid and left the café without a backward glance.

But she went after him, still clutching the rolled-up newspaper.

'I don't know what to do,' he said. 'Best would have been for you to stay right there at that table. But it would be pretty naïve of me to think you'd leave me alone.'

'Leave you alone?'

'Yes! Leave me alone! Did you think I'd let you draw me out? What is it you want from me? Why did you phone?'

'I'd have told you straightaway if I thought I could trust you.'

'So why don't you?'

They were walking down Laan van Middenburg, in the direction of Rijswijkse Weg.

'I'll tell you why I don't trust you. You've got a shady look about you. That pale face of yours, the pale hair and smooth cheeks. And then that high squeaky voice. It's not that I'm scared, mind you. You can guess what I think you are. But if I tried to run away you'd get out your pistol and shoot me. Go on then, take me to the police – I've had it. I've been set up.'

A tram with blacked-out headlamps rolled towards them, whistling persistently.

'If you're so sure I'm from the Gestapo,' said Osewoudt when the tram had gone, 'you might just as well tell me now why you left England to come here. Save yourself some torture later on.'

'No, I'm not talking. I'd rather be dead.'

'That would be a shame. You're a nice girl, although you seem to have taken a dislike to me.' He put his arm around her and whispered: 'I'll tell you exactly what I think of you. When I saw that weird pen you've got in your bag I thought: where did she get that from? Must have been in England. But the picture, you understand – no, it's got nothing to do with me.'

'So you don't believe I got it in England?'

'No.'

'Why not? If it's nothing to do with you, if you've never seen it before, why won't you believe I got it in England?'

Another two paces and she in turn put her arm around him. But Osewoudt drew back.

'I can't help you! I must get home! You'll have to fend for yourself!'

He turned his back on her.

'Don't go!' she cried. 'You just gave yourself away! You must have seen that picture before, or you wouldn't care whether I got it in England or not.'

When they boarded the tram together he had yet to make up his mind where he would take her. Amsterdam would be the best place for her to stay. But with whom?

He looked her up and down, then glanced around in the gloom of the tram car, which was lit only by a few bulbs largely covered in black paint. Was she wearing anything that might stand out? Wasn't her white raincoat rather unusual, and what about that bag with the shoulder strap?

When the conductor came she opened the bag and handed him a silver guilder for the fare.

The conductor held the coin between thumb and forefinger and said: 'Is this a real one?'

'No!' said Osewoudt. 'You can keep it if you like, but here's a paper one. A silly mistake, you understand, a mistake.'

The conductor held on to the coin for a moment longer, then accepted the note instead.

Osewoudt gave Elly a nudge.

'Didn't you say you were saving it to have it made into a pendant?' he said, a little too loudly.

'All right for some,' said the conductor.

Osewoudt gave him a zinc ten-cent coin as a tip. The conductor moved away.

'What was wrong with that guilder?' she asked.

'Where did you get that thing? Everyone handed in their silver guilders ages ago.'

'I got it in England.'

'They might just as well have sent you here with a label on your back saying MADE IN ENGLAND. How many of those guilders do you have?'

'Twenty.'

'Don't ever spend one again!'

As they went into the railway station in The Hague, he said: 'Wait there, by the ticket window.' He ducked into a telephone box, dialled his own number and waited with pinched nostrils in readiness, his pulse pounding in his forehead.

'Osewoudt tobacconists,' he heard Ria say. 'What can I do for you?'

'This is . . .'

His eye fell on an advertisement on the cover of the telephone directory. *Mijnhardt's Tablets*. He said: 'This is Mijnhardt speaking, could I speak to Mr Moorlag?' He kept pinching his nostrils.

'Meinarends, did you say? One moment please, I'll see if Mr Moorlag is in.'

He heard her lay down the receiver. Then came Moorlag's voice: 'Hello Meinarends, hello!'

'Moorlag! This isn't Meinarends. Don't say anything yet,

don't give me away. I'll speak as softly as possible, I'm afraid Ria may be listening. Can you hear me?'

'Yes.'

'I won't be coming home tonight, I have to go to Amsterdam, I'll be back tomorrow. I couldn't tell Ria myself, you've got to help me. Stop her from getting upset when I don't come home. I'll be back, though, at least I hope I will. I have to find somebody a place to stay. She says she arrived here from England yesterday, identified herself with a photo that was still in my hands a week ago. So I don't believe the photo came from England. But I can't leave her in the lurch either. Wait for me at the station in The Hague tomorrow morning at quarter to twelve. If I'm not there, take my Leica and all the papers and hide them as quickly as you can. Do your best, Moorlag, help me!'

He did not wait for a reply but dashed out of the telephone box: their train, the last to Amsterdam, was leaving in two minutes.

'Did you get the tickets?'

'No, I thought you said I wasn't to spend any money.'

He dragged her through the barrier; the stationmaster blew his whistle as they entered the carriage.

'Don't you have any paper money at all?'

'Yes I do, but it's all new. You've got me worried now. The notes could be fakes, maybe poor ones. There's something else, too, which I probably shouldn't tell you because it'll only make you more suspicious, but it wouldn't be fair not to, so I will. Back in England they gave me an ID card, obviously, but the people I stayed with last night said it was no good. I don't know about these things myself, but apparently ID cards have a watermark, a lion I think, and the lion in the thing they gave me is far too small.'

Osewoudt laid his hand on her thigh and squeezed it hard, as if this might encourage her to keep quiet.

'Let's not talk too much here. People will think: what are those two whispering about?'

She put her arm around him and brushed his chin with the back of her hand.

Osewoudt looked at Elly, and drew her towards him.

'I can't believe you're over twenty.'

'I'm eighteen.'

'You can't stay with me.'

'Well, perhaps I could do something for you in return, in spite of my money and my ID card being no good. Surely there's something you're short of?'

She turned her hand over and stroked his cheek with the tips of her fingers.

'Not razor blades though,' she said. 'No shortage there, obviously.'

'Razor blades! Who needs razor blades?'

'I've never met a man with a closer shave.'

Osewoudt let go of her, almost groaning. But he took control of himself and said, with his lips close to her ear: 'There's no stubble because I don't have a beard. I never shave – don't need to. Feel.'

He pursed his lips and rubbed his chin along her ear.

The train stopped in Leiden.

'Don't you mind my not having a beard?'

She smiled, dimples appeared in her round, white cheeks, and her wide-eyed look became veiled, as if he had made some strange, sophisticated proposition and she was considering whether it appealed to her.

'Well in that case,' he went on, 'tell me, have you ever met someone called Dorbeck?'

'I told you before, I've met nobody. I just went to the address I'd been given, and when it turned out to be useless I went to my aunt's.'

'So you didn't meet a man who looked very much like me – same sort of face, same height, but with dark hair?'

'I do wish you'd stop banging on.'

'I'm not. The thing is, you could have come across this person under an alias.'

'You still don't trust me. Is that what you're getting at?'

'It's not a matter of trust. It's just that I'd like to know if you've been in contact with a man who looks very much like me except that he's dark-haired, the same as me but dark.'

'Not that I recall.'

'Strange. You arrived in Holland only yesterday. Not much has happened since, so little that you ought to be able to remember all of it without any trouble.'

The ticket inspector arrived, Osewoudt explained that they had to dash to catch the train, the inspector didn't mind and wrote out two tickets, without adding a fine. Osewoudt paid for them.

When the inspector had left, Elly said: 'This is the first time in my life I've been on a Dutch train.'

'You mean you've never been in Holland before?'

'No, I haven't. Soon I'll be seeing Amsterdam for the first time, too.'

The railway station was dark. So was Prins Hendrikkade, which they crossed, looking out for the occasional car with blacked-out headlamps like glowing rivets.

But the white sign saying FÜR WEHRMACHTSANGEHÖRIGE VERBOTEN at the approach to Oudezijds Achterburgwal was as visible as ever.

'What does it mean?'

'It means,' said Osewoudt, 'that this part of town is unsafe for Germans, which makes it all the safer for us.'

Uncle Bart answered the door himself.

'What, no housemaid these days?' Osewoudt asked.

'No, there's no one left,' said Uncle Bart. 'What did you expect? That I'd just carry on, sell all my feathers to the Germans? My feathers on every German whore's hat? I'd rather starve.'

'So who does the cleaning?'

'No one. I've shut all the rooms. I've moved my bed into the office. I have everything to hand, stove, table, bed. What more does an old man need? Come on in.'

They sat down in the narrow little office on the first floor. Uncle Bart had grown a moustache and his breath was so vile you could smell it even when he wasn't speaking, or maybe you smelled it constantly because he didn't keep his mouth shut for more than a second.

'So you've done a runner with a girlfriend, Henri. Doesn't surprise me in the least. I know exactly what you'll say: that you've had it up to here with Ria, she's so much older than you . . . Didn't I tell you? I always said you shouldn't get married. Yes indeed, your old uncle here has done a fair bit of reading and studying in his day. Didn't waste his time in the cinema, the way young folk do nowadays. The laws of natural selection can't be broken with impunity! Darwin knew that back then. What am I saying? Schopenhauer! What's the age difference between you and Ria again? Never had proper relations with her, I shouldn't wonder! Don't look at me as if you think your old Uncle Bart's lost his mind! I know full well no other father-in-law would dream of saying such things to his philandering son-in-law! But that's because most people don't use their brains, because they refuse to think about nature! Me — I don't care whether I'm your uncle or your father-in-law, all my life I've tried to observe the world with the unprejudiced eye of the naturalist! That has always been my goal!'

He leaned forward and gave Osewoudt two hard slaps on the knee.

'She seems a nice enough girl to me,' he went on. 'Indeed, a nice girl!'

He shifted on his chair to get a better view of Elly.

They climbed the dark spiral staircase.

'Is he an uncle of yours?'

'I call him Uncle, don't I?'

'But is he your wife's father?'

'That too.'

'He's very broad-minded. Or is that because of the war? In England they say the war's brought down the moral standards of the Dutch.'

'He was like that before the war. He's in a world of his own. If he had any idea of what's going on he'd be the strictest moralist of them all. Falling standards has nothing to do with it in his case. In my case, it might.'

He pressed himself to her back and put his arms around her. His hands were on her breasts. She thrust the back of her head against his face. As one, they climbed the last two steps, then stood still for a moment in the dark, by the door to his old bedroom.

'In my case there does seem to have been a loss of moral standards,' Osewoudt repeated. 'I would never have gone in for any of this in the old days.'

He felt her nipples harden between the tips of his fingers; he pushed her against the door of his room, which was not properly shut and so swung wide open. They stumbled and fell across the bed, on which lay two flat cardboard boxes that gave way under their weight with soft plopping noises and a smell of mould, dust, and stale herbs.

He pushed up her skirt, she lifted her legs and crossed them over his back. A loose floorboard thudded dully like a diesel engine, great green bicycle wheels rotated in the gloom. The girl's mouth felt so much bigger than it actually was. Oh to be slurped up by her, followed by the thought: this girl has come all the way from England to get shagged by Resistance heroes.

He got off the bed, stuffing his handkerchief into his trouser pocket.

When he had switched the light on he saw brown cardboard boxes stacked against the wall, Elly on the bed with one hand pulling her skirt down and the other shielding her eyes from the light, and protruding from either side of her the burst cardboard boxes leaking hundreds of small, red birds' feathers. They were still drifting to the floor.

Osewoudt shut the door. Elly lowered her arm, burst out laughing and then sat up. She swung her legs off the bed.

'The things a girl will do to avoid suspicion!'

'This war turns everything into a performance,' Osewoudt said. 'Come on, get up. This place is a mess.'

He pulled her to her feet, took the boxes off the bed, knocked them back into shape and added them to one of the stacks against the wall.

Elly swept up the scattered red feathers with her hands. 'Is that all you've got to say?'

'You're crazy, that's what I think you are. Was that what you wanted to hear? Or something else? Forgive me, but I haven't known you long enough to form any other opinion.'

She caught him by his jacket lapels.

'Never mind. Time passes much faster these days. If you think you don't know me well enough, just ask me questions – anything, the kind of thing you wouldn't normally ask people until you've known them months, or years. What else do you want to know about me?'

'That aunt you stayed with last night, is she married?'

Elly blinked a few times, as if this were a problem she needed a long time to solve, then looked away while soundlessly moving her lips and crumpling his lapels. Then she gave them a sharp tug.

'Do you want to know the address?'

'I just want to know if she's married.'

'Yes, she's married, but her husband happened to be out of town.'

'That makes no difference. Your aunt isn't likely to keep it from her husband. Is she in the Salvation Army by any chance?'

'Salvation Army? Salvation Army? What on earth? In the Salvation Army! Whatever gave you that idea?'

'Nothing,' Osewoudt said. 'I'm only asking because of the photo. You know, the one you gave me. I met a Salvation Army woman a while ago, and she had exactly the same one. I can't see why the people in England would give the same picture to every person making contact with me.'

'Is that true?'

'Clearly it is. The people who sent you over here are a bunch of incompetents. They give you useless fake identification and a bag full of silver guilders no one would be seen dead with in Holland these days. They didn't even take that funny-looking pencil off you. Go on, open your bag. Show me what else you've got in there!'

She emptied the bag out on the bed. There were nineteen silver guilders, three zinc quarters, two zinc cents, six food coupons, five new hundred-guilder notes and ten new hundred-Reichsmark notes.

'Where did you get the zinc coins?'

'They're change from the guilder I paid on the tram to get to the terminal at Voorburg. Otherwise I haven't spent anything. I was at my aunt's house until this afternoon.'

Osewoudt unfolded the identity card and held it up to the light.

'You're right, it's a rotten fake.'

He folded the card again and pocketed it. He also took the silver guilders. He scrunched up the paper money and put it back in her bag. Then he reached for her coat.

'You never know! There might be a label of some London shop sewn into it! That would be good. Save the Germans a whole lot of time if they started wondering where you came from.'

He examined the coat closely, the outside, the lining, the inside of the loop at the collar, but there was no label, number or name anywhere.

'The stitching is different,' he said. 'It looks peculiar, un-Dutch somehow. Could be the kind of stitching they use for army uniforms.'

He laid the coat down and she let him help her out of her sweater. She took off her skirt and underwear herself. It was pink, sensible underwear, made of coarse material. He inspected all the seams but found nothing suspicious. Still holding her vest, he turned to look at her. She was sitting on the edge of the bed with her arms to her sides in an attitude that might say: I'm cold, or, more likely, perhaps: I know my body's a bit flabby, I bet you're disappointed.

He laid the vest down.

'Henri! Henri! Listen here!' called a voice from downstairs.

Osewoudt left the room and went down two flights.

Uncle Bart stood in the doorway of his room.

'Did you take that girl up to your old bedroom? You'd better sleep in Ria's room. There are sheets and blankets in the cabinet. You know I'm not prejudiced, but there are limits. You know what I mean. Not being prejudiced isn't the same as saying anything goes, is it now? If you don't want to stay with Ria that's your business, but not under my roof! Do you get my drift? The world's immoral enough as it is. There's nothing like a war for bringing down morals. What do you take me for? Ria is my daughter, after all! My only daughter!'

'Of course, Uncle. Good night then.'

Uncle Bart seized Osewoudt's hand and squeezed it firmly. He smiled with relief and said: 'I've just been listening to a broadcast from London. Things are looking up! The front in Normandy is on the move. In a few months we'll be liberated!'

Osewoudt withdrew his hand and went back upstairs.

The girl had got under the covers. He sat down on the bed and asked: 'How long are you thinking of staying here?'

'That depends on you, and on your uncle.'

'No, it depends on how much work you have to do in Amsterdam.'

'I don't actually have anything to do in Amsterdam yet, but I may later. There's someone I have to see in Utrecht first, so I think I'll do that tomorrow morning. The person's name is de Vos Clootwijk. He's a railway engineer. I'm supposed to get him to give us information about German troop movements.'

There were still three people ahead of him in the queue when Osewoudt reached into his pocket for the fare. He looked in his wallet, but it was empty. Then he realised he had spent all his money the previous evening on tickets for Elly and himself.

He patted his side pockets and felt the silver coins he had taken from her, the old Dutch guilders. Also something flat and stiff: her fake identity card.

He broke into a sweat, glanced over his shoulder; there were at least ten people behind him. The train was leaving in eight minutes. What to do? Risk using the silver guilders? A ticket office clerk would be relatively harmless, being stuck on his chair. But what about the other people waiting by the window? What would they think when they heard the chink of silver, a sound unheard since the war started? What if there were someone from the Gestapo among them?

Osewoudt began to mumble, hardly knowing what he mumbled, and left the queue. He walked out of the station, his head full of vague thoughts . . . change the silver guilders . . . find someone on the black market . . . but how? He didn't know anybody. Ask a random passer-by?

For a quarter of an hour he wandered over Nieuwendijk, but no one accosted him, nowhere did he see anyone resembling a black marketeer. Wait until the afternoon?

Ten minutes later he was back at the station. The train had

left, and there was no one waiting at the window marked DIREC-
TION HAARLEM.

In a low voice, in German, he asked for a one-way ticket
to The Hague and quietly laid two silver guilders in the tray.
The clerk pulled the tray towards him, deposited the ticket plus
the change and put the guilders in his pocket instead of in the
till.

As Osewoudt went up the stairs to the platform it occurred
to him that someone might be sent to follow him on the train
to The Hague. What would be the safest thing to do? He
couldn't decide, so he carried on along the platform and took
a seat on the train.

Nothing happened. His train arrived at The Hague on
schedule at 12.15 and no one took any notice of him when he
got off.

He didn't count on Moorlag still being there. What would
Moorlag have done? I think what I told him was: if I'm not
at the station exit by quarter to twelve, something's wrong.

But Moorlag was still there, keeping a sharp lookout. He
had already seen Osewoudt, who responded with a nod. But
no sooner had he done so than Moorlag turned and wandered
off in the direction of Rijswijkseplein. Once Osewoudt had
passed the barrier Moorlag looked over his shoulder, saw him,
but kept on walking.

Mustn't run. Why is he acting so strangely? Osewoudt took
long strides. It was clear that Moorlag wasn't trying to shake
him off; on the contrary, he let Osewoudt catch up, though he
didn't stop, even when he must have been able to hear footsteps behind him.

'Osewoudt! I've been waiting for you for the past half-hour!
I'm a nervous wreck. The Germans came at ten this morning.
They've taken Ria and your mother away. Bundled your mother
and Ria into a car. I had just got up, was still in my pyjamas.

I saw it all from the window. When they were gone I ran down to get your Leica. But while I was upstairs getting dressed they came back. They're waiting for you. I fled over the roof. I went back later to take a look. The whole neighbourhood knows what's going on. Anyone going into the shop gets arrested. It's terrible! I've got nothing but the clothes on my back! They'll take away my books next, and books are so hard to come by these days! We've been shopped by that girl you rang up about.'

'Calm down,' Osewoudt replied. 'Even if you go back now they won't arrest you! They let you get away on purpose! Don't you understand? They let you get away on purpose so you'd come running to tell me what happened!'

It was an absurd idea: using Moorlag as a tool in all this wouldn't occur to any German. They had let him get away by mistake. If Moorlag hadn't been at the station what else would I have done but go home to Voorschoten – and get caught?

But Moorlag fell for it.

'Oh they're a crafty lot! Now I get it! They thought if I told you about your mother being taken away you'd get in touch with them straightaway, of your own accord. They want to catch you by using your mother as bait!'

'Not by using Ria!' Osewoudt laughed. 'Have you got that Leica with you?'

Moorlag reached into his pocket and with some difficulty pulled out the camera. A white envelope came with it, which became crushed in the process.

'What's that letter? For me, is it?'

'Yes, it was lying on the mat last night.'

Osewoudt put the camera in his pocket, then felt the envelope between his thumb and forefinger. It didn't contain a letter, but something much smaller than a folded sheet of writing paper. He tore the envelope open. Out came a snapshot of six by nine centimetres. It was of three soldiers in pyjamas, side by side. They wore gas masks over their faces and had their arms around each other's shoulders.

On the back a message had been printed in pencil: PHONE AMSTERDAM 38776 SATURDAY 5 P.M. DORBECK.

He tucked the photo into the breast pocket of his jacket, and as he did so felt the other one, which he'd got from Elly. One more, he thought, and I'll have all three of those damn pictures again, just the one to go: a soldier in pyjama trousers, bare-chested, manning an anti-aircraft gun.

'Hey,' said Moorlag, catching him by the arm, 'I'll stick with you of course. I'll do anything to help.'

Osewoudt looked down at himself: there was a bulge on his left side because of the Leica, and, he thought, a bulge on the right too because of the pistol. He fumbled in his breast pocket, took the photos out again and memorised the phone number: 38776. Then he tore them both up into small pieces, crossed the street and dropped the pieces into the water of the Zieken canal.

'You need a disguise,' said Moorlag. 'That would be best. Couldn't you grow a moustache?'

'No. I don't have a moustache.'

'Oh, sorry. Do you want my glasses?'

'All right, give me your glasses.'

They huddled in a doorway, looking about them in case anyone was watching. Moorlag took his glasses off. Osewoudt put them on. Straight lines were now curved and misty, the colours of pavements, buildings, roofs and sky running together like splashes of watercolour paint. Every time he moved his head the world became elastic. He could feel his gullet tightening as if he were seasick; with each step he took the ground seemed to fall away.

'Can you see anything?' Moorlag asked. 'I'm very short-sighted, the glasses are pretty strong, minus four, and the right lens is also cylindrical.'

'I can't see a damn thing.'

'Nor can I. I'm no good without my glasses.'

'Let's stop playing around like this. Here, take your glasses back.'

'No, don't give up. What if some German turns up and recognises you? Come on, better keep moving.'

Osewoudt sensed that Moorlag was pinching his coat sleeve between thumb and forefinger. Swallowing hard to suppress his nausea, he walked on, with Moorlag bumping along beside him.

'I say,' said Moorlag, 'the glasses aren't enough, of course. You'll have to get a hat. Makes an enormous difference to a face.'

'Come off it. You'll be giving me a false beard next. Damn!'

'You'll have to get glasses of your own. I'm not saying that because I want mine back, you understand, it's just that you should get some with a black frame and plain lenses.'

'Come off it. What will the optician say?'

'No, I'll buy them for you, at least I will if you give me the money.'

'All I have is seventeen real silver guilders.'

'What?'

'Real silver guilders! From that girl I had to take to Amsterdam yesterday. She got them in England! To live on as a secret agent! God almighty!'

'Don't get all worked up for nothing. Give me the guilders, I'll go and change them for you. I'll make a profit, you'll see. I know somebody. The black-market boys are scared their paper money won't be worth a cent after the war. They give three times the value for silver guilders!'

'Mind they don't call the police,' said Osewoudt. 'Oh damn

it all. I wonder where they've taken my mother. Given her an injection straightaway, maybe – finished her off. They do that sometimes with cripples or mental cases. Damn and blast.'

'Stop swearing, Henri. Look, you can wait here while I do the errands.'

They were standing in front of a narrow display window. Osewoudt raised the glasses, blinked a few times and read the sign on the pane: EAST INDIAN RESTAURANT PEMATANG SIANTAR.

There was a white card behind the glass in the lower right-hand corner, which said, in Gothic script: FÜR WEHRMACHTSANGEHÖRIGE VERBOTEN. DER ORTSKOMMANDANT.

'Wait for me in there,' said Moorlag. 'No Germans allowed, and it's still early so it may be empty. No one will see you.'

Osewoudt opened the door.

'Let me have my glasses back for now,' said Moorlag, 'I can't do without them.'

Osewoudt handed back the glasses, went inside and took a seat roughly in the middle of the empty restaurant.

A smell of fried onion and garlic reached him.

A white-coated Javanese waiter with a batik cloth tied around his head enquired in a whisper whether he wanted his rice on the ration or off. But suppose Moorlag didn't manage to change the guilders?

'I'll have a glass of soda water,' said Osewoudt, rubbing his eyes with both hands, still unaccustomed to being able to see properly.

A gentleman and a lady came in, sat down and ordered fried rice off the ration. It was half past twelve. Four young men came in, also for fried rice off the ration. More people drifted in. By two o'clock the restaurant was full to bursting, but Moorlag had still not returned and Osewoudt was now sharing his table with three strangers, all having fried rice off the ration while he had nothing but his soda water to sip every ten minutes.

He kept studying the menu, from which he could glean nothing of interest except that a glass of soda water cost twenty-five cents. A relief. He still had three zinc ten-cent coins in his pocket. No need to run off without paying, in so far as running off without paying would be feasible in a crowded restaurant.

He leaped up when he saw Moorlag through the window at last and deposited his three ten-cent pieces next to his glass. Moorlag came in carrying a large paper bag in his left hand. He cast his eyes around the restaurant, barely looked at Osewoudt, shrugged as if to say the place was too crowded for his taste, and walked out again. Osewoudt followed.

'Did you manage all right?'

'Of course. I got forty-five guilders for them. I also ordered a pair of glasses with plain lenses, but they won't be ready until this evening. And here's your hat.'

Moorlag opened the paper bag. It contained a green hat of coarse felt.

Osewoudt took the hat from him, Moorlag screwed up the bag and threw it away.

Osewoudt walked along, swinging the hat nonchalantly as if it had always belonged to him and he just happened to be carrying it in his hand. Then he put it on.

'Moorlag, I know it's awkward for you, but let's stop in this doorway so you can give me your glasses again.'

Moorlag promptly took off his glasses and handed them over.

'We must get a move on, we're taking the tram to Leiden. I know someone there who's well connected.'

They staggered on, both of them practically blind. Nausea welled up in Osewoudt's gut; the world now consisted of bulging gelatine, his brains seethed under the hat, for he had never worn a hat before and the hooks of the glasses chafed behind his ears.

'That friend of yours with the connections, any chance he could get me a new ID card?'

'Of course, that's what I had in mind.'

'I also need another one for that girl I told you about.'

At Bezuidenhoutseweg they boarded the tram to Leiden.

Osewoudt sat by the window with his hand shielding his eyes to ease the headache, and also to raise the glasses slightly, so that he could look out from underneath.

Squalid, run-down tenements along Schenkweg. Prim, middle class free-standing houses on Laan van Nieuw Oost-Indië. Stretches of sodden grassland. Beyond that the railway track, on which an electric train was racing against the tram. Voorburg. The small white station. Further back, to one side, was where I first saw her, in her white raincoat, a rolled-up newspaper in her hand.

Stop. Conductors get off. New conductors get on. A low whistling sound. Under the floor of the tram an electric pressure pump begins to throb angrily.

The tram gathers speed. Shade: the Leidschendam viaduct. On the horizon three windmills in a row. Shimmering glasshouses.

He felt the sweat beading on his brow; the leather hatband on the inside was beginning to smell.

Voorschoten. The tram slowed down as it rolled into the street where he lived.

He was now covering his face almost entirely with his hand, but his eyes bored holes between his fingers.

EUREKA CIGARS AND CIGARETTES. He kept his eyes on the shop as they went past. No German car outside, no crowd. Not a soul. The blind over the door had been fully lowered, but the blind over the shop window had caught on one side and hung down lopsidedly like a half-open fan. That's how the blinds hang in houses whose occupants have left in a hurry:

from the street there is nothing much to see. You ask yourself why they didn't at least lower their blinds properly before they went. But the neighbours know that the back of the house has been torched and that only time will tell how long the front will stay up.

At a white stuccoed house on Hoge Woerd, Moorlag rang the bell. The fanlight was decorated with a realistic, life-size painting of a white duck. Osewoudt took off the glasses and rubbed his eyes. Moorlag noted this.

'Let me have my glasses back, all right?' he said.

A young man in a long grey dressing gown let them in. He was short with a domed forehead under a shock of curly fair hair.

'Hello, Moorlag, my landlady's out, or it wouldn't have been me answering the door.'

'Stands to reason,' said Moorlag, in a tone that was new to Osewoudt. 'May I introduce you to Mr van Druten?'

Osewoudt held out his hand.

The young man took it.

'Meinarends is the name. It is a great honour to meet you, but are you by any chance keeping something under your hat?'

Meinarends kept his left eye screwed up, thereby raising the left corner of his mouth.

'I beg your pardon, I'm not very well,' said Osewoudt, stepping into the hallway. Only then did he remove his hat.

Moorlag pushed the front door to.

'Don't tease, Frits. He's had a terrible shock. The Germans are after him. His wife and mother were taken away by the Gestapo this morning.'

'Well, well. Then I suppose this gentleman would like a new ID card?' said Meinarends.

Moorlag tapped him on the shoulder. 'Good thinking, my friend, but there's more to it than that. I've had quite a shock too. I've lost my digs. But if you go back to your parents in Deventer, I'd be able to move in here.'

'I can't leave now,' said Meinarends as they went up a flight of stairs. 'I'm far too busy. Have you matriculated, by any chance? Is that why you're so keen on living in Leiden?'

They both laughed heartily. Osewoudt began to feel left out. These were students, the pair of them, for Moorlag also counted as a student, in spite of not yet having matriculated nor living in Leiden. And what am I? A tobacconist.

He took a packet of Gold Flake from his pocket and said: 'Care for a smoke, Mr Meinarends? A real English cigarette. Do have one, I run a tobacco shop, you see.'

Meinarends took a cigarette without looking at the brand, and put it between his lips. They went into a room with half a metre of books neatly lined up on a shelf. The room was clean and tidy, except for a large table by the window, on which lay various small implements which Osewoudt could not identify.

They sat down.

Meinarends struck a match and said, 'You must understand, Mr van Druten, the university has been closed down by the Germans. I have no business here any more, strictly speaking. Which is why our theologian here is after my room. But first he ought to matriculate, in my opinion.'

Osewoudt twisted the hat in his hands, felt himself redden, put the hat down on the floor, but couldn't think of an answer.

'How long would it take, an ID card?' Moorlag asked.

'Not very long.'

'I need two. Apparently there's something wrong with the

watermark on this one,' said Osewoudt, producing Elly's identity card. 'And I also need one for myself.'

Meinarends unfolded Elly's identity card, gave it a cursory look, then said: 'Made in England.'

He put it in his pocket.

Osewoudt said: 'The photo and the name don't need changing, but on mine the name has to be different, as well as the date of birth and everything else.'

'Occupation, too. How about police detective? You've got the right kind of face for that. A German name? Or isn't your German up to scratch? A German name is safer.'

'Not a German name,' said Osewoudt, drawing his feet under his chair. 'I have something for you in return.'

He felt in his inside pocket, took what he judged to be half of Elly's ration coupons between thumb and forefinger, and gave them to Meinarends.

Screwing up both his eyes now, Meinarends studied them through a magnifying glass and said: 'These coupons are remarkably good fakes, I must say. Pity they were declared invalid just an hour ago. Haven't you been listening to the radio? Don't you know what's going on?'

'We've been on the go all day,' said Moorlag. 'How could we have listened to the radio? We've been running around like refugees, no home, no nothing, haven't eaten all day either. Couldn't you find us a couple of sandwiches?'

Meinarends and Moorlag left the room at about five, saying they would be back in a quarter of an hour.

Osewoudt stood up as soon as he heard the front door slam. He went over to the table and examined the array of implements. He had worked out what they were for, but not how they were used. I'm no good at this underground stuff, he thought, I've got the face of a home-grown Nazi working as a detective for the Germans. Then he lifted the telephone from the hook, dialled the code for Amsterdam, waited for the tone and picked out Uncle Bart's number. An extraordinary blaring he had never heard before erupted from the earpiece. He put down the phone and cast around for a directory so he could check what the extraordinary noise might signify, but didn't see one anywhere. Maybe I made a mistake dialling the number, he thought. He tried again, but there was the same noise. He tried a third time, and a fourth. The fifth time he spoke each digit out loud before dialling and then waited a few moments before touching the phone again. All he heard was that strange blaring noise.

He headed back to his chair, changed his mind, dialled the information service and asked the operator for the number of Bellincoff Ltd., Oudezijds Achterburgwal 28, in Amsterdam.

'48662, madam.'

'I'm not a madam. And that's the number I've been dialling, Miss, but all I get is a whining noise rather like an air-raid siren, do you understand?'

'That means the number's been cut off, sir.'

'Cut off? By whom?'

'The account has been cancelled, sir.'

He thanked her and rang off. He looked out of the window, but there was no sign of Moorlag and Meinarends. He dialled the information service again. A different voice answered this time.

'Could you give me the number of the Sicherheitspolizei, at Binnenhof, The Hague?' He found a pencil on the desk and wrote down the number.

He telephoned the Sicherheitspolizei straightaway. A female voice answered. He said: 'Could you put me through to the department dealing with persons taken into custody?'

When the department came on the line, he said: 'Dominee Verberne speaking. I would like to know what has become of old Mrs Osewoudt of Voorschoten, who was detained this morning along with her daughter-in-law.'

'Information of that kind is not released over the telephone, Dominee. You should visit our office in person!'

Moorlag and Meinarends returned, having made up their minds as to the best course of action.

For the time being Osewoudt would stay with Meinarends, until the identity cards were ready. Moorlag would return to his relatives in Nieuw-Buinen, and didn't even take his coat off, as he was going straight on to catch the train.

'You know the address, Osewoudt, in case there's any trouble. It's easier for a person to hide where we live in the country. More food there too.'

Osewoudt shook his hand, saying: 'Thank you for everything you've done for me.'

'I did it for my country,' said Moorlag. 'Don't thank me, it's me who's grateful for the chance to serve my country by helping you.'

Osewoudt put his hands in his pockets and beat a rapid tattoo with his feet.

'Oh Christ! He'll be speaking in tongues next! Lord in heaven! Strike up the harmonium!'

Moorlag chuckled softly.

'You're thinking of your mother. She'll be in my thoughts too, Henri, if you'd rather not hear me say I'll pray for her.'

'You're a good sort,' said Osewoudt. 'I mean it.'

He turned away even before Moorlag left the room. My country, he thought, what's that supposed to mean? The blue tram? The yellow tram? The service is the same as before, except for the lights being dimmed after dark. A tobacco shop with empty packaging in the window? Dr Dushkind? North State? Havana cigars? I still have a packet of real English cigarettes on me. If Dorbeck hadn't asked me to develop a film for him I wouldn't have got mixed up in any of this. I'd be at home, safe and sound.

'You're an odd bloke, aren't you?' said Meinarends, when Moorlag had gone. 'What I wanted to say, though – you have a Leica, isn't that right?'

Osewoudt went over to his raincoat, then held out the camera. Meinarends did not take it.

'We could do with someone who can use a camera. If you want to get involved, I could find you somewhere to stay. You can stay here tonight, and tomorrow night as well if necessary, but not indefinitely.'

'I'll go now if you prefer.'

'Certainly not. The ID cards won't be ready till tomorrow. The best thing would be for you to avoid going out during the day for the next week or two. Can't you grow a moustache?'

'I don't have a moustache, no beard either.'

'You don't? Curious. Then we'll get your hair dyed black.'

'Fine by me, the sooner the better.'


But the following evening he was still waiting for his hair to be dyed.

'Listen here, Meinarends,' said Osewoudt, 'you must realise that I hadn't bargained for anything like my mother and my wife being arrested. I have appointments to keep. I was supposed to be in Amsterdam this morning. I can't put it off any longer. I have the papers now, I have money, there's no reason for me to hang around here. That girl's desperate for her ID card.'

'You idiot! Your ID card says your hair's black! And it's still fair! Have you gone mad?'

'Maybe. Don't get me wrong. I tried phoning that address in Amsterdam. No reply. I haven't the faintest idea what's going on there and I need to know. You go instead of me if you must, but I have to know, I have to get some message to them, it's the least I can do.'

'Me go? I can't leave here.'

'Fair enough. But black hair or not, I'm going to Amsterdam.'

'No you're not. Do you think I'd risk my neck on your account? What's the matter with you? If they stop you and your ID card says you have black hair while it's fair, don't you think they'll want to know where you got the ID card?'

'It's a risky business. Think of all the risks involved if I don't keep my appointment. Why only consider the people at your end?'

'But you can't go now. Tomorrow, perhaps. I'll see if we can hurry things up.'

Meinarends went over to the table and picked up the phone.

When it was nearly dark outside, he took Osewoudt to a small hairdresser's in Breestraat, directly opposite the town hall.

'Well, you can find your own way back,' he said when the door was opened.

The light was not on in the shop, but Osewoudt could make out a girl in a white smock.

'We can't switch the light on here,' she said, 'but I've got everything ready out the back, don't worry.'

She fastened the door bolts and took him by the hand, laughing out loud in the dark.

'It's through here. I'm taking you to the ladies' salon. That's where we do the dyeing.'

'Fine by me,' said Osewoudt. 'Nice smell in here.'

'You're in good hands with me, I promise.'

She pushed open a door. An empty space, brightly lit, almost dazzlingly so, with metal hoods on stands down one side and cubicles made of white curtains on metal rails down the other.

'Do take a seat, we pride ourselves on our prompt service.'

He sat down, she remained standing behind him. He saw himself and her in the mirror. Her breasts were level with his ears. It was impossible to see what she had on under the white smock: the neckline of her dress was evidently lower than that of the smock. At her throat hung a red coral pendant from a thin gold chain. She had a long neck, and also long, wavy, pale blonde hair reaching down past her shoulders. Her mouth was so big that her teeth were almost permanently on view. Beautiful teeth. She had a naturally smiling expression in any case.

She took a handful of his hair, and with her free hand brought a strand of her own to hold against his.

'Such sweet fair hair, do I really have to dye it pitch-black?'

'Everything sweet turns sour in war,' he replied. 'You mark my words!'

She took a small basin from the washstand, turned on the hot tap and filled the basin.

He wanted to put his arm round her hips, but she swung round to face him.

'Are you a student too?' she asked.

'No. I'm in the tobacco trade.'

'I went to university for a year and a half, but when the Krauts closed the place down I looked for a job here in Leiden. I was already rooming with these people anyway.'

She stirred some sort of powder into the water, put down the basin, draped a large towel over his shoulders and began to tuck the edge into the collar of his shirt. The backs of her hands brushed against his cheeks, so he said: 'I don't need to shave, I don't have a beard.'

'Really?' She turned her hands over and he saw her ten red fingernails lying like geranium petals on his face. He wished he could bite her slender fingers. She smiled, gave his jaw a playful pinch and asked: 'Something to do with hormones?'

'Never thought about it.'

'Everything okay otherwise?'

'Big questions for a little girl like you.'

'Come on! I was a medical student!'

'Want me to strip to the waist?'

'No. Just keep your head over the washbasin.'

She pushed his head down, warm water streamed through his hair. He heard the soap frothing, not through his ears but directly through his skull, he felt her fingers on his scalp. Another gush of warm water. Maybe it was warming up his brains. I'll be a new man, he thought, it'll be a new life! Ria arrested, the tobacco shop closed down, Uncle Bart may well be gone, too. I'm being born again. Whoever ends up winning this war, I'll be among the winners. He now felt her squeezing the moisture from his hair, then her two hands pushing his head back until he was sitting upright. He opened his eyes and saw the girl in the mirror again.

'Do you mind telling me your first name?'

'My name's Marianne. What's yours?'

'Filip.'

In another dish she mixed a black paste. She divided his wet hair into narrow sections, dipped the comb in the paste and set about applying the dye.

'Will it be ready soon?'

'It'll take another twenty minutes or so.'

'This is all so ridiculous.'

She combed. His scalp turned a shiny black. Suddenly it hit him: Dorbeck! He was the spitting image of Dorbeck! Same black hair, same white face with red spots on the cheekbones. If I'd always had black hair, my entire life would have been different, even without a beard, he thought. A man who appears and disappears as he pleases, bound by nothing but his own will, a man before whom the world bows. As if by magic, Ria and the shop fell away from him; he dared to admit to himself it might not be such a bad idea if the Germans helped his unfortunate mother to a painless but better world. He burst out laughing, couldn't stop.

'Keep your head still,' said Marianne. 'Watch out, you'll get the dye all over you!'

'My hair's turning black, but apart from that it's all sweetness and light,' he laughed. 'You've put a spell on me. It's not just the colour of my hair you've changed, it's my whole face!'

'In that case you'd better put your head over the washbasin again. Time for the final rinse.'

When he was sitting upright again, she passed him the comb. He stood up and made a parting in his wet hair.

She stood beside him, washing her hands.

'Like it?' she asked in the mirror.

He put down the comb and caught her wet hands. He was still laughing. At the edge of his vision he could see the mirror, and in the mirror himself, laughing. He was certain his new laugh would get her to do anything he asked!

'You've done a wonderful job. Not only have I turned into someone else, you have too,' he said. 'Know what I mean?'

She put her hands against his chest and pushed him away.

'I think you're crazy.'

'Yes I'm crazy, crazy about you. I can't imagine you wouldn't let me thank you with a kiss.'

But she pushed him further away: 'It sounds so silly when you put it like that!' As his hands were gripping hers he was unable to pull her to him.

'You don't mean that,' he said. 'But I won't insist.'

'Just as well. I hope I can take you at your word.'

He laughed some more.

'Before the week is out I'll be back, perhaps even the day after tomorrow.'

She pulled her hands free and left the cubicle. He followed her, putting on his coat as he went.

'Your collar's not right,' said Marianne, smoothing it down for him. 'Come on, I have to switch the light off. They'll be wondering upstairs what's keeping me.'

She tugged at a cord and the lamp in the cubicle went out, but the rest of the room was still ablaze with light.

He followed her into the narrow corridor.

'You know,' he said with his mouth close to her ear, 'I've done every heroic deed in the book, enough to get me decorated three times over, but until now I never knew what I was doing it for.' He buried his nose in her soft, long hair.

She turned to face him. Her expression was more serious than it had been all evening.

'After all, how many people really know why they're against the Germans? The dominees in London safe and sound behind their microphones, they know exactly what it's all about: Justice and Faith and Queen and Country. But none of that stuff means anything to me. I'm only against the Germans because they're our enemies, because I refuse to surrender to an enemy. I'm only fighting in my own defence. War as such doesn't make any sense, there's not a single ideology worth taking seriously. Freedom! they cry, as if freedom were something that ever existed. All very well for people making lots of money talking into a safe microphone, not for the rest of us. Being exploited is the one thing I really won't have. I won't be told what to do by people I didn't ask for advice. I didn't ask the Germans for anything. That's why I want them kaput. It's as simple as that.'

They were at the door. She began sliding back the bolts. The moon was shining and a slab of light slanted in through the display window just in front of Marianne, so that all he could see was the white smock and the glistening hair framing her face. She pushed the door open.

'It's five to eleven. You'd better be quick or they'll catch you straightaway, my little hero.'

He took her hand and she let him pull her forwards. But the shadow of the door frame fell across her face, so that only her body was clearly lit. Osewoudt bit his lip and gripped her hand more tightly than he meant to, and his arm began to tremble.

'I'll be back as soon as I can.'

She made to close the door but he was still clinging to her hand. Suddenly she pulled him close, kissed him on the forehead and the next thing he knew he was out in the street and the door was shut. He heard the click of the safety lock. He took a step sideways, put his forehead against the window, shielding the sides of his eyes with his hands. He stared and stared, but couldn't see anything move inside, and anyway his view was largely obstructed by the short curtain at the back of the display.

He started banging on the glass, thought to himself that this was ridiculous, turned back to ring the doorbell. Then he took something out of his inside pocket.

The safety lock squeaked and the door opened.

'You again? You'd better get cracking, it's almost eleven!'

'There's something I forgot to ask you. Would you do me a favour?'

'What is it?'

'Go to Amsterdam tomorrow morning, early, to Oudezijds Achterburgwal, number 28, Bellincoff Ltd. Ask to speak to Mr Nauta. If he's not there, try and find out when he'll be back. If there are any Germans about say you're from some firm or other, doesn't matter where, and that you've come to choose some feathers for a hat. Tell them you're a milliner's assistant and you need feathers for a client. But if you get to talk to Mr Nauta himself, begin by asking him why he hasn't been answering the phone. If he has a satisfactory explanation you can carry on. But if he says he doesn't know what you're talking about, tell him to watch out, because Ria and her mother-in-law have been arrested by the Germans. Ask him where Elly is. Just ask after Elly. But if it turns out there's nothing wrong with the phone, give him this ID card. Put it in a sealed envelope first. Give him the envelope and tell him: from Henri. If he asks any questions, just don't answer them.'

He thrust Elly's new identity card into her hand.

Zoeterwoudsesingel did not have an even and an uneven side, the houses were numbered consecutively: 70, 71, 72. On the far side of the canal, which followed the zigzag course of the town's old defences, was a stretch of parkland with huge weeping willows.

Number 74 sat exactly in the crook of an angle in the zigzag waterway. The house was quite different from the houses to the left and right, which stood slightly further back. The windows and eaves were decorated with lavish woodcarving. There was no garden at the front, but next to the doorway there were iron railings enclosing a flagged space hardly big enough to park a baby's pram in.

The house next door was full of doctors, all of whom shared the same name. Their nameplates were set one above the other by the entrance.

Labare opened the door in person. He was about forty, and had a dented appearance, with hollow temples, hollow cheeks covered in a thick stubble of a mousy shade, and grey, spiky hair. He wore slippers. He extended an ink-stained hand and said: 'My name is Labare. Come in.'

'I'm Joost Melgers,' said Osewoudt, and shook the proffered hand.

He was quickly ushered upstairs. Labare drew him into a small, narrow room.

In it stood a narrow bed with a dingy white counterpane, a

straight-backed chair and a small table with an enamel basin and jug. On the wall: a framed picture of a family of ginger apes partially clothed as humans.

Labare sat down on the bed, and with a weary wave of the hand indicated by turns the chair and the space beside him on the bed. In his other hand he held a flat tin box.

Osewoudt sat down on the bed.

'Look here, Melgers, it's like this. You can sleep up here as long as nothing's going on, but in emergencies you'll have to stay in the basement. These are all strict orders. We have no time for amateurs, jokers, show-offs or blabbermouths here. There have been enough accidents already. Have you heard about the Dreadnought group? It's the firing squad for them all next week. That lot talked too much, they all knew exactly who the others were. The Germans rounded up every one of them in an afternoon at the same address. So we don't go in for chit-chat here. Like to roll yourself a smoke?'

'No thanks. Allow me to offer you an English cigarette.'

'You'd better hang on to those.' Labare opened the tin box and rolled a very thin cigarette with pitch-black, hair-like tobacco.

'So in an emergency,' he went on, 'you go straight down to the basement. There are bunks there too. Besides, that's where all the work is done. It would be safest if you stayed down there permanently, but that's a bit hard . . .' He paused. 'A bit hard . . . You might as well come down with me now. Could I see that Leica of yours?'

Osewoudt got out the camera and handed it to Labare. Labare crossed his legs and examined it with head bowed. He kept the roll-up between his lips, the smoke curling around his hollow temples. He was breathing through his mouth and began to cough.

'Not bad, new model. No close-up lens?'

'No.'

'Why not?'

'I've never had one.'

'Never had one?' Labare looked at him as if he thought Osewoudt had lost it, or even deliberately destroyed it.

'So what in God's name have you been doing with that Leica? Oh well, it's none of my business.' His voice tailed off. 'Rank amateur,' Osewoudt heard him mutter. Labare stood up with a sigh, then spoke out loud again: 'And is that Summar the only extra attachment you've got? No ninety-millimetre lens?'

'No.'

'You obviously have a lot to learn. Follow me.'

Halfway down the stairs to the basement Labare stopped abruptly.

'Take a look behind you, Melgers.'

Osewoudt turned to look.

'See that rope?'

Osewoudt saw the rope.

'If you pull that rope a whole contraption of iron bars comes down behind the door, a kind of grating, but much heftier. So anyone wanting to force the door from the outside has a hard time of it. That's what it's for, understand? No, don't pull the rope now, because once the bars are down it takes more than one man to get them up again. More than two, in fact. The windows in the basement are heavily barricaded too. So that could get very nasty.'

Labare went on down the stairs. 'Very nasty,' he repeated. At the foot of the stairs he stopped again, thereby obliging Osewoudt to remain standing one step up. Labare said: 'As you can see, it's very cramped here. We have to make the best of what little space we have. So we knocked up all these cubicles from hardboard. What's in those cubicles and what goes on there is none of your business. None. What would be the point of you knowing, anyway? It never does anyone any good to know about things that are none of their business. No good at all, especially not with the tricky kind of work we do here.'

He began to wriggle his way into one of the narrow passages between the board partitions.

'Getting around is a bit of a squeeze for me, but it won't be a problem for a small chap like you. I'll take you to where you'll be working, and then I'll show you where the emergency exit is, too.'

Osewoudt walked, or rather sidled, behind Labare. The passage became so narrow that it was impossible to advance by putting one foot in front of the other in the normal manner. Moving sideways, scraping between the partitions, they came to a black curtain no wider than the passage.

'You will have noticed,' said Labare, 'that every light bulb has a smaller one beside it that isn't switched on.' He pointed to the ceiling. 'Emergency lighting, in case the current fails. We've thought of everything. No messing about here.'

He pushed the curtain aside, took a step forwards and then stopped to hold it open for Osewoudt. Osewoudt looked past him.

The cubicle beyond the curtain was painted black all over: ceiling, floor, walls and even shelves, which were stacked with canisters and brown bottles. There was no window, not even a boarded-up window, but there was a small washbasin and a folding bed.

'In here,' said Labare, 'is where you'll be doing most of your work. I might as well explain right away. This is the darkroom. Nothing like a darkroom for shedding light, eh? Now don't go thinking that the things that come to light are any business of yours, just concentrate on making it happen. You can do it with your eyes shut, in a manner of speaking.'

He reached for a black ebonite container rather like a jam

jar, but slightly wider and not as tall. He removed the cover and took out a reel.

'This thing is your developing tank. Unfortunately it's the only one we have, so you can't develop more than one film at a time, and developing plus washing takes a full hour. All those boxes contain films that need developing. There must be about eighty, as there's been nobody to process them for the past fortnight or so and new films come in every day. We have a huge amount of documentation. But even when you've developed a film you're not done yet, because you still have to thin it. You probably don't have a clue about the technical side of photography, like most people who snap merrily away, so I'll tell you how it works.'

He shut the ebonite container and put it back on its shelf, then leaned back with his elbow resting on the same shelf to facilitate his standing delivery.

'A film, Melgers, consists of two things, mainly: a strip of celluloid which we call the emulsion base, and on top of that a thin layer of gelatine, which we call the emulsion. The emulsion is the photosensitive layer. Now, in thinning, we separate the emulsion from the base. The problem with that is the instability of the emulsion – once the gelatine falls apart the image is lost. So before we start thinning we have to toughen the gelatine layer.'

He took a bottle from the shelf.

'This is used for washing the film. When that's done we can start prying the emulsion off the base. We make sure the gelatine comes off in one piece, without tearing. That gelatine layer is extremely thin. Once it's properly dry it can be rolled up so tight that it can easily be hidden, inside a propelling pencil for instance. Not that we have any of that romantic stuff going on here. We thin down films mainly to save space. I can't abide romantic notions of any kind in this business.'

To mark his switch from the technicalities of film processing to philosophy, Labare slid the bottles together on the shelf and rolled himself another cigarette.

'You must think of this as an ordinary job, you don't want to get carried away thinking there's a war on and you're a hero or anything like that. Obviously, we have to make safety precautions and stick to them, but it's the same in peacetime, too. Down mines, in chemical factories. That is how you should see our safety precautions, it's as simple as that. We have no use for heroes. What is a hero? Someone who's careless and gets away with it. We have no use for careless people. I don't need men who keep shtum when they're interrogated by the Germans, but men who'll spill the beans – it's a question of making sure they don't have any beans to spill, that's all. Because if someone does know something, try holding a burning cigar to his balls and nine times out of ten he'll talk, and in the one case where he doesn't, well, he'll be stuck with burned balls for the rest of his life, which would be too bad.'

Osewoudt cackled shrilly, Labare laughed too, but inaudibly, only moving his lips, and he said in a nasal tone: 'Yes, my boy, that is how you must think of it.'

He shook his head.

'If anything happens, the first thing you do is pocket the finished films and switch on the light to expose the rest: they'll go black. You do that at the first signal. The second signal means it's time to leg it. I'll show you how it works.'

Labare put out his cigarette under his shoe and walked off. Osewoudt went after him, this time through another passage, one wide enough to walk down normally. It ended at a door.

'This door opens into the neighbours' house. Got that?'

Labare took Osewoudt back to the small darkroom, and said: 'You can start now. You know where everything is.'

\* \* \*

Osewoudt switched the light off, opened one of the canisters, had no difficulty loading the film on to the reel. He put the reel in the ebonite container, closed the lid, switched the light on again and began the procedure as explained to him.

While the successive baths took effect in the ebonite container, he sat waiting on a low packing case, elbows on knees, head bowed. Now and then he looked at his watch, undid the strap and fastened it again. It was very quiet, no sound from outside penetrated the darkroom, and there didn't seem to be anyone else in the basement besides himself. He reflected on all that had happened in the past week, starting with that phone call from Elly last Monday. He counted the days. It was Friday now! I have to be in Amsterdam tomorrow at five, make that phone call: number 38776!

Dorbeck has made a new man of me, he thought.

Not until half past eight that evening did Labare allow him to leave the house.

'I ought to keep you indoors all the time, really, as I have a feeling you're a risk outside, but I had one chap staying here who went clean round the twist being stuck inside twenty-four hours a day. And that was a sight more risky for us.'

Osewoudt had developed and thinned ten films, which had taken him ten hours straight. He hadn't even had a proper meal, just a piece of bread from time to time without interrupting his work.

The fresh air had a sweet smell. He couldn't recall the air ever smelling so sweet. He took deep breaths to empty his lungs of the lingering stench of chemicals and cigarette smoke.

Ten minutes later he rang the bell of the narrow hairdresser's shop. The glass in the door was not curtained, so he could see Marianne coming from afar. Rather than a white smock she had on a white blouse with a dark skirt.

He shook hands with her, and hesitated: I'd like to kiss her, he thought, but didn't.

'Hello Filip.'

She sniffed the air a few times, inaudibly; all he saw was her nostrils flaring.

'You smell of formaldehyde.'

'You smell of perfume. I wouldn't know what kind, though, I know nothing about perfume.'

'Cuir de Russie. Formaldehyde reminds me of the dissecting room.'

'Then it may not be such a good idea for me to come in,' Osewoudt said as he followed her up the stairs. 'I don't want you mistaking me for someone else.'

'Don't worry, you're not *that* pale.'

Then he asked: 'So how did you get on? Did you go to Amsterdam? Did you pass on that message for me?'

'Yes, of course.'

They went into a warm room, small but not particularly narrow, more or less square.

'Who did you speak to? Mr Nauta himself?'

'Yes, I did. There was nothing the matter.'

'Nothing the matter, you say? What about the telephone?'

'Your Mr Nauta said he'd had the phone taken out as he's giving up the business. He doesn't want to sell his feathers to the Germans, he won't have Kraut whores wearing his feathers. Why Filip, you look surprised. I thought he was a nice old gent, digging his heels in like that.'

Marianne laughed, reached out to him and began to unbutton his overcoat.

Osewoudt said: 'All right, all right.' He undid the last button himself and laid the coat over the back of a chair.

'How did you introduce yourself?'

'I said what you told me to say. I said: Henri sends his regards. I've brought an envelope for Elly. Wasn't that what you meant? That was what you told me to say, wasn't it?'

'Yes, that's fine. And did you get to see Elly?'

'No, she'd left a few days earlier, Mr Nauta said. He explained what happened. She arrived there on the Monday evening with a nephew of his, and the nephew was married to his daughter! Can you imagine? He said his daughter's much older than the nephew; I had the idea he wasn't very fond of the daughter, he thought she was mean and could imagine why his nephew would go off with someone else.'

'What was the nephew called?'

'He didn't say. What's it to you anyway?'

'Oh, nothing. Carry on. The nephew brought the girl to his house, then what?'

'I wish you'd sit down. You're not in a hurry, are you? No one ever comes to visit me here.'

Osewoudt sat down. Marianne dropped on to the divan. She folded her legs beneath her and rested her hand on them. He saw that she was wearing smart stockings; he took another good look at her, thinking she must have dressed up for him. Cautiously, he sniffed her perfume. Cuir de Russie.

'So Mr Nauta didn't know when Elly would be back, then?'

'No. It went like this. He said: I'm not prejudiced, I didn't mind putting them up for the night. I wouldn't have known where else to send them anyway. It was already close to eleven when they arrived. But I didn't feel like having them for weeks on end, he said. He said it wouldn't have been fair on his daughter.

'The nephew left fairly early the next morning. The girl stayed. She didn't go out all day. By eleven that night the nephew still hadn't come back. The girl then knocked on Nauta's door and asked if his nephew, or rather his son-in-law — I don't know how she referred to him — had said anything in particular. When he'd be back, for instance.

'At that point Mr Nauta apparently began to lose his temper. He said that he wasn't prejudiced, but that there were limits. The man wasn't prejudiced, he must have told me that a hundred times! Right then, no prejudices, but there were limits! The poor girl took the hint and left the next morning.'

'He sent her packing without an ID card?'

'Yes, I think so. She probably hadn't mentioned that she

didn't have one. Whatever. What are you getting worked up about?'

'Wouldn't you be worked up if you'd gone to a lot of trouble to get a good ID card for someone and they went off without it, just like that?'

'It's annoying, of course.'

'What did you do with the ID card? Did you give it to him anyway?'

'No, I'm not that stupid. Nor did I tell him about the Elly girl not having an ID card. Because people are bad and you don't find out just how bad until you're living under German occupation, like now. Don't you agree, Filip? I thought if I told that man she had no ID he might phone the police! Whether he's prejudiced or not! Or he'll let it slip in conversation with his daughter, and then the daughter . . .'

Osewoudt drew a deep breath and said: 'It was very sensible of you not to mention that. Did you pass him the other message, about Ria and her mother-in-law having been arrested, I mean?'

'No, you said I was only to tell him that if there was something strange going on with his telephone. So there was no need to.'

'It was more than just a password,' Osewoudt muttered.

'What did you say?'

'I didn't say anything.'

'Oh yes you did. Did I do something wrong? But I'm positive I said exactly what you told me to say! I didn't make any mistakes! I'm very careful about things like that.'

'Yes.'

'Don't you believe me?'

'But of course I believe you.'

'I say, Filip . . . did you ever meet this Elly girl, by any chance?'

'Never set eyes on her. Why do you ask?'

Marianne turned her hand briefly palm upwards, then laid it on her leg again: 'If you knew her you might be able to track her down. Mightn't you?'

Osewoudt got up from his chair. He looked at the three Japanese cups ranged on a sideboard of brown oak, he looked at the picture on the wall above: Whistler's *Portrait of the Painter's Mother*, complete with a prose poem beneath. Well, well, Uncle Bart, so you threw her out, he thought. So much for not being prejudiced.

'I say, Filip, do you know what I think?'

He went over to the divan and sat beside her.

'What do you think?'

'You're a nice boy, but it's as clear as daylight! She's gone to the nephew, of course, that nephew of Nauta's, the nephew-cum-son-in-law! She must have known where he was!'

Now Osewoudt burst out laughing, thinking: mustn't laugh, mustn't laugh, not now, and he tried to picture Elly standing somewhere with her hands up, surrounded by German policemen. But he couldn't stifle his laughter. Between gasps he managed to say: 'What if she was stopped on the way without an ID card?'

'Oh, come on, I'm sure she didn't have far to go. The nephew must have rented a room nearby! Where else could she have gone? Plenty of rooms to let around there anyway. She'll get herself another ID card, I'm sure.'

Marianne fumbled behind her back for her bag and slid it forwards. She took out Elly's identity card. She held it at arm's length, studying the photo.

'Not very pretty, is she?'

'No?' Osewoudt wanted to take the card from her, but Marianne clung on to it. 'I didn't look at her properly,' he said. Marianne's thumb and his thumb in parallel. Elly's portrait in between.

'She looks rather dim.'

'Yes, and so puffy.'

'No sense of humour in those eyes, not a flicker.'

'Not like yours.'

Marianne raised her eyebrows.

'You flatter me. I only hope you're right.'

'How do you mean?'

'What would I do without a sense of humour? Seriously, Filip, sometimes I'm afraid I'll lose it.'

'Oh, come on,' he said, his head almost resting on her shoulder. 'We mustn't lose our sense of humour!'

He let go of Elly's identity card and Marianne placed it on the divan beside her. He kissed her on the temple, nuzzled the hair above her ear. 'We've got to hang on to our sense of humour,' said Osewoudt. 'The best way of doing that is: make sure you don't know too much about people.'

'You're absolutely right. There's not that much you can discover about other people anyway.'

She let him hold her hand.

'Especially at a time like this,' he said. 'Knowing a lot about someone always backfires. The best thing would be for everyone to change their names.'

'Oh, Filip, I wouldn't want you to change your name. I think Filip's a nice name. Filip . . .'

He was now leaning his full weight against her and she was slowly yielding. Then he asked: 'I hope my name isn't the only thing you like about me.'

She began to laugh, her lips quivering and drawing away from her delicious teeth, and yet there was a touch of disdain in her laughter, as if she wanted to say: how silly to be carrying on like this. Or maybe: men are always after the same thing. With his head he pressed her head into the cushions, his lips on her lips, and his tongue found the warm softness of her mouth. His hand slid under her blouse and he felt her ribs beneath a thin vest. Averting her face, she said: 'I suppose I ought to say you're a bit fast, but who knows what tomorrow will bring.'

He slid his hand upwards and cupped her breast.

'Time runs so fast we have to be fast to keep up,' he said.

He swung his legs off the divan and sat up. He could feel his eyes narrowing, his ears ringing.

'I want you,' he said, taking her hand and pressing it to his crotch without quite knowing what he was doing.

Marianne was still smiling, but her smile had grown sad. Yet she said: 'You never know, maybe you can get what you want.'

In his mind's eye he pictured himself as a towering figure, demon and hero, or at least as a fairy-tale prince.

He unbuttoned her blouse and her skirt. She let him take off all her clothes, but he kept his on. He lay on top of her and thought: she is naked but I've still got my armour on. What would I do without my armour? He lifted his head to look at her face. Her eyes were hooded with arousal, but her lips were parted in a smile that now seemed pitying. Not wanting to see this, he smothered her smile with his mouth and thrust his tongue between her teeth. It was as if he held her body taut between two hooks, or between two poles of a battery, and he sent a high voltage current through her frame, making her jerk convulsively and moan as though under torture.

She lay with her back to him. He sat hunched on the divan, adjusting his clothes. Elly's identity card had fallen to the floor. He picked it up and slipped it in his pocket.

Then he leaned over Marianne and planted a kiss on the small of her back.

'You have the loveliest bottom.'

She rolled over towards him.

'Do I? Go on, tell me all the other things you like about me.'

He gazed at her from head to toe. Abruptly, his eyes widened and he laughed.

'Hey! So the colour of your hair isn't natural either! I had no idea you'd bleached it.'

'No?'

'Didn't you think black hair suited you?'

He laid one hand on the hair that was still natural. With the other he ran his fingers through the blonde hair on her head.

'Black hair would look very good on you, too. Very good. Good enough to eat.' He kissed the dark hair, nibbled it and said: 'I'll graze it all off if you're not careful.'

'I didn't bleach my hair because I didn't like the colour.'

'No? Then why?'

'Do you mean to say you don't know? Don't think you can fool me!'

'I don't know what you're getting at. And I don't want to know either. I thought we'd agreed that it's best not to know too much about people.'

'Oh how discreet we are all of a sudden! Go on, take a good look at me, Filip, take a good look and tell me you can't see why I bleached my hair.'

'I can't look at you for so long in cold blood, it gets me too excited.'

But she pushed his head away, drew herself up and remained sitting upright.

'Do you really mean there's nothing about me that makes you wonder?'

'Of course I do! That's no reason to get cross now, is it?'

She began to laugh, looked down at her body and then at him, but although she was still laughing her eyes were so sad that she seemed to have long since died, and she murmured:

'Can you really not tell that I'm Jewish? Had it not occurred to you?'

Her voice grew louder and very matter-of-fact.

'My father, my mother and my two brothers were rounded up by the Germans. I was already a lodger here at the time, and now I'm in hiding. Are you telling me you really didn't know? Be honest, didn't you guess ages ago?'

Osewoudt pulled a face.

'Anyway,' he said, 'the worst is over.'

'How do you mean?'

'Any day now the Americans will force a breakthrough in Normandy, and then there'll be no stopping them.'

'Do you think so? It's already a fortnight since they landed, with all that hoo-hah about the Germans being taken completely by surprise and the Atlantic Wall being a fiction and so on and so forth. And where has that got us?'

'You shouldn't be so pessimistic. A week's not a long time.'

At five past ten on a Saturday morning a figure in a pale beige gabardine coat emerged from Amsterdam Central Station. He wore glasses. He looked about him and noted that the trees were already tinged with yellow. He looked up at the clear sky. The sun shone, a fine day after all. These damn glasses keep getting dirty, he thought, took the glasses off and fumbled under his coat to extract his handkerchief, but thought better of it and put them on again without cleaning them. The glasses had a heavy black frame.

The man wore a dark green hat. In his inside pocket he carried identification in the name of Filip van Druten, occupation: detective; hair colour: black. The hair visible under the green hat was black.

This was how Osewoudt pictured himself as he took the familiar route to his Uncle Bart's house.

Ten minutes later he called from the bottom of the stairs: 'It's me, Henri!'

He removed his glasses on the way up, but kept his hat on as he entered Uncle Bart's small room.

Uncle Bart crossed to the stove, the coffee pot in one hand, a cup in the other.

'I thought it was some gent with glasses, but it's you.'

'A gent with glasses? You must be getting awfully old! You should have your own glasses checked some time.'

Uncle Bart set down his cup of coffee on his desk.

'I was about to pour you a cup, too, but if you carry on snapping at me like that I may change my mind.'

Uncle Bart was already on his way to the wall cupboard for another cup. The hat felt heavy on Osewoudt's head. He didn't dare take it off, nor did he dare sit down. If I sit down he'll only notice the hat and the fact that I'm wearing it indoors.

He remained standing, but started unbuttoning his coat.

'I'm in a terrible rush, Uncle, I must be off again straightaway. It's just that I have some really bad news to tell you.'

Uncle Bart turned to face him. He held the cup of coffee in his hand.

'Why don't you sit down? Keeping something under that hat of yours, are you? Well I never, he's got a new hat!'

He stared at Osewoudt and Osewoudt noted that his uncle was poorly shaven, as usual, and he thought: I didn't realise Uncle Bart was so old. He said: 'Sorry about keeping my hat on. But I've come to tell you that Ria and Mother have been arrested by the Germans.'

'What did you say? Why would they do that?'

Osewoudt shrugged. Everything here smelled of lonely old man. The book lying open on the desk was by Hegel; beside the book lay a stub of aniline pencil used for making notes in the margins, which were veined with multicoloured scribbles: red, black and blue, resembling the cross section of a tumour. That's forty years he's been reading the same book, forty years he's been writing in the margins.

'Go on, boy, answer me. Why were they arrested?'

'Why? They didn't tell me! I wasn't there! If I'd been there, I wouldn't be here to tell you! Do you understand what I'm saying?'

'But surely you could have gone to the police station to find out what was going on?'

'Me go to the station? Me? What do you think! They'd have

locked me up immediately. I can go to the police, but I won't come back! That's the way it is these days, understand?'

'There's no need to shout! You're behaving as if it's my fault! It wasn't me that ran off with some floosie, remember!'

Osewoudt went up to him and grabbed his arm.

'Come now, Uncle Bart, I didn't run off with anyone! You don't get it. Is Elly still here?'

'Elly? You have the cheek to ask me where Elly is? Your wife and mother arrested and all you want to know is where that girl is? Come all the way here to wind me up, have you, acting as if butter wouldn't melt in your mouth? Good grief, has everybody run mad? Eh? Henri? What have I done to deserve this?'

'You don't get it, Uncle. But I really need to know where Elly is. Now, this minute.'

'All right then! I'll tell you! She went chasing after you the next day. Just as well, too, that she left when she did, because you know me: I'm not prejudiced, never have been, but there are limits!'

'She didn't come after me at all — I haven't seen her since, I swear. And it's not true that I ran off with her, as you put it.'

'Are you saying you're not fed up with Ria? That you came here with a girl you didn't even fancy?'

'Uncle, listen to me, please. If it had been like that do you think I'd have come to you of all people for a place to stay?'

'Stop arguing with me,' said Uncle Bart. Clutching his side, he staggered to the desk and sank on to his chair. 'Good grief! My poor sister! What a life, what a way to go! But surely that's not possible! Even the Germans wouldn't be such brutes as to lock up some unfortunate old woman for killing her husband years ago in a fit of insanity? They certified her as being of unsound mind!'

*For killing her husband!* Should he disabuse old Uncle Bart? Offer him a more likely explanation? Never! The less he knew the better!

'Oh, Uncle Bart, you have no idea what the Germans have been getting up to, ever since 1933! People who've served their sentences for past crimes and who've been perfectly law-abiding ever since are being sent to concentration camps and done away with! *Berufsverbrecher*, professional criminals, that's what they call them!'

'I don't care what they call them, you must still do everything you can to secure your mother's release. It's your duty!'

Osewoudt sat down and slurped his coffee. Turning things over in his mind, it struck him that his uncle's assumption might not be so far-fetched after all. The Germans might indeed have come for his mother and not for him! What evidence could they have against him? Why would they have come to get her on Tuesday morning, at a time when Elly was presumably still safe with Uncle Bart? Even if Elly had already left by then, even if she'd been stopped in the street and the Germans had wrung his address from her, that still wouldn't explain their coming for his mother and Ria on Tuesday morning!

'Was there anything in the papers about it, Uncle?' he asked.

'About what?'

'Have the Germans made any announcement about detaining former criminals and the insane? Was it on the radio? You listen to the radio every day, don't you? Was it in a broadcast from London by any chance?'

'How should I know? You're the one talking about the Germans sending recidivists and people of unsound mind to concentration camps without trial, not me! All I said was that I can't see why they would arrest an old woman who had an unfortunate accident involving her husband ten years ago, who's been before the courts, who's been treated in an institution and who's never hurt a fly since! And what about Ria? What did she do?'

'I don't know, Uncle. Everybody's up to something, but not everybody's found out! Take yourself, you have a radio, you listen to broadcasts from London, that alone could get you two years hard labour. The Germans can arrest anybody they like, only for being in breach of some rule of theirs. Not that they abide by the rules – they just go around arresting people anyway! How could I possibly find out why they've taken Ria?'

'What's wrong with you? Are you daft? Grow up! Are you going to allow your wife and mother to disappear without lifting a finger? Damn you, didn't it ever occur to you to get hold of a lawyer?'

'A lawyer? But my dear Uncle Bart, it's not as if we're living under the rule of law. You must be mad. Do you want to be arrested too? The first thing they'd ask any lawyer requesting information is: who sent you?'

'He could say it was me!' Uncle Bart cried. 'Let him say I sent him, let the lawyer say: I am here on behalf of Mr Nauta, the brother of old Mrs Osewoudt and the father of young Mrs Osewoudt. I'll instruct the lawyer accordingly. Do you hear, Henri? I'm not afraid! And if the Germans consider someone like your mother a danger to the public, I'm prepared to reach a compromise with them. I'll do whatever it takes, but they're not sending her to some concentration camp! I'll offer to put her in a private clinic at my expense!'

Osewoudt's jaw began to twitch, he was barely capable of remaining seated. His forehead itched unbearably under the brim of the hat. Without realising what he was doing he took off the hat and wiped his forehead.

'What on earth?'

Breathing noisily, Uncle Bart leaned forwards, open-mouthed, stubble down to his Adam's apple.

'I said,' Osewoudt went on, 'that it's no use sending a lawyer because the Germans won't take any notice. Believe me, Hitler isn't the same as Hegel, even if they both begin with an H! If we could fork out 20,000 guilders, or 50,000, it would be different, then they might listen!'

Osewoudt didn't look at Uncle Bart. He twisted the hat round in his fingers as he spoke, or rather shouted: 'I also said that it's ridiculous to think they could have arrested Mother over *that*. The Germans have plenty of other people to arrest! Besides, public health issues aren't a priority. They must have had some other reason, I'm telling you, otherwise why would they have taken Ria as well?'

He saw stars before his eyes, which were fixed on Uncle Bart's shoes.

Then he felt a tug at his hair and looked up. Uncle Bart was shaking his head from side to side, foaming at the mouth.

'But you, what have you done to yourself? Have you dyed your hair? How come it's black?'

'Lay off, will you! What? Black hair? Yes, it's been dyed! And do you know why? Because it's me the Germans are looking for! It's me they're after, just me! Get it? They only took Mother and Ria because I wasn't at home!'

'Then you're a coward! How can you abandon your own wife and mother for your own safety? To think that you didn't go straight to the police and say: here, take me, just let my mother and my wife go, because they haven't done a thing!'

'I'm not a coward. But I can't possibly give myself up!'

'Not a coward! A degenerate, that's what you are!'

'Degenerate? Not that again! Degenerate – because I don't shave I suppose! Damn, damn, damn! Ha! Ha!'

It was not laughter, just the exclamation 'Ha! Ha!', as if he were reading a story out loud.

'I repeat,' Uncle Bart said, 'degenerate! What have you been up to? Why are the Krauts after you? Because you've been selling those filthy cigarettes on the black market? Did you think I didn't know? The fool goes and gets his hair dyed because he's scared! If it were anyone else I'd be splitting my sides. But my own flesh and blood! Who shared my home for years! I did everything to make a reasonable man of him! But he's in the black market! Selling cigarettes, the cancer of modern society! He's dyed his hair like some old woman! It's unspeakable. You make me sick.'

Osewoudt stood up. He put one foot forward, holding his hat over his groin. He withdrew the foot and put the other one forward. In a soft voice, more consoling than combative, he said: 'You've got it all wrong. I can't help being in this situation, it's just the way it is. I had no choice. I'm not in a position to go into detail now, but you really are mistaken. Don't go to a lawyer, Uncle Bart, because you might regret it, if not in the short term then certainly when the war's over.'

Tears welled in his eyes and in his nose; he had to clear his throat before continuing.

'Mother and Ria are innocent, they haven't done anything. The Germans will release them after a few weeks, I'm sure. But I beg you, stay out of this. Our enemies are making things bad enough for us as it is.'

But Uncle Bart grabbed his chair, lifted it up and set it down again violently, with the back to Osewoudt and the seat facing his desk. Then he sat down on it, bent over the desk and riffled the pages of his book as if looking up a particular passage, or no, as if trying in vain to locate a passage that might apply to the situation. He smacked the desktop with the flat of his hand.

'Oh for God's sake, boy, get out of my sight!'

Osewoudt stood up and said: 'I never knew you had such a low opinion of me. The fact that you don't understand proves that you have always despised me. It's because you've always despised me that you won't believe me!'

Uncle Bart refused to look at him. His hand kept striking the desktop, not particularly hard, but impatiently.

'I suppose you can't help it, boy, but I happen to know where you come from. I knew your father.'

'True, you knew him, I didn't. But you're talking complete rubbish. You should listen to what I'm saying instead of thinking about my father. You're as bad as the Germans: you can't think straight. But that's neither here nor there. I'm long past caring whether you believe me or not. But I beg you Uncle Bart: don't get mixed up in this, because it's asking for trouble, not only for you, but for me as well.'

Yet when he was out on the street again, he was plunged into such despair that he felt capable of going up to the first German he saw, saying: here I am! But there wasn't a German uniform in sight, which was hardly surprising in a part of town that was *verboten* to the *Wehrmacht*. He heard tapping on a window and turned to look. Beckoning him was a pale, fat whore. She sat behind the glass on a raised chair, her knees drawn up, her slip rucked up over her thighs.

'Too early!' called Osewoudt, blowing her a kiss. He laughed. It was not until he was going down Damstraat that he noticed he was still carrying the hat. He put it on and glanced around to see if he was being followed.

It was quarter past midday. What to do until five o'clock? Get something to eat for a start. He went into Restaurant De Gerstekorrel, removing his hat once inside. He picked a table at the back, hung his coat and hat on a peg in the wall, and sat down facing the leaded window. German music came from a radio. There were Germans occupying various tables: field-grey Luftwaffe officers, green SS ones, fat Germans in civilian clothes. And there were also fat Dutchmen with slim brief-cases, doing business.

The waiter came promptly to take Osewoudt's order.

'Can I order something with my ration card, or is that too inconvenient?'

'The only difference is the tip, which people don't always . . .'

'You can count on me.'

Osewoudt handed him two meat coupons and two butter coupons, and ordered steak, fried potatoes, peas and pancakes.

'Oh yes, waiter, and a large beer!'

The beer came first. He immediately gulped down half of it. In the meantime he tried to eavesdrop on his neighbours, but there was so much noise he couldn't catch what was being said.

Mother in prison, and me sitting here! Nice smell of food, though.

What sort of life would you have had if your mother hadn't lost her mind and you hadn't been obliged to look after her? Would you have married Ria? Would you, aged eighteen, have taken to running a tobacconist's like some retired navy officer or an invalid speed cyclist?

But if I hadn't done that I'd have been completely dependent on Uncle Bart. I certainly wouldn't have met Dorbeck! Dorbeck! Where would I be if it weren't for Dorbeck? My hair's black now, just like his. I've become his twin brother!

He checked his watch: 1 p.m. Must make that telephone call at five. Maybe I'll get to talk to him. Maybe I'll meet him again soon. What would he say if he saw me now? I know what I'd say: are you sure you're not looking in the mirror? What a laugh.

He looked up. An old woman stood at the table just beyond him. She had a flat basket on her arm and was talking to two Germans sitting side by side with their backs to him. She wore black, with a faded green scarf tied round her head. Short and shapeless, she stood out against the coloured panels of the leaded window, looking like a greatly magnified potato. She turned back the cloth covering her basket, and the Germans inspected the contents. The German nearest her even pushed his chair back the better to lean over and poke his nose in.

'Two guilders!' the woman cried. 'Good and *fett*!'

The man sat up again. A discussion with his companion ensued. The little old woman stood where she was with the cloth folded back, waiting for the Germans to make up their minds. In the end they shook their heads from side to side, loudly saying '*Nein! Leider!*'

The old woman covered her basket again, took a step back and looked at Osewoudt. Only then did he see that she was his mother, escaped from prison and now scratching a living hawking smoked eels from a basket. Don't give me any more of your warnings, Mother, please, Osewoudt muttered to himself. I can't help you, but you can't help me either. Your warnings won't get us anywhere.

The old woman drew level with his table and lifted the cloth again.

'Nice plump eels, sir.'

'I can see they're nice plump eels, but I can't be dealing with them just now.'

'Food is scarce these days, sir. Save them for later.'

'I'm going on a journey, I can't take them with me.'

'Well, what if I wrap them in newspaper?'

'No, thank you.'

He felt in his pocket and offered her a guilder.

'I didn't come here to beg, sir!'

She made her way past him to the table behind.

Half past one. He had finished his meal and couldn't very well linger in the restaurant. How to kill time until five?

Without really looking about him, he set off towards Dam Square, dragging his feet.

Uncle Bart must now be on his way to his lawyer, he thought, that old friend who's been his business adviser for the past forty years, an old man like Uncle Bart himself. And he'll say: of course, Bart, I'm entirely at your disposal! But you must understand, simply going to the Germans and demanding explanations, an old man like me, walking right into the lion's den . . . Look here, Bart . . .

And so he witters on. Doesn't go to the Germans. Better wait and see, he says. Here, take a look at this underground newspaper, I've got the latest issue of *Het Parool* for you. You can keep it, but don't leave it lying around! The Krauts are finished, that's what it says! Uncle Bart returns home, placated. How long before he gets restive again, though? A week? Probably less. He doesn't know what to think, but he's as pig-headed as ever, like in the old days when Aunt Fie finally got him to the registry office and they left Ria's pram with the porter! That was a good deed, to his mind, no: a Deed. With a capital letter! Something to be proud of later on. But why did he really do it? He did it because in those days you couldn't go around taking potshots at anyone you didn't like, not like now. Born at the wrong time, that was his trouble!

Osewoudt walked down Kalverstraat and turned right towards Spui. The electric clock on the corner by the church showed two o'clock. Osewoudt reached the University Library, just past the church, and stopped.

When I left secondary school, he thought, Uncle Bart talked about me going to university. If I had taken him up on it I might have been spending my days reading books in this very building. I wonder what it's like inside? Would it be open to the public?

He halted at double doors of pale oak. No signs saying

anything like RING or KNOCK. He pushed the right-hand door and it yielded. He entered a marble vestibule with a porter's lodge on the left, in which an old man sat pasting small circles of white paper on to the spines of books. Osewoudt doffed his hat, but the old man glanced at him only briefly before continuing what he was doing. Up a few steps and he found himself surrounded by oak; a strong smell of floor polish wafted towards him. Behind a counter sat a woman in a white apron, knitting. A sign at last: CLOAKROOM COMPULSORY. Osewoudt laid his hat on the counter and took off his coat. The woman put down her knitting, handed him a thick brass disc with a number, took his coat and hat and hung them on a rack.

An oak staircase, lit only by a leaded window on a small landing. More stairs. Glass doors left and right. He looked through the door to the left and saw a gathering of intellectuals, some standing still and others strolling about. He looked through the door to the right and saw long tables occupied by people reading books. But what shall I read? he thought, as he went in. The walls were lined with books, even the spaces between the windows were fitted with bookcases. Wooden stepladders stood here and there along the stacks.

An elderly scholar wearing pince-nez left his chair, moved the library steps to another stack, took down a book from a high shelf and returned to his seat. So you were allowed to take a book from any stack you liked! No need to ask anyone for permission either! Osewoudt had reached the first reading table. On his right he had seen a woman sitting at a vast desk, like a schoolmistress presiding over a classroom. The supervisor, apparently, but not a very watchful one, as she was engrossed in a book like everyone else.

Osewoudt paused deliberately for a moment or two, looking intently in her direction, almost hoping she would beckon to him and ask what he wanted. He hadn't yet decided what he would say. But the woman looked up from her book, saw him, and carried on reading. She had dark, fairly thick woolly hair, which looked as if it hadn't been combed but simply gathered at the nape of her neck. She was not particularly young, but her glasses were decidedly ancient: thick round lenses in a gold wire frame. She wore a green woollen dress, as green as the baize of her desktop. It could even be the same material, he thought, people run up clothes from the strangest fabrics these days, maybe there was some baize left over. She can't be earning much.

He advanced into the room. Some readers glanced up at him distractedly, their minds still on the books before them. He looked away, anxiously hoping to spot a title he would be bold enough to take to a vacant seat at one of the tables.

Some of the stacks had labels indicating the subjects ranged on the shelves. The labels seemed to demand his diploma, but he didn't have a diploma in any specialised subject. Once I'd done my school exams I never opened a book again. Flogged all my textbooks to the boys in the next year. Good riddance, I thought at the time. Am I sorry? He was now at the far end of the reading room and his gaze slid over the readers' backs. Why would I want to be like them? I might not have been bright enough for university anyway, or not bright enough to be brilliant. And then if I'd ended up at a desk like that supervisor I might well have thought: I'd just as soon be a tobacconist.

He now noticed the clock over the door through which he had come in. The clock said five past two. Three hours to wait; but not here. He retraced his steps as quickly as he dared. The supervisor now drew herself up and made to approach him, but he just grinned and went out of the door. At that moment someone emerged from the opposite door across the landing. It was Zéwüster, clasping a booklet.

'Hey!'

Osewoudt had raised his voice, but his cry was somewhat stifled.

Zéwüster stood with his hand on the banister and one foot already extended to go down the stairs. He gave Osewoudt a quizzical look.

'Hello Zéwüster!'

'I beg your pardon?'

'You are Zéwüster aren't you? ... I am ...'

His voice trailed off, against his will; it was as if Zéwüster's eyes transfixed him, as if he had lost the ability to move or speak. His forehead went ice-cold.

'I beg your pardon?'

'Yes, Zéwüster. Surely you remember?'

His voice faltered again, the last words trapped in his chest.

'You are mistaken, my name is de Bruin.'

Osewoudt now stood beside the other man, with his hand on the other banister, ready to start down the stairs, and a kind of rage made him overcome his paralysis.

'If your name isn't Zéwüster why not just say: I am not Zéwüster. Whether you're de Bruin or de Wit or anything else doesn't matter to me!'

A trio of students squeezed between them and went down the stairs. Zéwüster followed, quickening his pace and over-taking them without a backward glance. Osewoudt went down the stairs as well. The three students stopped to retrieve their coats. But Zéwüster did not stop at the cloakroom, he strode towards the marble vestibule, booklet in hand. Hatless and coat-less, he went out into the street.

Osewoudt collected his coat and hat and went after him. When he got outside Zéwüster had vanished.

It was my black hair that scared him witless! There he was, accosted by a man he's never seen before. Never? Why didn't he think I was Dorbeck, not even for a moment? Or is it Dorbeck he is scared of? Could he be a traitor? Has he switched sides? Is he working for the Germans? Has he gone to warn them? To telephone? Maybe he was caught by the Germans and they only let him go so he'd betray his accomplices. Which is obviously what he's gone and done: *I've got him! I've got him! One of the Haarlem gang! Quick, you lot! He's been found!*

Osewoudt ran to the other side of the Singel canal and down the steps to the basement urinal by the water. It was unoccupied. He had a good view of the lay of the land through the slits at the top, just above pavement level. He fumbled under his coat to transfer the pistol from his trouser pocket to his raincoat pocket.

Nothing unusual was going on. Trams came past at regular intervals, now and then a car, some bicycles. No cause for any anxiety. He stood there for a quarter of an hour, then thought: I might just as well have left immediately. The police aren't coming or they'd have been here by now, they know it's too late anyway.

At that moment he caught sight of Zéwüster.

Zéwüster was coming from Spui, walking along in his brown suit, looking exactly the same as before. He was alone. Both his hands were visible. The booklet poked ostentatiously from his jacket pocket. At the corner he looked in all directions as if he wanted to cross the street, but Osewoudt wasn't fooled. No, Zéwüster was not about to cross, he was simply on the alert. He made his way towards the University Library and halted by the entrance. Again he looked behind him and across the canal. Then he went in. Wait for him to come out again? Follow him inside?

But Osewoudt stayed put.

The library door swung open to let someone out. A moment later the door opened again, this time it was Zéwüster. Just popped in to fetch his coat, obviously. He paused on the pavement, again looking around him, then set off in the direction of Heilige Weg.

Osewoudt mounted the steps to street level, and walked slowly towards Koningsplein. Zéwüster knew who I was, he thought, and he was scared. Or he thought I was Dorbeck, and it's Dorbeck he's afraid of. He may not be a traitor after all, he didn't go to the police, he simply bolted and then came back for his coat.

Osewoudt did not go in the same direction as Zéwüster, although there was no particular reason to avoid a second encounter. He walked with his hands in his pockets, the palm of his right hand growing moist around the butt of the pistol.

He sauntered along Leidsestraat, crossed to the far side of Leidseplein and walked onwards, not knowing how else to pass the time.

On Overtoom he went into a shop selling fruit, after making sure there were no other customers within.

A woman with a red, chapped face stood behind the counter in a starched white apron.

'What can I get you, sir?'

Osewoudt lifted his hat, but did not take it off.

'I'd like to ask you something. Do you ever have occasion to make deliveries to people in prison?'

'Certainly, sir. We can make deliveries anywhere.'

'But if you're not certain which prison the person is being held in, is there a way around that?'

'I don't know, it certainly complicates matters.'

'The thing is, my mother's in custody, she was arrested by the Germans, and I think she's being held in The Hague. Would you be able to get a basket of fruit to her there?'

'Oh, sir, how very upsetting. And you don't even know exactly where they've taken your mother?'

'No I don't, they wouldn't tell me. But I'd very much like to send her something, as I'm sure you understand, only I don't know how to go about it. Even if they won't say where they've taken her, it might be possible for a parcel to reach her in prison.'

'Wouldn't it be better if you took it yourself? Then you'd at least be able to find out more.'

'That's just the problem, I can't get away at the moment, and I don't know anybody who could do it for me. Couldn't you help me out? I'll pay whatever it costs.'

'Oh sir, how dreadful it all is. You can leave it to me, no extra charge. I'll send my daughter. That's the best I can do. Only, we can't guarantee that the parcel will reach your mother.'

Osewoudt looked at her, contorting his mouth into a grin. The woman's eyes filled with tears. She wore gold studs in her ears, and he noted that her right earlobe had an extra piercing above an earlier one that had torn. Attacked in the street by a thief when she was a girl, he thought, possibly raped. She had a pencil tucked behind the same ear.

'What did you have in mind, sir?'

'Cherries would be best, I think.'

'That's all there is anyway. And in another week or so they'll be finished, too. We only get to sell fruit when there's a glut and there's so much the Krauts can't eat it all themselves. Yes, that's the way things are nowadays, isn't it?'

The woman crossed to the display, took handfuls of cherries from a propped-up crate and placed them in the scales. With her head to one side she read out the weight, slightly under.

'Do you want a card to go with it?' she asked.

'No, no, that won't be necessary.'

She took the pencil from behind her ear and set a very tall, narrow ledger on the counter.

'And what is your mother's name, sir?'

'Mrs van Blaaderen.'

'Van Blaaderen? But that's our name too! We're not related, are we?'

He looked at the shop window and saw the name in reverse on the glass – with two a's. He wanted to shout for help, but just stood there quietly.

'I don't believe we are,' he replied. 'We have no relatives.'

He undid the buttons of his coat and reached into his breast pocket.

'Oh no sir, I won't hear of it. You can settle up once the order has actually been delivered. We'll let you know how we get on. Your name, please?'

'F. van Druten,' Osewoudt replied.

'Van Druten, you say?'

She wrote it down. He now saw tears falling on her ledger. Meanwhile, he tried to think of an address.

The woman looked up.

'Oudezijds Voorburgwal, number 274,' said Osewoudt.

The woman stood her pencil upright with the point in the air.

'But sir! That's the address of the giro office! I should know – we're a sub-agent for them.'

'What did I say? I meant Achterburgwal, Achterburgwal.'

She began writing it down. Waiting for her to finish was torture, but he steeled himself.

Made a right mess of that, he thought, when he was back on the street. If it hadn't been for me saying the fruit was for my mother I could have given her my real name, no trouble. How could I be so stupid? I'll lose my wits altogether if this goes on much longer.

He could just hear the woman telling her family about him in her parlour: a man's mother . . . by the name of van

Blaaderen, same as us . . . no, no relation . . . the man's called van Druten . . . Oh, he was so twitchy . . . I didn't want him to pay in advance . . . he gave the address of the giro office, but he meant Oudezijds Achterburgwal, not Voorburgwal.

He visualised the daughter getting on the train to The Hague, carefully putting the bag of cherries in the luggage net . . . catching the tram to Scheveningen . . . asking the way to the prison . . . asking at the gate for Mrs van Blaaderen . . . being told she wasn't there . . . not believing them . . . flying into a patriotic rage, mouthing off about Hitler . . . being arrested herself, having the cherries thrown back in her face!

That must not happen. How could it be avoided? Oh, easily enough. *But it won't get my mother her cherries!*

He continued down Overtoom until he reached the T-junction with Jan Pieter Heyestraat. There was a public telephone in front of the technical college, and an electric clock across the street. There was also a tram stop.

Everything he needed for the next operation was at hand. Only, it was the wrong time: half past three.

So he walked on, turned left and came to Vondel Park. There he sat on a bench and waited for an hour and a quarter.

He was back at the telephone box at five to five on the dot, a precautionary measure in case it was occupied. It was not. To be on the safe side he went in anyway. He compared his wristwatch with the electric clock: they showed identical times. A woman with a brown leather shopping bag on her arm crossed the street and made her way towards the phone box. To justify his presence Osewoudt started leafing through the telephone directory. At his back the door was opened.

'Sir, since you're not on the phone, could I go first?'

'No! Clear off!'

'Charming, aren't you!'

Osewoudt grabbed the handle and forcibly pulled the door shut; fortunately the woman let go.

He held on to the door, using his free hand to lift the receiver, which he rested on the ledge while he fed a ten-cent coin into the slot and dialled the number. Then he picked up the receiver and listened. It rang only once before it was answered.

'Is that you, Osewoudt?'

'Yes, it's me. Dorbeck, is it really you? I say—'

'Shush! I recognised your voice. Forgive me for cutting you short, Osewoudt, but I want you to listen to what I have to say, just listen, you understand, I have little time.'

'But Dorbeck, I never get to see you, it's four years since you were last in touch. There's a lot I need to tell you, and a lot of questions to ask, too. Where have you been?'

'Some other time, can't go into that now. Just listen. I want you to be in the waiting room at Amersfoort railway station at 12.30 p.m. on Wednesday. Make sure you go to the correct waiting room, because there are two. Yours is the small one on platform one. Buy a return ticket to Wageningen beforehand. In the waiting room you'll see a girl in the uniform of a National Youth Storm leader. You go up to her and ask: haven't we met before? Aren't you Comrade Nispeldoorn's fiancée? If you've got the right person she'll say yes and show you a photo you'll recognise. Make sure you locate her before the train leaves for Lunteren. She'll give you further instructions. Good luck. And take some pliers with you! Mind you don't forget!'

'Dorbeck! Elly has disappeared! And how did she get hold of that photo I sent you? Wait, please listen—'

'Elly was betrayed in Utrecht by de Vos Clootwijk.'

The phone went beep, beep in his ear.

Beep, beep. Osewoudt hung up and hunted for another ten-cent coin.

'Still not finished yet?'

'No. Sorry. My business is at least as urgent as yours.'

He took the phone off the hook again, put the coin in the slot and dialled 38776. No reply. He hung up, the hook sank slowly with a rattle, the coin was returned. He dialled 38776 again. This time he heard a shrill tone, rising and falling. Wrong number, obviously. He hung up and started afresh, carefully dialling first three, then eight, then seven twice and finally six. Again the tone rising and falling, the same shrill tone as when he had tried ringing Uncle Bart from Leiden and his telephone had been cut off. The woman with the brown shopping bag now posted herself at the front of the box and pressed her nose against the glass, glaring at him.

Osewoudt hung up, dialled directory enquiries, got through to someone, and said: 'Could you tell me the name listed for number 38776?'

'38776. Just a moment.'

He waited. The phone made a very soft purring sound, like a gramophone record come to the end of the side. The woman went round to the back of the phone box.

'Sir! Are you doing this just to annoy me?'

He turned his back on her. She wedged her foot in the door and lunged forward, but as the box was a step up from the pavement she did not tower over him.

'You've been in there for over a quarter of an hour!'

'A quarter of an hour in a box is nothing these days, my dear madam!'

With his free hand he felt in his inside pocket and pulled out a card, which he waved under her nose, muttering: '*Polizei.*'

The woman let go of the door and made off without a backward glance. She walked stiffly and with her head thrown back, as if that was the only way she knew to keep herself from running.

He waited.

'Hello, sir?'

'Yes, Miss?'

'The number you gave is not listed, sir.'

At that moment a tram came into view. He ran to the stop and managed to catch it. By quarter to six he was at Central Station. He bought a single ticket to Utrecht and went to platform one.

In the telephone box he looked up the name: van Blaaderen, Vegetables, Fruits and Delicacies. The phone rang normally.

'Van Blaaderen speaking. What can I do for you?'

'This is van Druten. Do you remember me? I was in your shop a while ago to order cherries for my mother.'

'I remember, sir.'

'I have just heard that my mother has been released.'

'Oh that is splendid news! We'll deliver the cherries to her home address then shall we?'

'That won't be necessary. I'm sorry.'

He slammed the phone down. Shopkeepers! Money grubbers! And it's not even true that my mother's been released! She may be dead for all I know.

On the train to Utrecht he had ample opportunity to mull over his conversation with Dorbeck. The most plausible explanation was this: the first time, when he had actually got through to Dorbeck, the number he had dialled had been the right one. The second and third times he must have got the number wrong. But the right number never came back to him. He had torn up the photo with the number written on the back and thrown away the pieces. I memorised the number, didn't make any note of it, I was convinced it was 38776 but apparently not. What number did I dial the first time? 38876? 37886? 38667? 38676? 38677? 38687? 37886? He felt in his pockets for a scrap of paper and a pencil, found them, and began writing all the numbers down in the hope of recognising the correct combination if he saw it in black and white. But the train lurched so violently that he soon could no more rely on his handwriting than on his memory.

He screwed up the piece of paper, put the pencil back in his pocket and peered through the steamed-up window.

Utrecht. He had never been to Utrecht before, didn't know his way about.

On the platform he asked for a telephone box. It turned out he was standing practically beside one. He had already gone in when he saw that the directory was missing. A note had been stuck on the ledge, saying TELEPHONE DIRECTORY IN THE STATION CAFÉ.

At the café he ordered a cup of ersatz tea. He let it stand while he opened the directory at the letter V. But the name he was looking for wasn't listed under V. Under C then? Clooving, Cloppers, Cloppers, Clootwijk.

There it was: Clootwijk, J. B. G. M. de Vos, Chief Engineer Netherlands Railways, 21B, Stadhouderslaan.

Osewoudt paid and left the café without finishing his ersatz tea.

He asked directions, was told which bus to take.

It was half past six when he rang the bell at 21B Stadhouderslaan. Police, he said to the maid who answered the door. He lifted his right hand to the brim of his hat, but pulled the hat down over his eyes instead of removing it.

'Is Mr de Vos Clootwijk in?'

'They're having supper. I'll go and tell him there's someone to see him.'

'Very good.'

He didn't remove his hat until he was in the ill-lit hall.

'Do you mind waiting in there?'

The maid opened a door and went into a room. Osewoudt stood in the doorway. She went over to the windows and untied some cords. Blinds of black paper came down. She said: 'We're very strict about the blackout.'

'Quite right, too.'

The only light in the room now came from the corridor. Yet the girl didn't bump into anything on her way back to the door, where she turned a light switch. At the opposite corner of the ceiling, two small lamps with burgundy silk shades lit up. There were two more such lamps at the other corners, as well as a large ornamental lamp in the centre, but these remained unlit. The girl paused, her hand on the doorknob.

'Mr de Vos Clootwijk will see you presently.'

Osewoudt nodded, and she shut the door.

Over the mantelpiece hung a very large mirror, tilted forward slightly so that Osewoudt, standing in the centre of the room, could see himself from head to toe. The pale shade of his coat looked mauve in the burgundy glow of the ceiling lights, his face livid and luminous. He thought: it's true, I do look like the kind of sod who'd work for the Germans. The ghostly lighting, the oversized armchairs upholstered in purple-striped moquette, the lavishly carved, high-backed ebony chairs, the ebony cabinet, the almost uniformly dark-brown paintings, the luxurious light fittings, which also ran to a standard lamp with a satin shade and silk fringe — all this made on him an impression of invincible wealth. He wondered whether this visit would mark the beginning of the end. But he kept his eyes fixed on the mirror even when the door was opened. A portly gentleman entered, whom Osewoudt observed in the mirror before confronting.

The man paused after closing the door behind him, watching Osewoudt's movements. He was bald and bullet-headed; he wore a trimmed grey moustache. His jacket was unbuttoned and the pockets of his waistcoat were linked by a thin gold chain hanging down in two little loops.

Osewoudt made a fanning gesture with his hat, as if to dispel the atmosphere the man brought with him.

'Are you Mr de Vos Clootwijk?'

'What precisely do you want? I was at Maliebaan police station yesterday, and gave a full report of what happened. I have nothing further to add.'

The man stopped speaking, but went on working his mouth, the way people disturbed during a meal sometimes do.

Osewoudt took a step towards him.

'Did someone by the name of Elly Sprenkelbach Meijer get in touch with you?'

'As I said: I told them everything at Maliebaan station!'

'I have nothing to do with that station, I'm from the Binnenhof police station in The Hague.'

Osewoudt stepped sideways and dropped into an armchair. He gritted his teeth to stop them from chattering.

'It is annoying to be obliged to repeat the same story a hundred times.'

'But I haven't heard it yet. What happened, exactly?'

The man began to pace up and down at the far end of the room, by the window. He put his hands together and pressed them briefly to his nose.

'It was like this. Last Wednesday at about one o'clock, the maid came to tell me there was someone to see me. I was pressed for time, I went into the hall where the person was waiting. She made an extremely unfavourable impression. I told her I was in a hurry and had to be off in five minutes. She said she wanted to ask me something. And what do you suppose she asked me? Whether I would be prepared to give her information about trains being used for German troop movements, and if not, would I give her the address of some colleague who would. I told her she had come to the wrong man. So she left. But she had hardly been gone a second when the bell rang again. I was still in the hall, so I answered the door myself. It was the same young lady. She said: I am Miss Sprenkelbach Meijer. Please do not mention any of this to Mr van Stockum.

'I said I would not.

'My wife had been watching from behind the net curtains in the dining room, on the other side of the hall. My wife, too, formed an extremely unfavourable impression of her.

'I went to my office and reported the matter to my head of department, Mr Beuleveld. Mr Beuleveld contacted the police.'

'What for?'

Osewoudt stood up.

The man did not move.

'I suggest you ask Mr Beuleveld that, sir.'

'Did you think Miss Sprenkelbach Meijer was some sort of provocateur, sent by the Germans to give you a little test?'

'No I did not. She came from London! She also said her boyfriend was English. That is what she said.'

'So you believed her when she said she came from London?'

'Yes!'

'You believed her, did you? Strange. Then why did you turn her down?'

'Sir, I must protest! What makes you think I would pass on information to a complete stranger who turns up on my doorstep?'

'That wasn't all she asked for; she also asked, in the event of your being unable or unwilling to provide information, for the address of someone who might be.'

'But sir, do you really think that I, in my position—'

Osewoudt stepped forward. The man was not tall, but still taller than Osewoudt by half a head.

'Sir! You are, I believe, the right man in the right place at the right time! You occupy a senior and responsible post, but you're not sufficiently patriotic to run the slightest risk! You could easily have kept your mouth shut with your head of department, but you didn't even do that! Clearly it is not the place of someone like me to criticise your treatment of an emissary of the former government in London, but I must say: you have some funny ideas about our police methods! Thinking we would take it into our heads to send you some girl just to draw you out! You seem to have a strange notion of National Socialist values! Or, to be more precise: you seem to suffer from a mixture of base fear and a complete lack of political sense. What did you think – that the Germans have nothing better to do than send provocateurs all over the place to find out if any Tom, Dick or Harry might be persuaded to serve the very same government that they'd served until four years ago? As if the German police don't already have enough on their plate. The idea is absurd!

'The Germans only use provocateurs when they need evidence against people they already have reason to suspect. In other words, people who pose a threat, and whom they want to get rid of. But don't worry, you're not among them, you're too much of a coward.'

Osewoudt put on his hat and made for the door.

Mr de Vos Clootwijk stood rooted to the spot, working his mouth with increasing agitation, though by now he must have had time to swallow his food.

Osewoudt said: 'I dare say it surprises you to be addressed in this way by a plain traitor, a Dutchman assisting the German police. But I must advise you, sir, not to mention this conversation to anyone, not to the police at Maliebaan station and not to your head of department either. And if your wife happens to be eavesdropping you'd better tell her to keep her mouth shut, as you could be in great danger. I hope you survive this war, because I'd like to hear what you have to say for yourself when it's over and you are held to account. Thank you! I'll let myself out.'

He went out into the corridor, through the hall, and left the house. He ran off on tiptoe, darted into the first side street and then another. Only then did he slow down.

The train was still some distance from the station when Osewoudt posted himself at the carriage door. He swung it open before the train came to a halt.

He hurried down the platform, his fingers folding the lower half of his Leiden-Amersfoort return ticket. He ran up the steps of the railway bridge, down the other side, passed through the barrier and walked to a ticket window.

'Third-class return to Wageningen.'

He paid and straightened himself up, licking his lips which were parched from all the panting. He followed a party of cattle dealers into the waiting room.

There she was! The National Youth Storm leader! What luck! Beddable, smashing legs too! On her ash-blonde curls she wore a kind of Cossack cap of astrakhan with an orange crown. Symbol of the new Germanic Netherlands! Vestige of loyalty to the House of Orange, so recently forsaken! Her eyes were naturally slightly narrowed and her lower lip protruded somewhat, so that it seemed everything she laid eyes on was beneath contempt.

She stood by one of the doors to the platform, her hands in the pockets of her navy blue coat. She's on the lookout for me, thought Osewoudt.

He went up to her and tipped his hat.

'Pardon me, but haven't I met you before? Aren't you Comrade Nispeldoorn's fiancée?'

She merely turned her head slightly, keeping her body quite still.

'No, I don't know you, and I don't know Comrade Nispeldoorn either.'

She looked outside again, and this time changed her pose. Osewoudt raised his arm to her back in the Nazi salute, muttering: *Houzee*. Then he crossed to the farthest corner of the waiting room as quickly as possible. He checked his watch. Another twenty minutes before the train left for Wageningen. There was no other Youth Storm leader to be seen.

Again he studied the lovely creature at the door. Again she shifted her pose, slowly turning round as if the man who had spoken to her merited a second glance after all. Osewoudt stepped to one side so as to be obscured by a fat cattle dealer standing roughly in the middle of the waiting room. You sweet thing, he thought, spending a night of bliss with you and then doing you in would be right up my street, and a patriotic deed into the bargain.

The cattle dealer bent over to talk to the other dealers, who were seated at a table. Osewoudt could now see her profile, her nose, her stern chin, her disdainful lower lip, the mist of fair hair on her forehead. Even beneath her coat, her breasts were alluring. Then he thought: maybe she's sorry I left so quickly, but it's also possible that she suspects something. His throat tightened. The waiting room was stuffy and warm with a fug of steam, stale breath and unfermented tobacco. He wished he could go outside. If only I dared, if only I weren't scared of having to face that Youth Storm leader again. He had a vision of dozens of Youth Storm leaders swarming into the waiting room and him having to go up to each one in turn and ask: haven't we met before? Aren't you Comrade Nispeldoorn's fiancée?

The cattle dealers now rose from their table and moved to

the exit en masse. The moment they were gone he caught sight of another National Youth Storm leader. She was alone.

She seemed hesitant, glancing about warily while keeping her head as still as possible. Clearly she was looking for someone. That must be her. She had bandy legs, no figure to speak of, and her navy coat was ill-fitting. She too had fair hair, but it was thin and lifeless. She had a coarse face, almost like a man's. The sort of woman who has an invisible, but when it comes down to it, unmistakable moustache. She had sharp creases either side of her mouth, and yet she could not have been very old. Below the left corner of her mouth was a brown wart, starkly defined against her pale skin, which reminded him of the colour of boiled veal. He did not go up to her. Her gaze slid over him without apparent question. He looked again at the other youth leader, who at that moment stooped to pick up her travelling bag and left the waiting room. The ugly youth leader was standing by the stove, about three metres away from Osewoudt. He looked around: no one was paying any attention to either of them. Then he took a few steps towards her.

She noticed him coming and looked him in the eye. He knew there was no need for him to reel off his little piece, but did so all the same.

'Haven't I met you before? Aren't you Comrade Nispeldoorn's fiancée?'

She had no eyebrows, but raised the areas of her forehead where they should have been. She began to laugh quietly, and he noticed her face was filmed with curiously minute beads of perspiration.

'I am not engaged to Comrade Nispeldoorn, but I can show you a photo that will interest you.'

Osewoudt lifted his left wrist and pushed up his sleeve to uncover his watch.

'I think we'd better get on that train now.'

'Fair enough.'

They left the waiting room; the girl had no luggage.

As they drew near to the train she asked: 'Do you know what this is all about?'

'No, I don't. All they said was to buy a return ticket to Wageningen.'

'Oh. It's quite a serious business, actually. Let's get on the train first.'

He stepped towards an open carriage door.

'Are there two seats? Yes, you go on up then,' she said.

She stepped to one side and stood there, peering into the train with the same expression as when she had entered the waiting room. She seemed to be checking for someone else in the carriage she had to watch out for.

Finally, she too boarded the train, murmuring: 'I'm not really sure what's best.'

'What do you mean?'

'Oh, nothing. You stay there by the window, all right?'

He banged the carriage door shut. It was an old train, with wooden benches painted pale yellow and paired compartments.

The bench opposite them was unoccupied. Beside them sat an old lady with a spasmodic twitch in her throat, so that her head was never quite still.

'Now you can tell me what they've got lined up for us.'

The girl sat close to him, the suspected moustache now clearly visible.

She leaned towards him as if they had known each other for at least an hour.

'I'll explain. We aren't going all the way to Wageningen; we're getting off before then, at Lunteren. Lunteren is where someone called Lagendaal lives. He needs dealing with, he's a very dangerous individual, works for the Gestapo, has grassed on dozens of people. He lives outside the village, on open heathland. Used to run a bicycle repair shop before the war, but now he's got himself a nice bungalow. I know how to get there; I've done a recce, so you needn't worry about that. The thing is, he's had some sort of warning. In other words, he's on the alert, but isn't sure what for.'

'So what does he suspect?'

On the platform a whistle sounded, the train lurched into motion, a thick cloud of smoke floated past the window.

'He knows that something might happen at any moment. It's quite remote where he lives, or rather where his wife and small son live. He's not there most of the time. But he is today. The parents have decided to send the boy to stay elsewhere. A National Youth Storm leader is supposed to come and collect him.'

She smiled, baring large, even teeth, but they were closer to grey than white.

'So I go there first, to collect the boy. I take him to the station. Then it's your turn. Did you bring some pliers? You're to cut the telephone wires, to be on the safe side. When you've done that you go in and deal with the man.'

'I've got the pliers, I was told to bring them. What about the wife?'

'Obviously, you mustn't take any risks.'

He could tell from her expression that she knew the wife would be there. And it was equally clear what she meant by taking no risks.

'Oh, so you're the Youth Storm leader who's supposed to collect the kid,' he said. 'Are they expecting you this afternoon?'

'I hope so.'

He felt his teeth might start chattering. He saw her flare her nostrils, as if she could scent the future. She took his hand. Hers was ice-cold and dripping wet.

Osewoudt withdrew his hand and patted the back of her hand.

'So what happens to the kid afterwards?'

'I get off the train at Amersfoort, and there our ways part for good. Yours and mine I mean. The child stays with me.'

Then he said: 'Have you ever met someone—'

He was going to say 'called Dorbeck', but she cut in.

'No no, I haven't met anyone! Not anyone! Ever! Remember that!'

Of course she hadn't met Dorbeck, he thought, because if she had she'd have been startled when she saw me, someone who looked exactly like him.

'Do you know my name, by the way?'

'No, what is it?'

'Filip van Druten. And yours?'

'Oh, there's no point telling you, really. Just carry on addressing me as "you". Just say "Hey you!" when you need me.'

At the exit of Lunteren station they saw the other Youth Storm leader. The genuine one! Carrying her travelling bag! She'd been on the same train! Got off in Lunteren, same as them!

'See that girl?' he said.

'Doesn't mean a thing. Lunteren's crawling with that lot, didn't you know? Perhaps she's come to make the Leader's bed for him – he holds rallies here all the time.'

When they came out of the station the other youth leader was about thirty metres ahead of them.

'Which way?'

'Same as her.'

They followed the railway embankment up to the level crossing. The other youth leader was already on the other side. If she happens to look left now she'll see us, Osewoudt thought. But she didn't look left.

They too went over the crossing, and came to a wide road lined with boarding houses and the old-fashioned country homes of retired gentry.

'Is it around here?'

'No, much further on. God forbid, if it were here we'd have all the neighbours coming to the rescue. They do that sometimes. Did you know?'

'Yes, so I've heard.'

'A lot of people working for the Krauts have neighbours who take them for good patriots.'

'Naturally.'

'You know, the Germans don't even like using party members to do their dirty work, because then everyone would be forewarned.'

'Stands to reason.'

The other youth leader was still ahead, and had now increased the distance between them to fifty metres. But Osewoudt still had a clear view of her shapely legs in their black silk stockings, and of her trim waist in the custom-made uniform. He looked from her to his dowdy companion and thought: won't anyone seeing the first one go by, and then this one, think there's something fishy going on?

They came to a complicated intersection.

'This way?'

'Yes, we stick to the asphalt.'

The other youth leader had taken the asphalt road too. A greengrocer on a horse-drawn cart came towards them. When he was close by he made a filthy noise in his throat and spat on the ground. He glared at Osewoudt and his companion by turns, then half stood up on the box to look back at the other youth leader.

Further down the road the buildings petered out. On either

side were stands of trees, interspersed here and there with an old country house set in a garden.

'How far do we still have to go?'

'Another fifteen minutes or so, I think. See that letter box over there?'

He saw the shiny red letter box on a short post further along the road. Next to it stood an old-fashioned gas street lamp.

'Past there we turn left across the heath.'

To his consternation he saw the lovely, genuine youth leader turning left at almost the same instant.

'Where the hell is she going?'

The girl began to laugh, took his arm and pressed it to her side. She smelled of Lux bath soap.

'I believe you're a good sort, Filip. But shall I tell you what I think? She's going to the same address as we are!'

'To the same address? So what does that mean?'

'Isn't it obvious? She's going there to collect the little boy and take him to a safe place.'

'What about you then?'

'Well, things might get a bit awkward. We can't very well seize the boy from her by force. That would be overdoing the child-protection act a bit.'

'What do you think would be best then?'

'I don't know, that's for you to decide.'

'But you're the one who set the whole thing up! You did the recce! It's your plan!'

'I . . . I . . . That's a bit much. I didn't plan it all on my own! Besides, the order to liquidate Lagendaal came from London. To be honest, that girl's going to complicate matters. At least that's what I think. I was actually counting on her arriving on a later train, by which time we'd have gone.'

They too now reached the road branching off on to the heath. It was sandy and little more than a dirt track along a ditch, and apparently hard going for the other youth leader because she was closer than before. There were no houses along this road, although it was lined with telegraph poles. The poles carried only a couple of wires.

'If that's the way things are,' said Osewoudt, 'what did you reckon on doing with the kid?'

'The father has to go, the mother too if you can't help it, but the boy mustn't come to any harm.'

'But he's bound to scream if we snatch him off the youth leader!'

'Can't we think of some way of stopping her from getting hold of him in the first place?'

'Of course. Otherwise there wouldn't be any point in you having dressed up as a Youth Storm leader. Come on, let's get a move on, we need to catch up with her.'

Just then the other youth leader looked back; it was the first time she had done so. She even stopped for a moment, no doubt stunned by what she saw.

Then she walked on. Faster than before? Had she realised?

Osewoudt took Hey You by the hand. At first they looked like they were speed-walking, but soon they broke into a run, their feet landing awkwardly in the soft sand. The other youth leader glanced over her shoulder again, but apparently suspected nothing because she walked on. Osewoudt let go of the girl's hand and raced ahead. A smell of pine trees and manure penetrated deeply into his nostrils. His eyes were fixed on the youth leader. He saw her smile faintly, then her mouth open, but before she could scream his hands were around her neck. He was so quick that his forehead collided with hers and they fell to the ground almost as one. In falling he grabbed the hair at the back of her head so that she fell on top of him, but his feet, close together, were already planted against her stomach. He kicked out his legs without letting go of her hair.

She swung through the air and came down with a thud behind his head.

By the time the other girl came up, Osewoudt was back on his feet, patting the sand off his coat, stooping to retrieve his hat. The youth leader still lay on her back, legs flung wide, coat and skirt rucked up over the tops of her black stockings. Her cap was caught in her hair. Her eyes stared upwards through half-closed lids, her tongue lolled out of her mouth. Her bag lay at the side of the track.

The girl picked it up and looked inside.

'Empty! For the little boy's clothes, I expect. Is she unconscious?'

'No, not exactly. Come on, we can't leave her here like this.'

He looked about, nobody in sight. What did catch his eye were his spectacles, snapped in two. He picked up the pieces and pocketed them. The girl put the bag down again and helped him drag the youth leader's body away. Fortunately there was a stand of trees to one side of the track, but it didn't extend very far and the undergrowth was thin and sparse.

'She'll be found eventually, we just want to postpone the discovery.'

'Wouldn't it be better to take her clothes off and bury them somewhere?'

'What do you propose to dig a hole with?'

'Okay then, not bury them. Take them with us and burn them.'

The girl began undoing the buttons on the uniform. She held the coat while Osewoudt pulled out the limp arms. She folded the coat in four and laid it down.

Osewoudt unfastened the bronze swastika brooch from the dead youth leader's blouse and handed it to the girl.

Then they took the blouse off and started on her underwear,

but before she was naked Osewoudt said: 'Let's give up on this. Too much of a performance. We can't dig a hole, and where would we dump all her stuff?'

He didn't look at the girl, but kept his eyes on the dead youth leader, thinking how warm she had felt. He leaned forward to sniff her body.

The girl prodded his shoulder.

'What do you suggest we do then?'

'Clear off! Leave her! She won't be seen by anyone who happens to pass by. That's good enough. Give me her coat.'

'No, take mine instead.'

She quickly took off her coat, felt in the pockets to make sure there was nothing in them, and spread it over the dead youth leader. Then she put on the other coat.

'A perfect fit, I do believe.'

'Anything in the pockets?'

She checked them: 'Yes, a wallet.'

She opened the wallet. Five photographs of five different German officers. Osewoudt struck a match and they set fire to the pictures as well as the identity card. The wallet, which wouldn't burn, he tossed away as far as he could. The money (nine guilders in notes, no small change) went into his pocket. Finally he stamped out the flames and they walked back to the road. They paused for a moment and looked back. From where they stood there was nothing to be seen in the undergrowth.

'She's called Marchiena Siemerink. Quite a name!'

'Don't you think this coat suits me better than the one I had before?'

Osewoudt agreed without enthusiasm.

'How did you manage that so quickly?'

'I used to belong to a judo club.'

'Very handy.'

'Yes it is, sometimes. But in some respects it's a nuisance. My feet got completely deformed. I can't just go into a shoe shop and buy a pair of shoes.'

'Shoes are impossible to find these days anyway.'

'Not for me. If I want, I can get an extra coupon to have orthopaedic shoes made especially, no problem.'

'Must be expensive.'

'Cheaper than getting hold of a shoe coupon on the black market. A lot cheaper.'

'She was very pretty. Nice figure. Or didn't you notice?'

'Is this fellow Lagendaal's house still far?'

'I bet you'd have raped her if I hadn't been around! You should have seen your face!'

'Oh, belt up. I wouldn't mind a drop of cognac, though.'

'Maybe you'll find some at Lagendaal's.'

She caught his arm.

'Another two poles, and the one after that is where you cut the telephone wires. A little further on and you'll see the house.'

'Then what?'

'You wait for a bit. I go to the house and come back with the little boy as soon as I can. Just beyond the telegraph pole there's a clump of trees where you can hide. Once I've come past with the boy, you can go ahead. Look, here's the pole. And there are the trees. I'd better be off. Will you manage to get up to the wires?'

Osewoudt looked intently in all directions: not a soul. Then he began to climb. It wasn't easy. I should have taken my rain-coat off, he thought. Thank goodness his shoes had rubber soles, so he had some grip. The girl looked back at him and smiled. She jigged her thumb to say faster, faster.

At last he was able to grab the iron bracket holding the white porcelain insulators. With his free hand he took the pliers from his pocket. Down below he could see the girl heading towards the bungalow, swinging the bag as she went. He had never seen telephone insulators up close, had no idea they were so big. As big as a glass of milk. He cut the wires and watched them fall and spring back into enormous coils right across the way. He slithered down the pole, ran over to the wires and tried to get them under control in order to hide them in the ditch. With success. Then he slapped the front of his raincoat, but most of the dirt wouldn't go away. The pole had left a wide vertical black stripe on the pale cotton fabric.

Still slapping his coat he reached the clump of trees. He jumped over the ditch and plunged in among the bare larches, holding the branches away from his face. He worked his way diagonally through the trees. Before long he saw the house, which had to be Lagendaal's. It stood in the open, with just a few Douglas fir saplings dotted about the grounds, which were separated from the wood by a potato field. He saw the girl walking along, still swinging the bag. She had another 150 metres to go, at a guess.

It was a low, wooden structure. Well I never! Shutters painted the Dutch Nazi party colours: red and black!

Osewoudt sat on the ground with his knees drawn up, his hands crossed over his feet. The girl made her way to the house, no longer swinging the bag but with her hands in her coat pockets, including the hand holding the bag.

He took the pistol from his inside pocket, slid the safety catch back and forth and removed the magazine from the butt. He examined the magazine from all sides, blew on it, and slotted it back into the pistol. Then he lifted his eyes and saw a squirrel peering at him from the base of a beech tree, its forepaws poised on the trunk. Osewoudt slipped the pistol into the right-hand pocket of his raincoat and stood up. The squirrel bolted up the tree.

He looked at the house again, and a moment later the girl went in. He couldn't see who had opened the door. He thought: she must have known about Marchiena Siemerink being on the same train, because this fellow Lagendaal is bound to ask her name. Not only that, he is also bound to have been given the name of the youth leader coming for his son. So Dorbeck must have known her name, too, or rather: it was his business to know, and Hey You knew, too. Possible. And yet, I didn't notice a thing. So actually it's more likely neither of them knew, just which train she would be on, and that they counted on me getting rid of her. What if it had gone wrong?

He kept looking at the door of the house, but it remained closed. Ten minutes had already passed. Then he saw the girl emerge from behind the house. She was trundling a bicycle, a child sat on the carrier. The bag hung from the handlebar. Walking alongside was a man. He was bareheaded. Now say goodbye and get on the bike, he thought, for God's sake hurry up! But they did not say goodbye. The girl wheeled the bike and the man walked beside her, talking animatedly, apparently intending to see them to the road. Osewoudt noticed the man was talking more to the child than to her. The child had probably made a fuss about leaving his parents, and the father would be keeping them company to reassure him.

The man was stout and not very tall. He wore nothing on his head, nor had he put a coat on before leaving the house. His nose was sharply pointed, and so long as to run parallel with the creases beside his nostrils, while largely obscuring a small, lipless mouth. This made him seem to snarl every time he said something, but the little boy responded with peals of laughter. Osewoudt couldn't catch what they were saying. They came quite close, a stone's throw away, then vanished among the trees.

Osewoudt left the wood and sprinted in a wide arc across the potato field towards the house. He looked over his shoulder: the man was obviously still accompanying the girl and the child. Osewoudt trained his eyes on the windows, but could only make out the shapes of furniture inside. None of the windows had net curtains. The bungalow's name, De Hazenwal, was painted on the façade. Suddenly he noticed that the place was less isolated than he had thought. To the left, beyond the wasteland, was a farm; a white cow grazed nearby.

Miraculously, he made no sound as he advanced. Just as well there was no gravel surrounding the house. No effort had been made to create a garden, either. The house stood in the middle of a stretch of heath, which was only worn away in the immediate vicinity.

He had seen them emerge from behind the house, so there had to be a door there, probably to the kitchen. There was also a shed at the rear, he now noticed. Having come this far he could see the entire rear of the house. The eaves came low over a door, which was open. He ran to it. When he stepped inside, the kitchen seemed dark; all he saw was the light of a paraffin stove, then a woman turning to face him. Before she could make a sound she was on her knees. He held the back of her head by the hair and broke her neck on the edge of the draining board. Then he let her fall to the floor. A door stood open. He came into an unlit passage. This passage led to a small space that served as a hallway, because the front door was at the end. He posted himself by the door. It wasn't a proper front door; it had six small panels of glass, like the other doors in the house. No net curtain here either. Osewoudt looked outside, but the man was still nowhere to be seen. Would he be going all the way to the station with his boy and the youth leader? Plenty of time either way to get the woman out of the kitchen and hide her somewhere. Then the man would enter the kitchen unsuspectingly and go on in to look for his wife. If he saw her lying in the middle of the kitchen floor he might do a runner.

Risky to have to shoot him outside . . . Osewoudt took out his pistol and looked in all directions again. The cow on the farm was no longer alone: there were two men in cloth caps walking around it. What were they up to? Would they spend the next half-hour inspecting the cow, or would they move even further away from the farmhouse? Would they come this way? Drop in for a chat maybe? For the first time that afternoon it occurred to Osewoudt that he could still call it off and have another go the next day, or even the day after, when circumstances might be more favourable.

But the two farmers continued to occupy themselves with their cow. For a moment Osewoudt let his eyes wander, having made up his mind now to drag the body out of the kitchen. Then he saw Lagendaal approaching the house. Every thought of postponement vanished. It had to be done now, in the next few minutes. Come here! he ordered under his breath, recoiling from the door as far as possible while keeping Lagendaal in sight. As if he was afraid that Lagendaal would turn tail as soon as he took his eyes off him, the very *notion* of moving the body from the kitchen went from his mind.

Lagendaal took long, slow strides. He was poking around in his mouth. Something lodged between his back teeth, no doubt. Then he chewed his thumb. He kept his head down. His hair was thinning and greasy, his pink scalp showing through. He kept to the path, inasmuch as you could call it a path. Abruptly, he took a few steps to one side. He had seen something, and bent down to pick it up. Pliers! He stood still for a moment, lifted the pliers with both hands to eye level and opened and closed them. Then he returned to the path leading to his house. The pliers were in his right hand, and he kept opening and closing them. Osewoudt felt his teeth begin to chatter. He now had a clear view of Lagendaal's face, the thin elongated nose, the creases on either side. He also saw Lagendaal's eyes. The sockets were huge, and deep. He had thick eyebrows which were joined in the middle, each eyebrow a well-defined circumflex accent. Each eye seemed to sit in its own little house with a pitched roof. Watery, dull eyes they were, even the surrounding skin looked bloated. Without a glance towards the door, Lagendaal moved out of sight.

Osewoudt turned round, the pistol in his trembling fist almost level with his eyes. He positioned himself with one foot forward while keeping watch on the door to the kitchen, which was slightly ajar. He couldn't see into the kitchen because the door was at right angles to the passage. He should have left it open, he now realised. He listened intently, but could hear only the muffled sound of Lagendaal's footsteps approaching. Then came the thud on the kitchen floorboards. A cry: 'What on earth?'

'Help! Help!' yelled Osewoudt.

The kitchen door swung open and Lagendaal took a step into the passage. Osewoudt fired instantly. The whole passage lit up as if by lightning. But Lagendaal did not collapse. He ducked back through the door. Osewoudt sprang after him, and found him standing in the middle of the kitchen. Osewoudt fired again, but Lagendaal took another step. Osewoudt fired two more shots. Lagendaal fell but did not crumple up, his torso remained upright. One leg was doubled under him, the other kicking savagely across the floor. Osewoudt went up to him and, bracing his right elbow with his left hand, emptied the pistol into Lagendaal's back. Lagendaal keeled over, his head crashing on to Osewoudt's shoes. His mouth sagged, his eyes had stopped moving. Osewoudt looked up. Ribbons of blue vapour drifted towards the open kitchen door. He put the pistol in his pocket, stepped over Lagendaal and walked directly to the shed. It was not locked. Inside was a man's bicycle. He wheeled it out, slammed the shed door, and mounted. He set off, but braked almost immediately, got off the bicycle and left it lying there. He ran back to the kitchen and snatched the pliers from Lagendaal's clenched hand. Then he blew out the paraffin burner.

The two farmers, hands in pockets, were still chatting beside the cow. One of them stepped forward, patted the animal's rump. Then he stepped back and resumed his conversation with the other.

Cycling over the bumpy terrain was not easy. Osewoudt went past a rudimentary gateway made of two large stones painted white. He twisted round for another look. They had black letters on them. One said D E and the other H A Z E N W A L.

He rode on. He saw the telephone wires suddenly end and then begin again. He couldn't remember exactly where they had left the murdered youth leader. Standing up on the pedals he made quite rapid progress. Soon he was on the asphalt road. He sat back down on the saddle, relaxed, and rode on with one hand on the handlebars. He looked about him and whistled a tune: '*Mit dir war es immer so schön*'. There was the letter box, red and shiny as ever.

Then a heavy rumble sounded in the grey sky. Not far away field guns fired salvos of three shots at a time. A huge aluminium bomber hove into view, low over the trees. Osewoudt saw the glint of gun turrets, he even saw the circular shimmer around the four engines. Above the aircraft puffs of dirty brown smoke appeared, from bursting ack-ack shells. With his free hand Osewoudt waved to the bomber until it disappeared from sight.

He parked the bicycle against a tree by the station and made for the waiting room. There sat Hey You, with the little boy in front of her. The waiting room was a narrow space with a single bench running along the side, no refreshment counter. Not a soul about.

'Hey You! How are you doing?' called Osewoudt.

'Shake hands with the gentleman now!'

'I'm Walter,' said the little boy, putting out his hand.

'That's a very smart outfit you're wearing, Walter,' said Osewoudt.

He sat down beside Hey You.

'That's because I'm going away,' said the boy. 'Anyway, I like wearing my best clothes. Some children don't like wearing their good clothes, but I do. I like being neat and tidy.'

The boy was about five years old. His eyes were dark and his eyebrows thick and joined in the middle. The image of his father. Osewoudt tried unsuccessfully to remember what the mother had looked like.

'Did you find out when the train leaves?'

Hey You looked at him. She was paler than ever. She seemed to have difficulty opening her mouth.

'In half an hour. We just missed the last one.'

'I'm glad I'm going to Amsterdam,' said Walter. Holding on to Osewoudt's lapels for support, he got his right knee up on the bench.

'I'm a born traveller, you know. I think I'll go and live in Russia when the war's over. I want to have a big estate.'

'Since you're such a keen traveller, why don't you go and

see if there's a train coming? I can hear an engine. Go and take a look, I bet it's a goods train.'

The child let go of Osewoudt and wandered off through the open door to the platform.

'So how did it go?'

'Fine. The pair of them.'

'The woman too?'

'Yes. She was in the kitchen.'

'Any cognac on the premises?'

'Don't know. I didn't look, not for papers either. It didn't go very smoothly. But it's done.'

'I was afraid he'd come all the way to the station with us. I was telling him: you'll catch your death without a coat in this weather. You'll be laid up tomorrow if you're not careful. It's very cold for the time of year!' She did not smile as she said this.

The goods train came past, blocking out most of the daylight in the waiting room.

Osewoudt put his hand on the nape of the girl's neck and said: 'Come on, try not to think about it.'

'When he left I forgot to say *Houzee*.'

'What does it matter? It went pretty well, all things considered.'

'I wonder if the Germans will shoot hostages in revenge.'

Osewoudt felt his knees begin to quake. He asked: 'Where did you leave that bike he lent you?'

'At the left-luggage office. He said he'd come for it later. Why do you ask?'

'I've been a bit careless. I came here by bike too – I took his – but I left it outside. If anyone recognises it . . .'

'So what? It won't mean anything to them unless they've already been to the bungalow and have seen . . .'

'Damn, I wish that train would come.'

'Relax, will you. Even if someone has found out already,

why would they think of checking whether Lagendaal's bike was left outside the station?'

'No, but still, whoever finds out is bound to go straight to the village, in which case they'll go past the station.'

Walter came inside.

'I say! It was a very long train! Seventy-seven carriages! I expect it's going to the Eastern Front!'

'Yes Walter, to the Eastern Front, taking warm clothes for our soldiers.'

'I'm for the Russians,' said Walter. 'All us boys are for the Russians.'

In the train they sat the child between them, so there was no need for them to talk to each other. It was a carriage with a corridor from end to end.

The train stopped at Barneveld-Dorp and two women entered the carriage; all the seats were now occupied.

The train rode on. Outside, the drizzle was drawing thin streaks of wet on the window.

The train stopped again at Barneveld-Voorthuizen. The door opened and a large woman with a basket on her arm hoisted herself up.

'No seats left here?'

'No, all taken.'

Osewoudt stood up and pointed to his seat.

But the woman glared first at him, then at the child, and finally at the fake youth leader.

'No, thank you. I wouldn't take your seat if you paid me.'

'Good for you!' said one of the women who had got on at the last stop. 'People like that are best left alone! Get them used to being in solitary later on!'

The whole compartment laughed. Osewoudt sat down and looked out of the window.

The train set off again. Almost immediately, two men in long leather coats came in from the corridor.

'*Polizei! Ausweise bitte.*'

'Not that too!' said the woman who'd made the remark about being in solitary.

'Identity cards please,' said the man in front, extending his hand. The other man stayed in the corridor and kept looking left and right.

Osewoudt handed over his card. The man slipped it from its celluloid sheath, unfolded it, clapped it shut again almost at once, held it up with an air of complicity and gave it back.

Then the woman who preferred to stand handed over her identity card.

When everyone had shown their papers it was the youth leader's turn. The German smiled as he took her card, unfolded it, then frowned. He studied it closely, including the back. The second man peered at it over the first's shoulder, after which the first one folded the card and put it in his pocket.

'*Da stimmt was nicht. Kommen sie mal mit.*'

Something was wrong. As if expecting this, Hey You rose from her seat and went with the leather-coated duo. She did not look back.

Chuckles sounded in the compartment.

'Well, I don't mind sitting down now,' said the large woman, and sank on to the vacant seat.

'That's all right, but when Auntie Marchiena gets back you'll have to get up again,' said Walter.

The woman stared stonily ahead. The grins on the faces of the other passengers faded. They were puzzled. A leader of the National Youth Storm, a traitor, being led away by the German police? How was that possible?

After a pause one of the passengers burst out with: 'Plenty of gits among that lot too! Black market, who knows?'

'Where has Auntie Marchiena gone?' Walter asked.

Everyone grew still.

It took a tremendous effort for Osewoudt to tear himself away from the view through the window. All eyes were on him when he finally muttered: 'Hush now, Walter. We'll be arriving in Amersfoort soon, and then Auntie Marchiena will join us again.'

He checked his watch.

'Look, only another three minutes. We're almost there.'

Even before the train had come to a standstill he took the little boy's hand and held it firmly, ready to jump down to the platform.

Suddenly he realised that he had no ticket for the child. Of course Hey You would have bought him a ticket! Hey You still had it! He looked up and down the platform, but couldn't see her anywhere. Then he bent down to Walter.

'Look here, Walter. You stay put for a moment, don't move! I'll be back before you know it. You stay right here. Be on the lookout for Auntie Marchiena, will you? There's something I have to do. But you're to stay here, understand?'

He let go of the little boy's hand and ran to a door with a sign over it: THROUGH TICKETS. There he bought a one-way ticket plus a child's ticket to Amsterdam.

From a distance he could see that Walter was doing as he had been told. He was still rooted to the appointed spot.

Osewoudt thought: what have I let myself in for? What am I to do with the kid? Where in God's name can I take him? I should have left him there and taken the train to Amsterdam by myself. Damnation, how do I get rid of him?

But then, as if buying that half-fare ticket had made it his moral duty, he walked back to Walter.

'Well? Have you seen Auntie Marchiena yet?'

'No. Did you?'

'Yes, she's got an errand to run here in Amersfoort, some business to discuss with those two gentlemen. The train to Amsterdam will be here in five minutes. Auntie Marchiena will catch up with us later, she said. Take my hand, Walter, come along, let's go and find our train.'

Osewoudt led the child to the platform for departures to Amsterdam. The train arrived almost at once.

He found two seats.

'Travelling by train is best,' Walter said. He laid his hands either side of him on the bench.

'Is it? What else have you travelled on?'

'An aeroplane. I didn't like it much.'

'So where did you go on the aeroplane?'

'To South America. It's very hot there, you know!'

An old man sitting opposite joined in the conversation.

'That must have been before the war then, eh my boy?'

The old man winked at Osewoudt.

'It can't have,' said Walter. 'There's always been a war on.'

It wasn't until they arrived in Amsterdam that Walter started whining about Auntie Marchiena. 'Can't we look in the waiting room, see if Auntie Marchiena's there?'

'How could she be? Auntie Marchiena's still in Amersfoort. So she can't be in the waiting room. She'll be coming on the next train.'

'I hate it.'

'What do you hate?'

'I hate it here. I want to go to the children's home with Auntie Marchiena, like Papa said. I'm getting a belt with a dagger. You're a stranger and I've got nothing to do with you!'

At that moment a loud crackling erupted from the loud-speakers hung along the platforms, and a hollow but hoarse voice announced: 'Calling Mr Osewoudt! Mr Osewoudt! Will

Mr Osewoudt, believed to be arriving from Amersfoort, please report to the stationmaster's office to receive an urgent message. I repeat: will Mr Osewoudt, arriving from Amersfoort, please report to . . .'

Osewoudt felt as if he'd been dealt a violent kick in the groin. He had to swallow to keep himself from vomiting. He wished he could tie his handkerchief over his face. He squeezed Walter's hand. Walter said: 'Why are they calling that gentleman?'

'Because they need him, of course.'

He took out the tickets. He had three: the half-used return ticket for the Leiden-Amersfoort journey, the one-way ticket from Amersfoort to Amsterdam, and the half-fare ticket for the child. He examined each in turn, then put the first ticket back in his pocket and kept the other two in his hand.

'What do they need him for?'

'To give him a message, Walter. From his wife, I expect, or from his mother.'

'From his mother,' Osewoudt echoed softly as they shuffled forward in the queue for the barrier.

'What sort of message?'

'Maybe he promised his mother he'd buy her a basket of cherries and didn't get round to it. Something like that, Walter, something like that, maybe.'

'It's a funny sort of name. What does it mean? It sounds like the name of a wood. Is there a wood called Osewoudt, too?'

'No, there isn't. Not that I've heard of anyway. It's just a funny name, that's all!'

Walter's eyes kept darting in all directions.

'Is it still a long way to the children's home?'

'A very long way. You'd get too tired if I took you there

now. We're going to visit a very kind old gentleman first, we'll have a rest there. His whole house is full of birds' feathers, red ones, green ones, blue and yellow ones. He's got feathers from all sorts of different birds. You won't believe your eyes!'

They went over the bridge and started down Oudezijds Achterburgwal.

They were a few houses away from Uncle Bart's when he heard someone tapping on a window, more loudly than the way whores usually tap on their windows. Osewoudt stopped to look. From a basement window a whore signalled urgently to him. She had stood up from her stool.

Osewoudt took a few steps towards the open basement door. The woman came out, drawing her coat tightly around her with one hand.

'You're Mr Nauta's nephew, aren't you? Are you on your way to your uncle's?'

'Yes. Why d'you ask?'

'Listen! You want to get away from here as quick as you can! The Germans were here earlier and they took your uncle away. They ransacked the place, took everything away in a big lorry. I thought I'd let you know!'

Without waiting for a reply, the woman scurried back to her basement.

'What did she want?' Walter asked.

'Never you mind. Come along now. We're nearly there.'

Nearly where? He didn't know, hadn't a clue. He had meant to leave the child with Uncle Bart – on reflection a ridiculous idea anyway. He had to get rid of him somehow, the sooner the better! If only he could chuck him in the canal with a heavy stone round his neck.

He set off at such a brisk pace that the boy could hardly keep up. Osewoudt did not look up at the windows when he passed Uncle Bart's house. He kept his eyes on the pavement as he strode on. Here and there he saw a stray red feather lying by the side of the canal.

'What did that lady say?' Walter asked.

'Things that don't concern you.'

'Why not?'

'Oh, come on, Walter, pipe down, will you?'

'Why?'

'If you're a good boy I'll take you for a ride in a cart. Look, like that one over there. We'll go for a ride in one of those little carts!'

They had reached the turning into Damstraat, and were waiting to cross when a light metal cart came past, drawn by an emaciated horse.

'What a nice cart!'

'Yes, very nice. Handy, too, now there's no petrol for cars! When those carts were first invented they weren't pulled by a horse but by a man on a bicycle. Isn't that funny? But that's not allowed any more. Goes against human dignity, you see. Don't you see? Not to worry! We'll go for a ride in one of those carts, it'll be fun.'

He went down Damstraat towards Dam Square, pulling the child with him.

By the small archway leading from Dam Square to Rokin he stood still and said, giving Walter's arm a tug with each word: 'You stay right here in this archway! Do exactly as I say. Don't budge. I'll nip over to find us a cart, and then it'll come here to pick us up. Got it?'

He let go of Walter and sprinted towards Rokin.

He jumped on to the open platform of the first tram that came past.

Looking across the way, he noticed that Walter was not quite as obedient as he had hoped. The little boy had gone through the archway, no doubt driven by curiosity, and now stood with his hands in his pockets surveying the quiet side of Rokin, where no fewer than three carts were waiting. It was as if the carts were lined up there solely to increase the child's bewilderment.

Five minutes later he got off the tram at the Mint Tower. It was exactly half past six. The clock in the tower began to strike.

He saw Marianne at once. She was wearing a new summer frock. She saw him coming and smiled. He thought she was beautiful, and it felt as if nothing out of the ordinary had happened all day.

'Hello darling!'

She pinched his cheeks, he took her in his arms.

'You're very punctual,' she said. 'A man who keeps appointments — I like that. Where are your glasses?'

'Consumed by the flames of my ardent desire.'

'What did you do today?'

'A couple of errands. I also went to see Mr Nauta, you remember, Bellincoff Ltd. on Oudezijds Achterburgwal. He's been arrested by the Germans. They ransacked the whole house!'

'Really? Do you think that Elly woman had anything to do with it? Or that nephew-cum-son-in-law of his?'

'I don't know.'

'What did you do to your coat? The front's all dirty. You look as if you've been climbing a pole.'

'What?' Osewoudt looked down at himself and began slapping the dark streaks made by the telegraph pole. 'Must have been leaning against something,' he said. 'Everything's filthy these days. Nothing gets cleaned any more. The country's going to the dogs.'

'It looks like tar, or creosote!'

She reached out to grasp his raincoat and bent to sniff it.

'Don't!' he cried, pushing her away. 'You almost tripped me up. Where do you want to go?'

'Guess what! I went and bought two cinema tickets. Don't worry, not a German film. It's Czech, and it's called *Praeludium*.'

'Which cinema?'

'The Tivoli.' They crossed to the other side of the street.

'You can't imagine what it feels like,' she said as they walked down Reguliersbreestraat, 'going to the cinema like this. I have very strange thoughts. All those Aryans who won't set foot in the cinema by way of protest, and here I am, a Jewess going to see a film. Sort of perverse, don't you think?'

'No one can see that you're Jewish.'

'That's beside the point – I know what I am! My entire family have been rounded up, I haven't heard from them since. They may be dead for all I know, and here I am going to the cinema!'

'You don't want to dwell on that kind of thing,' said Osewoudt. 'Anyway, the rumours may be exaggerated, perhaps they're still alive.'

'But even so, they'll be in prison. They won't be strolling down Reguliersbreestraat like us, will they?'

'No.'

'The thing is, I can't believe how I can just carry on as if I didn't care.'

They joined the queue. Above the ticket window hung a notice saying FÜR JUDEN VERBOTEN! They shuffled forward over Persian carpets.

'You do care,' said Osewoudt. 'If you didn't you wouldn't have mentioned it.'

The lights dimmed and the newsreel began.

'Why don't the lights go out altogether?'

'It's been like this for a long time. If Hitler or some crony of his appears on the screen and someone whistles or jeers, they'll know who it was.'

Suddenly he thought of Hey You. What had they done to her? What could have been wrong with her identity card? Did they know anything about her? Would they ask her why she had gone to Lunteren? Would they find out that she had two train tickets, one for herself and one for Walter? Would she keep her mouth shut? It seemed unlikely she had told them anything on the train, or the Germans would surely have come back for Walter. Then it struck him that Hey You was supposed to have shown him a photo to prove her identity *and that he hadn't even asked her for it, that he hadn't seen it at all. That she must still have had it on her when she was arrested!* What would it have been of? Who knows, it might have been the third photo. The third photo of the set he had posted to Dorbeck, one of which Elly had, supposedly, given to her in England. What was the third one of? I can't remember, but that makes no difference. I'd recognise it if I saw it. Will it mean anything to the Germans? He was so preoccupied that he didn't look at the screen again until the voice and the music faded and the newsreel came to an abrupt halt.

The lights now went out completely, and something odd happened. A face appeared on screen, motionless but for a slight quiver because it was a film of a photograph. It was his own face. People coughed, the projector whirred, otherwise there was not a sound.

A typewritten summons accompanied the photograph:

500 guilders reward

Hendrik Maarten OSEWOUDT, born 23-4-20, retailer, last known domicile: VOORSCHOTEN, wanted by the Criminal

Investigation Office for robbery with assault. If you know anything about this man, contact your nearest police station immediately.

The audience was given ample opportunity to take it all in.

Where was that picture from? Probably from his original identity card, the duplicate of which would be at the civil registration office. Only, was his hair on that photo as dark as on this one? Or was it a photo of Dorbeck they were showing?

The picture faded. Melancholy Slavic music struck up and the feature film began.

'Filip! How very odd! That man looked just like you!'

'Listen carefully,' he whispered. 'Do exactly as I say.'

He felt in his pockets.

'I'm going to clear off, back to Leiden. But you must stay here until the end of the film, or near the end. I can't wait that long. If I leave at the same time as everybody else who's seen that picture someone will surely recognise me, some amateur sleuth eager to make 500 guilders. So I'd better go now. Take this.'

He gave her the pistol. 'Put it away now.'

'Hadn't you better keep it yourself, Filip?'

'No. I've used it far too often already. I should have got myself another one long ago. If the police catch me with it and they have some bullet they can trace back to it, then I'm done for.'

He gave her the pliers, and also the pieces of his broken glasses.

'Here, take these too. They're no use to me any more.'

He checked his pockets for anything else he was better off without, but found nothing.

'What's this? Pliers?' she asked.

'Bye now, dear Marianne. Don't worry. I'll see you later. It'll probably be okay, but you never know.'

'It's my fault,' she said. 'If only I hadn't dyed your hair black!'

He drew her towards him, then stood up, put on his hat and buttoned his raincoat.

At the far end of the auditorium an usherette was perched on a chair. She slipped out before he reached the exit.

Osewoudt came into the large foyer with the fitted Persian carpets.

'Sir!' called the doorman.

Osewoudt stopped. The doorman stopped too, further away from him than you'd expect for someone with something to say.

Osewoudt said: 'All right, what is it?'

The doorman said nothing. Osewoudt heard a clicking sound coming from the nearby ticket office. He couldn't see inside the window, but recognised the sound: a telephone number was being dialled. He walked out of the cinema. At his back the doorman shouted: 'Stop! Thief!'

A ridiculously theatrical yell in the unlit street. Osewoudt stood still, saw other people standing still too. When he saw the doorman rushing towards him he proceeded on his way, but did not run. He walked quite normally. The doorman clapped his hand on his shoulder. Osewoudt seized the hand, yanked it forward until the arm was stretched, twisted the arm round and bent down fast and low. Howling, the doorman smashed on to the cobbles with a force that could have broken his back. Osewoudt let him go, but in the meantime he was being hemmed in by passers-by.

Osewoudt took a step towards them.

'Why not let me through? That doorman's bothering me for no reason at all.'

'Identification, please.'

A Dutch policeman was barring his way with his bicycle.

Osewoudt handed over the identity card, the policeman switched on a pocket torch and inspected it.

'Well, well, in the Force yourself are you? Where's your other card?'

Osewoudt gave him the fake German police card. The policeman pocketed both cards, saying: 'You'd better come along with me.'

'Look here, I'm on an assignment, I don't have time to keep you company for no reason.'

'Maybe so, but I'm doing my duty.'

'And if I refuse?'

'I don't give a damn,' said the policeman. 'You're coming with me whether you like it or not. If you start running I'll shoot, mind.'

Osewoudt glanced over his shoulder. The crowd was growing. Running away was out of the question.

'All right then, I'll go with you. Since you insist.'

The policeman let go of his bicycle and fumbled in his trouser pocket. Click. Before Osewoudt could react, a handcuff was snapped on his wrist.

An about-turn was made. Without another word he was conducted to the police office on the corner of Halvemaanssteeg. The crowd straggled after them.

Not until they entered the police office did Osewoudt break his silence: 'Look here, officer. You may be a good patriot, I don't know. I'm not really in the German police. Those papers are fake. But I didn't commit any robbery with assault. It isn't me in the picture of the wanted man. I look a lot like him, but I'm not him. Different name, too.'

'True,' said the policeman. 'The man they're hunting is called Osewoudt, and your card says van Druten. But it's the same man in both pictures. Besides, your papers are fake, you said so yourself.'

'I didn't commit any kind of robbery. You must release me. It's a matter of life or death. You'll be sorry if you don't let me go. Give me back my papers.'

'Anyone could come out with your spiel.'

'Let me go. I'm wanted for political reasons. You'll be sorry for the rest of your life if you hand me over to the enemy.'

'If you ask me, sir, there's nothing wrong with your papers. You work for the Germans under an alias and now you've got into their bad books. Am I right?'

'No, the papers are forged, I tell you. You'll regret this.'

'And don't you think we'll regret it, here in the police office, if we let you go? I have a wife and children, sir.'

They sat him in the waiting room. They fastened the handcuffs behind his back. He was surrounded by four policemen and a sergeant. They nodded to everything he said. They offered him a cigarette, but he refused. His voice dropped almost to a whisper, but he kept talking.

Half an hour later two Germans came to fetch him in a small lightly armoured car.

Hands still tied behind his back, sitting bolt upright on the wooden seat of a badly sprung vehicle, his entire body quaked all the way to The Hague.

Osewoudt sat on a hard-backed chair. There were two desks in the rather smoky room, and two Germans bustling about with files; a third sat idle on a similar hard chair in the corner, one leg crossed over the other. A pistol was within his reach, but he didn't look at Osewoudt.

Osewoudt said nothing, asked nothing. His nerves still jangled from the shaking of the car. It was strange to see these uniformed Germans going about their business as if they were ordinary office clerks. It was even stranger to see them without their caps on while in uniform. It was as if he had never seen a bareheaded German before.

The German in the corner stood up, holstered his pistol and left the room. No sooner had he gone than a stocky little man entered, posted himself in front of Osewoudt, mimed a kind of comical amazement, and said: 'Herr Osewoudt! Have they given you a cup of coffee yet?'

The little man had left the door open and called out into the corridor: 'Coffee!'

Then he crossed to one of the desks, repositioned the office chair so that it was directly opposite Osewoudt, and sat down.

'Well now, Herr Osewoudt! I am Kriminalrat Wülfing. How nice to meet you at last!'

'Where is my mother?'

'I was just coming to that. Your mother is very well indeed! There are a variety of options, Herr Osewoudt. You could go and visit her, no objection whatsoever, we might even have no objection to letting her go – none at all! But first you must appreciate our position!'

He glanced at the door and called: '*Jawohl!*'

The door opened and a uniformed corporal entered with two cups of coffee on a tray.

Osewoudt took a sip of his coffee and half rose from his chair to set the cup on the desk. Kriminalrat Wülfing blew and slurped by turns, then puffed out his cheeks and blew hard.

'We are the subject of much slander, Herr Osewoudt, but, as I am sure you understand, it is not in our interests to behave like executioners or barbarians! What use would that be to anyone? We respect you as one respects an enemy on the battlefield! However, it is time you realised that, as far as you are concerned, the battle is over. It is time for you and me to have a talk! Man to man! Is there anything more pleasing in this life than conversation? Indeed, I wonder if there is any greater divide between man and beast than the ability to converse. And we are men, after all! Among men it is not the inescapable fate of the loser to be devoured! Cigarette, Herr Osewoudt?'

The German proffered a packet of English cigarettes. Osewoudt was almost certain they were his own.

'But among men,' Wülfing went on, 'among men of true humanity, battle is followed by conversation!'

He raised both hands in a gesture of modelling the conversation in the air. Then he drew on his cigarette, blew out the smoke and suddenly lunged forward.

'Kleine Houtstraat 32, Haarlem! We know everything! It's all come out! All parties involved have confessed! Where did you first meet Elkan?'

Osewoudt shrugged.

Elkan? The name meant nothing to him.

'There were three of you! We know everything! Who were the others?'

'I've never even heard of that address.'

'My dear Herr Osewoudt, don't talk nonsense. You were there from the beginning to the end! 23 July, 1940! Elkan, Osewoudt and Zéwüster empty their pistols into a number of individuals they had arranged to meet in a boarding house in Haarlem – at Kleine Houtstraat 32! We know everything! Who gave the orders for the shooting?'

'I don't know anything about it.'

'Why do you think we brought you here? Why do you think we found accommodation for your mother? Are you mad? Or do you think we are?'

Osewoudt thought to himself: he said there were three of us. Does he think Dorbeck's name is Elkan? Either he doesn't know everything, or he's setting a trap.

'Maybe you're the one who's mad,' said Osewoudt.

The German leaned forward, leaving his right arm extended behind him. By the time his right fist swung through the air Osewoudt had ducked. But an instant later he received a blow on the nose from the left fist. He had to fight down the urge to grab hold of the fist and wrench the arm out of its socket, but thought: then they'll know about my judo, and I might get a chance to use it to better effect later on. He sat up straight and resigned himself to snorting up the blood trickling from his nose.

Wülfing leaned back, knees wide, ankles crossed.

'Herr Osewoudt! Is it really necessary for us to lose our tempers as we sit here speaking man to man? Where is Elkan?'

'I don't know anyone called Elkan.'

'You spoke to him only three days ago.'

'I don't know him!'

'You met him at the entrance to Vondel Park in Amsterdam! Just off Leidseplein!'

'I don't know him.'

'You spoke with him at 3.30 p.m., at Vondel Park. Not only with him, either. There was a third man! Who?'

'Don't know!'

'But I do. He's here in this very building, in custody. He's called Roorda!'

'I've never heard that name either.'

'Perhaps so. His name is Roorda. Aliases: Steggerda, Heemstra, van Norden, Vervoord. You still don't know who we mean?'

'No.'

Wülfing reached over to the desk and pressed a button. Osewoudt felt in his pockets, but even his handkerchief had gone. The German understood what he was looking for, opened a drawer in his desk and gave him a small crepe-paper napkin. Osewoudt wiped the blood off his face.

Roorda stood in the room, with the policeman who brought him in holding him by one handcuff. Roorda showed signs of mistreatment. His suit was rumpled, all the buttons were missing, he had to hold up his trousers with one hand, the tieless shirt was soiled and torn.

'Who's that man, Roorda?'

'That's Henk Osewoudt.'

Henk? Who had ever called him Henk?

'Are you sure you recognise him, Roorda?'

'Yes. I saw him last Sunday afternoon at the main gate to Vondel Park in Amsterdam.'

'Well, Osewoudt, what have you to say to that?'

'I've never seen him before.'

'Who else was present on that occasion, Roorda?'

'Elkan.'

'What did you talk about?'

'The arms drop that was going to take place. Osewoudt said

he hoped there would be detonators with the stuff, because he was short of them.'

'That will do! Take him away!'

Roorda was dragged out of the room by the handcuff, like a dog.

'So you see, Osewoudt, we know everything. Why go on pussyfooting around? Let's get down to business. Then I shan't trouble you any more. It won't take long, half an hour and we'll be done. After that you can have a nice long sleep.'

'I don't know that man.'

'Not a thought of your mother, then?'

'I have never been to that address in Haarlem, I didn't do anything! I'll tell you something else, though. This evening I saw—'

'What did you see?'

'Nothing.'

'Yes you did. You were in the cinema! We know exactly what you saw! You saw yourself on screen, larger than life, that's what you saw! 500 guilders reward, it said! Your name too. And what did you do? You ran off! You left the cinema although the film had barely begun! Is that normal behaviour for someone with a clear conscience?'

'It was so smoky in there, I didn't feel well, I needed some fresh air!'

'*Quatsch*! It was not smoky in the cinema. Smoking is forbidden in cinemas for the duration of the German occupation! See? Pussyfooting around again.'

'I'm saying as little as I can!'

The German stood up.

'You forget that we have every means of making you talk.'

Not wanting to draw attention to his judo, Osewoudt did not duck this time. The blow landed on his cheek.

'Ach!' exclaimed Wülfing. 'What's this I feel? Such soft cheeks! *Wie ein Mädchen!*'

With the back of his hand, he felt the cheek he had punched, from chin to ear.

'Well I never! A nice bit of crumpet for Obersturmführer Ebernuss! Ha, ha! Like a girl!'

Osewoudt heard a rattling noise, then felt cold metal on his wrists as his hands were clamped together behind the back of the chair. The German sat facing him again.

'Let me give you some advice. When Obersturmführer Ebernuss arrives, stick a champagne cork up your arse, or you'll live to regret it! But what I was going to say is: we've been chatting for the past hour without getting anywhere. Who ordered you to go to Kleine Houtstraat 32 in Haarlem? We know everything; if you refuse to talk the consequences will be unpleasant only for you, not for us. We have plenty of time.'

'I have never been there.'

'Be sensible, boy. Obersturmführer Ebernuss will be here in an hour, because then I'll be taking a nap. And if you won't say anything to Obersturmführer Ebernuss, Obersturmführer Galovsky will take over eight hours from now. He will stay for another eight hours. And if you still haven't said anything by then it'll be me again. And so it will go on, day in day out, for as long as it takes. We have plenty of time, we'll be getting all the sleep we need, but you won't. No food for you either, for he that does not toil shall not eat, in other words, he that does not cooperate goes hungry. We could use the stomach pump for starters, but we're too kind. Nothing to drink either, no need for that, for he that keeps his mouth shut is not thirsty. Makes sense, doesn't it? Where was I? Ah yes, tell me where Elkan is.'

'I don't know anybody called Elkan.'

'Don't you now?'

When Obersturmführer Ebernuss came in, Osewoudt was lying on the floor. The handcuffs had been removed, but he had no idea when. He held his stomach with both hands, there was blood pouring into his eyes from a gash in his left eyebrow, and he kept spitting out the blood trickling from his nose on to his lips and chin. He could no longer open his eyes fully, nor could he shut them because of the pain. Ebernuss was a ghostly presence pacing the floor. Osewoudt thought: at least I haven't said anything.

Ebernuss switched off the desk lamp. Beyond the windows the sky was no longer pitch-dark. Dawn was beginning to break.

Then Ebernuss squatted down by Osewoudt's head and said: 'Look here, dear boy, I dare say you honestly don't know where Elkan is. How unkind of them to slap you about like this. Can you stand up?'

He smelled of violets.

Osewoudt shook his head, without stirring his limbs, without demonstrating his inability to stand up. I can, he thought, but I'm damned if I will.

'He can't even stand up!' cried Ebernuss, rising. 'Shocking, that is.' He switched the desk lamp on again, lifted a telephone and waited, holding the receiver to his ear.

At last Osewoudt was able to get a good look at Ebernuss: a pale face like his own, but much plumper, and no doubt he had a beard, a black one, since his hair was black, but he was remarkably clean-shaven. He's the biggest villain of them all, Osewoudt thought. Someone came on the line and Ebernuss began to speak into the phone in an affected voice, albeit with a menacing undertone. Then he replaced the receiver and picked out two cards from the papers on the desk. He put them on top of each other, held them side by side. One was the identity card made out to Filip van Druten, the other was the German police card bearing the same name and photo. Ebernuss unfolded the identity card and held it up to the lamp, then did the same with the police card.

Two policemen came in with a stretcher, which they put down beside Osewoudt. Then they grabbed him by the shoulders and feet and laid him on the stretcher. As they carried him away, Osewoudt saw Ebernuss place the two cards on the desk with an air of bemusement.

No one asked where I got those papers from, thought Osewoudt as he floated down the corridor on the stretcher. Why didn't Ebernuss ask about that? Why beat me to a pulp to find out what I know about Elkan, someone I've never met in my life? Why wheel out that Roorda fellow to say he knew me? What do they hope to achieve with that? And not a word about my forged papers!

The policemen rested the stretcher on a bench in the vestibule. One of them stepped outside, leaving the door ajar so that Osewoudt could see him look about in the gathering light, as if expecting a car to arrive any moment.

All at once Ebernuss was standing over him again.

'Osewoudt . . .' Ebernuss said in a low voice, almost whispering. He bent down low, his face no more than a hand's breadth away from Osewoudt's. The scent of violets was unmistakable.

'Osewoudt . . . don't you worry about a thing. You're going to hospital now, you can have a nice rest. It's a scandal the way they've manhandled you. I shall report the matter to Berlin at once, you can count on that. I am ashamed of my colleagues, please accept my sincere apologies. And while you're in hospital I advise you to think about the questions we've been asking. Consider how much easier things would be if you made a clean breast of everything. What have you got to lose? The game's up, you know, it's all kaput. Why not be sensible so you don't go kaput yourself? Come, shake my hand, and the best of luck to you.'

Osewoudt kept his arms quite still, but Ebernuss reached for his hand, drew it out horizontally by the fingers and patted it amicably with his free hand before turning to go. Just then a car pulled up.

No sooner had Ebernuss left than the two policemen hoisted the stretcher and went outside, dumped it on the pavement, and bundled Osewoudt into the back of the car. This was more painful than anything he had endured yet. Nevertheless, he took care to notice the view from the window as the car moved off. He could tell they were at Binnenhof, by the Parliament buildings, although he didn't recall actually having seen them before. To think he had posed as an agent working for the German police headquarters in this very place!

Where was the First Chamber? And where the Second? He thought: if only the old codgers from before the war were still here, deliberating for the public good. That would have saved me a lot of grief. Grief? Pain, rather. Gingerly, he flexed each limb in turn. All he longed for at that moment was for someone to wash the crusts of dried blood from his face. Cold, wet air blew into the car, and his teeth began to chatter. What had become of Marianne? Had she stayed in the cinema until the end of the film? He couldn't remember where he had said he was going. In any case, by now she would have gathered what had happened. She would have simply gone back to Leiden, to her room over the hairdresser's. She would have stayed up late, hoping to hear from him, but she hadn't. What would her reaction have been like?

Osewoudt pictured her lying fully dressed on the bed, her heart pounding, the bedside lamp switched on. She would have waited for it to strike eleven and then thought: eleven o'clock, everyone has to be off the streets now.

The car stopped. They had arrived at Zuidwal hospital.

Two male nurses took him to the first aid room; one of the German policemen accompanied them.

A young doctor came in and examined Osewoudt at once. The German sat on a chair in a corner.

'Doctor,' whispered Osewoudt, 'could you do me a favour? Could you telephone 22575, in Leiden? Ask for Marianne Sondaar. Tell her that Filip has been caught by the Germans, and that he's in hospital.'

'Of course I'll tell her. Leave it to me, I'll phone.' He smiled: 'You're lucky to be here. There are no serious injuries.'

'No. But Doctor, I feel very ill. You may not be able to find anything serious, but I'm in a terrible state.'

Osewoudt screwed up his eyes and thought: now he'll go and tell the Germans there's nothing wrong with me!

He felt much better now that the blood had been washed off his face.

The gash in his eyebrow was stitched.

He was bathed and put in a clean bed in a small room all to himself. The curtains were drawn but the light came in nonetheless. He was served ersatz tea and toast. The nurse told him there was a German guard in the corridor, and that the room he was in was on the second floor, so it was no good trying to jump from the window.

'You must be joking,' he retorted. 'I'm too ill, you can't

imagine the pain I'm in. Please give me a sleeping pill. I didn't sleep all night and I'm still wide awake.'

'The doctor didn't say anything about a sleeping pill. Try and relax, then you'll fall asleep of your own accord. There's nothing seriously wrong with you, some bruising and a bloody nose, that's all. Those stitches will hurt for a bit, but they can come out in a couple of days. We won't tell the Germans there's nothing wrong with you, you needn't worry!'

She smiled, stroked his cheek, then looked at him very earnestly while allowing her hand to linger on his face, as if she were trying to make up her mind about something. Finally she made for the door.

'I'm Sister Angela,' she said as she left. The name almost sounded like an alias. Her name might not be Angela at all, any more than Marianne's is Marianne Sondaar. How many people are still using their real names? Who can you trust? Perhaps the doctor is in league with Ebernuss, maybe the Germans are even now busy matching the telephone number I gave the doctor with the address, maybe Marianne will be arrested in the next half-hour. Maybe they only brought me here to see whether I'm witless enough to tell the doctor and the nurse everything they want to know.

Who can be trusted? Everyone's deceiving everyone else.

He wondered what had happened to the boy. How long would young Walter have stood there watching the horses and carts? Perhaps he'd grown tired after an hour and had sat down on the pavement, still hoping that 'Uncle' would reappear and take him to the children's home, and that he would get his knife with *Meine Ehre heisst Treue!* engraved on the blade. But he'd have become upset eventually, he'd have spoken to some grown-up, or some grown-up would have spoken to him: what's your name, little boy? Where are you from? Lunteren? Where are you going? To a children's home with Uncle? Did Uncle leave you all by yourself? What does Uncle look like? How did you get here? With Uncle and Auntie? By train? Where's Auntie now? Went off with two men in leather coats, on the train? And Auntie wore a uniform? A black astrakhan cap with an orange top? Uncle not in uniform then? What sort of uncle can he be, leaving you stranded in the middle of Amsterdam?

They go to Lunteren to investigate. They call the German police. In the meantime Hey You has told them everything she knows, which isn't much, but then maybe they've shown her my photo, which they're bound to do if they're showing it in the cinemas . . . The bodies of Lagendaal and his wife are identified, possibly in Walter's presence. The bullets are extracted. Where is the pistol that fired the bullets?

I know where it is, thought Osewoudt, Marianne has it. I gave it to Marianne in the cinema. But I wouldn't be surprised if they've arrested her already. Everyone I have anything to do with gets into trouble. There's no hope for me either.

No hope for me — the last thought of a drowning man as he sinks to the bottom. He could feel himself sinking.

But he did not sink to the bottom. He woke up to find the doctor standing by his hospital bed and the sun streaming into the room.

'I made that phone call, as you asked. Miss Sondaar told me to give Filip her regards.'

'Didn't she say anything else?'

'Yes! I know her family quite well, as it happens. They lived next door to us until I was about ten. She was a toddler when we moved away. They were very well-to-do. Her parents and her brother have been sent to Germany, because they're Jews.'

'That is very sad,' said Osewoudt.

'Look,' said the doctor, 'I didn't like to mention any of this in the first-aid room with the German soldier there, but it's an extraordinary coincidence.'

'My turning to you for help is even more of a coincidence.'

'Yes. It seemed a bit rash, especially for someone who's just been beaten up by the Germans for refusing to talk. And then, suddenly, giving a doctor, a complete stranger, the telephone number of a girlfriend who urgently needs to be informed of his arrest!'

'Who else is there for me to ask?'

The doctor smiled. 'So you rely on the kindness of strangers.'

'I don't have much choice. All my contacts are ruined. My sick mother and my wife have been arrested by the Germans. My uncle's been arrested. Two girls I know were arrested. There's no one left. You must understand, Doctor, they have it in for me. Chances are I won't get out of this alive.'

The doctor pulled out a chair from under the bed and sat down. He looked round at the closed door and said: 'We'll have to think of something. It's always easier to escape from a hospital than from a police station or a prison. Patients have been known to abscond from hospitals, after all.

'The stitches may still be painful, you may think you can't get up and walk, but believe me, there's nothing wrong really, no internal injuries at all. I'll lay it on a bit thick for the Germans so we can keep you here as long as possible, but it'll be more like days than weeks. As I said, it's a miracle they brought you here at all.'

Osewoudt remembered what Wülfing had said about Ebernuss' proclivities. But he was ashamed to think that that was the reason Ebernuss had wanted to spare him. He choked with rage at the idea. His next thought was: this doctor must have noticed immediately that I have no beard. What will he think if I tell him that's probably why the bloody Obersturmführer had them take me to hospital?

'Look here, Doctor.'

'Yes?'

'I haven't done anything, really. I'm innocent. I'd rather be a hero, but as it happens I'm innocent. Apparently there's someone going around who looks like me, very much like me, in fact. It's that person's crimes they're accusing me of. The Germans confronted me with another prisoner. He swore he knew me. I had never seen him before. That prisoner said he had spoken to me only a week ago, at the main entrance to Vondel Park in Amsterdam. I have never been there in my life. He insisted that we had talked about arms from England being dropped by parachute. He said I asked him about detonators. But I don't even know what detonators are, and it was the first I ever heard of arms being parachuted in by the English. It was that kind of waffle the Germans beat me up for, Doctor! I'm not a hero, I'm a victim. They have me mixed up with someone else. Last night I was in a cinema. They projected a man's photograph on the screen, along with my name. The photo looked like me. Wanted for robbery with assault, it said, 500 guilders reward. I was scared stiff, so I ran for it. As I left the cinema the doorman recognised me. He called the police, the swine. That's how the Germans got hold of me. I didn't do a thing, nothing at all. Tell me Doctor, is it true that it isn't too difficult to escape from a hospital?'

'Too difficult? That depends. You can't jump out of the window. And there's a German guard in the corridor.'

The doctor left and did not come back to see him all day. The nurse did look in at regular intervals to perform routine duties. Sister Angela. The last time was at half past eight in the evening. The sun had not yet set. The windows were open, letting in the moist heat, along with the smell of putrid canal water.

Sister Angela made to pull the door shut behind her and said, with her hand still on the doorknob: 'Time for bed.'

But the door did not close fully. On the contrary, it was

flung wide open and three masked men burst in. Sister Angela stumbled, but didn't fall because she was seized by two of the men and dragged to a corner of the room.

The third man strode towards Osewoudt.

'Get up! Where are your clothes? Put them on! Quick!'

It was a car powered by wood gas, and yet it was quite fast. Osewoudt kept looking back, but they were not being followed.

They were on the road to Leiden, which ran parallel to the blue tram line. Dusk was falling.

'Shall we drop you at home?'

'No, better near Leiden somewhere, if that's all right with you.'

'It's all the same to us. Right, Cor? We'll drop him near Leiden.'

'Plenty of time. We'll take him wherever he wants to go.'

'Quite a turnaround for you in the last fifteen minutes, eh?'

Osewoudt made no reply. So the man at the wheel was called Cor. He hadn't come into the hospital with the others, he'd been waiting in the getaway car. The man next to him hadn't said a word, he was the one who had tied up the nurse with the help of the man to Osewoudt's right. The man to Osewoudt's left said he was Uncle Kees. It had been Uncle Kees doing all the talking; clearly he was the leader. He had the same type of square moustache as Hitler, his eyes were almost square too, his face was a crossword puzzle.

'What did you mean, Uncle Kees, about dropping me off at home?'

'I thought you lived in Voorschoten. Don't you?'

'How did you know?'

'It's been in all the newspapers. Your picture, too! Rotten

of the Krauts to say "wanted for robbery with assault". If they'd said "wanted for murdering a traitor", no Dutchman would touch those 500 guilders.'

Osewoudt fixed his eyes ahead, without responding. My picture in all the papers, complete with my name and all the rest. I disguised myself with a hat and glasses, but I no longer have either. Free again, but for how long?

When they reached the outskirts of Voorschoten he repeated his thoughts aloud.

'Look here, Uncle Kees, what with my picture all over the papers and in the cinemas too, I can't show my face any more. I can't go anywhere I've been before, or they'll nab me again straightaway. I need to leave the country as soon as possible. Switzerland maybe, or Spain, and from there to England.'

The man at the wheel exploded with laughter: 'Think we're running a travel agency, do you?'

'Rescuing you not enough, then?' sneered Uncle Kees.

'All right, so you can't get me out of the country, but surely you can fix me up with an address where I can lie low for a while?'

He had a lump in his throat as he said this. Just then they drove past the tobacco shop. NORTH STATE CIGARETTES.

He saw that the blinds had been raised, both of them, the broken one over the window too. Who had done that? He was mystified, then thought: I don't really give a damn, anyway.

'He wants somewhere to hide, Cor!' said Uncle Kees.

'Good old Osewoudt!' said Cor. 'Wants it all handed to him on a plate! Listen, Osewoudt, kidnapping you from a hospital was risky enough, finding you a hideout doesn't come with it. We don't want anything to do with you, really, that's best for us, and for you too.'

He stepped on the accelerator.

The man on Osewoudt's right said nothing, nor did the man sitting beside the driver.

'Best for me?' said Osewoudt. 'Best for me to get caught again straightaway?'

'Leave off, Cor,' said Uncle Kees. 'Not everybody's as hardened to the job as you are. It's hardly surprising that he's looking around for help.'

Osewoudt leaned forward, so that his face was up close to the driver's shoulder.

'There's no danger in helping me. I'm not the man they're looking for. They've got me mixed up with someone else. You must believe me, I saw the photo myself in the cinema, that's what got me arrested in the first place. But it wasn't a picture of me, the picture looks like me, but it's not me. No such photo of me exists. But you may have met the man they're looking for. I know he exists.'

'How do you know?'

For the first time the driver looked over his shoulder.

Cor had dark hair with a heavy forelock, like a fire screen before the black embers of his eyes.

'Steady on, Cor,' said Uncle Kees. 'Don't ask too many questions. He's not asking questions either, he knows the rules. Hasn't said thank you either, come to think of it. Naughty!'

'How do you know it was someone else?' Cor persisted, keeping his eyes on the road now.

'Don't ask too many questions, Cor!'

'It's all right, Uncle Kees,' said Osewoudt. 'I have nothing to hide. The Germans confronted me with somebody who claimed to have met me at Vondel Park in Amsterdam. I've never been there, I'd never seen that man in my life.'

'Didn't they ask about that shooting in Haarlem, Kleine Houtstraat 32, back in the summer of '40?'

'I don't know about any shooting,' said Osewoudt and then, turning to Uncle Kees: 'Cor knows more about it than I do.'

'Oh, belt up, Cor,' said Uncle Kees. 'We ought to be raising a glass. He's just escaped death by the skin of his teeth, and there you go, pestering him with questions.'

'If he hasn't done anything why should we find him a hideout? No need for that, is there? We risk rescuing him and it wasn't even necessary, is that it? He's as innocent as a lamb. No use to the cause then, I take it.'

'I'm scared,' said Osewoudt. 'I don't want to get caught again. You saved my life. Perhaps you'll understand when the war's over.'

'Rubbish. Thousands of people who haven't done a thing get beaten up by the Germans. Which is unfortunate, but there's nothing we can do about it. We can only do things for people who matter to us. A question of economics. Poor sods who haven't done a thing aren't worth taking risks for, which again is unfortunate, but that's the way it is. Right then, where do you want us to drop you off?'

'Don't be angry. This isn't my fault, it wasn't me who ordered my rescue. It's a miracle you succeeded. At least I hope you're not planning to take me back there.'

Osewoudt gave a forced laugh.

'For God's sake, Cor, ease off,' said Uncle Kees.

'I had my doubts,' said Cor. 'I had my doubts the moment I saw him. I thought: is this really the big cheese we're after? He looks like a girl! I wouldn't be surprised if he isn't even Osewoudt the tobacconist. He's not a day over seventeen, I'd say.'

Osewoudt peered out of the window and saw that they were driving through the residential neighbourhood of Leiden, where the professors lived.

'You can drop me here,' he said. 'I'll find my own way.'

Cor looked round, swerved to the right and pulled up at the kerb. The man on Osewoudt's right did not stir. Then Uncle Kees opened the door on his side and got out.

Osewoudt made to step out of the car, and said: 'Thank you all very much, I can't tell you how grateful I am and why, but I hope I'll have a chance to explain some day.'

He stood beside the car. He shook hands with Uncle Kees and said: 'The Germans have arrested my old, sick mother, and my wife, and my uncle. I'm the only one in the family who's free.'

'The Germans,' said Uncle Kees, clasping Osewoudt's hand while lifting his left wrist to look at his watch, 'the Germans will be on the lookout for you. How will you avoid recognition?'

'I wore glasses for a while, and a hat, but I've lost them.'

'With that plaster over your eye they'll recognise you even if it's pitch-dark!'

Uncle Kees let go of Osewoudt's hand and reached out to rip off the plaster. Blinded by the pain, Osewoudt heard the car door slam and the engine revving. An acrid smell of burning wood gusted towards him. When he could see again, the car had gone. In the semi-darkness he saw the crumpled sticking plaster lying at his feet. He could feel blood trickling down his face.

A handkerchief!

In his trouser pocket he found the paper napkin Wülfing had given him. He held it to his face and started walking. Glancing around, he concluded that no one had seen anything. It was a very quiet neighbourhood.

At least Labare would have no reason to complain about his behaviour – he had, after all, kept his mouth shut. He had been rescued by friends of Labare's, of that he had no doubt. If they had been Dorbeck's friends, why would that fellow Cor have been so eager to know what the Germans had him in for? Why the snide remarks about his girlish appearance, and about them taking risks only for important people, not for poor sods beaten up by the Germans by mistake? Alternatively, maybe they knew the doctor, or knew both the doctor and Labare, or they knew Meinarends, or Marianne. But then where would Cor have got the idea that it wasn't for robbery that Osewoudt the tobacconist was wanted, as it said in the newspaper, but for a shooting in Haarlem?

The hairdresser's wife let him in.

Osewoudt had never seen her before, because until now Marianne had always answered the door.

The woman's face was still remarkably plump, considering how long the war had been going on. Her cheeks were ruddy, with a tracery of fine veins in a deeper red. She had a high forehead, slightly narrowed eyes and thin, frizzy hair.

'No, sir, Miss Sondaar is out, but do come in. You look dreadful, all that blood! Did you fall?'

'Yes, I tripped and fell.'

He stepped into the small shop. She motioned him to one of the two stools in front of the counter and said: 'Let me get some cotton wool.'

'Please don't bother. Just tell me where I can find Miss Sondaar. I'm in a hurry.'

But the woman went through to the back as if he hadn't spoken.

The display cases along the wall contained packaging and boxes of various soaps and hair lotions that had long since run out. Empty packaging. Would it ever be worth filling again? Everyone I have anything to do with comes a cropper. Why did they rescue me? He said nothing when the woman returned with a basin of water and a wad of cotton wool, and meekly submitted to having his face cleaned.

'There, you look a lot better now. But what's that over your eye?'

'Stitches. I had a fall the day before yesterday, too. Has Marianne been arrested?'

'Whatever gave you that idea? I certainly hope not! She'll be back later.'

'Where is she?'

'You're Mr van Druten, aren't you?'

'Yes.'

'That's what I thought, from the look of you. I was to tell you Marianne is at Mr Labare's. Number 74, Zoeterwoudsesingel.'

'Is that what she told you to say?'

'Yes, 74! But hadn't you better wait here? I could go and fetch her. You look so dreadful.'

What was Marianne doing at Labare's? How did she know him? Or had they known each other all along?

'No, thank you, no. It's quite a long way to where I live. If I wait here I won't make it home by eleven. Thanks anyway!'

He ran out to the street, which was now almost dark. Free, but a sitting duck. Every Tom, Dick and Harry who had seen his picture in the newspaper or in the cinema and wanted the 500 guilders reward could report him to the authorities.

Coming to a corner he paused, flattened himself against the building and looked in all directions. Not a German to be seen. Rounding the next corner he found he was no longer alone in the street. He was afraid any furtiveness on his part would arouse the suspicions of passers-by, but fortunately no one was paying any attention. So he looked about without pressing his back against the wall. But looking about wasn't enough, because the danger would see him before he saw the danger.

Twice a car of Germans came past, but they evidently had no orders to arrest him. A Luftwaffe officer asked him for a light and went on his way without another word. He arrived at Zoeterwoudsesingel unhindered.

When he caught sight of Labare's house, he thought: this is my last breath of fresh air. Anyone whose picture has been in the papers is useless to the Resistance. Wild horses won't drag me out of that house until the war's over. If Dorbeck wants me to do anything for him he'll have to come and ask me in person, and even then I may not be in a position to oblige. What's the use of blindly following his instructions? Anyone would think I idolise him!

Maybe he's been safe and sound in England all along. He sends me messages I can't make head or tail of. I have my hair dyed so I won't be recognised, but it's just as if I did it to make it even easier to confuse me with Dorbeck. My enemies make me pay for his actions, while my friends can tell at a glance that I'm not half the man Dorbeck is. To them I'm a seventeen-year-old with a girl's face, a wimp, a poor sod who gets beaten by the Germans more as a matter of routine than for any important secrets he might reveal.

I've lost my forged papers, not that I'd be able to use them now anyway. I'll have to sit tight until it all blows over.

His thoughts came to a sudden halt, and he was aware only of the aching in his battered skull.

Then the door of the house opened, without him having rung the bell. It was Marianne. He saw her standing in the hallway; she wore a raincoat of white Egyptian cotton belted tightly at the waist, her hair reached to her shoulders. She exclaimed when she saw him.

Osewoudt laughed out loud. He stepped forward and threw his arms around her in the hallway, without bothering to shut the door. He didn't explain what had happened to his face, only kissed her, and he saw tears rolling down her cheeks. Then he was seized with laughter again so that kissing was no longer possible. He kicked the door shut behind him with a bang.

She put her hands round the back of his head and said: 'Darling! I missed you so much that I couldn't bring myself to flee when I realised you'd been arrested.'

'Did you think they'd put us in the same cell if they arrested you too?'

'That would have been bliss.'

'Or did you think I'd be rescued somehow?'

'Rescued?'

'Yes! I was rescued. Abducted, in fact.'

'I thought the Germans had let you go. So you were rescued, then?'

'Yes! From the hospital! The doctor there said he knew you.'

'He lived next door to us, that's all.'

'So you know nothing about me being rescued?'

'Of course not. You're not disappointed in me, are you, Filip?'

'Then why did you tell the hairdresser's wife to say you were at Labare's?'

'I just hoped the Germans would let you go. Because it was all a mistake, wasn't it? You're not the man in that picture, are you?'

Osewoudt laughed and pressed her close.

'They certainly slapped you about a bit,' she said. 'Didn't they have any idea they'd got the wrong man?'

'No, first they beat me and then they confronted me with a man I didn't know. After that they took me to Zuidwal hospital to have me patched up. They kept me there all day. There was a German guard in the corridor. But this evening I was abducted by four men. They gave the German some injection and tied up the nurse. They brought me to Leiden by car.'

'And you didn't know who they were?'

'No. One of them was called Uncle Kees and another one Cor. The other two kept their mouths shut.'

'Hey, who are you talking to down there?'

It was Labare's voice, coming from the first-floor landing.

Osewoudt went to the stairs and called up: 'Yes, Labare, it's me! It's me, Melgers! I'll be right with you!'

He turned back to Marianne and said: 'Watch it, Labare thinks my name is Joost Melgers. Mind you don't slip up!'

He went on kissing her until he could tell from Labare's footsteps that he was halfway down the stairs.

Labare drew them into the back room, where Osewoudt had never been before. There was a man reading a newspaper, who introduced himself as Suyling. He wore glasses with thick, myopic lenses that made his eyes appear absurdly small. His voice had a snivelling quality.

'Look here Labare, this is not what we agreed. We can't have people who've had their fingers burned staying here. In any case, this Melgers or Osewoudt or van Druten, or whatever his name is, is believed to be the man in this picture. There is simply no point, not for us and not for him either, in letting him stay here.'

The newspaper spread out across Suyling's knees was the issue with the photo of the wanted man.

Looking Osewoudt up and down, he said: 'Yes, when you were in the darkroom you didn't get to see me, but I saw you all right.'

'No, I never saw you.'

'I didn't like the look of you one bit. I'm the only careful one around here!' said Suyling. 'The moment I saw that photo in the paper I said to myself: damn it, it's Melgers. Where has he got to? I check with Labare and Labare says: he'll be back this evening. We've been here all night with the pistols out on the table.'

Labare now intervened.

'Where he was last night is irrelevant. We know where he was. He was arrested. He kept his mouth shut about us or we wouldn't be sitting here. That much is clear. But one thing isn't: who were the gang who rescued him?'

'Are you telling me you don't know?'

'It's nothing to do with me,' said Labare. 'Meinarends rang

me up this morning saying you'd been badly beaten and that you were in Zuidwal hospital under German surveillance. He'd heard this from Miss Sondaar. So I asked Meinarends to send Miss Sondaar round so she could tell me herself. He said: fine by me, but then you'll have to find her another address. That's how she got here. All I know of the whole affair is what she told me. Your turn now. So you were rescued. By whom? On whose orders?'

'They wouldn't say.'

'And when you left the hospital and got in the car, what did you tell them?'

'They asked me where I wanted to go and I said I didn't want to go anywhere I'd ever been before. I asked them if they had a place for me, but they said that was out of the question. Then I said they could drop me in the outskirts of Leiden. I didn't mention any address. They stopped on some road, I got out of the car and they drove off straightaway.'

Labare slumped back in his chair, folded his hands over his stomach and twiddled his thumbs.

'Complete amateurs, obviously!'

He grimaced with such intensity that his hollow cheeks actually looked chubby.

'Blithering incompetents! Small fry! They go and kidnap someone from under the Gestapo's nose and then can't be bothered to take him somewhere safe! No! They wash their hands of him! Drop him any old where! Make off without even considering that he might bump into someone thirty seconds later, the law for instance, who'd say: what are you doing here? Your picture's all over the papers and I just had a phone call saying you've gone missing from Zuidwal hospital. You'd better come along with me. Abducted, you say? You can start by describing them! God, what idiots they must be! Asking for the firing squad, they are!'

Osewoudt felt himself redden. He opened his mouth to speak but said nothing.

'Well, what were you about to say?' asked Labare.

'What do you want me to say? They'd never done anything like this before. Friends of the doctor. The doctor let them in and showed them the way. The nurse was probably in on it, too, because she didn't say a word when they tied her up. Otherwise she'd surely have screamed, I mean any nurse would scream if three masked men burst into her tidy ward and made off with one of her patients, wouldn't you think?'

'It all sounds rather fishy to me,' said Suyling. The newspaper was still open on his lap. He looked from Osewoudt to the photo and from the photo to Osewoudt.

'Mr Suyling,' said Marianne, 'you're looking at him as if you think he really is a criminal!'

Suyling put the paper on the table and crossed his left leg over his right, but the leg wouldn't keep still. It went on swinging while he said: 'Oh, Miss, if I said all the things I think, there'd be no end to it. I'll give you an example: newspaper photographs are always a bit dodgy, but now that I've taken a good look at it I don't think the resemblance with Melgers is all that strong. How do we know that Melgers is indeed Osewoudt?'

'That's no concern of yours,' Osewoudt said. 'I am Osewoudt, but I am not the man in the photo. The photo is not of me, you understand, and the man the Germans are looking for is not Osewoudt but someone who looks like him. I am sure of that. The Germans confronted me with someone called Roorda who said he knew me. He'd spoken to me three days before, he said, in Vondel Park in Amsterdam. But I had never seen the man before, and I haven't been to Vondel Park for years.'

Suyling smacked his lips.

'Now let's assume for the moment that it's not only the

Germans making a mistake, but Osewoudt too. Like so: the Germans made a mistake arresting Osewoudt, but Osewoudt is making a mistake saying he was kidnapped from the hospital by four gangsters. How does that sound, Osewoudt? Eh? You've been doing a fair bit of embroidery, haven't you? Well, we've all done it. I don't mind. But d'you know what I think? I think the Germans realised they had the wrong man and simply let you go. It's not that I mind, you know, but I really don't see the point of spinning romantic yarns about masked men, cars powered by wood gas, Uncle Kees and Uncle Cor and all the rest.'

He clapped his hands three times, blew a raspberry and smirked.

Labare laughed quietly. Osewoudt didn't say a word, spread his knees, propped his elbows on them, and let his hands and his head drop.

Then Marianne said: 'How fortunate we are to have Mr Suyling here keeping the score. No possibility, however remote, is beneath the notice of his mighty brain. But Mr Suyling, if you're so keen on getting rid of him, if you think he's a liability, then I take it you know a safe address for him? Because I'm sure you don't need me to explain how important it is to prevent the Germans getting their hands on him again. He may have been arrested by mistake, he may not be the man in the photo, he may even not be Osewoudt the tobacconist, but that still leaves the fact that he can't have breathed a word about this place and what goes on here, otherwise you wouldn't be sitting here pontificating, would you, Mr Suyling?'

It was getting increasingly airless in the back room.

'Well, Suyling, do you know a good address?' said Labare. 'And can you take him there now, straightaway? It's already quarter to eleven, I'll have you know.'

Suyling did not reply. No one spoke any more. Quarter to

eleven, thought Osewoudt. Marianne would have to hurry. He threw her a look, but she made no move to stand.

Then the door opened and a boy of about fifteen burst in, waving a slip of paper. He shouted: 'The Americans are coming! We just heard it on the radio! The Germans are retreating at Caen! We might be liberated next week!'

Suyling did not let go of his newspaper on hearing this.

Marianne, Labare and Osewoudt sprang up from their seats. Labare snatched the slip of paper from the boy's hand. Marianne flung her arms around Osewoudt. She kissed him on his mouth, his neck and, very gently, on his good eye. But her kisses made him sad. Because if the Germans were beaten, what would a girl like Marianne still see in him: an uneducated, unattractive tobacconist, a man who didn't even need to shave and who, in a liberated Holland, would have lost every chance of being either hero or martyr? He screwed up his eyes and pressed her to him, working his hands up and down her back as if there had to be a way he could clasp her so tightly they would never be prised apart.

The voices of Labare and the boy shrieked in his ears. Suyling too made himself heard: 'How stuffy it is in here! If you would just shut up for a moment, then I can let in some fresh air.'

He switched off the light and opened the door to the back garden. All five of them went outside. Osewoudt had never been there before. He smelled the garden more than he saw it. There were no lights anywhere, and the neighbouring houses looked deserted too. Maybe the people who lived there had not been listening to the broadcasts from London and didn't know that the front line had started to shift and that the war would be over in a week. What was that fragrance? There would be a variety of plants growing in the central flower bed, which he could feel at his feet.

Together they looked up at the black sky. But there were no stars, and the blackness wasn't really black.

He pressed her face so hard against his that the stitches in his eyebrow hurt. She slipped her hands under his jacket and he felt them on his back, through his thin shirt.

He said: 'I missed you more than I ever thought I could miss anyone. You're going to have to spend the night here, as it's past eleven already. You'll stay with me, I have a small bedroom upstairs.'

These were plain facts, facts that were irrefutable, so much so that he had an instantaneous sensation of having checkmated her.

She said: 'Why do you put it like that? Even if I could go out all night, if I could come and go as I please, I'd still want to be with you more than anything else. Don't you understand? How suspicious you are.'

'Sometimes I think I'm afraid of you.'

'Getting arrested gave you a shock, so now you're scared of everything, for no reason.'

'Do you love me?'

'Yes.'

'And when the war's over, will you still love me?'

'Why ever not?'

He held on to her hair, knowing he was hurting her. He went up on his toes and had to kiss her to stop himself saying: I don't believe a word of it, because I know what I am, and I have a feeling I know what you are too. (I can't be sure, he thought, sometimes the strangest things happen, she may go on loving me, but it's unlikely, if only because things won't be so mad any more after the war. I can't keep on dyeing my hair for ever and even if I did it wouldn't make me the man Dorbeck is. We're alike, but not the same.)

A ghostly vision entered his mind. The war was over, and

he and Marianne were strolling hand in hand in some faraway countryside. Then they saw Dorbeck. Without a word, she went off with Dorbeck and left him standing there. No goodbye, no turning round to wave, just one quick look over the shoulder, only to call back to him: I knew what the man I wanted looked like. Forgive me for thinking it was you. Why must you look so much like him when you're not him? It's your own fault. Mine too, because I'm the one who dyed your hair, I made you fit the picture in my head. Now your hair's no longer black, what are you? A bleached rat.

Or, worse, they had a date one evening and he suffered an accident on the way, so couldn't be with her on time. By chance she would run into Dorbeck at the very hour they were supposed to meet. She wouldn't consciously notice the difference, but she'd say: I love you tonight more than ever before! And when he at last caught up with her she would say: now I understand. You're a fraud, you were always pretending to be someone else.

Marianne slid her mouth away from his and said: 'This is the longest you've ever kissed me.'

He let her go and looked about. Labare, Suyling and the boy had apparently gone back inside. The door was still open. They went into the unlit room, and he groped behind him to close the door. The house was quiet. Taking Marianne by the hand he drew her into the corridor and upstairs to the small room with the narrow bed and the dingy white counterpane, the straight-backed chair, the small table with the enamel basin and the enamel jug, and the framed picture of a family of ginger apes partially clothed as humans.

Their clothes lay in a heap on the straight-backed chair.

Marianne pushed him away and began to laugh.

'I say, didn't they give you a bath in hospital?'

'Yes, why?'

Her laughter became uproarious. He laughed as well and asked: 'What's so funny?'

'Didn't the nurses think it was funny?'

He stopped laughing. 'What do you mean?' he asked.

'You and I are exact opposites!' giggled Marianne. 'Don't look so glum! If they had noticed, the worst they could have done was tell some German they'd seen a patient who'd changed his hair from fair to dark. No harm in the Germans knowing that, is there?'

She made a grasping gesture with her hands, as though plucking the conclusion from the air: 'How bad could it be? They're looking for a man with dark hair and the man they arrest turns out to be naturally fair! So then they know they've got the wrong man!'

'No,' said Osewoudt, 'because they don't know how long I've been dyeing my hair. It might already have been dyed when that photo was taken. By the way, what did you do with my pistol? I gave it to you in the cinema before I left.'

'I've kept it with me all the time. It's in my handbag. Do you need it now?'

'You make me laugh.'

She planted swift kisses in the hollow above his left collarbone, and ran her fingertips over his throat. He raised his left arm to look at her body beneath him. He was aware of their bodies touching all over, and yet it was not as if she were another, separate being. Time passed at breakneck speed, and this, this would be happiness or eternity: bringing time to a standstill but keeping the breakneck speed. Marianne gave a moan, and it was as if he sank into her, or as if he was swallowed up by her and she by him.

Afterwards he lay beside her, his arm beneath her head; he pressed her cheek to his chest. A wave of despondency came over him.

'You know,' he said, 'I didn't tell Labare the whole truth.'

'What didn't you tell him?'

'I told him they didn't trust me, but there was more to it than that. That fellow Cor said he didn't think I was a day over seventeen. He didn't believe I was Osewoudt. He said there'd been no point in rescuing me, because I was just some poor sod the Germans had beaten up by mistake, and that they only put themselves on the line for people important to the Resistance, not for the likes of me. He said I looked like a girl. But I'm a man!'

'Of course you are.'

'It's true, I don't shave. I've been picked on for that ever since I reached the age boys start sprouting beards.'

'Oh, that's just some physiological peculiarity, or it could be a skin disorder, something minor that has nothing to do with the rest of you. I wouldn't feel the way I do if you weren't a man.'

She tickled his side, saying: 'Every time you see me you prove you're a man. And what a man!'

'Proving it to you is easy. But I can't go around proving it in public, can I now?'

'Just as well. I love being the only one to know. I'm very jealous. You shouldn't take any notice of what people say or think.'

'All the same, it got to me, almost as if I had a sneaking feeling they were right.'

'Why, for goodness sake?'

'The thing is, the man in the photograph actually exists. You're not going to believe this, but it's the truth. I met that man a number of times. His name is Dorbeck. We're the same height, and he looks exactly like me. Really, like a twin. It's hard to imagine how two unrelated people can look so alike, but we do. Only, his hair's black, and he shaves. Everything else about him is completely different. He was an officer in the Dutch army back in '40. When Rotterdam was being bombed he saw two Germans in the street. He had them shot immediately. So he was a wanted man from the moment we capitulated. He wasn't afraid of anything. He asked me to do things for him a couple of times. I did everything he asked. I had the feeling I was an extension of him, or even part of him.

'When I first saw him I thought: this is the sort of man I ought to have been. It's a bit difficult to put into words, but think of the goods being produced in factories: now and then a substandard article gets made, so they make another one and throw away the reject...

'Only, they didn't throw me away. I continued to exist, reject though I was. I didn't realise I was the reject until I met Dorbeck. Then I knew. That's when I knew he was the successful specimen, that compared to him I had no reason to exist, and the only way I could accept that was to do exactly as he said. I did everything he told me to do, which was quite a lot sometimes... quite a lot...'

Marianne sat up and leaned forward, propping herself up on her elbow.

'But Filip, aren't you getting a bit carried away? You could be imagining it all, you know, I mean about that man looking so much like you.'

'Imagining it? Why do you suppose the Germans arrested me if it's *him* they're looking for, why would they circulate his picture with my name? And how could Roorda be so sure he recognised me, when I know for certain it was Dorbeck he met? There's no other explanation than that Dorbeck is the spitting image of me, other than that we're like twins – identical twins even: same height, same build, one voice lower than the other but the same intonation, same gestures. I'm telling you: the only difference between Dorbeck and me is that Dorbeck has black hair and shaves.'

'But he's not you. Would you prefer to be someone else then?'

'Why not? Who am I? Do you think it's any fun being me?'

'Maybe I wouldn't be yours if you were someone else.'

'Maybe if you knew Dorbeck you'd rather have him than me.'

'No.'

'How can you say that? When you met me I was at Dorbeck's beck and call. It was only by doing what Dorbeck said that I got to know you. Without Dorbeck I'd still be stuck behind the counter in the tobacco shop. You'd never have met me. You've never known me the way I used to be. Ten minutes after we met my hair was pitch-black, like Dorbeck's.'

'Poor Filip. The one thing I can't give you is a beard. A stick-on moustache maybe, but that's all. Anyway, I don't like moustaches.'

'You're turning it into a joke.'

'What else can I do? It's almost as if you're telling me you're a fraud and that loving you is a mistake. You make it sound as if you'd offer me to Dorbeck on a plate the moment he turned up. How do you think that makes me feel?'

'You might fall for him anyway.'

'It's good to know where you stand, I must say. You obviously have a high opinion of me and my feelings.'

'That's not the point. The point is I can't help thinking: in reality she's in love with Dorbeck, even if she doesn't know it. She says she loves me, but she means Dorbeck, because Dorbeck's the genuine article and I'm the reject.'

'Your nerves are on edge, that's all. The black dye will grow out eventually. You'll see how much I love you when you're fair-haired again. I wish you'd believe me. Why don't you break contact with Dorbeck, if he's such a nuisance? Give up on him, be yourself. You can trust me. Try me.'

'What do you mean, break contact with Dorbeck? You don't know what you're saying! Give up on Dorbeck? That would mean betraying him. And how would I go about that? By going to the Germans and saying: you've got it all wrong. I know who you're looking for. His name's Dorbeck. His hair's black, mine's only dyed. That's not what you meant, is it, Marianne?'

'No, that's not what I meant.'

'And even if it was, it would still be absolutely impossible, because of all the things I did on his behalf. I developed secret films for him, I shot a man in Haarlem, I killed a Youth Storm leader, I shot a German agent and the agent's wife, I abducted their kid to Amsterdam . . .'

'But it was you doing all those things on your own, Filip, just you. Dorbeck wasn't there, was he?'

'No, Dorbeck wasn't there.'

'So if Dorbeck wasn't there, they were your own actions! What difference does it make that it was Dorbeck telling you what to do? Soldiers obey orders, too. Does that mean a soldier's actions aren't his own?'

'A soldier obeys whoever's superior in rank. He doesn't obey the man, he obeys the orders. But I can only obey Dorbeck, and no one forced me. Do try to understand: before I knew him I didn't have a life, really. I got married to a first cousin seven years older than me, it was pure chance. I did nothing, wanted nothing, left everything to chance. My uncle thought I should go to university, but by chance, when the time came, my mother was discharged from the mental institution, so the easy way out was to take over my father's tobacco shop and have my mother stay there. It looked as if I was making sacrifices for her, but that wasn't the case at all: I sacrificed nothing because I was nothing. I had no skills, no ambition. It wasn't until I met Dorbeck that I felt I wanted something, if only to be like Dorbeck, if only to want the same things as he did.

And wanting the same thing as someone else is a step up from not wanting anything.'

Marianne lifted her elbow and leaned diagonally across his body. She kissed his ear. 'Here you are, talking away, while I could do with some loving. Why can't you do what I want for a change? If you love me as much as you say you do?'

He pressed her to him, muttering: 'You're right. This is the answer. This is the only possible answer.'

He had an acute sense of how tired he was, but overcoming his weariness became in his mind a bid for glory. Everything that might happen from now on he would confront with this passion, as if life itself were a gigantic female, the tang of whose sweat alone would drive every virile male to unrelenting ecstasy. Not just once, but time and again, without respite, without rest.

He heard Marianne's shallow breathing and drew himself half upright, gritting his teeth. She gave a moan and opened her eyes wide, as though showing him how to fight and die with eyes open.

Neither spoke for the next quarter of an hour. He rose from the bed, switched off the lamp, opened the curtains and the window. Hardly any light came into the room from outside.

'Such awful things you've been telling me.'

'Yes.'

He lay down beside her again.

'That you're married to an ugly cousin of yours who's seven years older than you.'

'Was that what upset you the most?'

'Yes. Where is she?'

'Arrested by the Germans.'

'Is her name Ria?'

'How did you know?'

'Does her father live in Amsterdam on Oudezijds Achterburgwal?'

'Yes. What of it?'

'Then his name's Nauta. Of Bellincoff Ltd. I went there and said: Henri sends his regards, and Ria's been arrested. Don't you remember asking me to do that?'

'Yes, I do.'

'So you're the Henri who left his wife and took a girl to spend the night with him at his Uncle Nauta's?'

'Yes, that's me.'

'Where's the girl?'

'Arrested. Maybe dead. She was an agent from England.'

'How did you know her?'

'She had my address. I had to help her on her way. She showed me a photo to prove her identity.'

'Remember the ID card you asked me to take there? I can just see it now, with her picture on it. Well, well.'

Osewoudt gave her a fleeting kiss.

Marianne sighed: 'All those people getting shot.'

'You don't mind about that.'

'Of course not. In fact, it makes you special. If only you knew how much it means to me to be with a man who's actually done that kind of thing – me, a Jewish girl who's obliged to bleach her hair and take a non-Jewish name. Oh, Filip, sometimes I imagine you were only doing it for my sake.'

'So I was.'

'Then you got off to a very early start! But it's sweet of you to say so.'

'Maybe I wouldn't even be caught up in all this if I hadn't been destined to meet you.'

'Now you're exaggerating.'

She laughed. He laughed as well and rolled over on to his back.

Suddenly they heard cars approaching along the canal, slowing down and stopping at the house. It became light in the room; German voices sounded in the street. The beam of a spotlight came slanting upwards through the window and froze on the far wall, illuminating the ginger apes partially clothed as humans. Outside, heavy boots thumped on the cobbles. The spotlight remained fixed on the apes.

There was a commotion in the street, then the bell rang and someone started pounding the door with a heavy object.

Osewoudt slid off the bed, ducked under the light-beam and made for the straight-backed chair. He grabbed the heap of clothes, picked out his underwear, threw Marianne's on to the bed.

Alarm bells began to shrill all over the house. Orders were barked in German, more pounding on the door. Then the sound of breaking glass.

'Filip! They're coming in through the window.'

'Where's your bag?'

'Isn't it there?'

'Can't find it.'

Wearing only his vest and pants he crawled over the floor, seizing clothes and tossing them aside.

'Marianne, where's your bag? It's got my pistol in it.'

He searched the floor in desperation, even looking under the bed, but no handbag. No time to put on his socks and shoes. Barefoot, he opened the door and went out to the landing. He saw circles of torchlight sweeping over the walls. Voices came from the front room. Someone kept turning a switch on and off, click, click, but the light didn't come on. Labare must have disconnected the current at the mains.

Osewoudt leaned over the banister and looked down. He saw the Germans going in and out of the rooms on the ground floor, torch in one hand, machine gun in the other. One of them opened the door to the basement and called to someone else to take a look behind it. Cackles of laughter. Osewoudt was surprised to see the door opened so easily, as the portcullis was supposed to prevent that. He started down the stairs, and when he was halfway put his hands up and shouted: 'Don't shoot, I surrender!'

Three torches were trained on him as he completed his descent.

'I'm Osewoudt!' he said. 'I'm the one you're looking for.'

As he reached the bottom he felt machine guns jabbing him in the ribs. He was too blinded by the three torches to see the Germans' faces.

'*Stimmt. Ist der Osewoudt.*'

They manhandled him into the back room, where another two Germans were waiting. These were not in uniform. They pushed him towards an easy chair, and he sat down.

One of the Germans in plain clothes pulled up a second low chair, which he placed directly opposite Osewoudt. He sat down, but jumped up instantly as though stung, looked at the seat, flung Marianne's handbag into a corner, and settled himself on the chair. The bag hit the floor with a thud that sounded far too heavy for a lady's handbag.

'Why are the lights off?' the German asked.

Osewoudt couldn't tell him. The other German in plain clothes went over to the corner where Marianne's bag had fallen.

'*Verdammt*, Helmuth, come here with your torch, I need some light!'

Two torches remained fixed on Osewoudt, the third swung away to the corner where the German was crouching.

'Who else is in this house?' asked the man sitting opposite Osewoudt.

'There's no one, just me. Everybody's gone. I don't know where.'

'Werner! Take a look here! Some dangerous lady's forgotten something!'

Holding Osewoudt's pistol by the barrel in one hand and the handbag in the other, he came forward to display them to the man sitting opposite Osewoudt. At that moment a German came in with an acetylene lamp which spread a garish glow. He set it on the table. Marianne's handbag was turned upside down. They pounced on the identity card.

'Marianne Sondaar,' intoned the man called Werner.

'The pistol isn't hers, it's mine!' Osewoudt cried. 'I can prove that!'

'How interesting,' said Werner. 'We'll give you plenty of time to furnish proof. Take him away.'

He slammed down the pistol on the table beside the empty handbag, a powder compact, a lipstick, some zinc coins, a screwed-up handkerchief.

Osewoudt stood up. A German in uniform grabbed his arm and walked him to the door. The others stayed behind.

Coming into the corridor, Osewoudt saw there was no one about. The door to the hall was open, as was the front door. Outside, there was a fair amount of light, although the spotlight was not aimed at the doorway. He felt coconut matting under his bare feet, then the cold stone doorstep. He saw the waiting police van.

Was it because the stones hurt his bare feet? He stepped to one side and at the same instant seized the hand of his German guard. He yanked at the hand, dragged the arm it belonged to over his shoulder and bent down, so the German's feet were lifted off the ground. Osewoudt slung him away with all the force he could muster, twisting the arm until it was torn from his hands by the weight of the falling man. A cry sounded, like the squeal of a pig being dragged by the tail into a cattle truck. From behind the van another German came running, with hobnailed boots scraping the cobbles. Osewoudt dashed across the pavement, caught momentarily in the spotlight. Shots were fired and he ducked behind the vehicle, where the spotlight couldn't reach him. Further along, another car engine sputtered to life. Osewoudt crossed the road and ran down the grassy bank of the canal, while a volley of shots rang out behind him. He felt no pain and reached the water safely. It was knee-deep. Bending over, keeping his head down as far as possible, he waded on. His legs tore against dead branches on the bottom, or perhaps they were shards of metal. The spotlight slid past him several times. Spray from the impact of bullets made him blink. Now and then he had to wrench a foot free with his hands, so he seemed to be advancing on all fours. He had no idea how quickly or slowly he was going; he felt he was making no headway at all.

There were no bridges along this stretch of the canal. The Germans would have to make a considerable detour before they could close in on him on the other side. He heard an engine running, but the sound was not coming from across the water. It was too shallow to swim. Growing impatient, he straightened up to try and take big strides instead. Shots were still being fired, but the bullets weren't coming his way. A spotlight remained fixed on the top of a tree.

At last he was able to scramble up the opposite bank. The shooting stopped abruptly and a moment later the spotlight went out. A bird, probably roused by the noise, started to sing. Osewoudt ran on, bent almost double. The park was fairly wide; he ran through grass and across footpaths. Crouching behind a rustic bench, he focussed his eyes on the far side of the canal.

He had the idea the vehicles were still outside Labare's house; the lights were still on but he couldn't make out what was happening. Bending as low as he could he walked on. He came to the limit of the park. Another pavement, then a road. It was a narrow road with a bend in it, so he couldn't see to the other end. He looked up, scanning the house fronts for some sign of life, but every window was dark and shut. Everyone was asleep, no one cared. Or maybe they weren't asleep; maybe they had heard the gunfire and even now were shivering, with dishevelled hair and rumbling stomachs, behind their blacked-out windows.

There was no sound but the slap of his own bare, wet feet on the pavement. Then, faintly, he heard music. It was coming from a ground floor. He put his ear to a window. No, next window. He found the porch that belonged to the ground-floor flat with the window, felt along the doorpost, found the door-bell and rang. He began to shake uncontrollably. His hands were covered in mud and fronds of rotting water plants; he wiped them against each other and on his trousers. The music in the house was American. Osewoudt put his face to the letter box on the front door, and saw the light come on inside.

The music stopped, the door opened. The hallway was flooded with light. 'What is it?' growled the man who answered the door.

Osewoudt pushed him out of the way, stepped into the hallway and slammed the door.

People emerged from the front room. Two women in the lead, one holding a glass in her hand. There were also a few men, he couldn't tell how many because the corridor was too narrow for more than single file.

'Please hide me,' Osewoudt begged, stepping forward. 'The Germans are after me.'

Everybody started talking at once. Osewoudt tried to take another step forward, but no one stood aside to let him pass.

'He's been in the canal. He stinks!'

'Oh, how awful! How awful!'

'What did you think, that we could hide you? We wouldn't know where!'

'Look at the mess he's making!'

'Do listen to reason, sir! The Americans will be here in a couple of days, and the war will be over. You wouldn't want to get us into trouble for nothing, would you? If we hide you we'll all get shot pronto.'

'Help me!' shouted Osewoudt. 'My life's in your hands!'

'He's making everything sopping wet!'

'Can't you see him shaking? He's freezing cold.'

'He's covered in blood! He's bleeding to death.'

'Care for a drink, sir?'

'You're all talking at once! For God's sake! Let me through!'

From outside came the sputter of a motorcycle. Heavy footsteps. The doorbell rang continuously, rifle butts hammered on the door.

'Let me through!' shouted Osewoudt. 'Let me slip out through the back garden!' He held out his arms and tried to squeeze through the crowd. Just then the front door burst open. His arms were seized by two Germans, handcuffs were clamped on his wrists, and he was hauled backwards out of the house with his heels dragging along the ground. He was hoisted up and slung into the back of a van. He landed so awkwardly that a numbing pain shot up from his shoulder into his skull. He shut his eyes and drew up his knees.

They put him in a dark cell and left him there for a week. He had not been allowed to wash. The gash over his eyebrow had not been dressed. When he touched it gingerly with his finger-tips he felt thick, slimy crusts. He had a permanent headache.

No one came to see him. Tapping signals went unanswered.

But when the week was over he was released from the cell. They gave him a towel the size of a handkerchief and a lump of hardened clay for soap. He was allowed to wash under a shower from which issued boiling water, albeit only in a trickle, so it seemed the shower was turned off and leaking, rather than turned on.

'Will the Americans be here soon?' he asked the guard.

'Doesn't look like it.'

'Any chance of getting some cold water for a quick rinse?'

'I have to stay where I am. I can't go and get it.'

He improvised by catching the scalding trickle in his cupped hand and distributing it over his body with the infinitesimal towel. When he was done his hands were blistered.

Naked, he was taken to a bare cubicle that apparently served as an infirmary. Two nurses treated the wound with a stinging liquid, tore the stitches out and stuck a couple of plasters on his eyebrow. He was given his clothes to wear and was taken back to his cell, where the light was on.

Hardly five minutes had passed when someone came for him again; he was led down corridors and ushered into an

office where Kriminalrat Wülfing was seated behind a desk.
A small table with a typewriter was occupied by another
uniformed German.

'Well now, Osewoudt! The pleasure was brief. I am not
referring to your escapade. I am referring to our previous
conversation. Let us be grateful for the opportunity to pick up
where we left off. Your looks haven't improved since we last
met, I have to say. Ebernuss will be so disappointed.'

Osewoudt sat hunched forward on the straight-backed chair,
head bowed, handcuffed hands between his knees.

'Go on, say something. Do you know Labare?'

Wülfing pushed his armchair back with a loud scraping noise
and came out from behind his desk.

'No,' said Osewoudt.

'You seem to be suffering from amnesia. What will become
of you if things go on like this? Did you think we'd pack you
off to hospital again to cure your amnesia? No, dear boy, that
is a condition for which we have our very own remedy.' The
door opened. Osewoudt looked up.

A uniformed German pushed Labare into the room.

Labare did not look as if he had been mistreated, though
he did have a plaster cast on his left arm. He wore his ordinary suit and a clean shirt, only the tie was missing. He was
clean-shaven.

'Melgers,' he said. 'There's no need to keep quiet any more,
go ahead and tell them everything you know. They found all
the stuff at my place. I didn't have time to destroy the films.'

'I thought you were going to barricade the door.'

Labare now began to sob, lifting his good arm to wipe his
eyes. His whole body seemed braced to hold back the tears,
but his voice was barely audible.

'Melgers, things have gone terribly wrong! I was the last
one to go downstairs. I let the safety beam down but it didn't

drop automatically, and when I gave it a pull the whole thing came down on my arm. I was stuck. I didn't even get a chance to lock the door to the basement. That's how those bastards got me. They stood there laughing at me, they just laughed and left me lying there for at least half an hour. And that sod Suyling didn't lift a finger to help. He was hiding in a corner. Did he at any time ask himself: what's keeping Labare? Oh, no, not him! And I didn't want to give him away so I didn't call out. I thought: just let him get away with the films. But he didn't even manage to do that. You know, Melgers, I feel gutted. Truly gutted.'

Wülfing went up to him and patted him on the shoulder.

'Buck up, Labare! Ha, ha! The Americans aren't in quite the hurry to get here you thought, but maybe they'll get going one of these days, in which case your prospects will be on the up. You had a run of bad luck, that's all, because I must say your set-up was pretty sophisticated. Good work, Labare! I have observed your activities with admiration. And I should know. Guess what I did before the war? I wrote scripts for gangster films. Seriously! All my own invention – entire colonies of gangsters, in minute detail! Not one of my scenarios ever made it to the screen. If only I'd met you earlier. We would have made a far superior team than is possible now under the present, rather grimmer circumstances.'

He laughed at the ceiling and his right hand came up cupped like a lily, level with his head.

'Melgers, the whole thing's blown up,' said Labare. 'Everybody's been caught. Suyling, Robbie, Marianne, the lot! Don't be fooled, they know everything. If those bastards insist on hearing the whole story from you all over again, just go ahead and confess. They know everything already.'

Wülfing made a waving motion and the policeman who had brought Labare in opened the door.

'Goodbye, Melgers!' Labare cried. 'Take care! Maybe we'll meet again one day. Long live the Netherlands!'

He was interrupted by a kick to his backside from the policeman, but in the corridor, when the door was already closed behind him, he shouted 'Long live the Netherlands' twice more, and very quickly for someone whose speech was normally so slow.

Wülfing seated himself at his desk again.

'A good man and a good patriot. You heard what he said, Osewoudt, didn't you? There is no reason for you to keep your mouth shut any longer. Go on, tell me. How did you escape from that hospital?'

'I climbed out of the window.'

'Climbed out of the window? On the second floor? Pull the other one.'

'I jumped. I used to do judo, I know how to land properly after jumping.'

'Used to do judo, eh? I'll say you did. Breithaupt is still in the sick bay with a dislocated shoulder. Quite right. True confession. A judo buff. Got that, Gustaf?'

Wülfing looked at the German behind the typewriter, who was picking his nose. He extracted a gobbet, inspected it, then popped it in his mouth, muttering: 'Judo buff.' But he didn't touch the keys.

'Then what?' Wülfing went on. 'Then you were out in the street, I take it? In your hospital smock! Nobody noticed, I suppose, the guard we posted out there having conveniently absconded to have a drink, eh? Was that what you were going to say? You needn't bother! We know everything! Uncle Kees! Name rings a bell does it? Ever heard of Uncle Cor? Cor was driving the car that took you to Leiden. Did you think we didn't know? Let's hear what those two Resistance heroes have to say for themselves, shall we?'

He picked up the phone, pressed a button and said:

'*Bringen Sie Ome Kees und Cor.*'

After a pause he said: '*Was? Na also . . .*' and replaced the receiver.

'Uncle Kees and Cor are unavailable at the moment. But we have no time to wait for them, Osewoudt. We aren't running a variety show here, after all. There's no need for me to confront you with them all, Osewoudt, but you know I already know everything. Let's see – that shooting in Haarlem, in 1940. How many shots did you fire?'

'Not one.'

'You're a fool. We know, down to the second, at what time you fired, and also how many times. Right. Next question. What were you doing at Labare's?'

'I was developing films. I didn't know what was on them. I didn't know what they were for.'

'Ah, so you didn't know. But we do know.'

The door opened and the same policeman now pushed Suyling into the room.

Suyling looked distinctly the worse for wear. His face was unmarked, but his hair was matted and he limped.

'Well now, Suyling! Tell me, who's the man sitting over there?'

Suyling stared at Osewoudt, first with astonishment and then with loathing.

'Oh, now I understand! He's been telling tales! That's Melgers! But his name isn't really Melgers. He's the man whose picture was in the papers. I don't remember his name, but he's the one who was in the papers.'

Wülfing went up to Suyling, stopping about one metre short. He clenched his right fist, then beat it against the palm of his left hand.

'Quiet! Stop moaning! A prisoner who refuses to tell the

truth — I can deal with that. But don't give me cock and bull stories. Do you understand me, Suyling? You, not knowing the name of the man in the papers? It won't wash. I bet you know more than all the others put together.'

'I know nothing!'

'You know everything! I'm too much of a psychologist to be taken in by you, and you're not enough of one to come up with a lie that doesn't have exactly the opposite effect of what you intend.'

He took one step back and then two steps forward, standing so close to Suyling as to seem minded to spit in his face.

'Who's Uncle Kees? Who's Cor? What was the car's registration number?'

'I don't know anyone called Uncle Kees!'

'But you've heard of him!'

'No!'

'I know you're lying! Did Uncle Kees get Osewoudt out of that hospital or did he not?'

'Say yes, Suyling!' Osewoudt blurted. 'You can see they already know.'

'I'm saying no.'

'What good is it to you to deny things they know about?'

'What good is it to them to keep asking things they know about already? I won't be humiliated.'

Wülfing turned round, clicked his heels and went back to his desk.

'Well, well. Herr Suyling does not wish to be humiliated. Very good. Unterscharführer! Lock him up in the dark and make sure he doesn't overeat.'

Suyling was dragged out of the room before he could say any more. There was a lot of shouting in the corridor. There was also the sound of stumbling, or maybe it wasn't stumbling as much as kicking and punching.

Wülfing sat himself down on the desktop so heavily that it creaked.

'Well Osewoudt, what have you got to say for yourself? You can see I'm not stringing you along. All your friends have been rounded up. Would you like us to bring old Robbie in again? Well?'

'I hardly know him.'

'You hardly know him? And you were living in the same house!'

'No. I wasn't living there. I just happened to be there that evening.'

'You were still there at half past midnight! Nobody's allowed on the streets after eleven. And you were found in that house at half past midnight.'

'It was too . . .'

'Of course! You left it too late to go home! That's what it was! And so you decided to stay the night. Alone, I trust! Right?'

'It's none of your business!'

'None of my business? How can you say that? You make a rapid exit from the hospital just to spend the night in a place like Labare's? Now why would you want to do such a thing?'

He stood up, and walked solemnly around the desk.

'To sleep with a Jewess, Osewoudt! That's why! Am I right?'

'I don't know what you're talking about.'

'That'll be the day. But I have proof.'

'It's nobody's business who I sleep with. It's got nothing to do with politics.'

'Ah, you mean to say it has nothing to do with politics if you go to bed with a Jewess in possession of a forged identity card?'

'I know who you mean. But I'd never met that young lady before, and she wasn't Jewish either.'

'Are you telling me you didn't know she was Jewish?'

'It didn't occur to me. I met her for the first time that evening.'

'Well, well, straight off to bed was it? There weren't enough beds so you had to share, was that it?'

Osewoudt shrugged. Wülfing opened a desk drawer.

'Whose tie is this? No takers? And whose is this shirt? Nobody's? Going, going . . . And whose are these nice shoes? Not Osewoudt's by any chance? All found in Mirjam Zettenbaum's virginal bed!'

His voice dropped.

'Perhaps you should try them for size, Osewoudt. And whose is this Leica? Not yours either? Don't worry, the film that was in it has been developed. My word, you do take some charming pictures with your little box!'

He placed the Leica carefully on the desk and said: 'And I have another charming plaything just here.'

He bent low to the drawer and took out an automatic pistol, lifting it up with slow deliberation.

'This pistol, Osewoudt, was found in the handbag belonging to Mirjam Zettenbaum, also known as Marianne Sondaar. With whom you have never slept. And yet you lent the lady the toy pistol. Or are we to take it that it was she who pulled the trigger on 23 July, 1940 at Kleine Houtstraat 32 in Haarlem? Because you must understand, Osewoudt, establishing criminal responsibility is an exact science, not a game! The bullets found in Knijtijzen's body have been traced to this firearm. And that is not all. Once we've examined all the bullets we collect from dead bodies, who knows what else we'll discover?'

Osewoudt was taken back to his cell, where he was given half a litre of soup and a hunk of brown bread. The brown bread was surprisingly good: rough and moist, with plenty of coarsely ground wheat in it. At last he was able to eat his fill.

That evening, at seven, the cell door opened and Ebernuss came in. Ebernuss had a stone bottle of Bols genever under his arm, and in his hand a piece of sausage in greaseproof paper.

He looked as if he had shaved specially for the occasion, and had put on a freshly pressed uniform. His scent of violets overpowered the prison stench of rising damp, corrosion and dried urine.

He seated himself on the stool, reached into his pocket and produced two glasses, which he filled with genever.

'*Prosit*,' he said.

Wordlessly, Osewoudt took a sip.

'Let me explain. The reason I let Wülfing take you to task this afternoon was because Gustaf was present. I felt obliged to make my little contribution to the cause, especially with Gustaf there. But you mustn't think I have it in for you. Indeed, I rather like you. I took to you from the start. Anyway, the Americans will be here any day now. But even if they never get here, the war is lost. I am well aware of that. Go on, drink up. Let's have another.'

'I don't like genever.'

'Teetotal?'

'Not really. I just don't like it.'

'You're not ill are you, Osewoudt?'

'Nothing wrong with my health.'

'What kind of treat could I give you, then? A woman, perhaps?'

Osewoudt said nothing. He did not like Ebernuss' friendly tone, nor did he trust his air of familiarity. But there was something about the man's manner that gave Osewoudt a glimmer of hope, so he thought he'd better not antagonise him straightaway. It was not that he had any idea what he might yet achieve with this man, but what would Dorbeck think if didn't even leave the *possibility* open?

'Your girlfriend was a Jewess all right,' said Ebernuss. 'All that has been investigated in minute detail. Mirjam Zettenbaum. Personally, I have nothing against Jews. What do you say to that?'

'I think it makes sense, at least if you're convinced Germany's going to lose the war.'

Osewoudt lay back on the bunk, drew up his knees and rolled over, turning his back to Ebernuss.

'Slumbering Ganymede! What a pretty picture!' Ebernuss exclaimed. Osewoudt could not recall having heard the name Ganymede before, and thought: his mind's rambling.

'The whole treatment of the Jewish question,' said Ebernuss, 'amounts to nothing but a bid on the part of some high-ranking SS men to parasite the rest of Europe! It wasn't only the Jews they were out to rob, but us as well! Just think what all that shunting about of absolutely harmless, and moreover, useless people has cost us in terms of transport potential. The old, the sick, children, women, intellectuals – thousands of wagonloads, while the fighting troops were short of supplies! The worst the Jews ever inflicted on Germany was taking up all that space in our goods trains and cattle trucks.'

Ebernuss laughed. Osewoudt said nothing.

Ebernuss said: 'I may laugh, but I didn't mean what I said. Is it really impossible to envisage a world in which people do not go out of their way to kill each other? Surely mankind ought to be able to reach that minimum standard? Don't you agree, Osewoudt? Wasn't that why you joined the Resistance?'

'Yes it was! That was the only reason!'

'I never doubted it for a moment! The thing is knowing who your enemies are, and where to look for friends. Friends turn up in the strangest, most unexpected places. Remember that, Osewoudt.'

Osewoudt thought: he'll throw his arms around me next, but I'll kick him senseless, to hell with the consequences.

The spyhole opened, making a very soft clicking sound, almost inaudible. Osewoudt's head started. Each click of the spyhole made him jump. He did not look round at the door. He did not hear footsteps moving off, but was certain, after a time, that the spyhole had been covered again.

This meant, likely as not, that he would be left alone for the next half-hour. He got off the bunk and looked up at the corner of the cell next to the frosted glass window. He peered at the air vent and saw a string dangling from the grating. His heart raced as he clambered on to the bunk and stood up. He flexed his knees, jumped, and succeeded in getting hold of the grating with one hand and grabbing the string with the other, before dropping back on the bunk. At the end of the string was a pencil stub.

He sat down on the bunk and took a sheet of toilet paper from his trouser pocket.

He wrote:

Dearest Marianne,

I have been in prison for three months already. Nothing is happening, weeks go by without my being interrogated or seeing anyone. Once in a while they come to my cell to question me about things I know nothing of. How will all this end? Are the Americans coming? Or not? Sometimes I think I'll be murdered one of these days, like so many others, without trial, without any reasons being given.

I have found out you are in Westerbork transit camp. Do your best to stay there, avoid deportation to Germany at all costs. The war can't last much longer. Then we'll be together again. I think of you day and night, which is no exaggeration as I seldom get any sleep. Try thinking of me too, maybe that will help. I am suspected only of things I didn't do. They can't keep me here for ever. Goodbye my darling, I kiss you a thousand, thousand times.

A thousand times a thousand, he reflected, folding up the note as small as possible. He lay back on his bunk. Was that a lot – a thousand times a thousand – where kisses were concerned? How long would it take to kiss someone a thousand, thousand times?

He heard the click of the spyhole again. He got up, went to the door and stuffed the note into the round hole.

Nothing much happened for a whole month. Only, someone had been put in the cell next door, with whom he was able to communicate by tapping signals. This man claimed he had been caught red-handed stealing rubber stamps from a German police office. Osewoudt replied that he himself was entirely innocent of the crimes he stood accused of. Would the war go on for much longer?

His neighbour was in the know. From him Osewoudt learned that the Allies had already got as far as Arnhem.

That same day, the cell door suddenly swung open and Osewoudt was summoned. He was not handcuffed.

He went with the guards. He was positive that he would be released.

They opened a door and a wave of violet scent penetrated his nostrils.

A small office with bars on the windows and Ebernuss sitting with his back to the bars.

Ebernuss stood up at once, and hurried forward to clasp Osewoudt's right hand between his.

'Osewoudt! It's been such a long time! I have been very busy, very busy indeed! Not a day has gone by without my hoping to spare fifteen minutes for you! Something kept coming up! Do sit down! Cigarette? Real English ones, Gold Flake! Whole crates of them are dropped from the sky these days. Such a friendly nation, the British. Take the recent developments in Arnhem. You have heard the news, I presume? You thought the war would be over soon, did you not? Wrong! Those British! Did they get a thrashing from our SS! Lads of sixteen, just back from France for a breather. We pulled it off! *Jawohl!* My dear fellow, I was afraid I might never see you again. But we have not been deprived of each other's company yet, not by any means!'

Osewoudt dropped his eyes, saying: 'I haven't done anything. Nobody has produced any evidence against me. Why won't you let me go?'

Ebernuss propped his elbows on the desk and pressed his hands flat against his cheeks, the way older women sometimes do to tighten their jowls.

'Evidence. Oh, what a nice boy you are! Did you think we were keeping you here because we're gathering evidence? The world you live in ceased existing long ago.

'We only detain two kinds of people. The first kind are people we prefer to keep off the streets for one reason or another. The second kind are people who can supply us with interesting information. Nobody is released simply for a lack of evidence. Furnishing proof is the business of professors, not politicians. The only thing that interests a politician is achieving his aims. What would we achieve by accepting the lack of evidence against someone? Have some sense, boy! I'm telling you: for a politician it's more important to get rid of an innocent victim than to punish someone who's guilty, because the innocent victim, once released, will seek revenge, whereas a sinner who gets let off will be grateful.

'Do try to understand how the world works, Osewoudt!'

'Oh, Herr Ebernuss! What I don't understand is how you can make the National Socialists out to be such monsters!'

'Try telling your mother that!'

'I don't even know if my mother is still alive.'

'I do. She is no longer alive.'

'Are you sure?'

'I am sure.'

'And my uncle?'

'He has been sent to Germany, to a concentration camp, but nobody seems to know which.'

'And my wife?'

'That I do not know. I will enquire. Any other questions?'

'No.'

'You're lying. You want to know where Marian Zettenbaum is. It's no use denying it! You wrote her a note. Here it is. Here, here! You do make me laugh, you know!'

Ebernuss picked up a folder of papers, leafed through the contents and found the sheet of toilet paper on which Osewoudt had written his note. Ebernuss started reading it aloud: '"Dearest Marianne. I have been in prison for three months." Which is four months, now. "How will all this end? Are the Americans coming?" Yes, they're coming, but far too late for most people.'

'So you know what's happened to Marianne! You must tell me! Has she been sent to Germany?'

'"Goodbye my darling, I kiss you a thousand, thousand times."'

Ebernuss slipped the note back into the folder.

Osewoudt sat there, sobbing.

Ebernuss went up to him and tapped him under the chin.

'Let me tell you something. She is not in Germany. I saw to that. I'll tell you something else. She is pregnant. What do you say, Osewoudt? Pregnant! Congratulations, my friend! If it's a boy you can call him Waldemar, after me. Agreed?'

Osewoudt said nothing.

'By the way,' said Ebernuss, 'it's time you started calling me Waldemar, too. We have known each other for so long now, months and months . . . But that's not the only reason. You are alone in the world. Your mother is dead, your uncle is dead, so is your girlfriend Elly Sprenkelbach Meijer, so is Labare, and your friend Robbie is either dead or in a concentration camp which he won't come out of alive. Let me make myself clear: I too am alone. All my friends have fallen in battle. As for *my* mother, she is buried under the rubble of her house in Frankfurt. Who will do anything to help me when the Americans get here?'

Osewoudt sat up straight, gave Ebernuss a nasty grin and said: 'Nobody, I expect. The shoe will be on the other foot!'

'So what if the shoe is on the other foot? Will that bring back your mother and your friends? Well, what do you say?'

Osewoudt crooked the index finger of his right hand and bit the knuckle.

Ebernuss laid his hand on his shoulder.

'We are comrades in misfortune. I am prepared to help you, as a good comrade. I can arrange for them to let that Jewish girl go. Do you understand? So there will at least be one person waiting for you at the end of the war. What am I saying? One person? Maybe two! Possibly three, if she has twins. But you must help me in return, you must tell me something you know and I don't. Is the girl worth that to you? And the child? Or do you prefer to keep quiet and have her sent to Germany and end up in a gas chamber? Then who'll be there to say thank you when the war is over?'

Ebernuss stood up and raised his voice.

'No one in the whole world is going to say thank you! No one! Even if you're still alive when the Americans come!'

He took up the folder again.

'Look, I might as well tell you what I'm getting at. We have come up with an idea, something that sounds insane, but is apparently true. You needn't say anything, just yes or no. Are you sticking by your story that a meeting between you and Roorda at Vondel Park never took place?'

'Yes.'

'Quite. On the day Roorda says he met you at Vondel Park you weren't anywhere near there. Because you were with Meinarends in Leiden, were you not?'

'I can't remember.'

'They turned up the heat on Roorda and he changed his story slightly. Added to it, in fact. He says he met you in Amsterdam not once but twice, the second time in the waiting room of the public baths a few days later.'

'He's lying.'

'Quite. Because that afternoon you were not in Amsterdam. You were on the heath at Lunteren, where you shot Lagendaal and his wife. True or false?'

Osewoudt said nothing. The whole room danced jerkily before his eyes, and his thighs felt drenched in ice water.

'Well?'

'It wasn't me.'

'Stop fibbing like a schoolboy. The bullets from the bodies have been examined. They were discharged by the pistol found in the handbag belonging to your friend Zettenbaum. What more do you want? You're not going to tell me it was Zettenbaum who went to Lunteren to deal with Lagendaal? You're not shifting the blame on your girlfriend, are you?'

Osewoudt tried not to show how ill these words made him feel. If words could kill, he would gladly have dropped dead, but he did not: he saw Ebernuss' grim expression, heard everything Ebernuss said.

'Fine. So Zettenbaum didn't do it. It was you. Don't worry about it, we're not worried either. We can't go around checking every particular! But there's one question we would like to resolve. Who did Roorda meet? We have no reason to assume that Roorda is lying. In fact we can prove he is not. So if that man is not lying, he must have met someone. Who was it? It wasn't you. So who was it?'

'I wasn't there, as you said yourself. So how should I know who Roorda met?'

'You don't need to know. The solution is obvious: it was someone who looked like you. Who looked very much like you. Not your twin brother, because you don't have one, but still someone so like you that it's nigh on impossible to tell you apart. Same height, same shape, same mug, and so on and so forth. Well, there is one difference I suppose: he has black hair and yours is fair. It would be too much if he had no more beard growth than you, though that hardly seems likely, ha, ha. A man who shaves, then. Right. Who is that man, what is his name?'

'I don't know.'

'But I do. His name is Dorbeck. If he actually exists, then his name is Dorbeck. And you know him. Why else did you dye your hair black? You were acting as his double.'

'That's not true. If I'd known about somebody in the Resistance who looked like me I'd have been more likely to dye my hair red.'

'Don't give me that.'

Nevertheless, Ebernuss hesitated: what Osewoudt had said sounded reasonable enough.

'Come on,' Ebernuss continued, after a pause, 'let's stop beating about the bush. There is evidence that this man exists, and that he's in Holland. There seems to be some sort of clandestine club in Amsterdam for underground heroes. They meet in the attic of a canal house. The place is run by a theology student. His name is Moorlag. Don't tell me you've never heard of him, because you know him. He was your lodger in Voorschoten.'

'Moorlag?'

'Well then. Now you're reminded of Marianne again. I have a proposition to make. We take you to that club in a day or two. You go in, you have a chat with Moorlag. You pay close attention to their reactions. They might address you as Dorbeck, for instance, or say something like: hey, what's going on? We thought you got here a quarter of an hour ago.

'That's all you need to do. Plain sailing. I won't go with you, none of us will, you can be sure of that. All you need to do is have a drink in that attic. You won't be betraying anyone. And if you do as I say, I promise you they will release Marianne Sondaar and issue her with a genuine ID card, without the J on it. Think it over!'

He thought it over. Day in, day out he thought it over. Evidently they wanted to give him ample time to think it over, because Ebernuss did not send for him again. Could they be waiting for him to ask one of the guards to tell Ebernuss he'd thought it over and had agreed to do it ... ? Was that their way of getting him to collude of his own free will, so to speak, so that they could take it a step further and say: look here, you said you'd cooperate, you agreed to get us into that attic Dorbeck visits from time to time ... so what's the difference if you lure him away under some pretext and play him into our hands?

The prison was overcrowded, most of the inmates were five or six to a cell meant for two, but he was left alone, no company for him. The cell next to his was usually vacant, too. His was situated at the corner of the building, so there was only an exterior wall on the other side.

What would be the best course for him to take? If he refused to do as Ebernuss asked it would certainly be the end of Marianne. But if he agreed to do as Ebernuss asked Marianne might survive the war, and even if it looked as if he was in league with the Germans, the chances of Dorbeck being fooled were negligible. Dorbeck! He'd tip him a wink and Dorbeck would see through it all at once. What was the risk for Dorbeck? None at all. They'd sort it, one way or another!

One week of solitary confinement was enough for Osewoudt to make up his mind, but no one came to enquire.

A month later he thought: maybe they've managed to get hold of Dorbeck some other way. In which case they don't need me any more, I'm of no further use to them, so they won't be doing me any favours to have me cooperate. Marianne's been deported to Germany. She may well be dead. Everybody's dead, except me. It might even be an act of kindness on Ebernuss' part to keep me here and leave me alone. Once the war's ended I'll be released anyway. I may even receive an honour.

He could already picture himself behind the counter of his tobacco shop with a ribbon on his lapel. The window would be filled with cigarettes, cigars, shag and pipe tobacco. The best brands. All imported from America and the Indies. Yes, sir, all available again!

His clientele would expand by leaps and bounds. Everyone would want to buy cigars and cigarettes from the decorated Resistance hero. Suppose he had the shop refurbished and came up with another name for it? 'The Underground Tobacconist'? No. 'Cigar Emporium "Loyal Through the Ages"'. That was more like it.

The cash register would ring out. But for whom? Not for his mother, at any rate. For Ria? He leaped up and hammered the wall with his fists. Never, never, never.

What would it be like without Marianne, without Dorbeck, without Labare, without Meinarends, without Moorlag? No one would need him any more, everyone would go their own way. Maybe somebody would drop by every six months or so, to have a cigar and reminisce about the bad old days of the war. But even that would peter out over the years. What would he be? A nobody stuck behind the counter of a tobacco shop, a beardless youth in the clutches of a washed-out wife who helps herself to the till without asking. The glamour of his decoration would fade, and the new-found patrons would go back to their old suppliers. His unprepossessing appearance would not favour making conquests of any kind.

Ebernuss came to deliver the letter in person.

Dearest Filip,

I was released from the camp at Westerbork four months ago. I'm living at my old address again, but I now have a proper ID card without the J. So I'm as safe as houses. I've written to you at least twenty times already, telling you how it all happened, but never had a reply to my letters. All that is behind us now, so I won't go into it again. I just want you to know that I am fine. My dearest darling, I have some news to tell you, really new news that will never go stale, on the contrary, it's getting newer by the day. Darling, you'll never guess, but I am soon to have your baby! I'm so thrilled. Even if I never see you again I won't have lost you for ever. Forgive me, I'm sitting here crying as I write and I can hardly tell whether it's because I'm happy or sad. Oh my dearest Filip, sometimes I actually dare to hope we will be together after the war, but at other times I think: no, that's too much to ask, that's wanting it all, like a little girl getting applause for her role in the school play and thinking she'll be a star when she grows up.

The war can't go on much longer. They say the Germans are planning to flood the whole of Holland at the very last minute. But if that happens, you can be sure I'll reach dry land in time, and I'll take little Filip with me in a boat which I'll get someone to make from a wooden chest. Finding a chest won't be easy, though, because people chop everything up for firewood. Is it very cold in your cell? Oh my poor darling, how thin you must be if you have to get by on the standard ration of one slice of bread and three potatoes a day. Can you imagine, I'm actually entitled to extra rations because I'm pregnant! How about that? So don't you worry about me. Goodbye my darling. Someone said there might be some way of smuggling a note to the outside, from you to me . . .

Osewoudt folded the letter, stuffed it in his trouser pocket and lay down on his bunk.

Ebernuss offered him a ham roll.

'You are fully aware of how things stand, I hope, Osewoudt. We, for our part, have kept our side of the bargain rather splendidly. The mother-to-be lacks for nothing. Everything hunky-dory. But it'll be over in an instant if you don't keep your promise to me.'

Sitting beside Ebernuss in the car to Amsterdam, he couldn't believe his eyes. It was pitch-dark, and theirs was the only car on the road. It was as if the population had died out during his captivity. Even when they drove into the city he saw nobody in the streets.

'Is the food shortage that bad?'

'Food shortage!' echoed Ebernuss. 'Our soldiers are going short, too. They don't get more than five cigarettes a week.'

'So why aren't there any people about? It's still early, after all.'

'It is not early. It is close to nine o'clock, and by eight everybody has to be off the streets.'

They stopped at a junction, not to look out for other traffic, but because Ebernuss was not sure which direction to take. Now and then a heavy droning sounded in the sky.

'I don't see any searchlights,' said Osewoudt. 'What's up with them?'

'Searchlights aren't used any more. The latest thing is radar; invisible rays on long wavelengths. But whether those invisible rays allow us to see our enemies is doubtful. We never shoot any down nowadays.'

'Excellent,' said Osewoudt, 'then the war will be over all the sooner.'

'Quite. The sooner the better. What are your plans for after the war, supposing I get you through it alive?'

'I'll join the American intelligence service in Germany.'

'Very funny. What with our having spent so much time together, I've grown rather fond of you, Osewoudt. We must remain friends. When the Americans arrive, let's not say goodbye for ever. I have no one left in the world, just like you.'

'So you said.'

'It strikes me that you never call me by my first name. I would like to hear my name from your lips. No one ever calls me Waldemar now.'

Osewoudt made no reply.

'What you should have said,' Ebernuss went on, 'what you should have said is: you never call me by my first name either. To which I would have replied: I like your first name, but your surname's better. Besides, I'd rather not use your first name, because I realise there must have been plenty of people close to you calling you Henri. I wouldn't want to be forward.'

'It's over the way,' Osewoudt said, pointing. 'The odd numbers are on this side of the canal.'

Ebernuss braked, reversed down Ziezeniskade, then turned to cross the bridge. Slowly they jolted over the potholed Lijnbaansgracht.

'Did your mother call you Henri?'

'Yes, my mother called me Henri, but I'd rather not talk about her.'

'I thought you'd be glad of a chance to talk about your mother. It must be ages since you had an opportunity to talk about her with anyone.'

'I don't talk about her, even when there's an opportunity.'

'You must have loved her very much. A mother who murders the father — the consummate mother! Why would a woman need a man if she has a son? It's the same with bees: after inseminating the female, the male dies. I have a confession to make. I went to far greater lengths to save your mother than the Jewish girl. But it was too late. She had already committed suicide in prison. Had I been able to save your mother, I wouldn't have lifted a finger for the little Jewess. Not even to wring a promise from you, or to make you cooperate.'

Osewoudt leaned forward. They were at the corner of Spiegelgracht. Ebernuss stopped the car and switched on a spotlight. He beamed it on a house number and said: 'It would have been far better for you if I'd been able to save your mother instead of that girl.'

'The address is five numbers further on,' said Osewoudt. 'May I suggest you park by the entrance?'

Ebernuss laid his hand on Osewoudt's knee. He looked straight ahead, keeping the spotlight on the house number.

'You're not even listening to what I'm saying. Pity. I repeat: we are both alone in the world, and once the war's over there won't be a place in it for us. Not for either of us, do you hear? Not for me, but not for you either. I won't go into details, but remember this: in times to come, you'll have cause to think of me. If we leave each other in the lurch, neither of us will last long. Suppose the Americans get here next week – they're a hundred kilometres past the Rhine already, and the Canadians are advancing in the east. It's April now. I won't make it to the end of the year. But nor will you. You mark my words, and I don't need to read any tea leaves to make my prediction: you will have cause to think of me!'

'Christ, I wish you'd get a move on. What do you want to do with the car? Leave it here?'

Ebernuss switched off the spotlight, put the car in gear and drove up Spiegelgracht. He parked under a tree along the canal and they got out.

It was a small DKW with a sputtering engine which still ran on proper fuel, not on gas or wood. It was black and yellow, and had a Dutch registration number. There was nothing about it to suggest that it belonged to the German police.

Osewoudt stared up at the dark sky while Ebernuss locked the car. The drone of the invisible bombers now grew deafeningly loud, like a circular saw of gigantic proportions being drawn across the city.

'Here, take this,' said Ebernuss, grasping Osewoudt's hand. Osewoudt felt the chill of metal against his palm, and lowered his eyes.

'Your Leica. Put it away, or just hold it in your hand, as you like. There's a new film in it. If it had been up to me you'd have had your pistol back too. But there you are – not everything is up to me.'

'What is it you really want?' asked Osewoudt.

'I want out, Osewoudt. I wish you'd believe me. I've had enough. The war's over as far as I'm concerned. I regret everything I did for the German intelligence service. You think I have a hold over you, but in reality it's you who have a hold over me. You're the ones with power now, not us.'

'In that case, why don't you get in your car and drive back to The Hague or wherever you like. Just let me go. Leave me alone. After the war I'll see what my friends can do for you.'

'Letting you go wouldn't be enough. There's much more I want to make up for. Your case is nothing compared to everything else I have on my conscience.'

'Fine, but let's discuss that some other time.'

'No! No! It has to be now! There's something very important that you don't know. Do as I say: introduce me to those people, get them to fix me up with a hideout. You'll be sorry if you don't.'

'Is that a threat?'

'Why don't you trust me? Here! Take the car key.'

Osewoudt took the key and pocketed it.

'Why are you so cagey about taking me inside?' Ebernuss went on. 'You can tell them everything you know about me. I mean it! Do you hate me so much that you'd rather see me dead, along with the rest of Hitler's gang? What have I done to deserve that? I've always been decent to you, haven't I? I did everything I possibly could for you. I had them release your pregnant girlfriend from that camp. I never raised my hand against you.'

Osewoudt said nothing. He cradled the Leica to his chest as if it were a small pet he had just saved from imminent death.

'It's not only about me, you know,' Ebernuss persisted, pinching Osewoudt's sleeve between thumb and forefinger. 'Truly Osewoudt, it's of vital importance to you as well. You'll understand that later.'

'If it's so important, why won't you tell me now?'

'What good would that do? It's not *you* who needs to know, it's *them*. Not you, them. I wish you would believe me, Osewoudt.'

'I haven't any cigarettes on me,' said Osewoudt. 'Give me another of yours, will you?'

Ebernuss stood still, fumbled in his trouser pocket, and offered Osewoudt a cigarette.

'Why won't you believe me? The way things stand now, with everything falling apart – do you really think it makes sense for me to go on collecting evidence against you? Why do you imagine I still care about tracking down your Mr Dorbeck? He may or may not exist, you may or may not have a double, and I may or may not have accused you of acts perpetrated by him, but do you really think I care? Let the committees doling out medals after the war sort that out! Let them rack their brains as to whether Dorbeck exists or not, and if he does, then let them decide who the hero is, Dorbeck or Osewoudt – or both, for all I care!'

Osewoudt crossed to the pavement, followed by Ebernuss, who struck a match and gave him a light.

'I'm putting all my cards on the table,' said Ebernuss. 'All I'm doing is trying to save my own skin.'

They came to a house with a flight of five steps set into a wide porch. There were three front doors. Ebernuss pulled a string dangling from the letter box of the middle door.

The door opened. They entered a narrow hallway leading to a steep flight of stairs.

At the top of the stairs stood a figure holding a candle.

'Moorlag, is he here?' Osewoudt called out.

'Yes he is. What do you want?'

'I'm Osewoudt! I need to speak to Moorlag!'

He started up the stairs, leaving Ebernuss in the hallway. As he climbed, his view of the man at the top of the stairs improved.

'Moorlag, is that you?'

'Yes.'

Osewoudt now bounded up the stairs two at a time.

'Jesus, it's ages since we last saw each other.'

Osewoudt tried to laugh, without success.

'Yes, Henri, it's been ages. The last time was at Meinarends', I remember it well.'

'So do I,' said Osewoudt. 'Any news of Meinarends?'

'Yes. He's dead.'

'Really? Dropping like flies, we are.'

Osewoudt now stood face to face with Moorlag. Moorlag was holding the candle in his right hand, his left hand in his trouser pocket. He evidently had no intention to shake hands, so Osewoudt folded his arms over his chest, Leica in one hand, cigarette in the other. The aspiring theologian's appearance had altered considerably. He wore glasses with a heavy black frame, and had sprouted a large, frizzy moustache. He wore a thick jumper of lumpy, undyed homespun wool, with a tight collar rolled up to his chin. Osewoudt drew on his cigarette and cast an eye over the space. The stairs ended abruptly in the floor of an attic. A few small tables and wooden benches stood about. Sitting around one of the tables were several figures, whose faces were lit by a small, shadeless paraffin lamp in the middle.

Moorlag stood where he was.

'You're the last person I expected to see,' Osewoudt said. 'I thought you'd be sitting out the war in Nieuw-Buinen.'

'Oh.'

'You can't imagine what I've been through. Aren't you surprised to see me?'

'I heard about you. People talk. I thought you'd turn up at some point.'

Who had talked about him? Osewoudt eyed the group at the table: three young men and two girls, none of whom he had seen before. There were two piles of books on the table in front of them.

'Look here, I've got someone with me. He's waiting at the bottom of the stairs. Can he come up?'

'What does he want?'

'He has something to say to someone here, or who'll be here soon.'

'Who?'

'Dorbeck.'

It was so cold that his breath was distinctly visible in the candlelight.

'Dorbeck? Never heard of him.'

'Never heard of him? Can't you remember that time in Voorschoten? I'm sure I told you about Dorbeck back then. He asked me to develop some photographs, which I later got back one by one. You know, the army officer who looked so much like me!'

'I don't remember.'

'But you must remember the evening I went to Amsterdam with that girl who'd just arrived from England. Elly Berkelbach Sprenkel. She had real silver guilders and an ID card you could tell at a glance was fake. Called herself Sprenkelbach Meijer. An inconspicuous alias! I rang you up. It was the night the Krauts arrested my mother and Ria. You were at the station in The Hague next morning, waiting for me!'

'Certainly, I remember that very well.'

'When we met at the station you gave me an envelope that had come for me, and in that envelope was another of those pictures.'

'I vaguely remember something about an envelope. What's that you've got in your hand?'

'My Leica. Don't you remember . . . ?'

'Yes, yes. Still the same Leica, is it?'

'Ah, so you do remember that. Is it all right for that man to come upstairs?'

244

'What sort of man is he?'

'Keep quiet and don't tell anyone here. He's from the Gestapo.'

'Any other men from the Gestapo outside?'

'No, of course not. You have nothing to fear. It's me pulling the strings. He just needs to tell Dorbeck something, and then he'll vamoose.'

'I told you there is no Dorbeck here.'

'Let the man come up anyway, then he can see for himself.'

'All right then. Go and sit down somewhere. I've got things to do.'

Moorlag turned on his heel and disappeared into the unlit recesses of the attic.

Osewoudt leaned over the stairwell, called: 'Hey, you can come up now!' Then he made his way to the gathering at one of the tables, without waiting for Ebernuss to appear.

'My name is van Druten,' said Osewoudt, stopping one step short of the table.

The three boys and two girls were mumbling unintelligibly, and remained seated.

Osewoudt sat down with them, at the same table, although it would have been more natural for him to occupy a vacant one.

'You can say what you like, but Roland Holst's poems have been reprinted during the war, whereas you can't get a complete set of Rilke anywhere.'

The boy who had spoken laid his hand on the pile of Rilke: the complete works. Another boy took a volume from the Roland Holst pile.

'This isn't a reprint. You can tell by the paper. It's pre-war quality. But the binding isn't pre-war, it's cardboard. Oh well, as I said: I'll give you 300 guilders extra, but that's more than enough!'

'300 guilders? What can I get for that? A measly pouch of shag tobacco, at the most!'

'Fine, then you can have a smoke as you read Roland Holst!'

'Poor old Alfred! He'll have to read his Rilke without a cigarette. How very dull!'

'Culture is a mighty achievement of mankind,' said the third boy. He belched by way of conclusion. He had sunken, pimply cheeks and thick curly hair which stood on end.

The girl said: 'Hark at Simon's words of wisdom! He'd be worth his weight in gold if he didn't keep repeating himself.'

'Shut it, will you? Whore. Slut,' said Simon. The insults were uttered evenly. 'As I was saying,' he went on in the same toneless voice, 'listening to repeating is often irritating, always repeating is all of living, everything in a being is always repeating, more and more listening to repeating gives to me completed understanding. Gertrude Stein said that. Hey, what's going on?'

Everyone turned to look.

Ebernuss and Moorlag were approaching, Moorlag holding two stone bottles of Bols genever.

Ebernuss was introduced as Naaborg, after which he sat down.

Moorlag remained standing and gave Osewoudt a nudge on the shoulder.

'Come with me, you can help with the glasses.'

'Right. I'll be happy to!'

Osewoudt stood up and followed Moorlag to the back, where the candlelight barely penetrated.

'You're very well provided for! Genever!'

'We deserve a treat. Don't you agree, Henri?'

'Why are you acting so strangely to me? I've been through so much, a week wouldn't be enough for me to tell you. My mother died in prison.'

'The glasses are in there. Just open the door.'

Osewoudt saw a luminous rectangular outline in the gloom.

He fumbled, felt wood, then felt a doorknob, and opened the door.

The door opened into a sort of kitchen area, with crockery stacked on shelves along the walls. Beside the sink an acetylene lamp spread a blinding light. Despite the glare he could make out a figure turning away from the sink. He too wore a jumper, but it was black and round-necked. He was the same height as Osewoudt. He had black hair and a small pointed black beard. He twisted his head back, keeping his body still, and fixed Osewoudt with green eyes.

'Dorbeck! I didn't know you were here already!'

Dorbeck put down the reservoir of an acetylene lamp, which he had filled with tap water, and took a step towards Osewoudt. He gripped him by the elbows and continued to stare at him.

'There isn't time to talk now, Osewoudt. You're here with a German who's had you behind bars for the past nine months.'

'No. He'll do anything for me. He wants to desert!'

'We don't need him. Look!'

Dorbeck drew a tobacco tin from his pocket and took out a packet of Rizla cigarette papers. He put the tin away again, and opened the packet. But instead of cigarette papers, it contained a small quantity of sparkling green crystals.

'Put this in Ebernuss' glass. Wait a quarter of an hour, then you can leave. Here are the glasses.'

'But Dorbeck—'

'I realise you have a lot to tell me, but not now. Don't ruin everything by arguing now. So far you've done very well. You've been my surest ally. Just do this one more thing for me. Don't believe what Ebernuss tells you, he's a liar, he's playing games with you. The sooner he's got rid of the better.

Liquidating Germans isn't such a good idea, generally speaking, but this one knows too much. The glasses are up there.'

Dorbeck reached up to the top shelf and lifted off a tray with eight stem glasses.

'Don't put it in yet, you might make a mistake setting out the glasses. Wait until his third or fourth drink. See you later.'

Osewoudt took the tray with the glasses and went through the door, which Dorbeck held open for him. Picking his way with difficulty in the dark as he crossed the attic towards the table, he felt tears welling in his eyes.

'Damn,' he muttered, not understanding the cause of his tears.

He thought: I've gone soft in prison.

The young folk round the small table were passing his Leica around. Simon had already raised one of the stone bottles to his mouth for a quick swig.

'Let's take a picture,' he drawled, handing the stone bottle to the boy wanting to sell Rilke. 'Good souvenir for later! Here, pass me that Leica, will you?'

'No, it belongs to that gentleman,' said the girl.

Osewoudt took the glasses from the tray and set them out on the table, after which he sat down. Ebernuss took the other stone bottle and poured the liquor with an unsteady hand. All the glasses were filled to overflowing, each stood in a small puddle.

Now the girl was fingering the Leica.

'I've got an idea,' said Simon. 'Out with your matches, everyone. A bundle of matches is as good as flashlight.'

'That's a fact,' said Moorlag.

Ebernuss topped up the glasses while everyone searched their pockets for matches.

'I don't seem to have any,' said Osewoudt. He knew he had no matches, but fished about in his pockets anyway. He felt the Rizla packet containing the green crystals. He withdrew his hand from his trouser pocket, hiding the small packet in his palm.

A fair number of matches now lay before them. Simon gathered them into a bundle with all the heads at one end. He secured the bundle with an elastic band and set it upright on the table.

The boy wanting to sell Rilke reached for the Leica.

'All right if I take the picture? I've done it before.'

'Go ahead,' said Osewoudt. He stole a glance at Ebernuss, who was sitting beside him, but Ebernuss made no move to avert his face from the camera.

'Ready?'

The Leica was positioned on top of the pile of Rilke. 'Better not have the lamp on!' said Moorlag, and blew out the flame. Simon struck a match and held it to the bundle on the table, which hissed as it caught fire, all but went out, hissed again, and finally flared into a blinding light.

Swathes of green lingered in the gloom. The camera gave a loud click, as though gulping down the image.

Osewoudt held his hand above Ebernuss' glass, crooked his middle finger to open the Rizla packet, waited for the crystals to fall out, and put his hand in his pocket. Simon relit the paraffin lamp, while everyone coughed from the sulphur in the air.

'God almighty, what a stink! So much for Simon's bright ideas!'

'Drink up, drink up!'

'I hope my camera isn't ruined,' spluttered Osewoudt, taking the Leica from the pile of books and coughing even harder than before.

He got up, said: 'It's so stuffy in here!' and ran off, hugging the camera to his chest.

There was no one near the stairwell. No one was looking. Noiselessly, he went down the steep stairs in complete darkness.

'Is that you, Osewoudt?'

'Yes. Are you down there?'

'Yes, you're almost at the bottom now.'

Dorbeck opened the front door and stepped outside. Osewoudt went past him and down the five steps to the street. Dorbeck reached behind him and quietly shut the door. Dorbeck wore a long, dark raincoat, under which he was obviously hiding something quite large.

'Did you manage all right?'

'Yes.'

'Can I have the Rizla packet back?'

Osewoudt gave it back to Dorbeck along with the key to Ebernuss' car.

They sprinted along the canal, turned the corner, and got into the car.

'Here,' said Dorbeck, drawing the large object from under his coat. 'If anyone tries to stop us, just use this. Open the window on your side.'

Osewoudt laid the Sten gun across his knees and wound down the window.

It was close to half past six, day was breaking. People began to appear in the street, staring after the car, which was a rare sight in the starving city.

Osewoudt looked at Dorbeck, who sat hunched at the wheel, careering round bends with tyres squealing. In through the open window came a blast of morning air, mixed with the sour smell of refuse which lay heaped in the gutters.

'Been in England again?' Osewoudt asked.

'Not lately. My contacts are down south now, beyond the rivers.'

'What's life like there, in the liberated provinces?'

'Same as here: blackout. Waiting for the end of the war. I don't notice much, I mean about how people live. I'm restricted to army quarters, mostly.'

'But surely people can go out and about at will now, and they have plenty to eat?'

'Not plenty. Some things are available. They're already beginning to grumble, just like before the war.'

'What would be the best way of getting there?'

'Easy. You can go to any village and find someone with a boat to take you across.'

'Don't the Germans patrol the rivers?'

'Probably. But I have my own contacts, one hundred per cent reliable.'

'You've got it all worked out, haven't you?'

'Indeed. Well as far as I'm concerned, the war has been a successful operation. I didn't surrender on 14 May, 1940. I'm on the winning side. So are you.'

'Am I? It's ridiculous, but I can't get used to the idea that I'm free again. Maybe it's because this car belongs to Ebernuss, or used to. Christ, I'm tired. I've been in prison for nine months. Where are we going?'

'To Bernard Kochstraat. Do you know it?'

'No. I'm not very familiar with Amsterdam.'

'A quiet street.'

'What's it like in London? I've never been abroad.'

'What it's like in London? Plenty of nightclubs, plenty of rowdy airmen who think they're a cut above everybody else just because their predecessors, who fought the Battle of Britain for them, aren't around any more – they're all dead.'

'Couldn't you get me a job with the Allies?'

'I've been thinking about that.'

'I'd like to join the military. That's the only way I could

make myself useful now. Maybe, with the war still on, they won't be so fussy, maybe they won't mind my being half a centimetre too short.'

'Maybe.'

'I mean, I'm no use to the Resistance any more – that was obvious from the moment the Germans showed my picture in the cinemas. And I'm even more useless now. Besides, what'll happen when they find Ebernuss has gone missing?'

'The lads will see to it that he vanishes without trace. Don't you worry.'

'Right. But I can't stay in Holland. Nor can you, really. Because, you know, the picture they showed in the cinemas wasn't of me, even though my name was up there beside it. It was a picture of you. And Ebernuss had found out it wasn't me in the picture, he even thought I had a double.'

'So they interrogated you about things I had done?'

'I was confronted with someone called Roorda, a man I'd never seen in my life. He said he knew me.'

'Roorda. Ah. Interesting.'

'So you know Roorda?'

'I think so.'

'Tell me your contacts. I must get away from occupied territory. I want to take a friend with me, a Jewish girl who's in hiding in Leiden. I want to escape with her. Tell me the best way of making it across the rivers. Give me a password, or some means of identification. I want to escape with her, and I want to take as few risks as possible, for her sake.'

'I understand.'

The car turned into a drab-looking street with a line of trees on a central reservation. The house-fronts were tarred black, and the front doors, all identical, were painted moss green.

Dorbeck put the handbrake on and removed the key from the ignition.

'Leave the Sten behind, and wind up the window.'

Dorbeck opened a front door with a Yale key, which he passed directly on to Osewoudt.

'Here, this is yours.'

They went up a wooden staircase. The house smelled as if it had been unlived-in for months.

They came to a narrow corridor with three orange-painted doors off it. The doors were ajar. At a glance he could see that they led to a small kitchen, a bedroom with a made-up bed, and a parlour.

Dorbeck went into the front room, the parlour, and perched on the square table with his face to the window, which was more of a projecting bay set with small panes. Osewoudt just stood there, Leica in hand, looking at Dorbeck. Then he noticed a battered suitcase standing by the table leg. On one side of the room was a mantelpiece with a mirror reaching up to the lowish ceiling.

'Who lives here?'

'You do. Listen carefully to what I have to say, I don't have much time.'

'Must you be off again?'

'Yes, as soon as I can.'

'What a pity! This is a historic moment. It ought to be recorded for posterity.'

Osewoudt aimed the Leica at the mirror and adjusted the focus.

'It's much too dark in here,' said Dorbeck.

'No, it'll be fine. Keep still now!'

From the mirror Dorbeck stared back at him. Their heads were close together. Osewoudt's hair had grown quite fair again, but in spite of that, and in spite of Dorbeck's pointed beard, the resemblance between them was uncanny. It really did look as if it was the same man twice over, once in disguise.

Yet if you had to guess which one was real, you'd sooner take the pale, beardless one for the impostor. For a moment they were quite still, eyeing each other in the mirror. Osewoudt kept his finger on the shutter, rapt with emotion: now I am whole at last, if only in a photograph. The shutter clicked.

'Thanks,' he said.

Dorbeck slackened his pose and yawned.

'Why don't you take a look in that suitcase? You'll be surprised.'

Osewoudt put the camera aside, bent down and opened the suitcase.

It contained women's clothing: two vests, two pairs of white bloomers, two starched white pinafores, a black woollen cardigan, two slate-blue linen dresses, black stockings, walking shoes, a blue coat, a blue nurse's veil, and half a dozen white, starched caps with ribbons. Osewoudt held up one of the dresses. An enamel brooch with a yellow cross on it came undone and fell to the floor.

'But this is a nurse's uniform. What are you going to do with it?'

'Not me. You! You must put it on, and keep it on until the end of the war.'

'You're crazy.'

'What's the alternative? Hole up in this house and starve to death? Or go out into the street as you are and get caught? Don't count on my being able to rescue you again, you can't take that kind of thing for granted.'

'I realise that, and it's been twice already.'

'Twice? What do you mean?'

'Well, first you got me out of that hospital in The Hague, remember? There was Cor, and Uncle Kees.'

'I don't know any Cor or Uncle Kees. I had no hand in any of that.'

'Didn't you really? Let me tell you something. No sooner had we got in the car than they made it clear they weren't getting what they'd expected. They didn't say in so many words, but it was quite obvious: it wasn't me they thought they were supposed to rescue from the hospital, it was you, and they felt let down. They were disappointed, wouldn't even take me to a safe house. They didn't think I was important enough.'

'Ha, ha, what a laugh! You, not important enough? Wasn't it you who liquidated Lagendaal? Didn't you take part in the Haarlem shooting? Well then.'

'Of course, but I couldn't tell them that.'

'Whatever the case, it's a mystery to me. I've never heard of any Uncle Cor, or of an Uncle Kees for that matter.'

'Do you have any idea why the Germans had it in for me then? They were looking for me even before they knew Lagendaal was dead. They had my name broadcast over the station tannoy in Amsterdam. They knew about that business in Haarlem.'

'Poor Osewoudt! Don't tell me you don't know! It was your own wife who grassed on you to the Germans! It was Ria! Along with the chemist's son! She's back in the tobacco shop, with him! As if nothing ever happened. She tells everyone you're dead.'

'What? Damn, damn! After they'd got me out of the hospital and were driving to Leiden, we went past the shop and I could tell the place was lived in. I couldn't think who it might be. Damn! The chemist's son saw me boarding the blue tram in Haarlem. He followed me to Zandvoort. He struck up a conversation with me to draw me out. God almighty!'

'Ria got herself arrested just for show. That way she was able to get rid of your mother, too. Later on the Germans let Ria go, supposedly because there was no evidence against her.'

Osewoudt seated himself on the table beside Dorbeck,

and covered his face with his hands to think. Then he said: 'I want to go to England with Marianne and never come back.'

'Of course I'll help you to get to England. As soon as I can,' said Dorbeck. 'But in the meantime we'll have to think of something else. Look, you've got to put on that nurse's uniform. It'll fit, I've seen to that.'

'All right, if you say so. I'll put the stuff on when I go out in the street.'

'If I say so?'

Dorbeck got off the table and turned to face him, pressing his clenched fists to Osewoudt's chest.

'If I say so? You're not a coward, are you? You want to hide away in a corner for good, just because the Germans had you banged up for a bit? You seem to think there'll be others to pull your chestnuts out of the fire from now on. What's got into you? Put those clothes on, I tell you! I want to make sure they fit properly! What did you think I went to all that trouble for? Things might get tricky for me yet. I might need your help. And then what? Will you go out disguised as a nurse? Yes or no?' Dorbeck's clenched fists began to shake. Otherwise he kept quite still, fixing Osewoudt with his dark green eyes.

'I'm not a bloody woman!' shouted Osewoudt.

'Of course not. But you don't need to shave, and your voice is pretty high-pitched, too. Can you think of a better disguise for someone like you?'

'Oh, well, all right. Whatever.'

Osewoudt slid off the table, took off his jacket and pullover, loosened his tie and unbuttoned his shirt.

He shut his eyes as he put on the nurse's underwear, which smelled of lavender. Then he put on the dress and pinafore.

'Why are you putting my clothes in the suitcase?'

Unperturbed, Dorbeck stowed everything Osewoudt had taken off in the empty suitcase.

'I'm taking your stuff with me. Tonight or tomorrow I'll come and fetch you. You can change into your own clothes once we're across the rivers.'

'I want to take Marianne with me.'

'I said that was all right, didn't I? Give me her address. I'll pick her up.'

Osewoudt told him the address of the hairdresser in Leiden.

Dorbeck said: 'I'll get her to come with me. I'll be back tonight. Give me your socks and shoes too.'

Osewoudt took off his shoes and socks. Dorbeck slammed the lid on the suitcase.

'Oh, before I forget. Here's a ration book, and an ID card. All it needs is your fingerprint and it'll be impossible to tell it's a fake. Look at the photo – isn't it wonderful?'

Osewoudt studied the photo: his own face, framed by the white nurse's cap. He read the name he would henceforth go by: Clara Boeken. Occupation: district nurse.

'Go on, put the cap on, just for a laugh,' said Dorbeck. 'Then you can see how good the photo is!'

He held the identity card up beside the mirror.

Osewoudt put the cap on, grimaced, and took it off again.

'How come this outfit is exactly my size?'

'Dead simple! I tried it on myself!'

'That must have been quite a sight! With that beard!'

'Ha, ha, ha. Well, I must be off. See you tonight.'

Dorbeck took the suitcase and left the room without shaking Osewoudt's hand.

'I say, Dorbeck!'

Dorbeck didn't seem to hear, he was already on the stairs. Osewoudt wanted to go after him, but he had not fastened the underskirt of the nurse's uniform properly, and it slid down.

He almost tripped over it. By the time he had hitched it up, Dorbeck had shut the front door behind him. Gathering up the skirts, unable to find the fastening, Osewoudt staggered back to the room and looked down into the street through the side of the bay. He rubbed one cold, bare foot over the other. Ebernuss' car was still there. Osewoudt rapped loudly on the glass. But the car started up, gathered speed, and turned the corner.

'You might at least have left me a gun!' he cried. His voice sounded flat in the confined space.

He paused for a moment with his head bowed, then crossed to the mirror. He shivered with cold and began to adjust the nurse's clothing as best he could. The top was especially troublesome, because of the buttons being on the left and the buttonholes on the right. He even pinned the brooch with the yellow cross to his chest, and finally put on the black woollen stockings and flat shoes. Alarmed at the sight of his hair, which was too short for a nurse, he covered it with the white cap. Yes, now his face in the mirror exactly resembled the photo on the identity card.

He stood like that for quarter of an hour, gazing at his reflection. He didn't look too bad, he thought. He laughed, smiled, twisted round to get a view of his back, lifted each leg in turn to inspect his calves. Then he went back to the table and put on the black woollen cardigan. Only now did he see there was also a black shoulder bag in the suitcase. He opened the bag. It contained a clean white handkerchief, a stack of food coupons, a wad of banknotes, two packets of English cigarettes, matches, a comb and a knife of a type he had never seen before. It had a large handle made of black rubber. The blade was no longer than his thumb, but incredibly sharp and as wide as a cut-throat razor. It would not be difficult to inflict a fatal wound with it. The blade was fixed in the rubber hilt by a spring. It could be made to shoot out by pressing the thumb on the hilt. The purpose of this curious instrument was clear: it could be used to stab someone without anybody noticing, simply by setting the hilt against the person's body and then releasing the blade.

I'd rather have had a gun, he thought, but this is better than nothing. It seemed a handy sort of weapon.

He looked at his watch and saw that it was half past seven. This watch was the only masculine object he still possessed. It could give me away, he thought. He quickly removed it and, in case he forgot it later, put it in the shoulder bag. Then he decided to take a look around the flat.

In the kitchen he found bread, cold porridge and a knob of margarine on a saucer. Not much, but enough to survive for a day. At least he wouldn't have to face leaving the house in this get-up just yet. He struck a match and turned on the gas ring. No gas. Had even the gas run out in Amsterdam?

He went back to the parlour and peered into the cold stove. It was filled with dry wood and paper. A hod of coke stood further back. He lit the stove and heated the porridge.

By seven that evening Dorbeck had still not come to fetch him. Osewoudt went to the bedroom and lay down on the bed in his clothes with a blanket pulled over him. Now and then he dozed off. Each time he woke he struck a match to check his watch. Eleven o'clock. Then it was two. No Dorbeck.

The next morning he got up at half past nine, went into the kitchen and held his head under the tap. Then, with Marianne on his mind, he began wandering about the flat: kitchen, bedroom, parlour, and back.

When he had crossed the small landing for the tenth time he looked down over the banister. He saw something white lying on the mat by the front door. He crept down the stairs, telling himself: the neighbours think there's no one living here.

It was a small envelope. There was a slip of paper with a typewritten message in it: *Marianne Sondaar is in labour at the Emma Clinic, Oranje Nassaulaan 48. Dorbeck.*

The breeze played with his veil. Now and again Osewoudt had to brush it away from his face. It was finely textured and smelled new. It had been carefully ironed, the folds in which it had lain were still clearly visible, making sharp right angles.

There had been a brief shower a quarter of an hour before; the sun was now shining again, not all that brightly, but pleasantly enough. The wet, shimmering pavement made him blink.

All was quiet in the street, except for a distant dog and a pigeon. There were few people about. Each time he passed someone, he cast a furtive sideways look to see if they had noticed anything. But no one paid him any attention. They took him for an ordinary district nurse, on her way to visit a patient.

He did not feel cold, and although he had eaten hardly anything he did not feel hungry either. First time walking about on my own and free, he thought, it feels no stranger than if I had been ill in bed for a long while. I've pulled through! The Americans are in Hanover! The war will be over the day after tomorrow, or next week – soon, anyway. Everything will start completely afresh!

What would his own fresh start be like? Dorbeck had given him a new life. Start afresh with Marianne and the child! Soon, once the Germans were out of the way, it would be as if he'd been reborn as a grown man, a man who hadn't merely survived the war but who had come out on the side of the winners. A man who had risen to every challenge! What harm could possibly befall such a man in peacetime? Anything that stood in his way would shrivel under his gaze.

He tried the door of a florist's. The door was locked. He peered in the window and saw several empty vases and potted plants without blooms. He rang the bell, on the off chance. No one appeared.

On Willemsparkweg he found another florist. This one, too, was closed, and had nothing in the window. But when he rang the bell a little old man came shuffling to the door with a clay pipe in his mouth. The pipe was unlit.

'Good afternoon, Sister.'

'Oh sir, I hardly dare hope you'll be able to help me, as I've been to so many florists already without success. I realise that flowers are hard to come by these days, but I'd dearly love to find some. They're for a small child in hospital, you see. I'd hate to go there empty-handed.'

The old man took the pipe from his mouth.

'Yes, Sister, I understand. There's no trade in flowers any more. It's not that they aren't available, but you have to go to the Aalsmeer nurseries to get them. I'm bent double with sciatica, I've no tyres on my bicycle and just look how much weight I've lost!'

He plucked at the front of his waistcoat to show how thin he had grown.

'Maybe I can help you, though, seeing as you're a nurse. Step inside, will you. There isn't much I can offer, but it's the thought that counts, isn't it?'

Osewoudt stepped inside and the little old man fastened the door on the latch behind him. They went through the shop, which smelled earthy instead of flowery, to the living room at the back. An old woman dozed in an armchair; her head swayed slowly from side to side.

The old man took no notice of her; his wife began to mutter, without opening her eyes.

'Look,' he said, pointing to some crimson and blue hyacinths growing in a shallow basin filled with marble chips. 'I could let you have a couple of those. It's not much, but it's the thought that counts.'

He put his hand on Osewoudt's arm familiarly.

'I know how hard you nurses are made to work these days. One does what one can for nurses and doctors.'

He reached in his trouser pocket and brought out a large clasp-knife of the curved type used by florists, and asked: 'Is it a boy or a girl?'

'The colour doesn't matter, either will do.'

The old man cut off two red and two blue hyacinths and snapped the knife shut against his thigh. Holding the flowers aloft, he rummaged around the dresser with his free hand, grumbling: 'Not even any wrapping paper to be had these days.'

Osewoudt reached for his shoulder bag and opened it.

'How much do I owe you?'

'Let's see. It's not much, of course. Twenty-five guilders will do.'

With the hyacinths wrapped in a white paper napkin – very neatly, considering – Osewoudt made his way to Oranje Nassaulaan.

Is it a boy or a girl? he wondered. Maybe the child had already been born, or maybe it was being born even now. He hoped it would be a boy. He would tell Marianne that it would be good to call it Filip, as she had already said in her letter. But maybe it was a girl. What would Marianne prefer, a girl or a boy?

Then he caught sight of the enormous barbed-wire barricades

closing off part of Oranje Nassaulaan, where the villas had been requisitioned by the Germans.

His feet hurt because the shoes were a poor fit. They pinched his muscular judo-insteps, and he couldn't loosen them as they had buckles instead of laces. He could hardly expect Dorbeck to provide the custom-made shoes he was used to. Besides, in these tight shoes he took shorter steps than normal, and that, he thought, would make his gait more womanly. He almost laughed out loud, thinking how he, Osewoudt of the 500-guilder reward, was right under the Germans' noses, taking flowers to his child born of a Jewish mother. I've really pulled a fast one, he thought. Assuming that the child had already been born, he would shortly be peering into the cradle. Only your mother knew it was me, my boy, he'd tell his son later, everyone thought I was a nurse. The child's father *disguised as a nurse!*

He buried his nose in the hyacinths and inhaled the fragrance. Bastards, he thought, looking again at the barricades thrown up by the Germans, your final hour has come. Here I am, disguised as a sister of mercy with a bouquet in my hand, the same hand I shot Lagendaal with, the same hand I shook the poison into that drink for Ebernuss with, the sodding pansy. No, you'd never guess by the look of me, but I've been a sight more daring than all those manly men who've been talking down to me, pretending to have my interests at heart. More daring than Uncle Bart with his philosophical books, daring to call me a coward for not giving myself up when you lot arrested my mother. Bastards – I showed you, didn't I? I've dared more than those crybabies over in London, safely ensconced behind their microphones and too witless to give their agents decent identification or proper money instead of antiquated silver guilders, more too than all those people whining about German brutality, Fascist murderers and so on and so forth. Here I am, you bastards, come out from behind your barbed wire and get me!

He went up the stone steps to the entrance of the Emma Clinic.

The imposing building was a converted villa, not a purpose-built clinic, and he spent a moment in the vestibule casting around in vain for a porter's lodge. Then a young student nurse appeared in the corridor. He went up to her and asked: 'Could you tell me where I can find Mrs Sondaar?'

'Mrs Sondaar? Would you wait there for a moment?'

She pointed to the vestibule, where an oak bench stood against the wall.

Osewoudt did as he was told and sat down on the bench. He crossed his legs, rested his right hand with the flowers on his knee, and slid his left hand along his left thigh in search of cigarettes. Damn, he muttered, and bit his left thumb. On the wall facing him was a printed sign, reading: NOTIFICATIONS OF BIRTH TO BE MADE AT THE CIVIL REGISTRY OFFICE BY THE FATHER WITHIN 3 X 24 HOURS.

When a middle-aged nurse in a grey uniform came towards him he jumped to his feet, but had no chance to say anything. This woman was undoubtedly the matron, and not in the habit of exchanging pleasantries.

'You wish to visit Mrs Sondaar? That will not be possible for now, as she has finally got to sleep. Her condition is far from good. Sad . . . such a young girl.'

'Yes, very sad. But—'

'Would you like to see the child? You will have to wait a moment.'

The matron turned round and vanished down the long corridor. She thinks it's sad the child has no father, thought Osewoudt. This is insane. But why won't they let me see Marianne? He was confused by his own reaction, just standing there like an idiot offering the bouquet to the matron's receding back, not calling out to her, not asking what was going on, not even asking her to take charge of the flowers.

He sat down again on the oak bench, thinking: perhaps it's not a good idea to talk too much to a real nurse, under the circumstances . . . Suddenly he realised his teeth were chattering, thought of turning tail, leaving the flowers for the student nurse to deal with, coming back the following day. But he stayed where he was.

After ten minutes or so a morose manservant in a pink and white striped jacket came up to him and said: 'You wanted to see the Sondaar baby? Come with me.'

The manservant was carrying two buckets filled to the brim with ashes.

Osewoudt stood up and followed the man down the corridor. At the end of the corridor they went down a flight of stone steps; the occasional clank of the buckets against the steps echoed in the cellar.

Reaching the bottom, the manservant set the buckets on the floor. They were standing in a small hallway, dimly lit through a square of thick glass in the ceiling.

The man took a key from his trouser pocket and said: 'Very sad.'

He shot Osewoudt a quick look, then opened a door. On the other side it was dark. The man put his hand round the door frame and a weak light came on: a naked bulb suspended on a length of flex.

Together they went inside. It was a narrow space with pale, grey-painted walls. Along one side were dark blue stone slabs, upon which stood three coffins in a row. One large, the other two small.

The manservant stepped forward. On the lids of the coffins lay calling cards with names on them written in ink. He picked up the card lying on one of the two small coffins. Osewoudt craned his neck to read what was on it. It said: *Baby Sondaar, 4 April, 1945.* Then the man removed the coffin lid. The infant lay under a thin blanket. It was dressed in a shirt with elbow-length sleeves. The hands were folded on its breast. The tiny fingernails were dark brown, like fingernails that have been caught in a door.

The baby's face reminded him of a newly hatched bird: the upper lip protruded over the lower, making the mouth resemble a juvenile beak. There was some dried blood at the corners. The head had been propped up at a steep angle, presumably to keep the mouth closed, which gave the infant the appearance of looking down its nose. It wore an expression of infinite sadness, as if it had lived just long enough to mourn the fact that it would not survive.

The skull was pointed and deeply dented around the ears. Subcutaneous bleeding had already darkened the forehead.

Osewoudt's eyes filled with tears; the space around him became murky, as if a thick pane of frosted glass were being held before his eyes. He groped for the cold stone of the slab, laid down the flowers and, ignoring the manservant, went back up the steps and ran down the corridor. The tears kept streaming down, without him having the sensation of weeping.

The fresh air struck him in the face as he ran into the street. The screech of a car engine starting up made him look round as he crossed the road.

Two German soldiers opened the barbed-wire barricade and a small DKW with a sputtering engine slowly passed through.

The car caught up with Osewoudt and overtook him. It was a DKW of the same type as Ebernuss', only this one had been stripped of its peacetime gloss and painted with camouflage colours: dingy ochre, muddy green and rusty red. When the car was about twenty metres ahead, it slowed down. He saw the driver looking back at him. But Osewoudt walked on. Ahead of him was the car, behind him the barricade with the guards. The only alternative was to make a dash for it through the garden of one of the houses. His eyes widened with fear, he expected the German to step out of the car at any moment, pistol drawn.

But the car door remained closed; the engine continued to sputter. Osewoudt drew level and walked past. Then at his back he heard the engine revving. He walked on without a backward glance. He opened his shoulder bag; in it he saw the knife, the Leica, and the handkerchief. He took out the hand-kerchief, leaving the clasp of the bag undone. He held the handkerchief to his eyes, but instead of drying his tears it only made them worse. The DKW followed him in a low gear. Osewoudt turned a corner; the car continued to follow, suddenly accelerated, passed him, and stopped. The door swung open. A tall Luftwaffe officer got out. He was bareheaded. He left the car door open and walked somewhat unsteadily towards Osewoudt. When he drew near Osewoudt could make out the smell of liquor. He was roughly the same age as Osewoudt, twenty-three or so. He was very pale, his face had a greenish cast and the skin looked sallow and greasy. The cheeks were sunken, the mouth had no lips. He had a very thin blond moustache, not bristly but rather like floss silk.

Osewoudt felt his chin begin to quiver and the tears redoubling as the young Luftwaffe officer barred his way. He very nearly blurted: yes, it's me! All right then, take me away! I don't even care any more! Then the officer addressed him in clearly articulated German: 'Forgive me for bothering you, Sister! But I simply couldn't just drive on after seeing such lovely eyes filled with tears.'

His head swayed as he spoke.

'Please forgive me. You don't know me, and besides, you

hate me for being German. But believe me, the war is over, only the sadness remains. There is nothing for us now but to have compassion for one another and to offer consolation. You think I've taken leave of my senses, but I have not, I'm just very sad, like you.'

Osewoudt tried to sidestep him, wanted to make some reply, but was unable to do anything but bite his handkerchief in rage.

'Don't go away, please. Believe me, I mean no harm. Don't make me feel even worse than I already do. I am racked with remorse for everything my compatriots have done. I swear to you, none of it was my wish. I personally have not fired a single shot since the war began.'

Osewoudt stamped his feet but could not speak.

'There is no point in our remaining enemies,' the German officer persisted, linking the fingers of both hands and rhythmically pressing his stomach. 'We are both victims, Sister, victims! Please don't make me go without letting me do something for you. Tell me what I can do to help. I beseech you.'

A red mist rose before Osewoudt's eyes, and he said: 'I'm past helping.'

The sputtering car engine resonated at the back of his skull, as if he too were drunk.

The officer gripped the sleeve of the arm with which Osewoudt was holding up the handkerchief.

'I could at least give you a lift somewhere. Tell me where you want to go. I'm on my way to The Hague myself.'

Osewoudt made no reply

'I'll take you anywhere you like.'

'Well, if you insist,' said Osewoudt. 'You can take me to The Hague.'

'I can't tell you how grateful I am.'

The officer went to the car and held the passenger door

open for Osewoudt. His cap was lying on the seat, he tossed it in the back. Osewoudt got in. The officer walked round the back of the car like a taxi driver, slid behind the wheel, slammed the door shut and put in the clutch.

The officer, so eloquent in the street, drove off without saying another word. He seemed pleased with his catch. Now and again, especially when steering round corners, he took a deep breath. He sat hunched forward over the wheel, more so than drivers normally do. Steering the car cost him considerable effort. Yet he did not drive cautiously, carelessly, or too quickly. His wavy auburn hair had not been cut in a long time, but he wore it in a style popular among Germans: brushed rather than combed back from his forehead, and without a parting. On his collar he wore a star between two crossed sprigs of oak. There were no insignia on his blue-grey Luftwaffe jacket. He wore riding breeches with high brown boots and a brown military belt with a small holster attachment, the holster being barely big enough for a lady's pistol.

The roads were no longer wet. The sky had turned an even, late-afternoon blue, not a hint of cloud. Osewoudt put away the handkerchief and set the shoulder bag on his lap, without fastening the clasp. He briefly raised his rump off the seat to smooth the back of his skirt. Then he crossed his legs. The Luftwaffe officer gave him a fleeting, bashful smile. He began to talk: 'I am Dr Georg Krügener. The name is widely known. I am indeed a nephew of the famous Zeppelin captain. Personally, I have no claim to fame, thank God. I got my degree practically gratis because there was a war on. I'm in the Luftwaffe thanks to my uncle. I don't know what the inside of a plane looks like. My heart is too weak. Under normal circumstances I wouldn't have passed any medical examination. Now they've got me sitting in an office, in uniform. Why are you so quiet?'

They were approaching Schiphol airport. The fields were green. Here and there Luftwaffe listening posts pricked up their gigantic ears, but the sky was quite empty. Krügener now kept glancing at Osewoudt, and the car lost speed.

'My chatter doesn't interest you. You are still sunk in your sad thoughts. I am only talking to distract you, please excuse me.'

He stopped at the side of the road and switched off the engine. Then he reached under the seat for a bottle of rum and removed the cork.

'I haven't got a glass, I'm afraid. It would be in poor taste to offer you the bottle.'

He giggled like a child and took a swig himself.

Osewoudt said: 'Don't mind me. I don't drink.'

Krügener put the cork back in the bottle, and said: 'Now I can say what I've wanted to say all along. Please believe me, it is no coincidence, my speaking to you. I dreamt of you last night. I saw you sitting just as you are now, but you were dressed in black, with a black veil. Your hair was longer, it came down on either side of your face. You were sitting on a cart with two big wheels, drawn by a thin horse. It was on a lonely country road. You were holding out your hands and crying. You were on the way to the guillotine, although this was all happening in the present. There were American soldiers in front of the cart and also behind. They wore camouflage gear, and had automatic weapons and hand grenades hanging off them. Their helmets, covered with netting, had dry twigs poking out. They resembled walking storks' nests. It was like some kind of slow procession coming towards me. I saw everything from a low viewpoint, because I was lying in a ditch beside the road. I wanted to get up to save you, but couldn't move. The horse's hooves kicked grains of sand into my eyes. Can you make sense of a dream like that?'

Osewoudt shrugged.

Krügener took another swig; his hands were shaking.

'Do you know what dirty horse's hooves smell like? The smell was far worse than I ever noticed in real life. Oh! Hölderlin says: man is a god when he dreams, a beggar when he thinks.'

'Then I'd sooner be the beggar,' said Osewoudt. 'What happens to a god when he wakes up? He's either hanging on a cross like a scarecrow or lying in a ditch, like you.'

'My dream didn't end there,' said Krügener. 'I woke up briefly and then dropped off again, and it went on. Your head had been chopped off and came rolling towards me. I knew it was yours, though I couldn't see that because it had got wrapped up in the veil as it rolled. It came to a stop right next to me. More American soldiers appeared, advancing in loose formation. They had mine detectors, and were slowly and carefully scanning the ground. They took one step forward at a time, sweeping their instruments from side to side before taking the next step. I knew what they were looking for, but I kept quiet. They didn't notice me. When they had gone past, I unwound the veil. It was your head all right, only, at the same time it was the head of a man: a man with black hair. The cheeks had thick black stubble.'

He took another swig from the bottle.

Somewhere in the distance, out of sight, the drone of aeroplanes began.

'The Americans,' said Osewoudt. 'Let's drive on before they shell us.'

Krügener replaced the cork in the bottle, put it back under the seat, started the engine and drove off. The drone grew louder. There must have been quite a number of planes, because they were not in sight and yet made so much noise. There was the occasional flash as from a diamond in the sky, nothing more. Parallel white stripes began to appear overhead, as if the blue were being inscribed with musical staves, but the planes themselves stayed out of sight, and there was no shelling.

As they reached Leiden Osewoudt said: 'Since we're in the neighbourhood, I'd like to take this opportunity to pass a message to some friends of mine in Voorschoten.'

'Voorschoten? I don't know where that is.'

'I'll show you the way. You can follow the tramline, it'll lead you straight there. I don't suppose the trams are still running, but you'll still see the tracks.'

They followed the rusty tramline.

It was after six when they went past the silver factory. From there he could see the steeple of the Reformed church, which looked like an upended Zeppelin. Then the low medieval tower of the church of St Willibrord.

They passed the police station and reached the stop where the tramlines sidle towards each other until they overlap in a single track. He read the sign: NO OVERTAKING.

There were no vehicles or carts in the narrow high street, nor any oncoming traffic.

'Stop here!' yelled Osewoudt.

Krügener slammed on the brake, too drunk to pull over to the side of the road. The car stopped on the tramlines.

'Couldn't you borrow a glass from your friends?' Krügener whined. 'I'd love to pour you a drink . . .'

Osewoudt snatched the key from the ignition, got out of the car and made straight for the tobacco shop.

The first thing to catch his eye was a small notice: CIGAR-ETTE PAPERS SOLD OUT.

In the display he saw some open cardboard boxes containing strips of tightly rolled paper: CHEWING STICKS FIFTEEN CENTS. There were also a couple of paper bags on their sides, from which spilled green hay. The roller blind over the door-pane was up. He could see there was no one in the shop. He opened his shoulder bag, took out the knife and slipped it into his right-hand coat pocket. Then he reached for the door handle. It gave way.

The bell did not tinkle as he stepped inside. The leaded glass sliding doors to the back room were closed. Osewoudt pushed one of the doors aside.

There was Ria! She looked up from an ironing board and set the iron upright. Thin curls of steam rose from it.

Her jaw dropped, exposing her teeth which looked longer than ever, rather like matchsticks protruding from her jaws.

Osewoudt slowly shut the sliding door behind him, keeping his eyes fixed on Ria. His arms and legs began to shake; he felt the nurse's cap wobble on his head. From the corner of his eye he took in the rest of the room. The furniture had changed. It was new. Where had she got it?

Then a noise escaped from his throat, he didn't know what sort of noise it was.

Ria said: 'Sister! You gave me quite a turn! You reminded me so much of my first husband!'

Once her screams had stopped there was no further sound in the house.

She lay on the floor beside the ironing board. Osewoudt wiped the knife on everything within reach: clothes waiting to be ironed, tablecloth, lampshade, it was as if he wanted to spread Ria's blood all over the house. Then he stood still for a moment, panting, and stuffed the knife in his coat pocket. He went to the front of the shop, parted the short curtains at the back of the display, and peered outside.

Krügener's car was beginning to attract attention. Looking over it were two boys, lounging against the crossbars of their bikes, which had wooden tyres. Now and then they called out to the driver, and laughed. Three girls, arm in arm, came clattering along and halted in front of the car. They giggled at the boys.

Osewoudt took a step back and shut the curtains.

'Turlings! Turlings!' he called. But he had already guessed that the chemist's son was not there.

It grew darker in the shop because people were gathering in front of the window and perching on the sill. He could see their hair protruding over the top of the short curtains.

He took a deep breath, made for the door and seized the handle. Just above it the enamel plaque was still there: HAVE YOU FORGOTTEN ANYTHING?

He pulled the door open, shut it quickly behind him and ran to the car. The crowd of onlookers was swelling to mob proportions. Voices were raised, there was even some shouting. He didn't catch what they were saying. Osewoudt opened the passenger door. Just then Krügener threw the empty rum bottle out of the car window on the other side. He slumped diagonally against the seat back, twisted round to face Osewoudt, and said: 'I thought you were going to stay there, with your lover.'

Osewoudt leaned into the car, grabbed Krügener by the arm and dragged him away from the driver's seat. Then he slammed the passenger door, went round to the other side of the car and got in behind the wheel. He put the key in the ignition and started. The engine made a hollow, scraping noise like an empty coffee mill, but did not fire.

A boy shouted: 'Look at her! Wants a roll in the hay with a Kraut while she's got the chance!'

Again Osewoudt tried to start the car.

'See that? She's covered in blood!' the boy jeered.

Laughing hysterically, Krügener tried to lay his arm around Osewoudt's shoulders. Osewoudt shook it off and pressed the starter again. This time the engine responded. Osewoudt put it in gear. Jolting and grinding, he nosed the car through the crowd. The street widened. The door of the chemist's opened and a woman came out, but he didn't recognise her.

He looked at the sleeves and the front of his coat. On the dark fabric the stains were simply darker, not red. His left hand was sticky. He let go of the steering wheel and wiped his bloody fingers on the edge of the seat.

The posts supporting the tram wires flashed past. The sun beamed into the car at right angles to the direction they were going. The houses along the road thinned out, making way for the sprawl of glasshouses.

A furious screeching noise arose, and not far off a huge rocket shot up into the sky, swerved away in the direction of England, and dwindled to a glowing spark.

'Got no more to drink,' Krügener whined. 'And I asked you to get us a glass, too.'

Osewoudt pressed the accelerator to the floor, but the small car would not do more than forty kilometres per hour.

'The glass must've broken,' said Krügener. 'You've cut yourself, you've got blood all over you. Don't think I didn't notice, my poor darling.'

He laid a slimy hand on Osewoudt's cheek.

Osewoudt's right hand let go of the wheel, clenched in mid-air to a fist, and landed a blow under Krügener's chin, on the soft part of his throat.

Not a sound came out of Krügener after that. Osewoudt, tight-lipped, glanced at him from time to time. Krügener's eyes were shut, but he was not unconscious.

He had to stay alive. When would they be stopped at a checkpoint? There was bound to be one at the tunnel under the river in Rotterdam, in which case Krügener might come in useful.

The car drove through Voorburg, but nothing happened. Nor did anything happen in Delft. By the time he reached the outskirts of Rotterdam it was growing dark. He switched on the headlamps, but they were largely blacked out with leather flaps and shed practically no light.

It was long past eight o'clock, the streets were deserted.

He felt no excitement or fear as he approached the tunnel, but the sentries didn't even come out of their boxes. Without having to stop he rolled into the tunnel, which was unlit.

Once he left Rotterdam behind, the condition of the road worsened. It was badly rutted by tanks and heavy vehicles, and he was forced to drive even more slowly than before.

When they reached Dordrecht night had fallen. In the distance he saw a church. Osewoudt stopped at the side of the road a few hundred metres short of the church.

Krügener began to stir. He pulled in his legs and sat up. He gave a cry, threw both his arms around Osewoudt and tried to kiss him on the mouth. With his hands he fumbled under the veil at the back of Osewoudt's neck.

'Oh my darling,' he gushed. 'You are the first. It wasn't that I couldn't get any girls. But I've never felt so attracted to a woman as I am now, to you!'

He was almost sitting upright, bracing himself with one leg while kneeling on the passenger seat with the other. That way he loomed over Osewoudt in the low space.

'You are my angel,' stammered Krügener. 'My angel of deliverance! You are the first woman I have ever kissed! And I thought women meant nothing to me! How could I have been so mistaken! Give me your lips, my darling!'

Now Osewoudt managed to free his right arm. He put his hand in his coat pocket and found the knife. He butted his forehead like a ram, but couldn't prevent Krügener's lips from brushing his eyelids.

'Ouch!' gasped Krügener suddenly, recoiling. 'My back! A stabbing pain in my back!'

His embrace went limp.

'Oh! My back! My back!' he groaned. He reared up so high that the back of his head hit the roof of the car. His eyes boggled. His leg slid off the seat, his knees buckled. He tried reaching his arm behind his back to find the source of the pain, but the arm appeared to be paralysed. Osewoudt shoved him down into the space beside the steering wheel, where he remained, crumpled up. The knife stuck out of his back.

As Osewoudt made his way to the church, an artillery duel exploded on the horizon. White flames lit up the low bank of cloud.

The church was closed. Osewoudt walked around the building. With the pounding of field guns in his ears, he rang the bell at the rectory.

The priest himself answered the door.

'Help me,' Osewoudt implored. 'Over there, in that car there's a German, and he's dying! Help me, please, he tried to rape me!'

It was a cloudless morning. A flock of chickens ventured on to the road and fled squawking into the bushes as the old car approached.

'Will it be long now before the orchards begin to blossom?' Osewoudt asked.

'Not long now, I think. It's a good thing this last winter wasn't too severe.'

Dr Sikkens was in his forties. He wore rimless glasses and his sunken cheeks were hurriedly but closely shaven. He was at the wheel in a short duffel coat, the sort of coat doctors find convenient for getting in and out of their cars quickly. He also wore driving gloves, and spread a reassuring smell of coal tar. 'I'm run off my feet,' he said. 'I was called out twice last night. In all these years I haven't had a holiday, and the winters were the worst. It was bad enough with the war going on, but such hard winters! On the other hand, take the winter of '42. If that one hadn't been so cold, the Germans might have held out even longer.'

'Exactly,' Osewoudt said heartily. 'But if we'd had some more freezing temperatures last winter, the Allies might have been able reach us up north by crossing the rivers over the ice. If they had, we'd have been liberated by now.'

'I don't suppose you've had an easy time of it either, Sister!'

Osewoudt smiled, pouted, but kept quiet.

'When it comes down to it, nursing is an even more

demanding profession than being a doctor. I can't think where women like you get the energy. It never ceases to amaze me. I used to know a district nurse over there,' said the doctor, pointing to a distant church steeple to the left of the road. 'She worked until she dropped – literally! In the middle of the road. That was last year, a week before the Canadians arrived. Damn . . .'

He stepped on the brake.

A large sign made of rough planks stood in the verge. The wood had been painted black, with large white letters saying STOP.

Five foreign-looking soldiers stood guard beside it. Their helmets had mesh covering with dried twigs sticking out. They wore baggy fatigues with straps and belts, from which dangled all manner of metal equipment. Each of them held an automatic weapon under his arm.

One of them stepped out into the road. He seemed to recognise the car as the doctor's, and motioned it on with a raised thumb. Two others noticed Osewoudt in the passenger seat, put their fingers between their lips and whistled. The car set off again.

There were shouts of 'Hey! Hey! Hey!' as they passed the checkpoint.

'Our liberators seem very glad to see you!' said Dr Sikkens, accelerating. 'Is anything wrong? Not feeling carsick are you?'

Osewoudt sat, goggle-eyed and staring, with his legs spread and a hand clutching each knee.

'You're looking quite green,' said the doctor. 'Want me to stop?'

'No, no, please drive on. There's nothing wrong with me.'

'It's sure to be lack of sleep. You should have taken my advice and stayed at the house today. Crossing the Hollands

Diep in a boat last night, on top of all the other trouble you've had – you must be exhausted. It won't do, you know. Why are you in such a hurry to get to Breda?'

'I have an important message to deliver.'

Osewoudt now settled back in his seat, maintaining a relaxed posture.

'There's no need to slow down, I'm not feeling sick. Don't mind me, Doctor.'

'I'm not sure . . .'

The doctor angled his head so that he could shift his gaze from the road to Osewoudt at will.

'Notice anything in particular?'

'Just what I said before, Sister. I must advise you to rest as soon as possible. Can't you come back and stay with us after you've delivered your message?'

'That's not what I meant, Doctor. Don't say you didn't notice! Well, I might as well tell you. I am not a nurse. I am not a girl. I'm a man.'

'Ah. Yes. Well. Hm.'

The doctor faced forward again and concentrated on driving.

'Don't you believe me?'

'Of course, Sister. I believe you! Of course. I quite understand what you mean. A village doctor's work covers a multitude of fields, including psychiatry. Look here, it seems to me you're at the end of your tether. You really need to take a rest or you'll have a breakdown. People with your kind of perseverance, your bravery, are under great stress – a sudden breakdown is not unusual! You are an exceptionally energetic and active sort of person, and I'd be prepared to bet that you always have been. It is quite possible that there is a touch of maleness in your psychological make-up. I wouldn't be surprised if you preferred playing with boys when you were little, if you were a tomboy, got into fights. Maybe you even wished you were a boy now and then. In times like these, during a war, when the whole world is upside down, that kind of impossible childhood wish can rise to the surface in people who are otherwise completely mature. But it will pass once you have taken some rest.'

'That has nothing to do with it. The only thing wrong with me is that I don't have a beard.'

'What's that? Well, that is an aspect I would have to look into. I think the best thing for you would be to consult a specialist at the earliest opportunity.'

A long column of armoured vehicles towing heavy guns came towards them. A motorcyclist wearing a helmet rode in front; he waved them to the side of the road. The doctor steered the car to the verge and stopped. Amid the din of roaring engines the vehicles rolled past one by one, olive green, dented here and there, splashed with brightly coloured, incomprehensible signs. Heads in helmets protruded from the tops of some of the trucks; long, thin antennae swayed to and fro in the air. These were the Allies! Osewoudt saw them clearly now for the first time, but he hid his face in his hands and cowered in his seat to avoid the soldiers' notice.

'Doctor,' he said, when they set off again, 'you've got it all wrong. I only put this nurse's uniform on the day before yesterday. I'm going to Breda to volunteer for military service.'

The doctor made no reply. Was he concentrating on the busy junction on the outskirts of Breda, which they were now approaching?

'Doctor,' said Osewoudt as they drove into the town, 'I had a girlfriend in Amsterdam. She had a child by me. Do you believe me now?'

'Is it all right if I wait for you here?' said Dr Sikkens. 'Then you can come back with me straightaway. I'll see what I can do for you. My car is hardly the place for conducting a surgery.

But you can stay with us as long as you like. I wish you'd take my advice! My wife and I would like nothing better! We have the greatest respect for people like you.'

'But Doctor!' Osewoudt implored, almost choking, 'I have a man's wristwatch!' He showed it.

'Most nurses have them, because the dial's bigger.' The doctor laughed. 'Just tell me where you want to go. I'll wait for you in the car and then we'll drive back together!'

'I'll get out here,' said Osewoudt, and opened the door while the car was still running.

'Where – here?'

'Here! Here!' he shrieked, putting his leg out of the door. By the time the car came to a stop Osewoudt was already dashing across the thoroughfare, zigzagging between two bicycles. He ducked into the first side street, his veil flapping behind him, and ran so fast he had to hold on to his cap. He could feel it sliding down, the bow under his chin had come undone. Slowing his pace, he retied it.

He came to a large square bordered by low houses. He ran across it and turned into another street, where there were no gardens. At the end of this street he saw a crowd of people. He made his way towards them, boldly.

The street led to a main road. There were a lot of people about, massed on either side of the carriageway, holding small flags, orange ones and red-white-and-blue ones. The boys wore orange paper hats and the girls had orange ribbons in their hair. Every house had put out a flag.

'Excuse me madam, can you tell me what's going on?'

'Haven't you heard, Sister? The queen will be coming past in a few minutes.'

'Oh, how wonderful! I just arrived here from occupied territory, you see. I escaped. I feel as if I'm dreaming! I can't believe my eyes! All these happy faces, all the bunting! It's five years since I saw a Dutch flag! This is my country, my very own country! I feel as if I've been away for years, and have finally come home to my own people!'

He was shaking all over. He clung to the woman's arm as though seeking support from the branch of a tree.

'Will it be long now? I'd so much love to see the queen, but I have to deliver a message. It's very urgent.'

'She may be here in ten minutes, five minutes, who knows . . .'

'I need to go to the headquarters of the Netherlands Armed Forces. Is it far from here?'

'Oh, Sister! You're right on top of it, so to speak! See those barracks over the road? That's their headquarters. If that's where you have to deliver your message you'll be better off than us. The queen's going to stop there to inspect the guard of honour. If you're quick you'll get a grandstand view! Come along children, make way! Let the nurse through!'

'Thank you, you are very kind.'

Osewoudt said goodbye and crossed the road diagonally. Helmeted troops now began to form a cordon, but they let him through. Even the sentry at the barracks gate did not stop him. Skirts flapping, he strode to the main entrance, climbed the steps and went inside. He was confronted by three soldiers with white braid on their chests and a sergeant with a barrage of shiny medals.

'Sergeant . . .'

'What can I do for you, Sister?'

'I have to speak to the commander. It's urgent. I have an important message for him. Osewoudt is the name. Just tell him Osewoudt is here.'

'I'll go and check, Sister.' The sergeant swung round and vanished into the building.

Osewoudt smiled at the soldiers.

'Nice day, isn't it, Sister?' one of them said.

All three soldiers now began to pay him attention. They stepped forward, and the one nearest to him said: 'Nice weather for a swim.'

He looked Osewoudt up and down, grinning and squinting, gauging what the nurse would look like in a bathing costume. He was the tallest of the threesome, and bent low towards Osewoudt's face.

'Nice weather for a sunbathe, too, on the lawn by the pool.'

'A bit early in the season for me,' said Osewoudt. He turned aside and looked out across the forecourt to the road. What was that? Indeed, the doctor's car. The doctor must have followed him. Driving very slowly, he poked his head out of the window to scan the approach to the barracks, without, apparently, spotting Osewoudt. But then it was quite dark in the vestibule compared with the forecourt.

The cordon of troops tightened their control. An old-fashioned military policeman on horseback, in blue dress uniform complete with sword and fur cap, approached the car. He leaned down, motioning the doctor to drive on. A moment later the car had gone.

Then footsteps sounded in the corridor. It was the sergeant, hurrying towards him with an officer in tow. The sergeant signalled mysteriously to the soldiers as he advanced, and the lieutenant, who was lame in one leg, swung his good leg further forward than people who have the use of both legs do, so that it landed each time with a loud thud. In his right hand he held out a file card from an index system. He was as pale as plaster, and his bulbous eyes shifted from the card to Osewoudt and back again. He was now very close.

'Osewoudt! Osewoudt!' he exclaimed. 'Is this Osewoudt? Can this be Osewoudt?'

There was a photo glued to the filing card.

'Yes, I am Osewoudt. Do you know who I am?'

'Arrest him! Take him into custody! Search him! The man's dangerous! You stupid fools! He's no nurse, he's a spy!'

Two of the soldiers promptly seized him by the arms and twisted them behind his back. The third, who only a moment ago had wanted to go swimming with him, frisked him gingerly with one hand, as if he thought Osewoudt might be carrying dynamite. Finally he pulled off the veil.

They marched him down the corridor, or rather, they propelled him by the elbows, as if he were a dressmaker's dummy. They came to a hall with rows of low benches occupied by the guard of honour, sitting up straight with their rifles between their knees. Osewoudt was conducted down the aisle between the rows; he kept silent. The third soldier, who was leading the way, opened a door. The other two soldiers let go of Osewoudt, or rather, flung him inside. The door banged behind them and bolts were slid home.

The wall dividing this space from the hall was very thin. Voices were raised on the other side of the bolted door. 'Silence!' barked the lieutenant, and a hush descended.

Osewoudt stood by the door, his heart thumping. He shook his half-dislocated shoulders, passed his hand over his now capless head. He noticed that his teeth were chattering and his knees quaking, as if he had climbed to the top of a tower at the double only to find himself in a boarded-up belfry.

Yet it wasn't dark in the cubicle. There was a window, tall and narrow, like all the windows in the barracks. It was covered on the outside by a web of barbed wire.

He listened at the door. He could hear talking in low voices in the hall beyond, but couldn't make out what was being said. His eyes wandered round the small space. There was a bunk, a low table on rusty tubular legs, a rusty metal chair, and a wooden washstand with an enamel basin.

The noise from outside now reached him. He crossed to the window, which he could raise easily. There was so much barbed wire that not even a child would be able to poke its arm out without getting hurt. But it was easy enough to see through.

The window overlooked the forecourt. He was about half a storey above ground level. The woman had been right, he would have a grandstand view of the queen! Clenching his jaws to stop his teeth chattering, he fetched the chair and set it in front of the window. He sat down, put his hands on the sill, propped his chin on his hand, and gazed outside.

The road was now closed to traffic. The carriageway was completely clear, and lined on either side with infantrymen posted in front of the onlookers, alternately facing the road and the crowd.

Loud stamping sounded from the guardroom next door. A few moments later the guard of honour emerged in the forecourt to the accompaniment of drums. They marched four abreast, shouldering their rifles with bayonets fixed. At the gate the column split in two, each half describing an arc until they came to a halt on command. They now stood in two facing semicircles, with rifles grounded.

It was quiet for a moment, then in the distance the cheering started. Six motorcycle outriders came past in succession, rolling slowly over the carriageway. The cheering mounted. A flurry of waving hands and flags rippled above the heads of the expectant crowd. An open car drew up and stopped.

A military policeman opened the car door and the queen stepped out. She wore a grey costume with a fairly long, flared skirt. On her feet she wore sensible brown shoes. The officers saluted, the cheers became deafening. Osewoudt sprang up from his chair.

The old lady advanced slowly across the forecourt. In her left hand she held a small bouquet wrapped in paper, probably the offering of a child in the crowd. She held her right hand level with her temple, with the palm turned to her face. She made stiff little bows left and right, fluttering her raised hand in a gesture of fanning her royal aura towards her subjects. She smiled benignly.

'Hurrah! Hurrah!' Osewoudt shouted.

At that moment the queen happened to glance in his direction. He let go of the barbed wire he had been clinging to, and bowed. He had the impression the royal hand gestures were meant specifically for him. No doubt the queen, too, had a soft spot for nurses! Then the old lady's gaze moved on.

'Hurrah!' Osewoudt shouted once more. But his voice was drowned out by the cheering crowd, and no one looked up at his window.

Then there was some commotion on the other side of the partition. The door opened slowly.

Osewoudt had shut the window and was sitting on his chair by the washstand. He did not move.

A soldier put his head round the door.

'Christ! Is that him?'

The door was pushed to, and he heard the soldier say: 'I'd have sworn he was a girl!'

The door opened again, and another soldier looked in. His lips were smeared with whipped cream. In one hand he held a spoon, in the other a saucer with strawberries.

'Strawberries and cream!' he crowed. 'But not for dirty faggots like you!'

The door slammed and Osewoudt heard him say: 'Damn! There was me thinking: nice bit of stuff! A blonde bombshell! Damn!'

The sun was already setting when the door opened once more. A tall colonel entered, followed by the limping lieutenant and a corporal. Osewoudt got up; he stood facing the colonel.

'Colonel! This is an inexplicable misunderstanding. My name is Osewoudt, I'm from Voorschoten. I slipped through the German lines last night, and I . . .'

The lieutenant opened his mouth to speak, but the colonel motioned him to silence. Then, looking over Osewoudt's head and without paying him the slightest attention, the colonel said: 'Lieutenant, I think it most inappropriate for this man to be held here wearing female attire. What will the troops think? He must be issued with men's clothing at once.'

He turned on his heel and made for the door.

'Colonel, surely you wouldn't want to lay yourself open to ridicule? It's not what it seems – please, couldn't you listen to me for one minute?'

The corporal shut the door; Osewoudt heard the bolts being slid across. He ran to the door and shouted through the keyhole: 'Colonel! It's not my fault I'm in women's clothes! I never pretended to be a woman! Please listen to me! I've been locked up here for the past five hours! It's all an idiotic mistake! I am not a spy! I really am Osewoudt, honestly! I'm not a cross-dresser! Let me out! I can explain!'

Nothing happened.

He went to the window and looked outside. All was quiet. There were a few soldiers idling about, whose boredom was so great that it seemed to affect the entire neighbourhood. The road was littered with scraps of orange paper, the Dutch flags on the buildings hung motionless in the calm of dusk.

He heard footsteps. The sergeant and a soldier crossed from the barracks to the main gate, where they climbed into a jeep. The vehicle started, drove out through the gate and disappeared.

A quarter of an hour later the jeep returned. The sergeant and the soldier alighted. The soldier held a package wrapped in newspaper.

Soon after that the bolts were slid back and the door opened.

'Is there no end to this?' said Osewoudt. 'Are you quite mad?'

The soldier threw the package on the bunk. The sergeant laid a khaki vest, khaki underpants, a khaki shirt and two khaki socks beside it.

'Take off the skirts and put on this lot. The rest is of no concern to me. Got that?'

They backed out of the room and bolted the door.

Osewoudt undid the newspaper. Out came a rather crumpled suit: double-breasted jacket and matching trousers. They were not new, but had not had much wear either. The fabric was purplish with large blue checks; it looked fairly thin, but was stiff and hard to the touch. It gave off an almost numbing smell of mothballs.

Osewoudt took off the skirts. He flung the nurse's uniform into a corner and pulled on the khaki underwear. The shirt was also army issue, but the epaulettes had been cut off, and there was no tie.

The trousers fitted him perfectly and stayed up despite the absence of a belt. Straightening the jacket over his chest, he heard something rustling in the inside pocket. He put his hand in and drew out a fairly large sheet of paper. There was the American flag in full colour in the top left-hand corner, and a notice printed in blue:

GIFT FROM THE UNITED STATES WOMEN'S LEAGUE
The Young Ladies' Circle at Knoxville (Tennessee) congratulates the citizens of all nations oppressed by the

German barbarians on their liberation by the Allied troops.

LONG LIVE THE UNITED NATIONS!

It was completely dark outside when two hefty Negroes came to fetch him. They wore gleaming white helmets and blancoed belts hung with hefty revolvers in hefty white holsters. Osewoudt went with them without being told to. They said nothing, merely made chewing motions.

One MP walked in front of him, the other behind.

'You're mad, all of you!' Osewoudt yelled at a Dutch soldier he saw standing in the corridor.

'Steady now,' muttered the Negro behind him.

They came to the forecourt. The two MPs now went ahead together, as if trying to distance themselves from him. They made straight for a jeep, which was waiting with the engine running. One of them climbed in behind the steering wheel, the other heaved himself into the passenger seat. He was too massive for the vehicle, and his right leg hung over the side. He waved his thumb over his shoulder, without looking round. Osewoudt understood what he meant and felt his muscles stiffen. Should he get in? His eyes bored into the darkness, hoping for an answer. Then he saw a second jeep. It was waiting about ten metres behind the first one, and it, too, was occupied by two white-helmeted figures. The windscreen was down and a small machine gun had been mounted on the bonnet.

Clambering over the wheel, Osewoudt got in behind the Negroes. The jeep set off at once, drove through the gate and turned on to the road, where it rapidly picked up speed. Osewoudt crouched on the floor. He looked back, the wind tearing at his hair. The second jeep was following closely.

When they reached the other side of town, the second jeep

was still following. Now and then the moon shone through rifts in the clouds. It was too dark for him to see where they were going, but he surmised that they would be heading for the Belgian border. The second jeep switched its spotlight on at intervals, and then Osewoudt saw his own shadow playing on the shoulders of the Negroes in front of him.

They drove through unlit villages, they passed armed checkpoints unhindered, they pulled up at a sign saying STOP! CUSTOMS! after which a red-and-white barrier was raised to let them through. The road became bumpy and potholed, the landscape flat and desolate. Afterwards they drove through a wood and finally came to a moor, where a fair number of army trucks, tanks and field guns were assembled. The jeep stopped a little further on. The Negroes got out, signalled to Osewoudt to get out too, and took no further notice of him. He climbed down and stood beside them.

The driver offered a cigarette to his companion, and then also to Osewoudt. He struck a match and had to stoop to give Osewoudt a light. Then both men turned their backs on him. Soldiers sauntered about here and there.

There was not a normal building in sight, but a high tent had been erected, as well as two sheet-metal hangars with small windows, weakly lit from the inside. The muddy ground was covered with strips of metal tracking.

Osewoudt shivered in the cold night air. The jeep that had brought him drove off. From the tent emerged a number of men in civilian suits and overcoats; he counted nine. Helmeted soldiers marshalled them into a line beside Osewoudt, at arm's length from each other. One of the soldiers held a flat case in front of his stomach, like a tray. With the air of a surgical assistant, he trailed after a sergeant, who stopped behind each prisoner, pulled his hands behind his back, took a pair of small steel handcuffs from the tray and snapped them shut with a loud click.

The dark sky was thick with the roar of engines, and some distance away a plane landed. It taxied towards them over the metal tracking, a spotlight set in the blunt nose flooding its path. It came to a halt, but the engines were still running. The sergeant said something to the prisoner at the far end of the line, then walked to the plane. A hatch in the body swung open. A ladder was fixed to the inside. The prisoner mounted the rungs, followed by the others. Nothing was said. Osewoudt was the last to climb up. The gale from the propellers whipped his thin suit while he struggled not to lose his footing on the narrow rungs.

The plane's interior was lit by small light bulbs. The hold had been knocked together out of rough planks, like a chicken run. The prisoners sat on wooden benches facing each other. They talked among themselves; no one ordered them to keep quiet. They even shouted to make themselves heard above the roar of the engines. They spoke languages Osewoudt didn't understand. After a while the man sitting next to him suddenly addressed him, in Dutch.

He was lean and grey-haired, and looked as if he might be a doctor or a dentist. He wore a spotless white raincoat.

'Who are you?' he asked.

'What is it to you?'

The man leaned towards Osewoudt confidentially.

'I've been in this business years. I was already working for the British in the Great War. Never got caught by the Germans.'

'What are you doing here, then?'

'It's all nonsense! As soon as we get to England I'll get in touch with my contacts. The day after tomorrow I'll walk free.'

'Ah, so you know where they're taking us?'

'Manchester, of course. Section LI4. Check-up, that's all. Plain sailing as far as I'm concerned. No problem!'

'They made a mistake arresting me, too!' Osewoudt cried.

'They're always getting their wires crossed! Especially the Americans, they're hopeless at this kind of work. Rank amateurs.'

'It was the Dutch who arrested me. I had just slipped through the German lines in the night, and the first thing they do is arrest me. I only escaped from prison four days ago – the Germans had me locked up for nine whole months. I go straight to the headquarters in Breda and what do they do? Rearrest me. It's too absurd to be true. But I'll set it all straight once we get to England.'

'Who do you know in England?'

'No one.'

'Who were you taking orders from – SIS? SOE?'

'I'm not familiar with those names. I didn't have much to do with England. They just sent me agents from time to time, for me to help on their way.'

'So who are you, then?'

'I am Osewoudt. But—'

'My word! Are you Osewoudt? I thought I'd seen your face somewhere!'

'I've never seen you before.'

'No. But I've seen you.'

'Where was that?'

'Where? Warnings about you were put out five months ago! Your picture's been in all the underground news bulletins. Even the normal newspapers in the liberated provinces have carried reports about you – a highly dangerous individual, they said, who'd delivered hundreds of good patriots into the hands of the enemy. That's you, isn't it? The beardless youth? Damn it, it's just come back to me! That voice of yours! So high-pitched! The dangerous youth with the high voice – for the past four months or so people in the liberated zone have been talking about nothing else.'

The hatch was slotted into place. The whine of the engines rose in volume. The plane juddered into motion. It bumped up and down like a wheelbarrow on a stony path, making the prisoners topple off their benches and fall in a heap on the floor, heads knocked together. Suddenly the shaking ceased. Osewoudt looked about him, his eyes stung, his gut rose to his throat.

One by one they crawled their way back to the benches over the steeply sloping floor.

A bare room, stinking of stale cigarette smoke, a large desk roughly in the middle, a smaller desk to one side, bars over the big window looking out on a high, tarred wall.

Outside, a drizzle was falling, so light as to be almost indistinguishable from mist.

Osewoudt had lost count of the times he had found himself in a bare room like this, sitting on a straight-backed chair facing a desk, with welts on his wrists from handcuffs removed five minutes earlier.

Behind the smaller desk sat a young man in a mouse-grey suit. His hair had been cut in a way that gave him a thick forelock, the secret of which is exclusive to English barbers. He was smoking a cigarette in a long amber holder, his eyelashes were remarkably long. He inserted a fresh sheet of paper into the typewriter before him. Now and then he smiled at Osewoudt, then stared ahead again, blowing perfectly circular smoke rings.

The large desk was unoccupied. There was nothing on it, not even a blotting pad. It was an old desk of cheap wood, splintered and worn at the corners.

The floorboards were uncarpeted. Around the desks the wood was stained with ink and trampled cigarette ash, near the fireplace it was blackened by coal dust, with large scorch marks from burning coals that had spilled out of the grate.

Footsteps sounded in the corridor.

'The boss did not arrive early today,' said the young man in English. 'He seldom does.'

Osewoudt understood with some difficulty what he was saying, but did not trust himself to reply.

Then the door opened and a tall man in a brown tweed suit entered. He went up to the desk, on which he deposited a blue folder.

'I am Colonel Smears, by the way,' he said in heavily accented Dutch. 'I am very glad of this opportunity to have a little conversation with you.' Turning to the young man at the type-writer, he switched to English, saying: 'Well Percy, how is everything this beautiful morning?'

'Quite well, sir, thank you.'

The tall man blew on his hands, then slowly seated himself. He was bald except for a fringe of very long hair at the back of his head, which he wore swept up and plastered over his pate. His face was a shade of bluish pink, his eyes bulged and the whites were so yellow as to make the eyes themselves appear yellow, while the skin on his fleshy nose was red and taut like a rubber balloon. But most striking of all was his moustache. It was shaped like a sideways hourglass, and was the colour of brass after centuries of weekly rubbing with fuller's earth.

He propped his elbows on the desk and swayed his trunk from side to side a few times, left to right and right to left.

'Well, well, a fine day for the time of year,' he said, reverting to his anglicised form of Dutch. 'But we'll start with a drop of whisky, just a drop.'

He ducked under the desk and re-emerged with a bottle and a tooth glass.

'Just *one* drop of whisky in the morning works wonders!'

He filled the glass almost to the brim, then drank it down, slurping audibly. After taking a deep breath he exhaled so vigor-ously through his moustache that a cloud of alcohol formed in front of his face. Then he lit a cigarette without offering one to Osewoudt. The index and middle fingers of his right hand were darkly stained with nicotine; he was in the habit of holding the cigarette with the lit end cupped in his hand, so that the palm too was stained.

'We shan't keep you here long,' he said. 'You must return to your liberated homeland as soon as possible. I just happen to be interested in a few outstanding questions, which you may be able to shed some light on. Does the name Elly Berkelbach Sprenkel sound familiar, by any chance?'

'Yes.'

'Very good. How did you track her down?'

'I didn't track her down. She telephoned me. She had been given my address in England.'

'In England? Back then? I'm afraid you weren't quite as well known here then as you are now,' he said. Then, turning to his assistant, 'Got that, Percy?'

'Yes, sir.'

But Percy did not touch the typewriter keys.

'Thank you, Percy. So she had your address. How did you find out she was a British agent?'

'She told me herself. She needed a bed for the night. I found her one.'

'So you did, so you did. A fine bed, too, if I may say so, because she is still fast asleep. Forgive me for saying so, but I find your sense of humour a touch cynical.'

'What are you talking about? She was denounced by a senior official of the Dutch Railways. He went to the German police after she'd approached him for information. There wasn't anything I could do about it, was there?'

'Of course there wasn't. You are giving me information I have already gathered from other sources. But there is a subtle difference in your version. The fact is, you were at the time already working for the Gestapo. You went to see Mr de Vos Clootwijk, you said you were a German agent; you threatened him and forced him to go to the authorities – not that it was necessary, really, as your people were already in the know. You don't mind me making this slight correction to your story, do you?'

'Haven't you seen the reports of what I told Captain Slum? For the past three months I've been interrogated by a different person every week. But it's as I said it was: I took Elly Berkelbach Sprenkel to an uncle of mine in Amsterdam. On my way home afterwards I heard that my mother and wife had been arrested by the Germans. So I didn't go home, I ended up with some people in Leiden who provided me with fake papers, including the German police card. When Elly Berkelbach Sprenkel was arrested after that bloke de Vos Clootwijk turned her in, I paid him a visit in Utrecht to give him what for. First I pretended to be from the Gestapo, only to get him to tell me the whole story himself. I showed him the fake police card Meinarends had given me in Leiden. I had originally planned to lure him out of his house and shoot him in the dark. Then I thought he wasn't important enough. Now I'm sorry I didn't.'

'There are some slight discrepancies between his statement and yours. He claims you paid him a visit before Elly Berkelbach Sprenkel got in touch with him. It was from you that he heard she would be coming and also that the Germans would be watching for his reaction to her visit.'

'He's lying.'

'Well now, aren't you getting rather carried away? Why would a senior Railways official lie about something like that?'

'Why wouldn't he? What I've told you is the truth.'

'Telling the truth is one thing, establishing it quite another.'

'I told Captain Slum all about the set of photos, too.'

'Of course you did. Have you got that, Percy?'

'Most certainly, sir.'

He tapped a few keys with one finger.

'Thank you.'

At this point Colonel Smears had a coughing fit. His right hand, with the cigarette stub pinched between four fingers and thumb, rested on the desktop while his left was clapped limply to his mouth.

'You are the highest authority to have interrogated me,' said Osewoudt. 'I am entirely innocent. I am merely trying to answer your questions as fully as I can. For my own sake.'

The colonel cleared his throat noisily, leaned back in his chair and wiped his moustache with a large white handkerchief, which he inspected closely after each wipe.

'Well now, this uncle of yours. Where is he?'

'He was arrested by the Germans.'

'What, him too? Along with Elly Sprenkel?'

'No, a short while later.'

'And where is he now?'

'How should I know? He's dead, probably, or he may still be stuck in Germany somewhere. You are in a position to track him down, not me.'

'There's a limit to what we can do. We're up to our ears as it is.'

'Then why don't you summon Dorbeck? I've told you people umpteen times that he knows exactly how it all went, that it was Elly Berkelbach Sprenkel who contacted me and not the other way round. She had a photo with her which she'd been given in England, it was a picture which Dorbeck had asked me to develop and which I had sent off in the post a few days before, to an address given to me by Dorbeck.'

'Summoning the supposed Dorbeck would not be as simple as it sounds.'

'Why not?'

'According to what you have told me, Dorbeck was working for one of our organisations. If that was indeed the case it probably still is. So I would have to obtain permission from his immediate superior to hear what he has to say.'

'Well, why don't you, then?'

'It is impossible. If my theory is right, Dorbeck's chief would be bound by the Official Secrets Act. Meaning he would be under no obligation to provide information about the people he employs.'

'So what are you going to do?'

'Well. It is a little difficult to say. I have the impression, though no more than an impression, that your compatriots also have certain matters they wish to discuss with you.'

'It's no good discussing with me. Everything I did was according to instructions from Dorbeck. It was Dorbeck who got me out of German detention. Why would he have done that if I was the kind of traitor you take me for? When Dorbeck rescued me, my photo and description had been circulating for months, both in the liberated zone and among the Allied forces.'

'Even that is not as contradictory as you might think. It is conceivable that you were not so much a *prisoner* of the Germans as their *protégé*. It is likewise conceivable that Dorbeck got you out of that protective environment to make sure you wouldn't escape justice!'

'But in that case he could have shot me there and then.'

'Now, now, you're getting carried away again!'

'He was the one who gave me a disguise. A nurse's uniform.'

'How charming. Got that, Percy?'

When Osewoudt was taken back to his cell, the warder handed him a parcel that had already been opened. He couldn't discover who had sent it. It contained a small loaf of Dutch gingerbread. He took a bite and his teeth hit on something hard. What was it? A bit of wire? No, a fretsaw. He pulled it from the loaf.

He had often heard and read about various kinds of implements being smuggled into prisons so that inmates can escape by sawing through thick iron bars or making holes in ceilings. He looked around the cell: the walls were made of granite blocks, which were so big that it would be impossible for a single man to dislodge them, even if they hadn't been cemented. He looked at the window: it was barred inside and out, and moreover far too high up.

He bent the saw double and used it to pick the wax from his ears.

The warder who brought him his rations spotted the saw, said nothing, and didn't bother to confiscate it.

Osewoudt asked for a pen and paper and was given one folio sheet and a biro.

Nevergold Prison, Manchester<br>29 June, 1945

Your Majesty!

For the last time I seek to draw your attention to the fact that I have been kept a prisoner without cause since my arrival here over two and a half months ago. This treatment is wholly uncalled for, indeed mistreatment would be a better word.

On 5 April of this year I escaped from German captivity with the help of a secret agent by the name of Dorbeck. This British agent provided me with a nurse's uniform to disguise my identity. On 6 April I travelled in disguise from Amsterdam to Dordrecht, where I appealed to the priest of the Church of St Ignatius for help. This priest gave me shelter for one day. On the night of 7 April I was fetched by members of the Dutch Resistance and taken to Willemsdorp. From there other people, whose names I do not know, took me across the Hollands Diep in a rowing boat, then left me with a doctor by the name of Sikkens in Hogezwaluwe. Upon my arrival there at 4 a.m. the doctor offered me a bite to eat and a few hours later drove me in his car to Breda, where I reported to the army headquarters at the Graaf Adolf barracks. I was taken into custody at once. Believing this to be a normal security measure, I hardly protested against my arrest. That same night I was put on a plane to England. On that flight I learned that my picture and description had been circulating in the liberated zone for several months, and that I was a wanted man. The only possible explanation for this is that the Gestapo had put some trumped-up information into the hands of the Allied intelligence services in order to arouse suspicion against me.

That, at any rate, was what I thought initially, given that the Germans in the occupied zone had already issued a warrant for my arrest in 1944, at which time the cinema newsreels showed my picture along with my personal details, accusing me of robbery with assault.

It comes as a great shock to learn that certain people in the Netherlands have been making damaging statements about me which are based on nothing but lies and distortions of the truth.

I believe it is my given right to be heard by the Dutch authorities regarding these matters. In 1940, after the German invasion, I put myself at the service of the nation entirely voluntarily. Relying on the competence of a Dutch military cadre, I blindly carried out the instructions and orders issued to me by Dorbeck, who was an officer in the Dutch army. Many of my associates and friends, my mother, my uncle and my fiancée, have been murdered by the Germans. This might not have happened had I, like so many Dutchmen, stayed on the sidelines.

I am well aware that I was only a small cog in a much larger wheel. Finding myself in a situation where I am

unable to make this understood to those interrogating me
is causing me great anguish. The exact course of events
is not known to me, and never was. It is Dorbeck who
has the information, but it seems he cannot be found. The
British Secret Service refuses to disclose his where-
abouts . . .

A week later, the warder showed a gentleman with a black briefcase into his cell. The warder left the door open.

'I have come from the Netherlands Embassy in London in connection with the letter you wrote to the queen.'

The warder returned with an upholstered chair for the visitor to sit on, after which he went away, locking the door behind him.

'Has my letter been sent on?' asked Osewoudt.

'Sent on? Do you really expect us to forward letters written by people like you to the queen? What did you think? That a Resistance fighter in a German concentration camp could write to Hitler and complain about his situation?'

'I can tell,' said Osewoudt, 'that you have never been a prisoner of the Germans. No, not you. But I have. The Germans kept me in prison for nine whole months. They beat me about the face – look, you can see the scar. And may I add that I wouldn't dream of comparing the queen to Hitler.'

'I did not come here to listen to your quibbles, but because we are subjects of a state where the rule of law prevails. There can, however, be no question of passing on your letter to Her Majesty. What's all this nonsense about your fiancée having been killed by the Germans? To our knowledge, you were married to Maria Roelofje Nauta on 25 August, 1939. Your wife was found dead in her tobacco shop in Voorschoten on 6 April. You were not divorced from her. How can you have had a fiancée?'

'Oh,' said Osewoudt, 'was my wife found dead in Voorschoten on 6 April?'

'Don't change the subject! I am referring to your so-called fiancée. How dare you mention such a relationship in a letter to the queen?'

'Should I have written "my mistress", then?'

'You should not have written at all. You are doing yourself no service behaving so impertinently. I have some news for you: you are to be returned to the Netherlands in a day or two, and will then learn all the charges that have been made against you. The list of crimes is appalling!'

'Can you tell me how my wife died?'

The gentleman cast an eye over his papers.

'No, it doesn't say.'

'My wife denounced me to the Germans; does it say anything about that?'

'No.'

'She was living with the son of one of the neighbours, a Nazi. Doesn't it say anything about that either?'

'No, no mention of that either. Besides, it is no concern of mine. I only came here to explain to you that the sort of letter you wrote does not qualify for consideration. You are entitled to information concerning such a decision, but that is all you are entitled to.'

He put his papers into his briefcase and rose to his feet.

Osewoudt, too, rose and took a step towards his visitor. The man's eyes widened with fear and the briefcase almost slid from under his elbow.

'Keep your hands off me!' he shouted. 'Don't do anything foolish now. Where's the alarm bell?'

'I have no intention of laying a finger on you! Look, I'm putting my hands in my pockets. But you know as well as I do that without Dorbeck the truth will never come out. Where is

Dorbeck? Why has Dorbeck not been traced? Surely there is something you could to do help? You could put pressure on the British to get a statement from Dorbeck! I've done nothing wrong. I've been behind bars for months on end. In the meantime Holland has been liberated, the war has ended and I'm stuck here. I want to cooperate in every possible way with every possible enquiry. But isn't there some way you can get me out of here?'

The door opened. Like a shadow, the gentleman slipped past the warder and was gone.

The torpedo-catcher's siren blasted three times in succession, shrill and piercing like a bird of prey. The wild pulsations of the propeller-shaft casing, which extended down the middle of the steel compartment, travelled on through all the surrounding steel. Then silence. The tin water bottle hanging on the wall no longer swung to and fro. The electric light went out for a moment, then glowed again, but at no more than half strength. The deep throbbing that had filled Osewoudt's ears for he knew not how long did not come back. A diesel engine rumbled in a remote part of the vessel.

Osewoudt wiped his sticky hands on each other, and swallowed. Then he took a gulp of stale water from the tin bottle and replaced it on its hook. Footsteps. More footsteps. Finally footsteps becoming very loud then stopping abruptly. The rattle of keys against the steel hatch.

Two military policemen in khaki burst in. 'You're coming with us, Osewoudt,' they said, and put a black sack over his head.

He followed them through the steel innards of the vessel, a pair of handcuffs dangling from each wrist. Peering down his nose, he caught a glimpse of daylight. Underfoot steel plates gave way to steel gratings. Then up some stairs: wooden steps edged with strips of brass. The air he inhaled became cooler and fresher. He glimpsed a wooden floor, then wood with raised bars across it. A sagging sensation at the knees told him that this was a downward ramp. They stepped on to a paved surface, and finally he caught the smell of a car.

'Watch it! Up the ladder!' said the policeman on his left.

He went up the ladder. A door was slammed. The hand-cuffs were removed from his left wrist, then his hands were fastened behind his back with the remaining pair. Finally they pulled the sack off his head and left without a word.

He was sitting on a wooden bench in the back of some kind of prison van. There was an air vent in the roof and a small barred side window of frosted glass.

He heard the engine start up, felt the vehicle drive off. He had lost track of time, but noticed that it was getting dark.

'Where am I?' he asked when he was let out of the van.

'In Drente. Camp Eighth Exloërmond.'

It was long after sunset. The open air smelled of rotten eggs. He could make out a few soldiers standing about, armed with Sten guns. He saw a high barbed-wire fence glaringly lit by sodium lamps. That was all he got to see before they hustled him into a building, down a passage and into a room.

The desk was piled high with files. A man with black hair slicked down from a central parting, a high forehead and slack, lined cheeks, pointed to a straight-backed wooden chair and said: 'Sit down, Osewoudt. I am Inspector Selderhorst. Let's begin by reviewing your case from A to Z. It's a complete shambles.'

He waved at the stack of files.

'No one can make sense of it any more. I want to give you every chance to justify yourself.'

'So what do you want to know?'

'There's that business with the photos to start with. How did you get them?'

'It was that day in May 1940 when the Germans invaded. Dorbeck turned up in my tobacco shop. I had a notice in my window saying that films could be left with me for developing and printing. Dorbeck gave me a film and said he'd be back to pick it up.'

'And did he come back?'

'No. It wasn't until much later, in 1944, that I got a note from him saying I should send them to a post-office box in The Hague. PO Box 234, it was. So that's what I did.'

'How do you know the photos arrived?'

'I posted them early and then went to The Hague myself later that afternoon. I kept watch by the post-office boxes.'

'Why did you do that?'

'I was hoping to speak to Dorbeck.'

'And did you?'

'No. A Salvation Army woman came to open the box. I went after her to find out who she was, but when I went out into the street she had vanished. The next day I went back to the same post office, hoping someone would show. No one did. Not the following days either. Later that evening I received a phone call from Elly Berkelbach Sprenkel. I met her at the yellow-tram terminal in Voorburg. She had one of the photos with her to prove her identity. She said it had been given to her in England. I found that hard to believe, as she had arrived from England the previous night and there could hardly have been time for the picture to get there before she left. But I did believe, and rightly as it turned out, that she had come from England. So I assumed she must have got the picture in Holland but didn't want to tell me who had given it to her. I never did find out who it was. I never had an opportunity to ask Dorbeck, either.'

'Stick to the point, will you? How many photos were there in all?'

'There were three.'

'Three? But there are eight on a roll.'

'Several of them didn't come out.'

'Do you remember what those photos were of?'

'Yes. A snowman wearing a helmet. Three soldiers in pyjamas and gas masks. One soldier manning an anti-aircraft gun.'

'Did you send off the negatives as well?'

Selderhorst rummaged among the documents, glancing enquiringly at Osewoudt now and then.

'No,' said Osewoudt. 'I kept the negatives.'

Selderhorst opened a large envelope and shook the contents on to the desk. They were the photos Osewoudt had developed – multiple copies of each.

'Are these them, by any chance?'

'Where did they come from? How is that possible, because I—'

'They were in one of the German dossiers! The Germans used them to infiltrate underground organisations. They gave them to double agents to identity themselves.'

'I can't help that. The Germans must have found the negatives when they arrested my mother and my wife.'

'Well, well. Did you come across these photos again at any time?'

'Yes. Moorlag gave me one that had been delivered to the shop in an envelope, on the day they came for my mother and my wife. I was away, taking Elly Berkelbach Sprenkel to Amsterdam.'

'Which was that?'

'The one of the three soldiers with gas masks. On the back there was a phone number which I was to ring a few days later. I tore it up straightaway.'

'What about the picture Elly Sprenkel had?'

'I took it from her. I tore that one up too.'

'Were there any others?'

'No.'

Selderhorst slid the photos back into the envelope, put it aside and took up another file. His suit was a dingy grey, his shirt unwashed and his tie twisted like the skin of an eel.

'A few days after the time we are discussing, a girl was arrested by the German police on the train from Lunteren to Amersfoort. Her name was Annelies van Doormaal. She was wearing the uniform of a National Youth Storm leader. This Annelies van Doormaal turned out to have one of the photos you mentioned — the one of the soldier in pyjama trousers manning an anti-aircraft gun. It says so here, in a German dossier! The identity of the girl was not established until later, because she committed suicide by taking poison almost immediately after her arrest. How did the girl get that picture?'

'I don't know.'

'You don't know, Osewoudt? But she must have been with you when she was arrested! The pair of you had murdered a National Youth Storm leader that very afternoon, on the heath in Lunteren! The body was found in the woods a month later. It was the same afternoon that Lagendaal and his wife were shot. Yes or no?'

'Yes.'

'How did Annelies van Doormaal come to be in your company?'

'I told you: there was a phone number written on the back of the second photo. I rang the number from a telephone box in Amsterdam. I got Dorbeck on the line. Dorbeck told me to go to the waiting room at Amersfoort station at such-and-such a time, where I would find a girl who would identify herself with a picture. I did as he said. That girl was Annelies van Doormaal, so you now tell me.'

'So how did she get hold of that photo? Why didn't you take it from her?'

'As I remember, she only said she had the photo. She didn't actually show it to me. I was too nervous later on to think of asking for it.'

Selderhorst planted his elbows on the table and, bowing his head low, brushed his hair back with both hands. Then he looked up.

'Ah, Osewoudt. But there is another hypothesis. According to that hypothesis, the girl called Annelies van Doormaal was in possession of the picture not so that you would know who she was, but so that the Germans would know. The Germans had to find it on her so they would know they had the right person. Because there were lots of girls wearing the National Youth Storm uniform at the time. We seem to be getting somewhere. It was you who planted the photo on her.'

'How could I have done that? As I told you before, by that time I had already sent off all the photos in the post.'

'You said yourself there wasn't enough time for them to have got to England.'

'No, but I'm sure Dorbeck received them. He sent a Salvation Army woman to collect the envelope. I saw her with my own eyes!'

'And what if Dorbeck never existed? What if you dreamed him up, like everything else?'

'That's ridiculous. If that's what you think, there's no point continuing this conversation.'

'Ridiculous?'

Selderhorst patted the stack of files.

'There are hundreds of documents here with incriminating information! If I were to discuss them all with you we'd be at it for years. The most horrific incidents are reported in these files, and not a word about Dorbeck! I can pick any one at random! At random!'

He pulled another file from the stack. He flicked through it briefly.

'Ever heard of Labare?'

'Yes, I stayed in his house.'

'Labare is dead. How did that happen?'

'He was shot by the Germans.'

'Exactly. Arrested by the Germans in his own house, a few hours after you arrived. How come they arrested him and not you?'

'I got away when I was taken outside by one of the Germans. I used to do judo, you see. I floored the German and jumped into the canal in front of the house. Half an hour later they caught me anyway.'

'Well, well. Where had you been that evening before you turned up on Labare's doorstep?'

'In Zuidwal hospital. I'd been rescued by a group of Resistance people.'

'Rescued by a group of Resistance people . . .'

'Yes. Four men with a car. One of them was called Cor, another one was called Uncle Kees. I never saw them again.'

In the meantime Selderhorst had picked up the phone. 'Yes, you can send him in now,' he barked into the mouthpiece.

'Rescued by the Resistance,' he said, putting the phone down. 'I don't know whether I ought to feel sorry for you, or whether you're just plain lying. Who gave the order for you to be rescued? The elusive Dorbeck, I suppose?'

'No, not Dorbeck. I asked him about that later, but it was the first he'd heard of it, he said, he hadn't been involved.'

'So whose idea was it, do you think?'

'There are two possibilities. First I thought it would have been someone who knew my girlfriend Mirjam Zettenbaum, or who knew Meinarends, then I thought it more likely that a friend of that doctor who treated me in the hospital was behind it.'

There was a knock on the door and Selderhorst's eyes left Osewoudt. A soldier ushered a German into the room. The German wore a uniform stripped of its markings. There were also a few buttons missing. He didn't wear boots, but a pair of old gym shoes.

'Do you know who this is, Osewoudt?'

Osewoudt looked at the man, the hands, the face. The German glared back at him, then at Selderhorst.

'I've seen so many Germans,' said Osewoudt. 'I may or may not have seen this one before, I'm not sure.'

'I'll tell you who he is. His name is Gustaf Malknecht. Does that ring any bells?'

'No, none at all.'

'He was doing the typing on the days you were interrogated by Wülfing and Ebernuss.'

'Oh. I really can't remember.'

'Malknecht! Tell us how Osewoudt was rescued from Zuidwal hospital.'

Malknecht stood to attention, his little finger aligned with the seam of his trousers. Osewoudt sat forward on the edge of his seat, his back arched in suspense, his mouth half open.

'I was there when Osewoudt was first brought in to see Wülfing. Wülfing confronted Osewoudt with Roorda. Roorda recognised Osewoudt, but Osewoudt refused to recognise Roorda. Then Wülfing slapped Osewoudt about a bit. Afterwards I heard that Wülfing had made a deal with Ebernuss. It was Ebernuss' idea. Ebernuss went to see Osewoudt and said: dear me, how dreadfully they've mistreated you! . . . you need to go to hospital! That was that. Osewoudt was taken off to Zuidwal hospital. We carried out the so-called rescue the same day. *Eine tolle Geschichte!*'

'Were you there, Malknecht?'

'No, not me. All I did was type up the reports of the interrogations, I wasn't particularly interested in Osewoudt.

I didn't hear about the so-called rescue until later. It was talked about, because of course we didn't normally go in for that sort of thing with prisoners. It was like this: Wülfing was sure Osewoudt had met Roorda, but Ebernuss was not so sure. Then Ebernuss said: why don't we let Osewoudt escape so we can see where he goes? There's no risk, because we'll get him back quite easily thanks to the 500 guilders reward. We may be able to catch some others while we're at it. I clearly remember Osewoudt being part of an extremely complicated plot.'

'Then why didn't they simply discharge him?'

'That would have looked suspicious to Osewoudt's friends, obviously. They would have cut him off immediately. So they had to think of something else. In the end they decided to stage a rescue operation. It was carried out by two Dutch provocateurs working for Ebernuss – Massing and Kolkgoot – and there were also two Germans, policemen in civvies.'

Osewoudt leaped up from his chair.

'Where's Roorda? Where's Roorda? It was Dorbeck Roorda met, not me! It was *true* that I didn't recognise Roorda. It was the honest truth! I had never seen him before. But Roorda recognised me. Because it was Dorbeck Roorda had spoken to, it was Dorbeck!'

Malknecht looked straight ahead, saying nothing.

'Right then,' said Selderhorst. 'Tell him where Roorda is.'

'Roorda was shot when he tried to escape.'

'He's lying.'

'Don't you believe that Roorda is dead?'

'Yes, I can believe that he's dead. But not the rest, not what he said about how I got out of that hospital!'

'There is no doubt about that,' said Malknecht. 'But there is more. Wülfing believed Osewoudt had information, presumably because Ebernuss had given him that idea. Ebernuss and

Osewoudt became very pally later on. So it's likely that Osewoudt was in on it. Massing and Kolkgoot drove him from the hospital to Leiden, where he asked them to drop him in a suburb. Obviously they kept him in their sights, and Osewoudt went straight to Labare's house. That was how we knew where to strike. Next morning we not only had Osewoudt back, we also had his Jewish girlfriend, the Zettenbaum girl, as well as Labare, Suyling, and a teenage boy called Robert Meier, who was a half-Jew.'

Osewoudt was now shaking on his chair. He could hear the soles of his shoes tapping the floor. He clamped his right hand on his left, but was unable to stop his limbs from trembling.

'Surely you don't believe,' he moaned, 'that I could have shopped my girlfriend just to do Ebernuss a favour?'

'Well, Malknecht?'

'I can't say. I don't know what promises Ebernuss might have made to him. They were very close in the end. Maybe Ebernuss said: if you do this for me, then I'll make sure you get through. And he did, as you see.' Malknecht pointed to Osewoudt. 'By the spring of 1945 Ebernuss had had it up to here with the war. He'd lost all hope. He said as much on various occasions. One day he was gone, on 5 April, that was. Deserted. Took Osewoudt with him, too.'

'Is that true, Osewoudt?'

'Partly true. Ebernuss asked me to put him in touch with Dorbeck.'

'So Ebernuss was aware of Dorbeck's existence?'

'He had found out. He was bound to find out! I'd already been in prison for months! Dorbeck was not in prison. In the course of his enquiries, Ebernuss must have come across descriptions of someone who looked like me. Maybe Roorda started having doubts, too, later on. Maybe Ebernuss realised that the picture they circulated with my name attached was not a picture of me. Because when I was arrested my hair was dyed black, and the man in the photograph had dark hair, but after I'd been in prison for a bit it obviously became clear that I was actually fair-haired.'

'What happened to Ebernuss?'

'He's dead. I poisoned him. I poisoned him myself! He took me to Amsterdam in his car, to a house at Lijnbaansgracht, which he knew certain people were using as a meeting place. He did say something about deserting, but I didn't take him seriously. We were allowed in, because I knew the tenant — Moorlag. Ebernuss sat down, drinks of genever were passed round. I went to the kitchen and found Dorbeck there. He gave me the poison in a Rizla packet, and told me to put it in Ebernuss' drink. So I did. Afterwards Dorbeck took Ebernuss' car and drove me to a house in Bernard Kochstraat. That's when he gave me the nurse's outfit. He took my own clothes away as he was afraid I'd refuse to wear the disguise, and he feared for my safety. He said he'd come back later to take me through the lines to the liberated zone, but he never turned up. That was the last time I saw him. He just sent a note saying my girlfriend was in labour at the Emma Clinic.'

'Not that old story again,' said Selderhorst.

'If Marianne were still alive, she could confirm all this.'

'She is still alive.'

'Where is she, then? Why don't you track her down?'

'She's gone to Palestine. She's in a kibbutz.'

'In a what?'

'In a kibbutz! Don't you know what a kibbutz is? Do you or don't you? A kibbutz is a farm surrounded by trenches and barbed wire, and around that a horde of Arabs armed to the teeth. How do you expect us to get her out of her kibbutz and answer questions?'

'What about Moorlag? Where's Moorlag?'

'Moorlag's body was found back in May, in Spiegelstraat. Shot through the heart. D'you know, Osewoudt, I'm not so sure you're telling the truth about poisoning Ebernuss!'

'What did you say? Is Moorlag dead? But then that means everyone who ever knew Dorbeck is dead!'

'Precisely! They're all dead, and you're the only one who's still alive.'

'How dare you make insinuations like that! One day you'll be ashamed you ever detained me. Someone like Dorbeck, who did so much, who went all over throughout the war, here and in England, who met hundreds of people – someone like that can't just vanish without trace. That's not what I'm worried about. But to suggest I connived in my own so-called rescue from that hospital is ridiculous. If I had, why would I have tried to escape that night when they surrounded the house and arrested Labare? I fled down the street half naked. They fired at me with machine guns. I jumped into the canal and swam to the other side. I ran to a house and rang the bell, but it was too late – the Germans had followed my wet footprints.'

'Perhaps you were doing it all just for show, and that's why you weren't hit. They were obviously firing over your head!'

'For show? Go and ask the people whose bell I rang, they'll tell you what sort of state I was in! Why don't you go and ask them?'

'Good idea. What street did they live in? What was the number of the house?'

'I didn't notice the name of the street. I wasn't familiar with that part of Leiden. It was a street with a bend, like a crescent. I'd be able to find the house easily enough if I were back in the neighbourhood. It was a house with a porch.'

The next morning at about eleven he was taken from his cell and shoved into a waiting car.

He had to sit in the back, next to Spuybroek. Osewoudt was not handcuffed; he had been given a clean shirt and even a tie. Only Spuybroek was in uniform. Selderhorst was at the wheel, in his shabby grey suit. If it hadn't been for the escort of two helmeted and armed outriders, they might have been going for a jaunt.

Even the sun was shining when they arrived in Leiden three hours later.

'Why are you grinning?' asked Spuybroek.

Spuybroek was a young MP, roughly the same age as Osewoudt.

Osewoudt said: 'Because this is my first look at the fatherland since the liberation. See that? The funny little old tram's still running, with the same old sign on the front saying OEGst-GEEst with the same old variation in type size. No change there.'

He looked left and right.

'Turn left here!' he cried. 'Don't go over the bridge!'

The motorcyclists were already halfway across the bridge. Selderhorst braked and hooted twice. Then he turned left past Dingjan's Steam Laundry, and drove up Zoeterwoudsesingel.

'Labare's house is exactly on the first bend to the right,' said Osewoudt.

The motorcyclists caught up again and overtook them.

'There, on the corner, that's it!'

Selderhorst sounded the horn again and then parked by the canal, under a tree. The motorcyclists swerved round on the asphalt and stopped, one in front of the car and one behind. They remained astride their vehicles with the engines running.

Selderhorst got out, followed by Spuybroek and Osewoudt.

Osewoudt raised his clenched fists and stretched his arms, taking deep breaths.

'Watch out,' Selderhorst said. 'He knows judo.'

Spuybroek said: 'Really? So do I.'

'You too?'

Osewoudt and Spuybroek stood facing each other. Spuybroek was more than a head taller than Osewoudt. They bowed, made feints, then grabbed each other's hands and pushed, their arms quivering with exertion. Osewoudt's forehead was covered with sweat, but the tension in his arms snapped. Spuybroek pulled him over his hip, swung him through the air like a lasso and laid him carefully on the road.

'Have you two finished?' Selderhorst said.

Osewoudt scrambled to his feet, gasping and coughing. He wiped the sweat from his face with the sleeve of his jacket.

'I'm out of practice,' he said. 'Besides, my feet hurt. In the old days I had my shoes made to measure.'

Selderhorst surveyed Labare's former home from top to bottom. It had been converted into some sort of office; there were no curtains over the bay windows. An array of drawing boards could be seen on the first floor.

'Ah,' said Selderhorst, 'so you were in better form back then, when you dealt with that German, eh?'

'I gave him a hip throw and lobbed him over the railing. Their van was parked right here, and I crept behind it and then dashed across, in that direction . . .' Osewoudt demonstrated his moves. He crossed the road from the house towards the canal. He pointed to the grass sloping down to the water and the clump of rhododendrons on the bank.

'I went into the water just past those rhododendrons.'

'But this is the widest part of the canal,' said Selderhorst, staring at the tall weeping willows on the other side.

'I didn't swim across, the water wasn't deep enough.'

'Right. So when you got to the other side you climbed up on to the road again?'

'Yes, and then I went through the park. I'm not sure which way, because it was dark. There were bits falling from the trees, brought down by bullets.'

'Right. I suppose the street where you rang that doorbell must be over there, beyond all those trees?'

'Yes, a fairly narrow street with a bend. I don't know what it was called. I don't know this part of town very well.'

'Let's go and take a look. See if we can find your street.'

Selderhorst held the passenger door open, the motorcyclists revved their engines and put them in gear.

'Which way do we go?' Selderhorst asked. 'This way or that way?'

'The two bridges are equally far, which was lucky for me as it meant that the Germans had to make quite a long detour. If those people hadn't held me up, I'd have got away.'

They were now driving on the other side, which was called Plantage for part of the way, and then Plantsoen.

'Here, all these trees — is this the park you ran across?'

'Yes.'

'It's quite a distance from the canal to the houses. Where's that street of yours? I don't see any street. Here, directly opposite Labare's house, there's no side street at all!'

They drove past the stately old houses with large front gardens. No spaces between them, not a single side street.

'No sign of your street,' said Selderhorst. 'You ran a pretty long way in your bare feet, I must say. Was it here by any chance?'

He braked.

Osewoudt looked out. The street was called Rijnstraat. It was straight, and led to a bridge.

'No, this can't be it. It was a street with a bend, and I didn't see a bridge at the end of it either.'

Selderhorst put in the clutch.

'When people get jittery they run faster than they realise,' said Osewoudt.

'How about this street, then? It's called Kraayerstraat.'

'No! Damn it, this one's straight, too, and it has a bridge at the end of it like the other one! They're all the same!'

They turned around and drove all the way back along Plantage.

'What about this one?'

Selderhorst didn't bother to stop the car, but slowed and turned into the street. The two motorcyclists buzzed about them like giant bumble bees.

'This one's called Levendaal. Was it here?'

It was a straight thoroughfare and so wide that it must once have had a canal running down the middle. On one side stood a row of small houses with stepped gables, hundreds of years old, on the other side were factories.

'Not this one either, eh?' said Selderhorst. He accelerated, turned right into Rijnstraat, where they had already been, and thus they came to Hoge Woerd.

'This it, then?'

'No, this is Hoge Woerd. This is where Meinarends used to live, a tram runs down it. I'd have known this street by the tramlines, even at night. It was a different street, one with a bend, and the house was a house with a porch.'

'A house with a porch . . . No houses with porches as far as I can see.'

Selderhorst put in the clutch, reversed, stopped, put in the clutch again. Osewoudt poked his head out of the window. He read the name: Vierde Binnenvestgracht. It was not a canal, but an alleyway. There was a bend in the alley, but it was more like a sharp angle than a bend. Selderhorst took a right into Rijnstraat and then a left into Tweede Haverstraat.

'Well, is it this one, Osewoudt?'

'No, not this one either.'

'Damn it, Osewoudt, where can it be?'

Selderhorst accelerated; they screeched round one corner after another, back into Kraayerstraat, Tweede Gorterstraat, Derde Gorterstraat, Pakhuisstraat, until they arrived once more in the wide street called Levendaal.

'Damn you, Osewoudt, I'm getting fed up with this! You spin all these yarns and expect me to take you at your word. Who do you think you are? What are you playing at? Your case was wrapped up long ago, you're a liar, a cheat and a traitor, but since we live under the rule of law nowadays, I've done my level best to discover something in your defence. But you? You've been taking me for a ride. All this stuff about a street with a bend and a house with a porch. I bet you've never even set foot in this neighbourhood. There's no street with a bend, and no houses with porches either! Do you see a porch, Spuybroek?'

Selderhorst was so enraged that he seemed unable to drive. He banged his fists on the steering wheel.

'I just don't get it,' wailed Osewoudt. 'I was panicking – which way could I have been going? It must have been somewhere around here, it's got to be, but I don't recognise a thing. If anyone had told me there was a rough area so close to those posh houses by the park I wouldn't have believed them. How can this be? Where's that blasted street? It's got to be here somewhere.'

He opened the car door before Spuybroek could stop him, and got out. But he didn't run for cover. He went to the middle of the road and stood there, scanning the stepped gables for any recognisable feature. Then he looked across the way to the factory buildings. The motorcyclists were on either side of him, engines sputtering.

'Everything I've ever done is slipping through my fingers! The people I worked with during the war are all either dead or missing, and even the streets I used to know no longer exist. It's beyond belief. I feel I'm in a different world, where no one will believe me. What am I to do? How in God's name can I ever justify myself at this rate?'

Osewoudt paced to and fro. The motorcyclists revved in anticipation.

Then Spuybroek took hold of Osewoudt's left hand and left elbow and straightened the arm, but without hurting him.

'No one said you could get out of the car,' he said.

Muttering under his breath, Osewoudt allowed himself to be led back to the car. He got in; Spuybroek got in beside him and pulled the door shut.

Selderhorst said nothing, put in the clutch and drove off. He drove like a madman, racing down alleyways with NO ENTRY signs, screeching round corners until finally they found themselves in Hoge Woerd again. From now on he slowed down at everything resembling a lane or side street.

'Was it here, Osewoudt? Here? Wielmakersstraat? No? Not good enough?'

He drove on.

'What about here? Nieuwebrugsteeg? Was it here by any chance? Anyone see a house with a porch?'

'No, not just yet,' said Spuybroek. 'But we're bound to see

one round the next corner, aren't we, Osewoudt? Round the next corner, eh, because we don't want to be going round too many more corners, do we, or we'll be in a different part of town altogether!'

Selderhorst stopped at an alley called Koenesteeg, and then again at the next one, called Krauwelsteeg.

'Well Osewoudt? Any ideas?'

Osewoudt looked dutifully in all directions. At the entrance to this alley was a sign saying NO BICYCLES and further along a shed with a sign saying BICYCLE PARK. Those were the only distinctive features in Krauwelsteeg.

They drove on, and passed the house where Meinarends used to live.

'Look!' cried Osewoudt. 'That's where Meinarends lived. There's a life-size picture of a duck on the fanlight over the front door. See? I told you I wasn't making it all up!'

'If it had been a picture of Dorbeck over that door, we might be getting somewhere!' said Spuybroek.

Selderhorst, tight-lipped, was still braking sharply at the entrance to every lane and alley.

He continued to do so even in Breestraat.

'How about this alley, Osewoudt? Plaatsteeg, is it?'

Now Spuybroek burst out with: 'Look, it's got a bend in it! Damn it, there's a bend!'

Spuybroek got out, pulling Osewoudt after him. Selderhorst also got out. People stopped and stared.

They walked into the alley; Osewoudt kept his eyes on the ground. But the sides of Plaatsteeg were for the most part wooden fencing. There were no more than three front doors, and none had a porch.

Selderhorst stood still, hitched up his trousers and took a deep breath.

'Well! Now what do you want? Do you want us to go to

Voorschoten and dig up that uniform of Dorbeck's, or shall we skip that part? Eh? Shut your trap, don't contradict me! Make up your mind, Osewoudt! Do you want us to go to Voorschoten, yes or no? But I'm warning you. If we go to Voorschoten and there's nothing there, the uniform's been eaten by maggots, or the whole back garden's vanished into thin air, then I'll see that you get a damn good hiding! I'd rather have you strung up on barbed wire than deal with any more of your nonsense! Understand?'

'I understand. I want to go to Voorschoten.'

The sun had stopped shining, great clouds were massing in the sky. The blue tram, the yellow tram – both were running again. Cows grazed in the fields.

The car followed the route of the blue tram, one motor-cyclist in front, one behind. They passed the silver factory, and as they drove into Voorschoten it started to rain. At the point where the tramlines sidle towards each other until they overlap, the first motorcyclist turned right towards the police station.

'Are you sure you'll be able to find your house, Osewoudt?'

A blue tram approached from the opposite direction, sounding its whistle. Selderhorst steered the car close to the houses to avoid the tram.

'The shop is at the other end of the high street,' said Osewoudt tonelessly. 'I'll show you where it is.'

After a minute he said: 'Stop here.'

They stopped right in front of the shop. Planks had been nailed across the door-pane and the display window had been bricked up with old bricks from a demolition site.

The rain now poured down with almost supernatural force.

Selderhorst made no move to get out. Now and then he glanced in the rear-view mirror. The motorcyclist who had gone to the police station returned. Close behind him came two policemen on ordinary bicycles. One had a spade tied to the frame.

The policemen leaned their bicycles against the shop front. The one with the spade untied it from his bicycle, the other began to break down the door. Osewoudt recognised him. He got out of the car and said: 'Officer, do you remember who I am?'

'Certainly. You're Osewoudt.'

'Do you remember that evening – it was at the start of the German occupation – when you came to the shop? There was a thunderstorm, and it was raining as hard as this. You came to check up because the light was on and the blackout blind wasn't down. Do you remember that? You had only just been posted here.'

'Yes, I remember.'

'Didn't you see someone leaving the shop?'

'It's possible.'

Osewoudt now turned to Selderhorst and said: 'That was the night Dorbeck brought me the pistol.'

Selderhorst drew a cigarette from his pocket, tapped it on his thumbnail and put it between his lips. He kept his hand over the cigarette to shield it from the rain. The door opened. Selderhorst was the first to enter.

Inside, it was less dark than you would expect for a house with bricked-up windows. The shop had been entirely gutted. There were holes in the floor, the sliding doors were open, and most of the leaded glass had gone. So had the glass in the French windows opening from the back room on to the garden. The walls were stained with soot, there had obviously been a fire, but it could not have lasted long.

The rainwater apparently collected on the flat roof and came straight down through the upper storey and out of a hole in the ceiling of the back room, in a gushing, clattering stream.

Dodging the waterfall, they headed towards the back garden.

The place was overrun with nettles and broom; it was beyond recognition.

'Well,' said Selderhorst, 'I think I'll wait inside. Tell them where to dig.'

Osewoudt took two steps into the garden, halted, and pointed to his feet.

'Here.'

The policeman swiped his spade to clear the nettles, and began to dig. Osewoudt turned up the collar of his jacket against the rain and watched closely. Spuybroek lounged in the doorway with his thumbs in his belt.

The soil was black and lumpy. The spade turned up a large bisected worm. Then a piece of newspaper.

'There it is!' Osewoudt cried. He bent down; the policeman stopped digging.

Osewoudt squatted down and continued to dig, using his hands. The newspaper disintegrated into slimy shreds at his touch. In the end he managed to pull away a handkerchief-sized piece, which he held out to Selderhorst.

Selderhorst took it and stepped outside. His shoulders darkened instantly in the rain. Both Osewoudt and the policeman were now squatting. The uniform emerged: tunic, breeches and boots. The fabric had gone completely black, and soft as a spider's web, the insignia were rusty, and also the buttons had turned green. When they picked up the boots, the soles stayed behind in the mud.

'What did I tell you?' said Osewoudt. 'Here it is: Dorbeck's uniform. See the two pips on the collar? The crossed cannons? It's the uniform of a first lieutenant in the artillery, just as I said. This is the uniform that belonged to Dorbeck. See for yourself. It'll fit me, because Dorbeck and me were the same height.'

He snatched the jacket from the policeman and held it to his chest to show that it was his size. But the fabric was so far gone that the garment fell away in rags, and they had trouble collecting the buttons, which had rolled away.

This cell wasn't really a cell. It was a good-sized space, if not high. It was half buried underground, so the only source of daylight was a double row of glass tiles just below the ceiling. An electric light covered with a griddle remained on all day. It wasn't cold, because there were thick central heating pipes passing through it, but dank due to the absence of a window. An enamel bucket with a wooden lid stood in the corner.

Things could be worse, Osewoudt thought. From time to time cries and groans sounded overhead, where a large number of political prisoners were being held. He was relieved to be on his own.

It would not be long now, he told himself, before everything came out in the open, enough at any rate for them to let him go, regardless of whether Dorbeck ever showed his face again.

He got up and took a newspaper from the small table, on which all his worldly possessions were gathered. The newspaper was much smaller than normal – no bigger than a pre-war weekly. He knew everything in it off by heart. On page three was his own picture, captioned:

500-guilders reward for anyone able to provide information concerning the individual pictured above, going by the name of DORBECK, who was sighted repeatedly during the

Occupation in various locales (Voorschoten, Amsterdam) passing himself off as an officer in the Dutch army.

A description of the wanted man followed, along with a list of official addresses where such information could be handed in.

A key turned in the lock, and Spuybroek stepped inside.

'Still reading that newspaper? Well, you'd better come with me. Apparently somebody's come forward at last with some information.'

Osewoudt stood up and coughed.

'Put a scarf on,' said Spuybroek. 'The wind's blowing from the potato-meal factory.'

Osewoudt pulled a faded but thick woollen scarf from the table and wound it around his neck.

'Who is this person who's come forward?'

'An old man in a wheelchair. Spent a long time in a concentration camp.'

Osewoudt followed Spuybroek out of the cell. They went past the central-heating furnaces, and then through another basement area filled with rusty machinery. The building was an old milk factory that had been shut down in the early days of the German occupation. They went up a flight of crumbling concrete steps and out through a small door.

An expanse of cracked concrete sloped down to a canal. The water was fenced off with barbed wire. Across the water was the potato-meal factory, beside which rose a mountain of pale, rotting foam like beaten egg white, so poisonous that dumping it in the canal was prohibited. Black clouds hung low over the flat, bare countryside. It was raining steadily; the stone terrace was full of puddles.

Osewoudt was racked with coughing again, and stood still. He cast a nervous eye over his surroundings.

On the chimney of the factory the word COOPERATIVE was still legible in a column of faint white letters. Beyond the concrete yard there was a second expanse of concrete, divided from the first by a tall screen of barbed wire. A small factory producing flavouring extracts stood there. When the weather was fine there was usually a breeze from that direction, carrying the smell of vanilla.

'I hope for your sake,' said Spuybroek, 'that we have a mild winter, otherwise you'll have a hard time of it here in the peat-cutting district.'

'I'll be out by then, with any luck.'

Osewoudt put away his handkerchief.

'Where will you go when you're free?'

Osewoudt looked about him and saw the armed guards by the entrance, who had nothing better to do than follow his every move.

'I wouldn't know,' he replied softly. 'I've no one left in the world.'

They went into a building which, had it been surrounded by a garden, would have resembled a villa. Formerly home to the factory boss, it now served as the camp offices. Spuybroek handed a note to one of the Sten-wielding guards, and they went inside.

Spuybroek knocked on a door, poked his head in, then beck-oned Osewoudt.

Osewoudt stepped inside. In the middle of the room stood a wheelchair, occupied by a man with long snowy hair. His head lolled on his chest; he seemed to be asleep. He wore a heavy black overcoat and had a rug tucked round his apparently lame legs. Beside him stood a woman, resting her hand on the back of the wheelchair. She wore a coat with a fur collar, and a nurse's cap. She had purple, cracked cheeks and hard, beady eyes, like a hen. She eyed Osewoudt with scornful interest, then gave the old man's shoulder a shake.

'Mr Nauta, here he is.'

'Uncle Bart! Is it really you?'

Osewoudt moved up close to the wheelchair.

The old man raised his head, but his chin stayed on his chest. White threads of saliva dripped on his coat, his pale tongue protruded over his bluish lower lip. He had a horrible scar at the left corner of his mouth.

He focussed his eyes on Osewoudt and said something, but he was unintelligible.

'What did you say?'

'Mr Nauta says he knows you.'

Inspector Selderhorst now stood up, took his chair and pushed the seat against the back of Osewoudt's knees.

Once seated, Osewoudt was able to put his head close to his uncle's, whose mouth emitted a vile smell, as if his entrails were rotting away.

'Uncle Bart, I didn't know you were still alive.'

Uncle Bart nodded and again tried to say something, but his lips barely moved. His voice was altered beyond recognition; the sounds he produced were more like grunts than words. Osewoudt had to strain to make out what he was saying.

'Yes, everyone's dead, but I'm still alive, Henri! I gave those Krauts a piece of my mind, so they tried to cut out my tongue. But I can still talk.'

'Uncle Bart, do you remember that I came to your house one night with a girl called Elly Berkelbach Sprenkel?'

'Yes, I remember that.'

'Do you remember what I told you about her, later on?'

'Henri, lad, I always knew you'd come to a bad end. I did everything I could for you.'

Selderhorst, too, rested his hand on the back of the wheel-chair and bent low towards Uncle Bart's ear.

'Mr Nauta, nothing has been proved against your nephew as yet. We just have a couple of things we want to put straight.'

'I never knew what the girl's name was. He came to me with a girl after he left his wife. That's all I remember, what does it matter, anyway?'

'Why were you arrested by the Germans?'

'I had a row with a German in the street.'

'Didn't they ask you about the girl? Didn't they want to know whether she had stayed in your house?'

'No. Oh, Henri, that it should have come to this! You, in this place! Your poor mother's dead. My poor daughter's dead, too. Murdered – and no one knows who did it! What a terrible world I've been living in. But there's a better world in store. I'm a socialist in every fibre of my being, I will never lose my faith in humanity. My sacrifice has not been in vain. Sacrifices are never in vain. The time will come when there will be no more war. Peace, liberty and prosperity for all men. We now have an excellent government. Before long, everybody will be receiving old-age pensions – an ideal that was regarded as a fantasy when I was young. In the longer term there will be family allowances for everybody, and that, too, is a very fine thing. We ought to pay more attention to the good things in this world. Oh, Henri, you who are still so young – that you should have thrown away your future like this!'

'Mr Nauta!' shouted Inspector Selderhorst. 'Was he working for the Germans?'

'Working for the Germans? What does it matter? All I know is that he never had ideals. Always taking the path of least resistance. I offered to send him to university, but all he wanted was to hang around in a tobacco shop doing nothing, when everyone knows that nicotine is a dangerous poison. All my life I have fought against alcohol, tobacco and the excessive consumption of meat. Total disarmament was my ideal, but as a boy he was too lazy even to address the envelopes for my temperance meetings.'

'Did you suspect him of anything?'

'I brought him up as my own son. Why would I harbour suspicions against him? The mere thought of him acting dishonourably was intolerable to me. What I do know, though, is that when his mother was arrested he made no effort whatsoever, none at all, to secure her release. I said to him: why don't you go to the Krauts, why don't you say: here I am, take me instead of my mother? But he wouldn't hear of it.'

Osewoudt got up from his chair, as if he were not close enough to Uncle Bart already. He put his hands on the armrests of the wheelchair and, leaning so far forward he seemed minded to kiss the old man on the forehead, he cried: 'Uncle Bart, I'm sorry about everything, but I am innocent of the crimes they suspect me of. Do you remember me telling you about Dorbeck?'

Uncle Bart's head fell again, but he made a final effort to lift his eyes to Osewoudt.

'I am tired. I would rather go now!'

His eyes filled with tears and he began to sob audibly, while his nurse took a folded napkin from her bag, shook it out, and wiped the dribble from his lips and his coat.

'Uncle Bart, this is extremely important to me. Do you remember the name Dorbeck?'

A kind of whimpering rose from Uncle Bart's throat, as from a dying dog after being hit by a car. He was too choked up to speak any more. His head jolted sideways and reared up again. Then it lolled to the side once more.

Osewoudt stood up straight. He held his hand out to Selderhorst.

'He's shaking his head no,' he said imploringly. 'Shaking his head, saying no, he can't remember. But what does that prove? He's an old man. The Germans have maltreated him. He can't help it that his memory's gone. What does this prove against me?'

Each morning the prisoners had to do half an hour of gymnastics in the factory yard. Running, leapfrogs, belly-crawls, rolls, vaults. It was Osewoudt's first time. He ran harder than the others, leaped further, crawled faster, rolled like a marble and vaulted higher. As a punishment the others had to keep it up for an extra quarter of an hour. Osewoudt was allowed to sit and watch.

Spuybroek wandered on to the yard, caught sight of Osewoudt and squatted down beside him.

'I've got a secret,' he said. 'Important news! Listen to this! That picture of you we published has been getting some response. Your uncle isn't the only person to have come forward. We've had word from a British army commander in Germany. They've excavated a mass grave somewhere near Oldenburg. It seems they've found a body that fits the description.'

'Hardly surprising, is it? And I suppose you want me to provide proof that it's Dorbeck? Me furnish proof? I'm the one nobody believes, remember? How can I prove anything about a corpse that's been buried for at least six months?'

'Shut up for a minute, I haven't finished. Do you remember mentioning the name Jagtman to me? Jagtman . . . the name passed on to you by Dorbeck, along with an address. You were to send photos there. Legmeerplein in Amsterdam, it was. But when you went to follow it up you found that the building had been destroyed by a plane crash the night before, and the whole Jagtman family had been killed. Wasn't that what you told me?'

'Yes, more or less.'

'Well, then. Do you know who's come forward? The family dentist. He knows exactly what the teeth of the various Jagtmans looked like. Now if the teeth of that body in Oldenburg can be matched with a member of the Jagtman family, we'll be getting somewhere. It would go some way to explaining why no one's heard of Dorbeck. Then it would be reasonable to assume that Dorbeck was an alias and that his real name was Jagtman. Let me tell you something: ever since you actually turned up the remains of that uniform, back in Voorschoten, my opinion of you has changed.'

'Oh really?' Osewoudt said. 'So tell me, if that body in Oldenburg is in fact the body of a Jagtman, how am I to explain what it's doing in Germany when the entire Jagtman family was wiped out in Amsterdam by the plane that came down on their house? Every time there's a chance, however slim, of proving that Dorbeck really existed, fresh complications arise. What use to me is a dead Dorbeck in Germany? The living Dorbeck is what I need, to come here and prove my innocence! And I'm certain he's still alive! Colonel Smears, who interrogated me in England, never denied his existence either.'

Spuybroek began to whistle, straightened up, and walked away. Osewoudt stared at the prisoners running round in circles. The sun was shining, the wind was blowing from the flavouring extracts factory, and it smelled of vanilla. If the dentist was able to identify the body in Germany, what would the consequences be?

After a shout from the sergeant in charge, one of the prisoners left the group and came to sit beside Osewoudt.

He was young, seventeen at most. He had a high forehead

and the green, shallow-socketed wolf's eyes of the wildest Germanic tribes.

'You're Osewoudt, aren't you? Interesting to talk to you. Everyone's heard about your case. If you ask me, the hunt for Dorbeck's like walking through quicksand: every step you take you sink deeper. What's your view?'

'That's none of your business.'

'If you ask me, Osewoudt, you're a real bastard. I'm not saying that to have a go at you, it's the truth. You know the trouble with most Dutchmen? They never learned to think. Take me. I joined the SS a year ago. I'm a theorist, an amoral theorist. A theorist, because I can't stand the sight of blood, and besides, by the time I joined, Germany was already losing the war and there were SS men running for cover with the Resistance. It wasn't that I believed in the SS, the 1,000 year Reich, or any of the other tripe the papers say every SS man believed in. But what I do believe is that moral values are nothing but a temporary frame of reference, and that once you're dead morality is irrelevant. I don't suppose you've done much reading, have you? I have. I'm an intellectual. Not many of them in the SS, either. A pack of idiots, like everybody else. Some of them thought the world of Himmler! Himmler, I ask you! A sea cow in pince-nez! They thought Hitler was a genius! Hitler! The epileptic schnauzer! They believed in a better future, for God's sake! If it were up to me, I'd have them all put against a wall, now, here, this minute!'

He pointed to the exercising men.

'See how they run! Ridiculous. You know what it is? You know what it all boils down to? It all boils down to the fact that man is mortal and doesn't want to admit it. But to anyone who accepts the reality of death there is no morality in the absolute sense, to anyone like that goodness and charity are nothing but fear in disguise. Why should I behave morally if

I will get the death sentence in any case? Everyone is sentenced to die in the end, and everyone knows it.

'The crackpot philosophers who shaped our Western civilisation thought there was a difference between guilt and innocence. But I say: in a world where everyone gets the death sentence there can be no distinction between innocence and guilt. And all that rot about compassion! Of course you've never read a decent book in your life, like all the other imbeciles in this country. But if you get a chance, you should take a look at Shakespeare's *Richard III*! Shakespeare, now there was someone who understood. What happens when Richard's kingdom is on the verge of collapse and he must prepare for the decisive battle?

'He sleeps, and in his dream appear all the friends and relations he murdered so that he could take the throne. Do you know what they say? Well, what do you think? Do you think they say: Richard, it was awful of you to kill us off, but what's done is done, there's no way we can come back to life, we forgive you for what you did to us and hope that you'll be spared our miserable fate, because even if you are punished for your crimes, it won't do *us* any good ... Do you think that's what they say, Osewoudt? No, my friend, that's not what they say. *Despair and die!* is what they say. *Despair and die!* Women, children, old folk. *Despair and die* they all say! Shakespeare knew what he was talking about!

'Take Dostoevsky. In Dostoevsky you'll find people who are gentle, kind, high-minded, generous, saintly – but they're all insane, every one of them. That's what it boils down to! Man is only good out of calculation, insanity, or cowardice.

'And this brings me to the point I'm trying to make: this insight is gradually gaining acceptance. The old prophets and philosophers who claimed otherwise are losing ground. The truth can't be kept at bay by autosuggestion. Man will have to learn to live in a world without liberty, goodness and truth. It'll soon be taught at primary school! This war is just a fore-taste of what's in store! The world is getting far too densely populated for there to be room for madmen, do-gooders or saints. Just as we no longer believe in witches, just as sexual taboos are disappearing, so our great-grandchildren will have no qualms about allowing things to happen that would horrify your taxpaying, vote-casting populace of today.

'The carnage of this war, the millions of defenceless people who have been gassed, beaten to death, starved, doused with burning phosphor from aeroplanes, that's just a start. Our grandchildren won't understand the hue and cry in the papers over such things. The persecution of Jews? You mark my words! In twenty years' time the British, the Americans and the Russians will have the Jews exterminated by the Arabs, if it happens to suit them. May I wish you the very best of luck with your case, Osewoudt?'

The prisoners were marshalled into line. The young SS man jumped up to join them. But after two paces he paused, looked back at Osewoudt and said: 'Or they'll have the Arabs exter-minated by the Jews, if that makes you feel any better!'

Not until the car pulled up at the entrance of the British army base in Oldenburg did Osewoudt get a chance to exchange a few words with the dentist, whom they had collected on the way.

'I gather you were a close acquaintance of the Jagtman family,' said Osewoudt.

'Yes, they were all patients of mine.'

'And did any of them look like me?'

'I should say so. That was why I phoned the police when I saw that picture of Dorbeck in the paper. But you must realise that it's five years since I last saw him. I don't keep a photo album of my patients.'

'What exactly was his name?'

'Egbert.'

'Egbert. Did you see him at all after May 1940?'

'That's a bit of a problem. The last time he came to see me was in August 1939. He was called up after that.'

'Was he in the artillery?'

'I wouldn't know for sure.'

'How old was he?'

'Twenty-three.'

'What if he'd had a lot of work done on his teeth by another dentist, while he was in the army?'

'Oh, the distinctive features of a person's dentition aren't affected, under normal circumstances. The chance of that happening is incredibly small.'

The dentist opened a small case he had been holding on his lap throughout the journey. Just then Selderhorst got in the car again, after having a word with the British commander. He started the engine. The British sentry waved them on. They drove very slowly down a track that was completely ploughed up by tanks, towards a low shed.

There were more British soldiers standing about, unarmed, with their flat helmets pushed back at a jaunty angle. They directed the car to a parking space among their own vehicles.

Selderhorst, the dentist, Spuybroek, and Osewoudt got out.

The dentist put down his case on the grass and opened it. He took out a large, buff-coloured card. It was a diagram of a full set of human teeth, several of them annotated, in two facing horseshoe shapes. On the left were listed the patient's particulars: surname, first name, date of birth, dental appointments, and so on. The dentist happened to be holding the card in his left hand, thus obscuring most of the list, but Osewoudt was able to catch a glimpse of the words Jagtman and Egbert, and a date: 3 December, 1916. There were three addresses, two of which were scored out.

The dentist pointed to the chart.

'A diagram like this,' he said, 'gives a complete record of everything that has been done to a person's teeth. It represents a unique combination. Rather like the combination which opens a safe. For example, here we have an inlay in the third molar in the bottom left, a filling on the inside of the second molar, an extracted eye tooth (necessitated in this case by a childhood accident – he was hit by a flying stone), three fillings in the third molar on the right, et cetera . . . No, no, the chances of this combination occurring in anyone else are negligible.'

A British lieutenant came up to them with a soldier in tow, who set down four pairs of rubber boots on the grass. The lieutenant was already wearing rubber boots, as was the soldier.

'Well now, gentleman,' said the lieutenant, 'would you be so kind as to follow me? That's very kind, because I can't say this is going to be a pleasant undertaking. The storage of the exhumed bodies leaves much to be desired, not least due to their poor state of preservation. The mass grave was discovered purely by chance ten days ago. It's not far from our base, which has simplified transportation.'

He produced a key, put it in a padlock on the shed door, and said: 'As far as we can tell, the majority are Belgian and Dutch servicemen.'

'Were they in uniform, then?' Osewoudt asked.

'Some were. The others had nothing on – another kind of uniform, so to speak.'

In a nearby field stood a diesel generator, blowing blue vapour into the misty air. There were cables running from the generator to various sheds, including this one.

The dentist put away Jagtman's dental chart and put on a pair of rubber gloves. From his case he took a long stainless steel spatula, almost as long as a crowbar, and a curious kind of clamp. The clamp consisted of two flat hooks, as big as spoons and with the convex sides turned outwards. The two hooks could be made to move apart by adjusting a screw. After casting an eye over each of these instruments, he put them all back in the case, which also contained a small mirror on a long handle and a pocket torch.

The door swung open and a sickly stench of decaying flesh mixed with formaldehyde wafted out. The officer turned a switch. Two inspection lamps suspended from the eaves flipped on. The dentist picked up his case.

There were so many bodies in the shed that there was hardly room to walk. Many of them were piled up on each other, so that only the faces of the top ones were visible.

'Don't worry,' said the lieutenant, 'we've marked the one we think fits the description.'

Looking left and right, he led the way for the others. Their rubber boots squelched in the black slime underfoot.

All the way at the back lay the marked body. There was a cross of red lead paint on the pale blue, distended belly. The eyelids were parted, but the sockets were empty. There was thin black stubble on the cheeks. The hair on the head was black, too.

'Is this Dorbeck?' Selderhorst asked.

Osewoudt hesitated.

The dentist sank to his haunches, inserted his spatula between the closed jaws and prised them apart. In his other hand he held his torch.

'I've seen enough!' he said, straightening up. 'Not a tooth left in his mouth!'

It was mid-November, and many weeks since Osewoudt had last been called for questioning. One morning when Spuybroek came to inspect his cell, he raised the subject.

'Couldn't you ask Selderhorst to give me another hearing?'

'What for? What would be in it for you? Don't you think they've got enough files on you already?'

'But there are still so many details that haven't been discussed!'

'You're mad. It's sheer madness on your part to think that more discussions will help. Incriminating evidence is, oddly enough, rather like cork. Sink a ship with a cargo of cork and the cork will come up again, whatever you do.'

'Still, I'd really like to speak to Selderhorst. Ask him when I can see him.'

At half past eleven that evening he was taken from his cell and conducted to Selderhorst's office.

Selderhorst's desk was stacked so high with files that he could barely see over the top, which was probably why he leaped to his feet when Osewoudt came in through the door.

'You again! What do you want? I didn't send for you.'

'That's exactly why I'm here!'

'I have no intention of losing any sleep over you. Did you think I still don't know enough about you to have you sentenced to death three times over?'

'No, in actual fact you know nothing about me! You never

brought up any of the facts that speak in my favour. The country's been liberated, and yet here I am, behind bars with a bunch of traitors, spies and black marketeers. Don't I have a right to be free? Did I not do my bit for the liberation? Did I not liquidate the monster Lagendaal?'

Selderhorst stamped his feet with rage.

'Damn you! How dare you talk to me like that?'

He waved at the files.

'There isn't a minute of your existence during the German occupation that is not documented in these files. For every time you scratched your arse I can produce ten sworn statements! What's the matter with you? Why did you come here? To tell me yet again that it was you who liquidated Lagendaal? Take a look in the mirror, you creep. Look in the mirror and then tell me you're the kind of man who would have had the guts to liquidate Lagendaal.'

He picked up the phone and shouted: 'Bring me a mirror! Now! This minute!'

He slammed down the phone, took his chair from behind the desk and set it down back to front before Osewoudt. He sat astride the chair, resting his arms on the back. He was still wearing the same shabby grey suit, his eyes were red from lack of sleep, his cheeks were covered with grey and black stubble, but on his feet he wore a new pair of army boots, brown and lavishly studded with nails.

'There is no proof whatsoever that you killed Lagendaal! All the records pertaining to his murder come from German sources. How can we trust them? Those same Germans who had you abducted from the hospital by their own people so you would lead them to the Resistance – how reliable can their version of who killed Lagendaal be? It's far more likely they did it themselves; maybe he was asking for too much money. Maybe it was the girl who did it, Annelies van Doormaal, the poor girl the Germans arrested with one of your photos on her! What the Germans have to say about Lagendaal's murder is of not the slightest interest to us.'

'What about Lagendaal's young son?'

'The Lagendaal boy said you took him to Amsterdam by train, along with Annelies van Doormaal. She was arrested on the way, and you abandoned the boy on some pavement, on Rokin it was, I believe. And besides, even if it's true that you killed Lagendaal, how is that going to back up your Dorbeck story?'

'Lots of people knew Dorbeck. They can't all be dead, and even if they are, they must have mentioned him to other people before they died.'

'Who would those people be?'

'For instance the people I did the job in Haarlem with, at Kleine Houtstraat 32.'

'Aha! Aha! At last!'

Selderhorst jumped up from his chair; the chair teetered.

'At last Mr Osewoudt here has decided to be more forthcoming! Kleine Houtstraat, number 32! Let's hear what he has to say for himself.'

'It was one of the first jobs I did for Dorbeck. He'd called at the shop a few days earlier. I asked the policeman who was there when we dug up the uniform, remember, and he said he'd seen him.'

'He saw that the light was on in the shop, that's all.'

'He saw someone leaving the shop. Dorbeck had been to see me; he'd given me a pistol. A while before that, he'd sent me a couple of Leica films to develop. Which I did, but there was nothing on them.'

'Really? Nothing? Are you sure? How could you tell in your darkroom?'

'I didn't have a darkroom.'

'You didn't have a darkroom? Go on, tell me more.'

'There was nothing on those Leica films. Dorbeck came to see me and told me the films had been planted on him and his friends by the Germans, by German provocateurs. He had decided to liquidate them. So he had made an appointment with them in Haarlem, at Kleine Houtstraat 32. He wanted me to help. So I did. There were three of us: Dorbeck, Zéwüster and me. Dorbeck stayed outside, on the lookout. Zéwüster and I went inside. We were received in a back room by three people. We shot them immediately.'

'Exactly,' said Selderhorst, taking out a file. 'Do you know the names of the victims?'

'No, we didn't bother with introductions.'

Selderhorst opened the file and flicked through it.

'Well, as it happens, I do have their names. They were Olifiers, Stoffels and Knijtijzen. Ringing any bells?'

'Why would those names mean anything to me?'

'They don't? Then I'll explain. Olifiers was on the level, Stoffels and Knijtijzen were working for the Gestapo. Olifiers didn't know that, through no fault of his own. Why was Olifiers shot too?'

'How was I supposed to know Olifiers was on the level?'

'I'll tell you something else. Those films came from Olifiers originally. And there was something on them all right. Photos of secret German documents. But after they'd been developed, the films were blank. How did that happen? You know more about this. Did you or did you not develop those films?'

'I developed them, it's true.'

'Did you develop them properly?'

'I didn't have a darkroom.'

'Ah, you didn't have a darkroom. So perhaps you made some mistake, causing the images to be lost. Did you mention that when you sent the negatives? Did you put a note in with them saying: there's nothing on them, but that could be my fault?'

'No.'

'And when you heard that those people had to be liquidated because there was nothing on the films, you still didn't say anything?'

'No, I didn't. I didn't say anything, because Dorbeck had sent two men to tell me there was no need to develop the films since there was nothing on them.'

'Dorbeck! Not Dorbeck again?'

'Dorbeck knows exactly how it all went. Anyway, even if there had been anything on those films, it doesn't change the fact that Stoffels and Knijtijzen got what they deserved. You said yourself they were working for the Gestapo.'

'But Olifiers was straight, and Zéwüster has testified that it was you who shot Olifiers!'

'Is Zéwüster still alive then?'

'He was caught later on by the Germans; he was shot. But I have the statements he made to the Germans right here. Zéwüster said he didn't trust you from the start. He even said he'd seen you again some time later, at the University Library in Amsterdam. He had the impression you were following him. Zéwüster was studying accountancy. He thought: what's someone like him doing in a university library? He must be looking for me.'

'What did the Germans say to that?'

'They said you'd already told them everything.'

'They just said that to mislead Zéwüster, to get him to make a confession.'

'By that time you and Ebernuss were rather good friends, weren't you?'

'Zéwüster lied,' said Osewoudt. 'He may have lied to save me, because the man I shot was Knijtijzen. The Germans removed the bullets from Knijtijzen's body, and they were traced to my pistol.'

Selderhorst slapped the papers down on the desk, and in doing so upset the pile. The whole mass of files toppled over, spilling on to the floor in a large, multicoloured fan.

This was ignored by Selderhorst, who seated himself astride his chair again, his forearms on the back and his chin in his hands. 'Tell me, Osewoudt, what did the man you shot look like? Can you remember? You'd better tell the truth, because those people weren't killed outright, they had time to make statements before they died.'

'It was the man who let us in, a man with a red, bald head. He was standing to my left. I had the pistol in a rolled-up beach towel, which I held in front of my chest.'

'Damn you!' said Selderhorst, rising once more. 'All right then, so it was Knijtijzen you shot at. What's the difference?'

Osewoudt gulped for air; his face oozed perspiration.

For the next few minutes they stared at each other wordlessly. Then came a knock at the door.

'Yes!' said Selderhorst.

A guard entered with a small, somewhat tarnished mirror.

'You asked for a mirror, sir?'

'Yes! Hold it up to that man's face, will you?'

The guard went up to Osewoudt and obediently held up the mirror.

Was this the face of a man who could ever have been mistaken for Dorbeck?

He looked like an office girl, the kind who knows she'll never get a man, thirtyish – and he was only twenty-four. His nose was upturned and small, with wide, thin nostrils. His eyes seemed to be narrowed even when at rest, and yet they were not the eyes of a keen observer, they had the blank, uncomprehending look of the short-sighted. The pale, thin skin around the eyes was crinkled, and his mouth, with its thin upper lip and non-existent lower lip, appeared to be permanently set in cantankerous mode. He lifted his eyebrows, making lines appear on his forehead, which continued to shine with the white gleam of a porcelain washbasin. And then there were the thin bat's ears, still rosy even now. And the pale, silky hair, which was still pale though greasy and matted. The cheeks smooth and round as a baby's bottom, the jaw seemingly boneless. And to cap it all: the dimple in the middle of the chin.

He pushed the mirror away, and said: 'But don't you have the photo circulated by the Germans with my name next to it? That wasn't a picture of me, it was a picture of Dorbeck. It was quite obvious that it wasn't me in the picture. Surely you could use that to track Dorbeck down with instead of a photo of me?'

'Did you honestly think we didn't have that photo? We showed it to twenty experts, side by side with yours, and eighteen out of twenty were positive that it was the same person in both photos.

'What good would it do to start circulating the other photo at this stage? We'd only get more people coming forward saying that they'd met Egbert Jagtman at some point in their lives, and where would that get us?

'Because Egbert Jagtman was the officer who ordered the summary execution of two Germans during the bombing of Rotterdam in May 1940! After the photo was published in the papers he gave himself up to the Germans; he said: here I am! Do what you like with me, but I'm not sorry! I'm an officer in the Dutch army. When the bombs were falling on Rotterdam the German lines were still a long way off, so I was authorised to have any German soldier shot as a franc-tireur; I don't care if he was dropped by parachute or not, your modern techniques of warfare don't change a thing. That is what Egbert Jagtman said in his statement, it's all in the files.'

Selderhorst gestured behind him.

'What happened to Egbert Jagtman?' asked Osewoudt.

'They sent him to a concentration camp without trial. We can't prove that the body we saw in Oldenburg was Egbert Jagtman's, but that the man is no longer alive is not in doubt.'

'What if he was posing as Dorbeck, what if he'd managed to escape from Germany? That way he could have gone on being active in Holland until the end of the war, couldn't he?'

'Don't talk rubbish! When did you first meet Dorbeck? Was it on 10 May, yes or no?'

'Yes.'

'Did he call himself Dorbeck then?'

'Yes.'

'What reason could Jagtman have had to introduce himself as Dorbeck in the first shop in Voorschoten he happened to go into?'

'Maybe he liked a bit of mystery.'

'Rubbish. You're the one with a taste for mystery. Let's see, that shooting incident in Haarlem — was Dorbeck there, yes or no?'

'Yes he was, he was on the lookout.'

'Ah. The shooting took place on 23 July, 1940. Yes or no?'

'Yes.'

'Right. But we know that Egbert Jagtman had already turned himself in to the Germans on 20 July, and that he was deported to Germany two months later. In other words, Egbert Jagtman was behind bars on 23 July. In other words: the man you saw in Haarlem on 23 July cannot have been Egbert Jagtman. Do you follow?'

'Christ almighty! It wasn't my idea that Dorbeck and Jagtman were the same person! I never said he was Egbert Jagtman. I said his name was Dorbeck. And if Jagtman and Dorbeck were in fact the same person, how do you explain the following? As I told you before, when I first met Dorbeck he gave me a roll of film he wanted me to develop. That's where those three stupid photos came from: the snowman with the rifle, the three soldiers in gas masks, and the soldier in pyjamas behind a machine gun. But there was a fourth exposure.'

'So where did it get to? You never mentioned it before – all your statements refer to three photos, not four.'

Osewoudt paused before replying. He lowered his eyes, put both thumbs in his mouth and chewed them like a little girl.

'Well? What was the fourth photo of then?'

'It was of Dorbeck. He had two girls with him, and it was taken outside Kleine Houtstraat 32. The number was clearly visible, and also the street name, because the house is on a corner. If Dorbeck was in fact Jagtman, and Jagtman had no connection whatsoever with that address or with what went on there, why would he have had his picture taken in front of that particular house?'

'That depends. First tell me what happened to the photo.'

'Something went wrong. Just as I was taking it out of the developer, my mother came in and switched on the light. I switched it off at once, but the photo was ruined – it had gone completely black.'

'Dear me, how sad! How could you have had such rotten luck! The only photo with Dorbeck on it . . . and that was the very one that didn't come out.'

'And yet I swear to you on everything sacred to me that I saw it.'

'Swearing won't get you anywhere. Listen here, you halfwit, if we had just one photo of someone who might possibly be Dorbeck I'd be prepared to think again.'

'But there *is* one of Dorbeck! I just remembered! I took a

photo the morning after Dorbeck rescued me, on 6 April, in the house he took me to in Amsterdam! We're in it together, in front of a mirror!'

'Really? So where is it now?'

'I lost my Leica when I fled. I had a shoulder bag, it was in there. I lost the bag on the way.'

'Christ, I'm exhausted. I never get to bed before three nowadays. If you promise to stop whingeing, I'll see if we can do something about your lost Leica.'

'You're just saying that to get rid of me. What do you expect? That camera was swapped for cigarettes with some Canadian soldier ages ago. It'll never turn up. And anyway, if it did turn up the film would never still be in it.'

Selderhorst stood up, groaning with fatigue. He took a sheet of paper and picked up a pencil from his desk.

'What did that Leica look like?'

'I can even remember the exact serial number,' Osewoudt said. 'It was a Leica IIIa, number 256789, and the lens was a Summar 222456.'

Selderhorst wrote down the numbers and then held the paper under Osewoudt's nose.

'That right?'

From the daily newspaper *Het Vrije Vaderland,* 18 October, 1945:

HERO OR TRAITOR? *(from our special correspondent)*

Of all the insalubrious episodes that have inevitably come to light during the post-war administration of justice, the mysterious case of tobacconist O. is by no means the least significant. We have the impression that the investigation, in so far as it has been effectively conducted at all, is sorely lacking in logical reasoning.

O. took part in various underground missions during the German occupation. Keen observers did not fail to notice that sooner or later everyone who had dealings with O. fell into German hands, while O. himself always managed to escape in miraculous fashion. Indeed, shortly after his arrival in the liberated provinces of our country in April 1945, he was taken into custody by the Allies on suspicion of high treason.

O., for his part, denies everything, claiming that a man named Dorbeck was behind it all. This Dorbeck has never been found, despite repeated efforts to trace him. According to O., Dorbeck is a Dutch officer working for the British, and by coincidence they resemble each other like two peas. No lack of coincidences in this affair! A third mysterious figure has since surfaced: one Egbert Jagtman, likewise a Dutch officer and likewise bearing a striking resemblance to the apparently chameleonic O. Because a photograph published in the press (of O.? of Dorbeck?) was recognised by none other than Jagtman's dentist! Prior to that, O. had already claimed to have sent secret documents to the said Jagtman's address, which he alleged had been passed to him by Dorbeck.

Whatever the case, it is now generally accepted that Jagtman himself is no longer alive and that a body found in a German mass grave is indeed Jagtman's. Is it fair to infer from this that the third pea in the pod, so to speak, has been eliminated? Possibly.

There is more.

According to O., Dorbeck asked him to develop some photographs, which he, after having heard nothing from Dorbeck for four years, posted to him. Only four days after doing this, O. was contacted by a young lady by the name of Elly Berkelbach Sprenkel, who called herself Sprenkelbach Meijer. She identified herself with one of the pictures O. had put in the post, claiming that it had been given to her in England. But the photo had still been in O.'s possession three days earlier. She also claimed to have been put ashore the previous night at Scheveningen, where she had gone to stay with an aunt. But by June 1944 Scheveningen had already been evacuated by the Germans, and the beach was heavily guarded in anticipation of the Allied invasion. Moreover, at that time communications between England and occupied Dutch territory were hardly good enough for a photo to be able to travel there and back in two days. A mystery . . . Elly Berkelbach Sprenkel was in effect a British agent, but how she had obtained the picture O. could not explain. Did the man called Dorbeck exist after all? Was it he who played it into Elly Berkelbach Sprenkel's hands (in Holland, presumably), instructing her to tell O. that it came from England? Theories abound, but what is the truth? Not long after this, Elly B. S. was caught by the Gestapo, and later shot. To make matters worse, it transpired after the war that the Germans possessed multiple copies of the relevant photographs . . .

Whatever the case, the possibility of Dorbeck's existence should not, in our opinion, be ruled out.

But then where is he?

The answer to that question appears not to be forthcoming from the authorities. We, for our part, believe it is incumbent upon us to take the matter in hand.

### Women

Numerous women are implicated in the present affair. One is O.'s girlfriend, named Mirjam Zettenbaum, who went into hiding during the war as Marianne Sondaar. She is now residing in Palestine and efforts to contact her appear to have been unsuccessful. Why is this? Why has she not come forward to clear her former lover's name?

The judiciary have shown remarkably little concern about this situation, possibly with good cause, as we shall see.

Mirjam Zettenbaum owes her life to the treachery of O.

She was apprehended by the Germans in Leiden along with O. Being Jewish, she was promptly imprisoned in the Westerbork concentration camp, and her fate in a German *Vernichtungslager* would have been sealed had O. not saved her.

O. saved her life — this is, by all accounts, not in dispute.

For the Germans had come to the conclusion, on the basis either of O.'s statements or their own findings, that the arrest of O. had not dug out the root of the plot. They believed (or knew???) that although O. was behind bars there was still someone at large who matched O.'s description! So they said to O.: tell us who this person is, and we will ensure that your girlfriend Marianne comes to no harm. Thus they persuaded O. to betray Dorbeck.

There can be no doubt about this, in our opinion. O. led the Germans to the address where Dorbeck was staying. The house concerned was rented by a student of theology named Moorlag, an old acquaintance of O.'s: he had previously been a lodger with the O. family at Voorschoten. No one in the world knew O. better than this Moorlag, but he too is dead. His body was found in the street a few days before the liberation, round the corner from where he lived in Amsterdam . . . Coincidence? By no means! Moorlag is dead, and Dorbeck certainly existed, *but he too is dead*! Both betrayed by O.

*Hidden truths*

That the judiciary has failed to make these simple deductions may seem strange, but it is well to bear in mind the following. No prisoner ever tells the whole truth during interrogation. Nor will those conducting the inquiry, in their turn, reveal all they know, in the hope of drawing out the suspect. Thus O. lied to the Germans, the Germans lied to him, and afterwards O. did not tell the whole truth to the British or the Dutch, while the Germans, of course, do nothing but lie when interrogated by their former enemies. They have no interest in helping the Dutch authorities, or in bringing to light the historical truth, their sole commitment being to save their own hides.

Consequently we recommend taking no statement whatsoever at face value, but rather bringing reason and logic to bear in fitting together the pieces of this puzzle.

## *Love*

The Germans kept their promise to O.: his girlfriend was not sent to Germany. They expedited O. himself, disguised as a female nurse, to the liberated south. He was driven there by a uniformed German officer in a small car: a DKW. This car was later found in Dordrecht containing the body of the officer, who had been stabbed to death by O.

These facts were conveyed to us by the priest of the church of St Ignatius at Dordrecht, with whom O., still disguised as a nurse, had sought refuge. What better way would there be for O. to remove all suspicion from the minds of the Allies than by killing the German officer?

However, this is not all. On his journey southwards O. paid a visit to his tobacco shop in Voorschoten, where his legal wife Maria Nauta, his first cousin and seven years his senior, was still living. This woman had a relationship with a Nazi sympathiser named Turlings, which was common knowledge in the locality. On the day of O.'s journey, his wife was found dead in her shop. She had been stabbed. Local residents reported having seen a German officer and a nurse leaving the scene in a car prior to the discovery of the body.

We are aware of the objections to our line of reasoning: that all these circumstances give rise to complications that are beyond the judiciary's remit, who are, after all, concerned exclusively with establishing irrefutable proof against O. They have no interest in composing his biography – a daunting venture by any standards, given the complexity of the affair. Whatever the case may be, O. is not entirely innocent, but neither is he as guilty as some of our countrymen believe. He started out in good faith, and that his wife and her Nazi lover betrayed him is beyond all doubt. In so far as O. was a traitor himself, it was out of love for his friend Mirjam Zettenbaum. It was to save her that he denounced Dorbeck and Moorlag to the Germans. Small wonder that Dorbeck has not turned up.

Hoping to come out of this alive, O. seized the opportunity to take revenge on his wife, no doubt with the half-formed intention of starting a new life with his girl-friend after the war.

Let us return to our first question: why is Miss Zettenbaum keeping silent in Palestine? In the light of the foregoing, does this question merit further investigation? No! The answer is obvious.

She is keeping silent because there is nothing she can say in O.'s defence. Assuming she were actually able to prove that Dorbeck existed, she would at the same time be proving that he was betrayed by O. She is silent out of love for O.

It is probably best for O. if she remains so.

To: Miss Mirjam Zettenbaum
In a kibbutz
Palestine

Camp Eighth Exloërmond
19 October, 1945

Dearest Marianne,

It was only last week that I heard, to my amazement, that you are still alive. I was told by the police. My joy is impossible to describe. This is the first chance I have had to write you a letter. I was convinced you were dead. I went to visit you in the Emma Clinic in Amsterdam, on 6 April. The matron said you couldn't see anyone. But they did let me see the child. Oh, Marianne, I can't tell you how I cried, and now that I'm writing this I am crying again. I have nothing, not a single thing, left from the days when we were together, and they were such happy days. The happiest days of my life, and nothing will ever be the same again. Oh, Marianne, I can't bear to think of you being so far away, but I don't think I could still make you happy.

Things have gone terribly wrong for me. I am a prisoner. The war has ended, all the occupied countries have been liberated, but I have yet to have a moment's freedom. I have been through so much, more than I have the strength to tell you, but my suffering is without name. I stand accused of treason. The basest, most evil motives are attributed to me, and everything I do to try and prove my innocence only backfires. Everyone who could have testified in my favour is either dead or impossible to trace. And you know as well as I know – and as my other close friends knew – that I was acting on Dorbeck's instructions at all times. I'm sure you remember my telling you about Dorbeck, that night at Labare's, before the place was raided by the Germans. You consoled me, remember? I told you about my absolute dependence on Dorbeck, that without him I was nothing, less than nothing, even. You contradicted me, you said I was a person in my own right, with my own worth.

But, dearest Marianne, things have turned out otherwise. Dorbeck has vanished. Dozens of attempts to track him down have been made, so far without success. There is no trace of him. Sometimes I think he must be dead, then I think the British must be hiding him. And so what I told you was true: without Dorbeck I am nothing, without him coming forward to explain my actions, everything I did in the Resistance can be twisted and distorted into crime and betrayal.

I am not at all well. I have a fever. I cough day and night. I am not being badly treated, but I rarely, if ever, see daylight. The interrogations sometimes go on all night, but I still can't sleep on the other nights. And yet I am privileged, because I have a cell to myself. The prison camp is an old milk factory. The other rooms are filled to bursting with all sorts of lowlife, former members of the SS, provocateurs of the Sicherheitsdienst and other traitors. It makes me laugh sometimes to think of the company I am in, and then I say to myself: why make such a fuss? It's all a big mistake, just one insane coincidence on top of another, that's all. Dorbeck could turn up at any moment, and then everything will be fine.

But I must confess, Marianne, that I sometimes get more worried than is good for me, which is why I want to ask you this: couldn't you write to the Public Prosecutor of the Special Court and tell them I was definitely in contact with Dorbeck during the German occupation? That I talked to you about him, et cetera. That he really exists. Because the people dealing with my case are so badly informed it sometimes seems they are out to convince me that I made him up.

Turlings, the Nazi who reported me to the Germans, is the only person still alive to have seen Dorbeck. It was after the shooting in Haarlem, at Kleine Houtstraat 32. He saw a man in a grey suit. He thought it was me. When he saw me wearing white shorts a few minutes later, he said: you got changed very quickly! He had seen Dorbeck instead of me.

But I can't very well ask them to get a statement from a traitor like that, can I? What would the judge think of me? So I'm keeping quiet about him.

And, Marianne, please write back. I would so love to know how you are getting on in your kibbutz. They say you people play recorders and tambourines out there. Perhaps you haven't forgotten me yet. I hope you don't think I abandoned you. At least now you know why you haven't heard from me. Once I'm free I want to try and save some money (except I don't know how, as the tobacco shop no longer exists), but if I can lay my hands on some money I'll come over to you, Arabs or no Arabs.

The new matron, Sister Kruisheer, was a gaunt woman in her fifties with a clearly visible blonde moustache.

She bent over the hospital bed, removed the thermometer from Osewoudt's mouth, and said: 'Thirty-eight point nine. Lucky you. Thirty-eight point five and you'd have had to go.'

With her left hand she held a tray with medicine bottles and glasses. She added the thermometer to the others in a tumbler of sublimate solution. Then she took from her tray a tin dish containing a Gillette razor and a dab of shaving cream, and said: 'Time for a shave.'

'I don't need a shave.'

'Nonsense.'

'I don't have a beard. Want to feel?'

She gave him a wide-eyed stare, and slowly removed the tin dish. 'Lucky you,' she said, with a mean smile.

Bleak morning light filled the ward, which had walls of pale blue distemper covered in stains and blisters from the damp. There were no windows, but the roof consisted of double-pitched toughened glass. This had originally been the bottle-rinsing room. Taps for hot and cold water abounded, even in the most unexpected places, hence its conversion into a sick bay. Not only were there taps on the walls, there were pipes running down the middle of the space upon which more taps were mounted, some dripping and others constantly emitting puffs of steam.

The patients lay in metal beds. The majority were malingerers.

Whenever one addressed Osewoudt, he shouted: 'Shut your trap, you dirty traitor!'

The uproar that ensued could only be calmed by the guards going down the aisle between the beds, lashing out left and right with rubber truncheons. Osewoudt was not spared, of course, but to him it was worth it.

Thirty-eight point nine, thought Osewoudt, four tenths too many. What could he do to make the fever go down, so that he would be sent back to his own room in the basement?

He felt his damp sheets, sniffed the smell of engine oil that came from the steam, looked up at the dingy glass ceiling and thought: I'll never get better here. His cheeks bulged suddenly, he threw himself over on his side, writhing with pain, and tried to smother the cough in his pillow, but his lungs felt as if they were bursting, and his chest muscles contracted in rib-cracking convulsions.

'Hello Henri Osewoudt!'

He turned over on his back and looked up.

An elderly gentleman stood at his bedside. In his pale, liver-spotted hand he held a black trilby. His large head hung forwards at an angle, forced into this position by a sickly red swelling on his throat.

'I am Dr Lichtenau. You don't know me any more, but I still know you. A lot has happened since then, but I still recognise you very well.'

Sister Kruisheer came up with a chair and Dr Lichtenau sat down. He laid his hat on his knees.

'I am the psychiatrist who treated your mother when she was in the institution. I remember you used to come and visit her, with your uncle.'

'Really?'

'Indeed I do! I asked you: what do you want to be when you grow up? and you said: a nurse!'

'Did I say that?'

'Yes. You were about five years old at the time. You haven't changed very much, really. Your father was still alive then.'

Dr Lichtenau stared into space and shook his head.

'Did you treat my mother again later, when she went back to the institution after that business with my father?'

'At first, yes. The murder of your father did not in fact shed any fresh light on the diagnosis. She herself did not feel responsible for what she did; that was nothing new. There was a voice, a "something", an "it", telling her what to do.'

Dr Lichtenau made two small gestures, as though seeking to portray the 'something' and the 'it' while indicating that he did not believe in their existence. 'She would sometimes disguise herself, tear a strip off a sheet and tie it over her face like a mask, and say: there it is again, I'll just chase it away.'

He looked intently at Osewoudt; he had watery blue eyes with sagging lower lids, and seemed to be wondering if his simple résumé had sunk in.

'She used to do that later on, too,' said Osewoudt.

'Indeed. That was her peculiarity – that she did things at the behest of some external agent. She did not like this, it frightened her. So she would try to chase the "something" or the "it" away. Clearly, she did not always succeed.'

'I suppose you heard about the Krauts finishing her off, Doctor?'

'Yes, Henri. Yet she was not incurably insane. She was a perfectly normal woman as long as she did not feel threatened by the "it". But tell me, you must have been very fond of your mother, no?'

'Need you ask? The only way I could take care of her was by moving into the flat over the tobacco shop and running the business. I was only doing it for her.'

'Then why did you put her at such risk by getting involved in underground operations?'

'I wouldn't . . . If I'd never met Dorbeck . . .'

'This Dorbeck business, do you believe in it yourself?'

'What do you mean?'

'Do you really believe that Dorbeck existed, that you met him several times, and that he gave you all sorts of assignments? Look here, Henri, please don't interrupt! I don't mean that you're not well in the mind, not by any means! But the war has been a time of enormous strain for all of us. It could be that in periods of great fatigue you came to believe that Dorbeck existed, that he telephoned you, sent you messages on the back of photographs, and so on and so forth. Come now, Henri, we who both knew your mother so well need have no secrets from each other. What I'm saying is that we all have our moments of weakness. You don't believe in Dorbeck yourself, if you ask me! There were times when you did believe in him, such as when you were suffering from mental exhaustion, but you don't believe in him any more. You are only sticking to your story because you are in a tight corner. What do you hope to achieve by that? The judiciary have obliged you in all sorts of ways. Tons of paper have been used up on your case – and that at a time when paper is in such short supply. The files keep piling up. The search for Dorbeck has extended to every country in the world, every person who might have met him at one time or another has been questioned, but he is nowhere to be found. If the authorities had not gone to such lengths to trace him, they would never have called me in. It is only because they have been scrutinising your entire past as well as your family's that they found me. No, don't contradict me, Henri, let me finish. The brief for your case is now as good as complete. It won't be long now before you are brought before the judge. What course will you pursue then? Saying you knew that Dorbeck didn't exist won't help, because you will not only be held responsible for everything, but the judges will also be greatly annoyed with you for having misled the police inquiry for months on end. Let me give you some advice: from now on, say as little as possible. Stop contradicting them, just let them get on with it. Remain silent in court. I shall draw up a report for the judges saying it was all a delusion in your mind, a hallucination. I shall say that you yourself were convinced Dorbeck existed. Dorbeck was simply the personification of certain inclinations embedded in your own soul. I shall say that this in fact reveals moral instincts on your part, in that you could not tolerate being responsible for your criminal inclinations, so you stepped outside of yourself, so to speak, by attributing them to Dorbeck.'

'So you want to declare me of unsound mind?'

'It's not me declaring you of unsound mind! It's you, by placing all the blame on Dorbeck, by saying that Dorbeck was behind it all. It's not me saying that, not the prosecution, it's you. If Dorbeck is indeed responsible, the only logical conclusion is that you are not.'

'No! No! No! I was obeying Dorbeck's orders, but the fact that I obeyed him does not mean I'm of unsound mind! You're confusing the issue!'

'What do you expect, if Dorbeck doesn't exist? He is a figment of your imagination. You invented him – not deliberately, of course, you had no choice. That is what I am talking about: your invention of Dorbeck was involuntary, the will did not come into it. That is why your case qualifies for a plea of, no, not insanity – of diminished responsibility.'

Osewoudt was seized with another coughing fit, and when it subsided he sat up straight, so that his head was almost level with the doctor's. In a voice that could only whisper, he said:

'Doctor, don't listen to a bunch of lazy coppers who are too stupid to find Dorbeck. Don't believe what they say about Dorbeck never having existed. I gave them proof. I showed them where his uniform was buried in my back garden, and they dug it up.'

'What does digging up a uniform prove? It wasn't a uniform marked with Dorbeck's name, was it?'

'Who else could it have belonged to? I always said Dorbeck and I were as twins, we were exactly the same height. And the uniform they dug up in my back garden was exactly my size. What more do they want?'

'How do you know the uniform was your size? Did you try it on?'

'No.'

'Why not?'

'It had decomposed in the soggy earth. It fell apart at the touch. But it was clearly the right size.'

'What is the value of a piece of evidence that falls apart at the first touch? Of course I knew about the uniform. I went though all the documents pertaining to your case before I came to see you. Look at my throat: swollen from all that reading. I have all the details. There is nothing left of that uniform of Dorbeck's, just the brass buttons, green with mould.'

'That piece of evidence is only the start,' said Osewoudt. 'I set about proving that Dorbeck is or was real – with some reluctance, actually, because by doing so I was in a sense giving weight to the notion that he never existed. But what does all that matter? If Dorbeck is still alive and news reaches him of the situation I'm in, he'll come forward to set everything straight. And if he's not still alive, which is quite possible, what with thousands of people vanishing without trace during the war, it may be because he was blown up by a bomb, or travelling under an alias on a plane that crashed into the sea, or burned to death in a tank, or he may even be in prison some-where, like me. Who can say?

'You, however, know nothing about it! You've never seen him, that's why you think he doesn't exist. What makes it all so complicated is the secrecy that I was bound to. I didn't talk about Dorbeck for security reasons. That went without saying. And the only person I ever told anything about Dorbeck is now in Palestine, and she's not replying to my letters. But do you think I care whether you believe in him or not? I can't help it that my mother was mad. Think what you're doing, Doctor. Ask yourself whether you have the right to deny Dorbeck's existence only because you happen to know that my mother suffered from delusions.'

Dr Lichtenau leaned back in his chair and shut his eyes.

'The death sentence. Do you realise what you are looking at, Henri? The firing squad. There is not a ray of hope for your case as it stands. If only you would admit that you were afraid, that you gave in under the Germans' appalling torture. But no! All the time that was available to explain your behav-iour has been wasted on a hunt for a non-existent Dorbeck.'

Osewoudt leaned over to pat the doctor on the knee.

'It was very kind of you to come and see me, Doctor. I know you mean well. But you've got it all wrong, like every-body else. Let me tell you something: I took a photo of Dorbeck and me together, side by side in front of a mirror. I took it myself, in the house at Bernard Kochstraat in Amsterdam. There's still a chance of it being found. Even now they keep confusing photos of me with those of Dorbeck; they think they're of the same person. But once that photo is found, every-thing will be clear. The ultimate proof that Dorbeck and Osewoudt are two different people will then have been deliv-ered. The camera I took the photo with got lost when I fled. The film was still in it. But let's imagine, just for a moment, that it's found. Imagine they develop the film and find the picture of the two of us together, when I'd gone and let you declare me of unsound mind! If I did that, then I'd really be of unsound mind! I'd rather die!'

A young Catholic priest in a threadbare cassock had been bustling about the ward all morning. On his left arm he carried a large basket containing holly and candles. He pinned a sprig of holly to the wall over each prisoner's bed, and on each night-stand he left a stub of candle tied with a red bow.

'Such a shame, such a shame,' he muttered at each bedside. 'The forecast isn't for a white Christmas this year. Such a shame! But it would have been too good to be true – a white Christmas in the year of our liberation!'

'Yes, Father,' the former SS men intoned meekly. 'Such a shame!'

'Well, it can't be helped, I suppose' said the priest. 'Father Christmas must have been too busy to make snowflakes. There's not much we can do about it. We'll just have to take it in our stride.'

'Yes Father! We'll take it in our stride!'

'We'll practise "Silent Night" again later, shall we, lads?'

They promptly started singing.

'No, not now! Later, I said! Hush now!'

He came to Osewoudt's bed.

'I'm Father Beer,' he said. 'Such a shame we won't be having a white Christmas this year.'

'Yes, a shame,' said Osewoudt, pointing up at the ceiling of toughened glass. 'We'd get snowed in.'

'Come now,' said the priest, 'if it got too dark we could light the Christmas candles.'

He set one down on Osewoudt's night-stand.

'Oh, take it away, please,' said Osewoudt. 'I wasn't brought up with that nonsense.'

'It's never too late to learn. A sprig of holly and a candle can't hurt.'

'That's as maybe, but I don't want them anyway.'

'What did you say? How can that be possible! Most of the lads here are well on the way to being converted. And you, talking like that? I must get to the bottom of this!'

He put down his basket, pulled up a chair and seated himself at Osewoudt's bedside.

Father Beer was not much older than Osewoudt. He had a round face and cheery, round eyes of a pale brown shade.

'How did you end up in this camp?'

'I'm innocent,' said Osewoudt. 'Not scum like that lot over there.'

'Who are you, then?'

'My name is Osewoudt.'

'Well, well. Osewoudt. So you are Osewoudt. I've heard about your case.'

'So has everyone else.'

'It's been in the papers.'

'I know, but I gave up reading them long ago.'

'Let's have a serious talk. Perhaps there's something I can do for you.'

'You don't need to do anything for me. Once Dorbeck turns up, I won't need anyone any more. My innocence will have been proved, clear as daylight.'

'Any help I might be able to offer would have no bearing on the legal proceedings.'

'I quite understand. All these sods who used to be in the SS are now singing "Silent Night". They go along with being converted to save their skins.'

'You have a point there. But what difference does it make? Even the worst sinner has the right to try and save his skin.'

'Even through hypocrisy?'

'Even through hypocrisy. Only, as I'm sure you'll appreciate, a priest cannot accept a hypocritical conversion. He must redouble his efforts until such time as hypocrisy makes way for true faith.'

'And get a stay of execution while he's at it, I suppose, in case the true faith doesn't reveal itself.'

'It is always better not to have put a fellow human being to death than to have done so, however depraved that human being may be.'

'Well now,' said Osewoudt. 'Allow me to give you some advice: get the Pope to endorse the abolition of capital punishment the world over and the release of all prisoners too while he's at it, including those who haven't converted. So much better than you having to run around wangling one false conversion after another.'

'Of course that would be better, but there is only so much one can do. I am only human, I can't do any more than lies in my power. And I have no say in the policies pursued by His Holiness.'

'If I were to convert, what would that prove?' asked Osewoudt. 'I'm innocent. How could I become any more innocent by being converted?'

'Not more innocent, but if you did convert, the people holding you here – and the judges who will sentence you because they don't believe in your innocence – might think: there's some goodness in him after all. They might even allow redemption to prevail over justice.'

'I can do without redemption. If I've sacrificed everything

for the good cause and all I get is redemption, what have I lived for? And why should I have to go on living?'

'Because life is a gift, and it is not to be cast aside. For we must go on living, even if we don't know why.'

The sheet was rumpled up under Osewoudt's nose. He pulled his arms out from under the covers and straightened them. 'By the way,' he said, 'don't you hate having to go around in skirts like that? I fled from occupied territory disguised as a female nurse. It was horrible. Like having your legs tied together.'

Father Beer began to laugh heartily.

'It has never occurred to me.'

'There's something else I'd like to ask you, something I've been curious about all my life. That little circle on the top of your head, do you maintain it with a razor, or are there special tonsure clippers for priests? Are there optional courses in tonsure maintenance?'

Father Beer was now choking with laughter.

'Is it hard to learn?' asked Osewoudt. 'Does it involve taking exams?'

'That is one of the best kept secrets of the liturgy,' said Father Beer. 'I would risk being defrocked if I told you.'

Osewoudt did not laugh. He said: 'I am boring you, and you are boring me. Conversation between you and me is pointless. You go around with holly and candles. If it were up to me, everybody in this building would be taken outside and shot, Christmas or no Christmas. They might still gain redemption after death, anyway. My case and theirs don't compare. My presence here is a strange accident. I feel no hatred for the people holding me here. If someone gets a falling rock on his foot and the foot has to be amputated, his entire life will be changed for ever. Yet he won't hate the stone. It's the same with me. It happens in every war, apparently, that soldiers get hit by their own side. My situation is a bit like that. But once

Dorbeck's existence has been proved, everything will be different. That is all I hope for, nothing more exalted than that.'

'You are being presumptuous,' said Father Beer. 'You are putting justice above redemption. But suppose justice is too long in coming?'

'It makes no difference to me.'

'How can you say that? Or is it because, in case Dorbeck turns up after you're dead, the people who have your death on their conscience will be consumed by remorse? Is that what you want?'

'Don't make me laugh! What's in it for me, once I'm dead, if someone who knew no better feels consumed by remorse years later? Besides, I don't believe in being consumed by remorse, as far as I'm concerned it doesn't exist. During the war I killed the father and mother of a small boy with my own hands. The father was scum, but the child had done nothing. I caused that child great sadness, I changed the course of his life, but I had no choice. I don't feel remorse. In the same way, the people mistreating me will always insist they had no choice. And if I'm not shot and it takes another ten years, say, for them to find Dorbeck, I'll still have spent ten years behind bars for nothing. Ten years which can never be made good. Ten years in prison is one of the heaviest sentences going. But if they let me out they'll act as if I should be grateful.'

Osewoudt burst into a coughing fit, stuffed the sheet into his mouth to stifle the noise, but it didn't help.

'After ten years in prison for nothing, there would only be one way for you to get on with your life,' said Father Beer. 'You would have to forgive those who trespassed against you. Do you see? Whatever happens, it all comes down to redemption in the end.'

Osewoudt shook his head.

'Whether I forgave them or not wouldn't matter a hoot to them, because—'

'You don't understand! It's not about other people, it's about your *own* welfare!'

'—because the reason they've put me in prison is not that Dorbeck can't be found, the reason is that I have a high voice like a castrato, a face like a girl and no beard. I've been imprisoned in this body all my life; my appearance has made me what I am. That is the answer to the riddle.'

Father Beer's face flushed a deep red; he began to blow his nose on a filthy handkerchief which he had whisked from his skirts as if by magic.

Then he said: 'But if what you're saying is true, then how else could you be saved than by redemption?'

'What's the point of my life,' replied Osewoudt, 'if I was born under a curse which can only be lifted through being redeemed? Is that what I'm living for – to have two gifts bestowed on me that cancel each other out, when I never asked for any gifts in the first place? I never asked for anything. I never asked to be born, I never asked to be cursed at birth, nor do I ask to be redeemed at death. And if there's nothing left for me but to die, I won't be needing redemption anyway: the end of my life will mean the end of the curse. You may be able to wangle redemption for your converted traitors and murderers, but what could that kind of redemption mean for me? Let's give it a rest. You have tired me out. I'm ill, I have a fever, and I've been in this stinking ward for over a month already. I don't care about the afterlife. All I care about just now is finding the camera I used to take a photo of Dorbeck. Once that's been found, once I'm able to present Selderhorst with a genuine picture of Dorbeck, I'll be halfway to salvation. Then at last he'll have eyes for Dorbeck, not me. That's all the salvation I ask for.'

'We'll talk again some time then,' said Father Beer. 'I'll be praying for you.'

'What about?'

'I'll pray for the Leica to be found. I'll beseech all the saints for its recovery.'

Osewoudt turned over on his side, muttering: 'I wish they wouldn't sing "Silent Night".'

On Christmas Day, before the carol singing started, Father Beer appeared at Osewoudt's side and said: 'I've been praying for you. I prayed for the Leica to be found.'

Osewoudt couldn't think of anything better to say than: 'That was very kind of you.'

When Father Beer made to leave after the carols, he said, in passing: 'I shall pray for you again. Times like these tend to be most auspicious for the granting of special prayers. I will be back tomorrow; we'll have some more singing. You needn't join in if you don't want to, you know!'

Father Beer kept his word and returned on Boxing Day. Carols were duly sung, and some parcels were handed out. There was nothing for Osewoudt, because there was no one to send him anything.

Father Beer came to sit at his bedside.

'I prayed to all the saints on your behalf. I'll go on praying until that camera is found. God's goodness is infinite, and we must not despair.'

But Osewoudt turned over on his side and said: 'Well, if it's all the same to you, I have a headache. I'd prefer to rest. You and I were never destined to see eye to eye.'

On the morning of 27 December, Selderhorst came into the ward. Sister Kruisheer followed, holding a brown woollen dressing gown over her arm and a pair of slippers in her hand.

Selderhorst carried a small cardboard box with the flaps open. 'Well now, Osewoudt, guess what's in here!'

Osewoudt sat up in bed and held out his hands for the box.

'A present from Father Christmas,' said Selderhorst, lifting the box teasingly just out of his reach.

'It's not my Leica, is it?'

'You never know. Have a look.'

He put the box down on Osewoudt's knees.

Osewoudt pushed the flaps aside and lifted the camera out of the box. His high tenor shrilled out in the ward.

'When was it found? This morning?'

'Oh no, we've had it for a week or so. Is it yours?'

'Yes! It's mine!'

Osewoudt turned the rewind knob.

'And the film's still in it!'

'It must be yours. At least, the serial numbers match those you gave us. And it's still got the film in it.'

'Then why haven't you had the film developed? If you had, you'd have seen that Dorbeck's on it!'

'Have it developed? No! You'd better do that yourself – you being such an expert developer! You did pretty well with those films of Olifiers, remember? Now you can have a go developing a film of your own.'

'How am I to do that? I don't have any equipment.'

'But we have. We've fixed up a very nice darkroom for you. Come along.'

Sister Kruisheer held out the dressing gown.

Osewoudt kicked off the covers and sat on the edge of the bed. It took a moment for him to get his arms in the sleeves of the dressing gown because he couldn't bear to let go of the Leica.

At last he stood up unsteadily beside the bed, his feet in the slippers. A woollen scarf was tied round his neck. Sister Kruisheer took his arm to hold him up. He pressed the Leica to his chest with both hands.

'I always knew it would be found! How did it happen? It's a miracle! Did they say where they found it?'

His eyes were riveted on the camera as he shuffled out of the ward, flanked by Sister Kruisheer and Selderhorst.

'It's damaged, they must have thrown it about. There's a crack in the lens. If the worst comes to the worst it can be mended, I'm sure,' Osewoudt muttered to himself.

On the stairs, he said: 'When I'm released I'll take a farewell photograph of you all.'

His teeth chattered as he went down the chilly ground-floor corridor.

They led him through the basement to the cell he had occupied before. Awaiting him there were Spuybroek, another guard, a man in an overcoat and a man in a white lab coat.

'This gentleman is an army photographer,' said Selderhorst. 'He's made everything ready for you. The glass tiles by the ceiling have been covered over. You'll find everything you need over there, on the table. It's all up to you now.'

On the table stood a small tank and bottles containing fluids.

Osewoudt read the labels on the bottles and said: 'The light has to be switched off.'

They gave him a chair and switched off the light.

He unscrewed the camera in the dark and felt with the tips of his fingers that the film was still in it. He took out the film, wound it on to the spool of the tank, and put the cover on the tank.

'We can have the light on again now,' he said.

They switched the light on.

'It's the same film,' he said. 'I can tell by the cassette.'

He held out the empty cassette. They nodded, but did not take it from him.

'Has anybody got a watch?'

He was slumped forward on the table, giving the tank a shake from time to time. His ears throbbed with fever.

The gentleman in the overcoat said: 'How fascinating this photography business is! I take photographs myself in my free time, but this is the first chance I've had to see a film being developed!'

Osewoudt looked at the watch, poured the contents of the tank into the first bottle and filled the tank with the second bottle.

Ten minutes later he said: 'It should be ready now.'

They all crowded round as he unscrewed the lid.

He stood up, took the spool from the tank and began to unwind the film from the spool.

The first length of film to emerge was blank.

'It was a film that had hardly been used,' Osewoudt said.

He had now drawn a metre of film from the spool, and still it was blank. Finally, on the last bit to unwind from the spool, there was a small dark oblong.

Selderhorst snatched the film from Osewoudt and held it up to the light.

'I'll be dammed! What have we got here? It's you! It's you, isn't it? And the bloke sitting next to you – who's he? Oh, but that's Obersturmführer Ebernuss! Ebernuss, for Christ's sake!'

Osewoudt grabbed hold of the wet film with both hands and pulled, but Selderhorst would not let go.

Osewoudt began to scream: 'That's a different photo! That's a photo taken in Moorlag's attic, when I was there with Ebernuss. But the next picture must be the one of me with Dorbeck! It must be further along the film!'

Selderhorst, Spuybroek, the gentleman and the photographer

put their heads together and stared at the single dark oblong on the long strip of clear celluloid. They were all at least a head taller than Osewoudt.

Osewoudt tugged again at the film, although he had already seen that there was just the one exposure on it.

'All right, see for yourself!'

Selderhorst let go, Osewoudt scrutinised the film. Then he said: 'It's not possible! Where's Dorbeck?'

Selderhorst said: 'I think Dorbeck's with your friend Marianne in her kibbutz! If he's as much like you as you say, she won't have noticed the difference.'

'How is this possible? The whole world is against me, even the light has let me down.'

He backed away, although no one said anything, no one moved.

'What are you staring at like a bunch of idiots? Go and find Dorbeck, I tell you, Dorbeck knows everything. Everything, I tell you. Without Dorbeck I am nothing, I don't mind admitting it. Dorbeck is everything.'

Osewoudt turned round.

Trailing the film on the floor behind him, he took a few steps towards the door.

'Damn you, Dorbeck, where are you? Why won't you show your face? Perhaps he's right here in this building. Perhaps he's being held in another section. I'll track him down all right. He planned it so the Germans would go looking for me instead of him, and now I'm in prison for doing as he said. It can't be possible!'

He opened the door and went into the passage.

Laughter broke out at his back, but no one stopped him.

He walked the length of the basement and found the exit.

'Where do you think you're going?' shouted the sentry, without going after him. 'Hey, runt! Come back!'

A thin drizzle was falling on the factory yard.

Gesticulating wildly, waving the film in the air, Osewoudt pressed on.

'Dorbeck! Come here! Yes, Dorbeck, it's me, Osewoudt. No, I won't listen. You must listen to me. Before we go on, I want an explanation!'

He lost a slipper, but limped ahead over the muddy concrete.

A motor barge with a cargo of peat was approaching along the canal.

'Where's Dorbeck?' screamed Osewoudt. 'He must be found! He must! He must!'

He lost the other slipper, then broke into a run.

The heavily laden barge slowly drew near. The diesel engine chugged deeply, puffing blue circles of smoke straight up into the misty air.

Only now were shots fired, a brief salvo from a Sten gun. When the second salvo rang out Osewoudt toppled forward, grabbing the barbed wire along the canal as he fell.

The building rocked. Windows were being shattered. Hundreds of voices clamoured simultaneously for help. Glass came tinkling down on to the yard.

They had laid Osewoudt out on the floor of the corridor, not far from the open door. Two guards sat on chairs close by, their rifles between their knees.

A pool of blood was spreading around Osewoudt.

'It's a foul business, all the same,' said one of the guards.

A sergeant came hurrying towards them.

'Sergeant,' called the same guard, without getting to his feet, 'Sergeant, is there a doctor coming?'

'The doctor of the Sixth Exloërmond is on holiday, and the doctor of the Fifth Exloërmond is out. His wife says there's always a rush after Christmas because of all the boozing.'

'Damn. Are they sending reinforcements?'

'Never you mind. Just do your duty!'

The sergeant drew his pistol and ran into the corridor.

The tumult continued unabated. The walls shook.

'Murderers! Murderers!' yelled the SS insurgents.

Bunks and chairs were being smashed. The whole building seemed on the point of collapse.

One guard stood up and bent over Osewoudt. Then he sat down again, and said to the other guard: 'He's still groaning.'

The other guard rested his rifle against his knee and brought out a packet of cigarettes.

'It's a foul business, all the same.'

'What did you say?'

'A foul business! Don't you ever read the newspaper?'

'Not me.'

'I believe in that boy. It's a foul business. He knows too much, that's why they're letting him bleed. Dorbeck did exist, he may even still be alive, I'm convinced of that. Not that the papers tell you everything.'

Skirts flapping, Father Beer came running down the corridor.

He fell to his knees in the puddle of blood and slid one arm under Osewoudt's head, as if he wanted to hug him.

'Osewoudt! Osewoudt!' he cried. 'Is there anything I can do for you?'

Osewoudt's eyes opened halfway.

'Dorbeck knows everything. Find Dorbeck. Dorbeck must be somewhere. Dorbeck knows everything.'

'But Osewoudt—'

'Dorbeck must be found. The photo didn't come out, but what does that prove? Tell Dorbeck . . . Ask Dorbeck . . .'

'You must stay alive, Osewoudt! If Dorbeck is to be found, then you'll have to hunt him down yourself, because no one else will find him for you!'

Osewoudt said no more and his eyes closed again.

'Osewoudt, don't give up! Osewoudt, can you hear me? Don't give up! You can't die like this. You must get away. Osewoudt, can you still hear me? You can have my cassock to escape in! What's keeping the doctor?'

Father Beer looked about him, but saw no one apart from the guards, hunched forward as they smoked their cigarettes. They paid no attention to Father Beer; they had their eyes on the gate. With chains clanking, two armoured vehicles drove into the factory yard, their guns trained on the front of the building.

'The bleeding must be staunched!' cried Father Beer.

He parted the front of Osewoudt's dressing gown and undid the buttons of the pyjama jacket. But the fingers on Father Beer's hands numbered fewer than there were bullet holes in Osewoudt's body.

Voorburg, May 1952
Groningen, July 1958

## Postscript (1971)

I can look for him when he is not there, but not hang him when he is not there.

One might want to say: 'But he must be somewhere there if I am looking for him.'

Then he must be somewhere there too if I don't find him, and even if he doesn't exist at all.

Ludwig Wittgenstein